DOWNLOADABLE

JILL THRUSSELL

CONTENTS

"The past is our lesson and our guide, the present lives within us and is our constant companion but the future is our unborn child of hope." ~ Jill Thrussell

THE HIDEAWAY LAB

Just on the outskirts of the busy, bustling city of Shuttlesburg, Professor Heisner's laboratory had finally found and established its home, quite a distance away from the usual hustle and bustle that usually accompanied and adorned the rather hectic, busy city streets. The location that Professor Heisner had selected had in the end been absolutely ideal for his very confidential and ground breaking scientific work that required not only an element of solitude but also very deep levels of intense concentration for its actual realization and he'd felt extremely satisfied with his choice.

A small office block had been recommended by the real estate agent which Professor Heisner had then purchased with the intention of converting the building into a state of the art scientific clinic and for the most part it had been one decision that

Professor Heisner had definitely felt completely at peace with. In terms of the building itself, it nestled gently into some hills which sat just behind it that it seemed to fit almost like a shoe that had been fitted onto a foot it had been very specifically measured for and the building suited the Professor in much the same manner. Almost everything about the building had been perfect in the end, including the price which had been very reasonable indeed and the Professor had enthusiastically snapped it up as soon as he'd been shown around the interior by an eager, young, very ambitious female real estate agent.

"I'll be converting the entire building into a laboratory and clinic." Professor Heisner had mentioned to the female real estate agent as he'd briefly outlined his requirements during a guided tour of the property.

"Well Professor Heisner, the building itself will need quite a bit of work but I think it's absolutely perfect for your needs. It's in a very discreet location which is essential for your clients, in order to provide them with a confidential environment." Amelia the estate agent had immediately pointed out as she'd discreetly urged the Professor to accept the property which had rather frustratingly, actually been on her hands for a while. "A lot of our clients prefer buildings situated right in the heart of the city, so this property really is a bargain just because it's on the actual outskirts."

"Actually, I think you're correct Amelia, it is almost perfect." Professor Heisner had finally agreed as the real estate agent had rounded off her guided tour and they'd stepped back inside the reception area. "I'd like to take it."

"Great Professor Heisner, I'll get the paperwork drawn up for you by Monday." Amelia had promised as she'd sighed internally with sheer relief.

Quite fortunately for Amelia, the final sale had in the end actually been rather straightforward and relatively easy but this particular property had definitely been a thorn in her side for a while. In the run up to the Professor's appointment, Amelia had even actually begun to think that she would never get rid of it and so the Professor's positive attitude, interest in the property and his enthusiasm had finally managed to restore her hope in her ability to sell any property that she'd actually been allocated to as long as she could find the correct buyer.

"That'll be absolutely perfect." Professor Heisner had agreed.

"That way when you come into our offices on Monday morning Professor Heisner, you can just pick up the keys, sign the paperwork and then get settled in straight away." Amelia had mentioned.

Professor Heisner had immediately nodded his head in response. "That'll be lovely Amelia. Thank you very much." He'd replied as he'd started to rummage around inside his grey wrinkled overcoat as he'd searched for his small notepad gadget which contained some very precise detailed information about the actual physical dimensions required from the building for the work of his actual clinic. "It certainly seems to meet most, if not all of my requirements and it even actually seems to exceed some. I'm very impressed." Professor Heisner had reassured Amelia as he'd admired the quite large, very spacious reception area.

"Yes and it's only still available really due it's very remote location, if this building had actually been situated in the heart of the city, it would have been triple the price and it would have been snapped up in a week." Amelia had mentioned as she'd glanced at the Professor's slightly disorganized, quite chaotic, rather rough looking appearance and smiled.

Predominantly, Amelia usually found corporate properties for very ambitious businessmen that sought out prime properties in the heart of the city for cut throat commercial activities and Professor Heisner's objectives had differed vastly from that usual criteria and so too had he. The Professor's very ruffled exterior had struck her as slightly unusual as most of Amelia's time was usually spent with very smart looking clients that would be suited in corporate attire from head to toe.

Over the Professor's body there was a large grey, very wrinkled overcoat that seemed to be at least two sizes too big for him which hung down from his physical frame that almost seemed to match his hair in terms of its color as Amelia had silently inspected his rather untidy appearance. The lack of attention to his external appearance however hadn't seemed to bother the Professor in the slightest and that had amused Amelia slightly. One thing that had really pleased Amelia immensely however had been the fact that she was just about to get rid of a very difficult property that had been placed rather heavily upon her young shoulders which had quite frankly been, a complete pain in the butt and the potential sale had lifted her spirits tremendously.

An appreciative and very grateful smile had adorned Amelia's face as she'd discreetly rejoiced in Professor Heisner's acceptance of the property that she'd shown him around that Friday afternoon as she'd accepted his acceptance with a huge internal sigh of relief. Absolutely no one that Amelia had shown the property to so far had actually wanted it and she'd almost given up hope that she'd finalize a sale on the property completely. Finally however, Amelia had managed to strike gold and she'd actually found a client who's requirements perfectly suited this very tricky, remote venue and finally, quite fortunately, the

5

strange location and the facilities on offer had been appreciated and wanted so much so that the building would actually be purchased and for that Amelia had felt, extremely grateful.

Personal failure wasn't something that Amelia coped with easily in life as she'd always been quite an ambitious person and now that she'd reached her late twenties, those deep seeds of ambition that she'd always carried around inside of her had grown and had fully blossomed. Her sharply cut chestnut brown, shoulder length hair that neatly crowned her face had flapped gently against her neck as she'd walked the Professor towards their parked cars in the parking lot situated just at the front of the building as she'd silently rejoiced in the deal she'd managed to seal that day.

Unlike the Professor, Amelia had dressed that day in a very sharp black, corporate looking city dress with crisp lines which had matched her very determined attitude that had been very focused upon delivering actual commercial results. For once it seemed, Amelia's power dressing had actually paid off and the irritation of failure had now fled from her being as she'd sauntered towards the Professor's vehicle with a very cheerful smile upon her face as she'd prepared to bid him farewell.

The sale that day had not actually just made Amelia's day but also her weekend and month as it had meant that now, she could actually face her boss again with her head held high as the absence of a sale had in recent times actually become a source of embarrassment. At least twenty prospective buyers had viewed the property before that day and absolutely none of them had wanted it and she'd really tried her best to sell it but that hadn't made the slightest scrap of difference at all. Finally however, someone had wanted it and Professor Heisner had politely agreed to take it off her hands and this rather remote, awkward hideaway building had finally become something that someone actually wanted to purchase and that had really brightened up her day.

Just a few months later and once the building had been modified very specifically, according to Professor Heisner's precise and rather unique requirements, Professor Heisner joyfully prepared to actually open up his actual clinic which he'd decided to call Restructure. Some relevant and essential pieces of high tech equipment had been ordered, purchased and installed and two months prior to the planned grand opening, Professor Heisner had recruited and hired most of the staff that he'd felt he'd needed and he'd then trained them extremely thoroughly as he'd prepared his clinic meticulously.

Absolutely everything that Professor Heisner could think of had been very carefully prepared in advance for the clinic's grand opening which he'd hoped would be an event that would not only mark the actual realization of his goals but that would also celebrate the opening of his clinic's doors to its first very real human clients. In terms of the Professor's life, playtime had now finally come to an end but he definitely felt ready to take his very first step out into the corporate human world with his precious research which he hoped to utilize to benefit real human beings and society at large, for a price of course.

Due to the objectives of Professor Heisner's work and clinic, he'd decided to name the Download clinic Restructure as that was in essence what the clinic was actually designed to do. The various pieces of equipment inside it would allow the Professor to restructure a client's physical DNA through actual Downloads which would provide each client with a more favorable physical appearance, according to their wishes and their budget.

Inside Professor Heisner's mind, in the run up to the actual day of his grand opening, he'd felt very optimistic about the actual launch which he'd hoped would not only be a tremendous success but also usher in a hugely successful corporate scientific venture. He'd really gone out of his way to ensure that both the building and the staff that occupied it would be very well equipped and thoroughly prepared for the actual launch of his experimental venture and he'd literally thought of everything he could think off but the implementation of those plans were as the Professor knew, just the first step in a long corporate journey to success.

In terms of the Professor's knowledge, he had actually studied many of the fields that he'd chosen to specialize in for years and years and he was a renowned scientist that was quite well known within scientific circles for his work. His main area of specialization had always been physical bodily enhancements which he intended to realize through a rather delicate combination of both technology and science as Professor Heisner sought to enhance human existence and ultimately, humanity's physical appearance in a way that people would both fully enjoy and actually appreciate. The Restructure clinic itself would actually be the real realization and the manifestation of all the knowledge that Professor Heisner had so carefully accumulated over the years, from his very dedicated and tireless devotion to his chosen areas of expertise and as the day of Restructure's actual opening neared, Professor Heisner became extremely excited about the dream he'd worked so very hard, for so very long to actually achieve.

Initially, regarding the actual launch of Restructure, Professor Heisner had decided to recruit just a few staff in the end but they were all definitely required as he'd felt that they would help him bring some order and structure to the clinic as his own approach at times could be, slightly chaotic. When it came to Professor Heisner's own personal skill set, his organization skills were really quite weak as he tended to focus more upon his scientific achievements than the practicalities of commerce and he would quite often work in a very haphazard manner that completely ignored the practical realities of life.

A very warm friendly, polite Receptionist in her late forties had been hired called Yucala that the Professor had recruited to greet his clients every working day and to manage the daily administrative affairs of Restructure on his behalf as when it came to actual administration, he was absolutely hopeless. Another female member of staff had also been recruited as a Bodily Enhancements Consultant, Talitha and she had been recruited to service the needs of his first group of clients as Professor Heisner wasn't particularly good with people and he tended to prefer spending his working day inside his laboratory conducting experiments as opposed to facing actual real human beings.

In terms of the clinic's other staff, there was already a Laboratory Assistant in place called Moses that formed part of Professor Heisner's team and Moses usually assisted the Professor with the more technical, scientific areas of his work. Due to the fact that Moses had already worked alongside Professor Heisner for years, he'd not actually been recruited and had simply been incorporated into Restructure's staff. Despite his rather enthusiastic corporate ambitions however, Professor Heisner had in the end decided to keep his initial team actually quite small in terms of numbers as he'd been very disciplined in his approach to Restructure's daily operations.

When it came to the actual appointment of a Bodily Enhancements Consultant Professor Heisner had held a series of interviews and he'd invited several candidates along but one had impressed him slightly more than others and hence he'd chosen Talitha almost immediately, to fill the vacancy on offer. In his opinion, Professor Heisner had definitely felt that she would be extremely well suited to his work and his clinic as Talitha had some prior experience that was extremely relevant and she was also very cosmetically pretty which really suited the image that Professor Heisner wished to present to the world. Although Talitha hadn't actually been involved in any scientific work in the past, or even worked for an actual scientist before, she had worked for various beauticians and cosmetic surgeons and that suited Professor Heisner right down to the ground.

Being a key member of his team, Talitha would

be tasked with being the human face of his work and that meant, she would greet, practically deliver and interact with his clients every working day and that she would represent the physical manifestation of the Professor's research in its entirety. Every single one of the interviews had been conducted by Professor Heisner himself and he'd been extremely impressed by not only Talitha's resume but also her positive attitude, professionalism and her skill set.

"You'll be changing people's butts, breasts and noses quite a lot and a whole lot of other things in-between, so you'll really have to be the height of discretion and some clients will be very demanding." Professor Heisner had explained throughout Talitha's initial interview.

"Yes Professor Heisner, those physical features were usually quite a high priority for most clients in the cosmetic surgeries that I've worked for in the past." Talitha had acknowledged as she'd smiled at the Professor's blunt and very frank explanations. "Don't worry, I'm very discreet and I've done quite similar work before, so it shouldn't be a problem for me." She'd immediately reassured him. "I don't get embarrassed very easily."

"My work is very experimental in nature." Professor Heisner had warned as he'd peered at Talitha's face across his desk over the top of the pair of glasses that sat delicately balanced against the foot of his nose. "Is that something that you'll be comfortable with?" He'd asked as he'd quietly inspected the woman slightly more closely that he'd essentially be trusting with his clients and his work. "And some of your clients will be extremely difficult."

"Yes, this is exactly what I'm looking for, something a bit more challenging and something a lot more interesting." Talitha had replied enthusiastically as she'd eagerly nodded her head. "I'm used to difficult clients, I've met lots over the years."

Absolutely everything about Talitha's physical appearance ticked all the right boxes inside Professor Heisner's mind more than once as she was in her early thirties which meant, she was definitely mature enough to command respect. In terms of her physical presentation, she possessed a wide beautiful, very warm smile, a perfectly symmetrical face and sparkling crystal white teeth and the vision of physical beauty was considered a huge asset by Professor Heisner. Essentially, Talitha's appearance would provide the perfect marketing message and a physical endorsement for the clinic itself and he'd therefore effectively killed two corporate birds with one stone as her past experience actually aligned quite nicely with Restructure's corporate requirements.

Various forms of physical perfection were in

essence what Restructure ultimately wanted to sell and offer to its clients and Talitha's physical beauty fully aligned with that image and so in many ways, she was the ideal candidate for the role and the perfect living advertisement for the services that Restructure would be offering. Some clients, Professor Heisner had felt, would be prepared to spend vast sums of money, in order to actually achieve the levels of physical perfection that Talitha physically verified were really actually attainable and hence she fitted his needs very precisely.

Due to the fact that the Professor himself was actually rather homely looking and situated a million miles away from what most people might classify as attractive or handsome, at least one of his staff had to present that image of beauty to the world and he was under absolutely no illusions at all, it certainly couldn't be him. When it came to the Professor's own image, regardless of his rather chaotic approach to life and his ignorance in relation to some of life's practicalities, one thing he did know for sure, an image of physical perfection was not one thing he could actually provide to anyone, not in his current physical form.

"When can you start Talitha?" Professor Heisner had asked as he'd prepared to end Talitha's interview. "I really need someone that can grab hold of the reins and steer the horse right away as to be perfectly honest, I'm tend to spend most of my time inside my laboratory, so I don't really have much time for client interactions." He'd explained. "And to be perfectly frank, I'm probably not the best advertisement to clients for the services that Restructure will be offering."

Talitha had smiled. "I completely understand Professor Heisner." She'd replied. "I can start immediately."

"Great, I think you'll be an excellent fit Talitha." Professor Heisner had confirmed as he'd enthusiastically nodded his head. "At Restructure we promise to provide our clients with physical perfection, so appearance really is quite important and you also have a lot of experience in a similar field, so those two assets will go hand in hand."

One thing had however, slightly worried Professor Heisner about Talitha's appointment as he'd prepared to conclude her interview and offer her the actual role and that had been her attitude towards the various moral and ethical issues that he'd known at some point would definitely present themselves to her. Quite often, it could actually be difficult to gauge and determine where exactly people stood or sat upon the spectrum of human moral judgments as at times people could be very unpredictable in terms of their reasoning, their subsequent judgments and their reactions. Despite the Professor's desire to fill the vacant position quite quickly, he had felt extremely worried about the possibility of actually recruiting someone that would essentially end up being an obstruction to his actual work but he verbally tiptoed towards the issue rather delicately, so as not to worry Talitha too much.

"Occasionally Talitha, some of the work that you might be asked to perform at Restructure could be what some people might consider slightly unethical." Professor Heisner had mentioned as he'd discreetly sought further clarity regarding Talitha's attitude towards moral issues. "For example, a client might ask you to give them a physical transformation in order to enable them to achieve something slightly dubious in nature. How would you feel about that?"

"Professor Heisner, I have worked for some cosmetic surgeons in the past and some of our clients weren't exactly what I would call angels. At the end of the day, it's their life really and whatever they chose to do with that life is essentially their own problem and their own responsibility." Talitha had replied as she'd smiled.

"Good because I really can't have my staff worrying about other people's decisions, we're just here to provide a service and to enhance humanity's existence on this earth as much as is scientifically possible." Professor Heisner had explained. "Ethics can be such a poor master when it comes to making a living and is far better suited to being a servant to the romantic passions in life and quite frankly although some moral standards can be really useful that usually tends to be when they seek to protect your heart as at other times, they can be a real pain in the butt."

Talitha had grinned.

Once the Professor had satisfied himself that Talitha would not be morally overbearing, he'd quickly offered her the position and then had concluded her interview. The last thing that Professor Heisner had wanted to do was to recruit someone that would be plagued by moral or ethical issues which might at some point obstruct his client's levels of satisfaction and their subsequent happiness. Restructure and his work definitely required someone that had a very flexible attitude and someone that would be appreciative of the new areas of scientific development that his work explored and he had absolutely no desire at all to recruit a obstacle to his scientific goals. A very high price would be paid by each of his clients for the work that Professor Heisner had scientifically developed for years and for the procedures that Talitha would ultimately perform upon them every working day and that high price would be paid for what clients wanted and not for moral lectures.

Finally, the day of Restructure's planned grand opening arrived and as Professor Heisner walked towards the clinic doors and main entrance to the building as he prepared to invite human guests inside his clinic for the very first time, he felt extremely excited about their pending arrival. Deep down inside himself, Professor Heisner silently acknowledged his achievement as he walked and quietly congratulated himself as he straightened up the very smart suit that he'd worn earlier that day for the actual event itself. Very unusually, in preparation for the wine and buffet evening ahead, Professor Heisner had actually been fitted for a suit and he'd even attended an actual barber shop to have a haircut, just for the occasion and for once, he actually looked quite physically smart and extremely presentable.

Everyone that Professor Heisner could think of had been invited along to Restructure's opening, colleagues from his professional field, potential clients, staff and their partners and even a few potential financers as he'd sought to provoke an early interest in his groundbreaking, very corporate application of science. Potential clients had already been sought out for the services that Restructure would offer in advance and various advertisements had been placed that were very discreet and that only hinted quite vaguely at the range of services that Restructure would offer to prepare for the grand opening but the response had been extremely favorable. Most of the adverts that Professor Heisner had placed had been featured inside lifestyle and health magazines and upon similar websites as Professor Heisner had quietly sought out his market from within the city's fairly large population rather discreetly.

A client waiting list had also actually been created as the response from Professor's advertisements had been absolutely phenomenal but he'd managed to narrow down the large list to just six external clients that he'd identified as suitable for Talitha to actually start off with. Some preliminary client meetings had then taken place with each of the potential clients as Professor Heisner had conducted client suitability checks which in his mind had been absolutely necessary as not everyone that had responded to the adverts would be a suitable client for the clinic and Professor Heisner fully appreciated that reality. Another seventh client had also been added to Talitha's list but she was actually the daughter of one of Professor Heisner's personal friends and so a client suitability check had not actually been performed for her as he'd simply accepted her as a client and reassured his friend that he would assist his daughter in any way he possibly could.

Some people had in the end actually been totally excluded from the waiting list and marked as unsuitable clients for Restructure's services as those people had very deep psychological issues that Professor Heisner knew, could not simply be

19

resolved with a simple Download procedure. Not every problem in life could be resolved by the Professor's Restructure clinic and he fully accepted that reality, no matter how much he actually wished it could be. The work of his clinic really couldn't stretch to certain lengths and the areas of science he'd focused upon were very precise which meant, the solutions offered really couldn't meet the needs of everyone as the provisions offered at Restructure were quite inappropriate when it came to some people's needs.

At approximately seven that Friday evening as was expected, several people began to step through the doors of the Restructure building and enter inside the reception area where Yucala very politely greeted them with a warm smile just as Professor Heisner had planned. Each guest was then politely shown into the large meeting room, just on the left hand side of the reception area that Professor Heisner had set aside, specifically for the evening's event. A wine and buffet reception had been meticulously planned and approximately fifty people in total had been invited to attend and the quite large meeting room had been radically transformed by Professor Heisner and the catering company that he'd hired earlier that day in preparation. The catering company's assistance had in the end been a tremendous help to the Professor as he wasn't really much of an interior decorator and had absolutely no idea at all how to dress a room.

Inside the large meeting room, a sea of pleasant smiles and happy cheerful grins which adorned his guests faces greeted the Professor as he entered inside the room and then began to circulate as he welcomed each of his guests with a polite handshake. Once most of the guests that the Professor had invited were finally present, he actively sought out Talitha's face, who'd he'd also invited along to the event that evening with Bryson her fiancée. Just a few seconds later, Professor Heisner managed to spot the couple and he quickly strode across the room towards them.

"Good evening Talitha." Professor Heisner boomed as he greeted the couple with a friendly smile. "And it's lovely to meet you Bryson, thank you for coming along." He quickly extended a hand politely towards Bryson as he spoke.

"Good evening Professor Heisner." Talitha replied as she smiled and then nodded her head. "I must say, you've done tremendously well, this is a very prestigious looking reception and you're looking very smart yourself." She observed.

"Well, sometimes I do have to try and conform to society's expectations of me, especially when I want their money." Professor Heisner teased in a quiet voice.

Talitha giggled.

"It's very nice to meet you Professor Heisner, Talitha's told me a lot about you." Bryson replied as he shook the Professor's outstretched hand.

"Well Bryson, you really can't believe everything that women say at the end of the day as sometimes, they can be such terrible gossips." Professor Heisner teased. "As a general rule I would just work on the assumption that if something good was said about me then you can believe it, if it was bad then that's just hearsay and gossip and that's my scientific approach."

Bryson smiled. "It was all good Professor Heisner, not a bad word was spoken." He quickly reassured him.

"Did the advertisements that you placed get a good response Professor Heisner, it certainly looks like they did? Did a lot of clients sign up?" Talitha asked.

"Absolutely loads but don't worry Talitha, I filtered out all the really complicated, difficult ones, so your first group of clients won't be too much of a headache." Professor Heisner gently reassured her.

"Wow, it sounds like your work is in demand Professor Heisner." Talitha replied enthusiastically.

"It sure is but I'm fully equipped and absolutely ready for this as I've waited for this day for a very, very long time, almost a decade in fact." Professor Heisner explained.

"Yes, I can see that you've really made an effort Professor Heisner and that hair cut is absolutely fantastic, it really suits you." Talitha said as she encouraged and acknowledged the Professor's efforts.

"The pains we human beings go through to present an acceptable face to the rest of society, necessary but not always preferred. I actually prefer my rather messy locks, they were way more comfortable, far less maintenance was required and the chaos that usually sits on top of my head that one usually refers to as hair, tends to keeps my neck warm in the cold winter evenings." Professor Heisner explained.

Talitha giggled

"Okay you two, I better go and circulate as apparently this evening, I'm actually supposed to be the host." Professor Heisner joked. "Enjoy your evening and Talitha please feel free to network with anyone here as some of these people will one day, probably be your clients."

Talitha nodded.

Despite the rather large reception and the huge interest in Professor Heisner's work as he walked around the packed meeting room, he felt extremely grateful that evening that he'd actually decided to keep his initial client intake and current operations quite small to start off. One thing Professor Heisner definitely lacked in life was corporate experience and hence in his mind, managing a small enterprise which would then grow organically, was definitely preferable to jumping into a much larger, corporate entity right from the word go. Problems would quite definitely arise and the Professor wanted to be able to respond to those problems quickly and manage them effectively before they escalated into huge mountains of trouble. Once Restructure was up and on it's feet and once it was financially sustaining itself and the services that the company offered had been fully developed, Professor Heisner quietly concluded, he would then perhaps seek to expand his client intake and hire more staff as the demand from the market certainly seemed to be there.

For Professor Heisner, Restructure ultimately represented his first dive into what could be at times, the very murky pool of commerce and he'd deliberately avoided the much deeper end of that pool as he'd chosen to tread water quite carefully, just out of his depth and his usual comfort zone. A bit more experience would definitely have to be accumulated before Professor Heisner could actually venture out more bravely into the deeper, very unfamiliar depths of a full scale corporate adventure and he fully appreciated and accepted that reality.

In terms of his lifestyle and his finances, Professor Heisner had spent most of his life living off various sums of research funding that he'd been awarded at various points in time and that had predominantly financially sustained him. Over the past ten years, another source of income for him had been his various teaching assignments which had occurred at the various educational institutions that specialized in science where he'd taught a variety of scientific subjects to students that he'd been particularly knowledgeable about. At various points in time, Professor Heisner had also received a few laboratory grants to deliver specific, very specialist pieces of research work but this corporate venture, Restructure which was very commercial in nature and extremely different to anything he'd ever done before. Essentially, this would be the very first time ever that Professor Heisner had to actually trade his own knowledge and earn financial compensation directly from the public at large and that excited him but also slightly scared him.

"Would you like a glass of wine Sir?" A polite male voice suddenly asked.

"Sure that would be great thanks." Professor Heisner replied as he glanced at the male Server that had paused right next to where he stood in order to offer him a glass of wine from a silver tray which he held inside his hands and then smiled.

"Would you like something to eat Sir?" He enquired. "I can fix you a plate of food if you like."

Professor Heisner gently shook his head as he internally shook of his thoughts which he'd actually become lost in for a moment. "No don't worry, I can do that myself." He insisted. "But thanks for offering."

"No problem Sir." The Server replied as he nodded his head and then began to walk away.

"Is everything okay Professor Heisner?" Talitha suddenly asked as she approached the Professor from one side of the room and then gently placed her arm on his. "You look a bit lost."

"This is just a huge step for me Talitha that's all." Professor Heisner explained as he smiled. "This is the first time ever that my work is actually being applied in practice to real human bodies and human beings."

"No more lab rats and guinea pigs." Talitha teased.

Professor Heisner smiled. "Yes and now, I actually have to interact with real everyday people not just brainiacs and science nerds, the cross I have to carry is so heavy at times." He joked.

"Well, we aren't all that bad, sometimes everyday people can actually be rather nice." Talitha teased. "Though sometimes, some people can be a total pain in the butt too."

"Yes. Some people can be rather nice at times." Professor Heisner agreed. "This will probably be quite good for me in the long run. I might even manage to find a serious girlfriend now and one day, I might even get married."

"Didn't the fields of science provide you with one? I mean biology is science and isn't that what it's all about, human physical interactions and our reproductive systems?" Talitha asked.

"Nope, I've actually found that most of the women I've met in a professional capacity tend to be rather focused upon my work and their own scientific careers. I'm not the best looking button in the box, so that probably didn't help much." Professor Heisner admitted as he smiled.

"Women can be very fickle at times." Talitha quickly pointed out as she nodded her head in understanding. "Sometimes, you're just seen as a step up on the career ladder. It happens to quite a lot of people in different professions."

"Yes indeed, well they definitely wanted a step up in life but not an actual step up the aisle, at least not with me." Professor Heisner agreed. "Never mind, the past isn't usually a good place to live, so I should really try to focus on the present and the future which as yet, remains completely unwritten and unexplored."

"Yes and everyone here seems to be really enjoying the food and the wine, so I'd say Restructure's grand opening has been a tremendous success. You should go up to the front of the room Professor Heisner and make a short speech or something and ask everyone to toast the opening of the clinic." Talitha suggested. "That way, you'll be the center of attention whilst you're looking your best."

Professor Heisner smiled. "Very true Talitha, being tidy, smart and quite well organized isn't something that usually happens for me very often, I really should make the most of it." He agreed.

Talitha giggled as she raised her glass. "Here's to the successful launch of Restructure and here's to me starting my job as an actual Bodily Enhancements Consultant on Monday." She announced.

"Yes and thank you very much for all your encouragement Talitha. You've been a great source of support to me this evening." Professor Heisner replied as he raised his glass in the air and then knocked it gently against Talitha's glass. "Here's to a great commercial future, the success of Restructure and maybe one day, my romantic success."

Talitha smiled. "Romance is much harder than it looks really, it took me quite a while to find Bryson and I had to kiss a few lizards on the way." She explained.

"Yes, perhaps that's where I went wrong, I gave up far too quickly really, perseverance that's the key." Professor Heisner replied. "Romance just became a lost cause for me and something that I couldn't quite scientifically perfect, or even attempt to try and figure out."

"It'll happen one day Professor Heisner when the right person comes along." Talitha gently reassured him.

"Or perhaps, it might actually happen when I notice that the right person is actually present as sometimes you don't always see what's right in front of your face." Professor Heisner suggested.

"Now that is actually very true, we do spend a lot of our lives looking everywhere for some kind of ideal partner when quite often what we really need can be right in front of us." Talitha agreed.

"I better go and give that speech you suggested." Professor Heisner insisted. "Before everyone forgets why they're actually here and perhaps Mrs. What I Really Need is here right now and she might even be watching."

Talitha immediately nodded her head in agreement. "Yes, I really think you should." She encouraged. "And don't be nervous Professor Heisner, everyone is here because of your work and because of your achievements which are absolutely amazing."

A proud smile spread out across Talitha's face as she watched Professor Heisner walk towards the front of the room and then step up onto the small stage and approach the podium which had been placed inside the room that day especially for the grand opening. Sometimes, Talitha suddenly realized as she watched the Professor, men weren't always just automatically naturally confident and confidence it seemed, was a suit you had to wear that quite often, someone else tailored for you with a needle of kindness and the threads of encouragement.

When the following Monday morning arrived, Talitha prepared for her actual first working day with real clients at Restructure enthusiastically as she got up, showered and then dressed as she readied herself to leave home and make her way to work. Five uniform dresses had been ordered for Talitha the previous week and on the Friday afternoon, Talitha had actually had to visit a store in the heart of the city that Professor Heisner had sent her to in order to collect them. One of the very smart looking black and white uniform dresses had been slipped over Talitha's head and then quickly zipped up and as she admired it in the long mirror inside her bedroom, she decided that it really wasn't the worse uniform that she'd ever worn and that in fact, she actually really quite liked it.

An excited smile pleasantly adorned Talitha's face as she stepped out of her front door as she greeted the morning and the surrounding streets with a very joyful heart. For Talitha, it felt absolutely great to be in full time employment once more as she was actually going to be paid at the end of each month which was something that hadn't happened for a while, prior to her appointment at Restructure. The sky outside was bright but the air was slightly breezy as it suddenly hit Talitha's face and then whisked itself around her body as she walked towards her car which as usual was parked in the driveway right next to her home.

"Life is going to be so different now." Talitha muttered as she unlocked her car door. "Now I'll actually have my own client list and I'll not just be waiting around to look after someone else's clients and my very own consultation room." She reassured herself as she entered inside the vehicle and then glanced inside the mirror. "This uniform actually looks quite good, it's warm and it's not ugly or clunky at all."

The engine of the car was quickly started and then Talitha began to roll the vehicle gently forward as she drove towards the open gateway at the bottom of the drive and towards the actual road. Outside the garden gates, Talitha found the city streets very quiet and clear as she drove rapidly through each one and headed towards the highway as that day, she was actually headed out of the city and not straight into its heart.

From the speakers inside the car, a tune beat out in a continuous rhythm as she drove and Talitha began to gently tap the steering wheel in time with the music as she sang quietly along to the words of the song. Due to the fact that Talitha's voice wasn't that great, she avoided a more noisy rendition so that she could appreciate the sound of someone else's voice that could actually sing as that was preferable to her ears than her own out of tune efforts.

Despite the fact that the building which Talitha would now officially call her working home was situated only twenty to thirty minutes drive away, she'd left home at about quarter past eight that morning, just to ensure that she actually arrived on time. Realistically, the actual drive itself would probably only take Talitha around twenty minutes as she was headed out of the city and it was quite early in the morning which meant, she was actually going in the opposite direction from most of the morning traffic that was headed straight into the city centre. Sometimes on her way to work, Talitha liked to stop off just to purchase some breakfast and that usually added at least ten more minutes to her journey time. The route to the Restructure building was actually quite familiar to Talitha by now as she'd driven to Restructure and back at least sixty times during her training period and so now she knew it like the back of her hand but she'd left slightly earlier than required that morning, so that she could stop off en-route to collect some breakfast.

Everything about Talitha's new job, in her

opinion, seemed to be absolutely perfect in that she'd been given her own consultation room in which to see clients and it even had a coffee machine inside it which was another positive aspect of her working accommodation. In terms of her boss, Professor Heisner was quite quirky and slightly eccentric but he appeared to be very laid back and possessed a cheerful disposition which made him very approachable and extremely easy to talk to and work for. The other two staff that worked for Restructure that Talitha had already actually met were the Receptionist Yucala, who seemed to be extremely helpful and very polite from what Talitha had seen of her and the Laboratory Assistant Moses, who seemed pleasant enough although he was rather quiet and slightly odd at times.

One of the most important elements of Talitha's working day however, was the actual fact that she would now actually be responsible for her very own client list, instead of merely showing someone else's clients into a consultation room and that really excited her. Despite the fact that it was a much heavier work responsibility than Talitha had ever had in the past, it absolutely delighted her that Professor Heisner had chosen to employ her to perform such an important role in his organization and she joyously embraced the trust and confidence that he'd placed in her abilities as she drove.

For two whole months prior to the clinic's grand opening, Talitha had actually been trained personally by Professor Heisner himself and it had been very intense as she'd spent the entire time diligently preparing for her new position. The Professor had provided Talitha with very detailed information about his work during that time and various reading materials which she'd even taken home some evenings and at times, she'd spent an hour or so at home just giving them a read through in preparation for her responsibilities as an actual consultant. In Talitha's mind, this was definitely more than just a job to her as it would actually be the very first time that she would actually apply very elaborate cosmetic changes to a person's human body and so she'd wanted to ensure that she fully understood those very complex, intricate procedures before she actually performed them in person.

Every single part of Talitha's work had been fully explained to her and she'd been briefed by Professor Heisner on absolutely every possible task that she would have to perform which meant, all that really remained now was Talitha's first application of what she'd learnt to an actual human body. The actual Downloads themselves had been explained and even illustrated inside the Restructure system and the preparation of client notes had been demonstrated many times which had to be submitted almost religiously after every client session. Various counseling methods had been discussed at length and taught to Talitha and she'd learnt about a variety of other pre-Download and post-Download procedures that had to be adhered to and applied as required. Deep down inside, Talitha now actually felt fully equipped to step into her role as she'd been very thoroughly prepared for it and so she really felt that she could now handle any difficulty or eventuality that might present itself as she internally prepared for her first official week alone as a consultant and her very first group of human clients.

Several of the beauticians and cosmetic surgeries that Talitha had worked for in the past had simply given her a small space just behind their main reception area in which to work from and at times, it had actually been quite cramped and she'd often felt that it hadn't really projected a very professional image. Since Talitha had already spent two months training inside the Restructure building however, she'd actually spent some time in her own actual consultation room and she'd been absolutely delighted and extremely motivated by both it's size and the various facilities it offered.

The consultation room that Talitha had been given was actually quite large and it even managed to house a small kitchenette inside of it which was situated at one side of the room, along with a coffee machine and a small fridge. At one side of her consultation room, there was a small boardroom meeting table and a very large, wafer thin screen which sat just above it that clung to the wall right behind it. A small bathroom and toilet adjoined onto her main consultation room and at the very rear end of the main room, there was also another small adjoining room where she'd been instructed, she would actually perform the actual Download procedures for each of her clients.

Once Talitha had stopped off and collected her breakfast, a bacon bap with lashings of brown sauce, she quickly resumed her journey as she rejoiced in the fact that she was headed out of the city, against the flow of the usual rush hour traffic. The drive to work each working day, since Talitha had been recruited to work for Restructure had been a refreshing change and extremely fast due to the clinic's remote location as opposed to Talitha's past positions of employment which had been slap bang right in the middle of the city, not just outside of it.

Many years had gone by where Talitha had literally had to struggle and fight each morning just to actually arrive at work on time, not just against the cars but also against the very frustrating city traffic lights which seemed to change at the most inconvenient times and usually delayed her journeys even more. Quite fortunately for Talitha however, Professor Heisner's clinic Restructure was situated just on the outskirts of the city and that meant, there would no longer be huge lines of traffic to fight through every working day and absolutely no stubborn, difficult traffic lights at all to wait impatiently behind.

On the actual highway itself, there were very few vehicles headed in the same direction as Talitha as she drove and she silently rejoiced in the fact that the roads that morning were delightfully clear. Eagerness and enthusiasm silently began to accumulate and grow inside Talitha as she neared her intended destination and as the ripples of excitement flowed through her body, her skin began to tingle. Suddenly, it actually struck Talitha that for the very first time ever, since she'd actually graduated, she was really looking forward to attending work for once and that was a great feeling indeed.

Apparently for Talitha's very first client intake, she would actually be assigned seven clients of her own and Professor Heisner had provided her with a short briefing about each one the week before. Every one of her client's circumstances intrigued Talitha and she definitely felt as if she would be challenged immensely by their various situations. Although it was very exciting for Talitha to actually have full control over her own client's procedures, it was also a huge professional responsibility and deep down inside Talitha fully appreciated that fact. Part of Talitha felt extremely excited about her client list as it was actually very challenging but part of her also felt quite worried as she completely understood the seriousness of her role and the fact that she now owed a huge duty of care towards her clients and that, that duty of care was not something that she could take lightly at all.

The parking lot was almost empty when Talitha arrived and only two vehicles sat inside it and as she quickly parked her car inside the space that had been allocated to her, she noticed how very quiet it was unlike the previous Friday evening when it had been filled to the brim with vehicles due to Restructure's grand opening. Once the car's engine had been switched off, the vehicle immediately fell silent as the music immediately stopped playing and Talitha began to internally prepare herself to enter inside the large corporate looking building that now stood directly in front of her. Today Talitha knew, would definitely be very different and today, the building that looked very much like an office block on the exterior would now become the scientific Download clinic that Professor Heisner had intended it to be. Real work would now begin as Talitha's training period had definitely ended and that meant, life had just become a lot more serious.

A deep breath was taken as Talitha inhaled as she stepped out of her car, today was the beginning of a new era in Talitha's life and huge clouds of potential now dangled deliciously from the sky just above her head as she walked towards the entrance to the building. Every breath Talitha took was filled with eager anticipation as she prepared to grab opportunity firmly by the hand and walk through the doors of Restructure for the first time as an actual consultant. Her entrance through the doors directly in front of Talitha would ultimately represent her stepping through a new door in life as her responsibilities changed and her professional challenges grew. Now Talitha would actually have the kind of duties and benefits that she'd only ever dreamed of having and the winds of change had finally blown in her favor in terms of her career and brought something very positive into her life.

Directly in front of Talitha, two smoked glass doors silently guarded the entrance to the white stone and glass Restructure building and as she prepared to push them open, an excited gasp suddenly escaped from her lips. One of her hands was armed with the latte that she'd purchased on her way into work but the bacon bap that she'd bought earlier that morning had already been hungrily consumed. Life was definitely improving for Talitha and she'd definitely jumped on the right train of opportunity when she'd applied for the position at Restructure and then actually attended her interview and now, she just couldn't wait for her professional journey to actually commence.

Just a few seconds later, Talitha decisively pushed open one of the smoked glass doors directly in front of her and then stepped through the door as she entered inside the building's reception area. Once inside the main reception area, Talitha immediately noticed Yucala who was seated behind the reception desk, equipped with a very wide, warm, large, friendly beaming smile and a pleasant demeanor. In terms of Yucala's build, she was actually quite a large and heavy set woman and Talitha estimated that she had to be in her late forties but despite her size, she had the softest, sweetest mildest voice that Talitha had ever heard which seemed to be in direct opposition to her physical frame.

Whenever the two women actually spoke, the sound of Yucala's voice would usually make Talitha smile as it was so unusual and so very soft and her voice, for some unknown reason, Talitha also found was extremely comforting and soothing. The second Talitha stepped inside the reception area however, before she could actually greet Yucala or attempt to depart from it, Professor Heisner suddenly appeared as he entered the area from a nearby hallway and then politely greeted both women as he quickly strode across the reception area towards them both.

"Good morning ladies." Professor Heisner boomed.

"Good morning Professor Heisner." Yucala immediately replied.

Talitha smiled. "Good morning Professor Heisner and good morning Yucala." She said as she drew closer to the large, dark grey reception desk that Yucala was seated directly behind.

Every word that the three spoke to each other that morning seemed to decorate the air almost like a song as every syllable clung to the particles of air around Talitha as she quietly absorbed her new beginning. The huge welcoming smile on Yucala's face and the pleasantness of Professor Heisner's greeting were indeed a refreshing change from the usual rough grunts and head nods of tolerance that Talitha was used to receiving at work on a Monday morning and the very warm reception absolutely delighted her.

"Good morning Talitha." Yucala quickly replied as she turned to face her.

Despite the fact there was no actual heating inside the reception area that Talitha could see, a very warm glow seemed to emanate directly from Yucala's face as she smiled. Each of her cheeks seemed to shine in a similar manner to the gentle rays of sunshine which shone down across a lake on a bright summer's day that made it sparkle and glisten. Between Yucala's lips Talitha could see slight traces of her crystal white teeth that sparkled as she spoke and it was almost as if her smile was attempting to break through the last remaining dusky particles of the morning as it attempted to chase away the final remnants of the darkness from the previous night. Yucala's smile seemed to spread warmth and happiness to everyone around her and it immediately lifted Talitha's spirits as she silently appreciated Yucala's warmth.

"How was your journey this morning Talitha?" Professor Heisner asked enthusiastically. "How was the traffic, not too heavy I hope?"

"There was very little traffic on the road Professor Heisner, since I was heading out of the city, so my journey was actually quite quick." Talitha quickly clarified.

"Good, I'm glad to see that you managed to get here bright and early as we have a lot to do this week." Professor Heisner quickly pointed out as he began to nod his head. "Right, I have to get back to my lab and Talitha we have a briefing later today just after lunch." He mentioned as he prepared to leave the reception area. "I'll speak to you both later and have a good morning."

Much to the amusement of the two women, just a few seconds later, the Professor quickly scampered off back along the corridor from which he'd come as he headed back to his laboratory and his day's work. The Professor's rather abrupt departure immediately prompted Talitha to think about her own as she interpreted his disappearance as her cue to start making her own way towards her consultation room. A day's work lay ahead of Talitha and hanging around inside the reception area certainly would not help her to achieve that and so a polite nod was quickly given to Yucala as Talitha prepared to vacate the reception area and actually begin work.

Technically because Talitha's training days were now officially over that meant, she was actually slightly unsure as to when she would see Professor Heisner each working week, apart from the direct briefings between the two that he arranged directly with her. A thought suddenly crossed Talitha's mind as she walked quietly along the white corridor towards her consultation room that some days now perhaps, she might not even actually see Professor Heisner at all. Predominantly, Talitha's working days would now be spent with her actual clients and her own actual workload and that meant, it was highly unlikely that she would spend very much time with Professor Heisner and that transition it appeared had officially begun.

From that day forward, the focus of Talitha's working day would now be her clients, their needs and their requirements instead of her own as her training period was now, officially over. Although the prospect of the day ahead filled Talitha with excitement, it also made her feel slightly nervous and her body began to tingle inside as she walked towards her consultation room door as eager anticipation surged through her veins. Finally, Talitha's first independent day as a Bodily Enhancements Consultant had arrived and although it was a change, it was an extremely pleasant and very welcome one.

For Professor Heisner, his Monday morning had already been meticulously planned as most of his working days were and as he stepped inside his laboratory and prepared to start work that Monday morning was certainly no exception. Fortunately, Moses was already inside his laboratory and waiting for him to arrive, so that they could proceed with the experiments they'd planned to perform that morning. The week ahead had already been scheduled by Professor Heisner and it promised to be extremely hectic as it was officially the first week that the doors of Restructure would be open for business and that spurred him on as he strode briskly across the large room towards the hidden enclosure at the foot of his lab.

Before lunchtime arrived that day, Professor Heisner had to not only face but also complete a huge mountain of tasks which meant, Moses would definitely be required to assist him all morning.

Inside the Professor's laboratory, in a hidden enclosure at the foot of the large room, there were some creatures that Professor Heisner usually housed there which he often utilized to perform experiments on and that particular morning, those creatures would also definitely be required. Some essential, very urgent experiments and tests had to be conducted that day by Professor Heisner which were necessary preparation for the actual clients that Restructure would be servicing and that meant, delays were not a viable option and could not possibly be allowed to occur.

True to his usual form, Moses's appearance was very much like the Professor's own and he looked quite untidy, rather rough, crumpled and slightly disorganized but their external chaos didn't seem to bother either of the two men as they politely nodded their heads at each other. A few grunts were quickly exchanged as the two outwardly acknowledged each other's presence and then silently began to prepare for the work they'd planned to perform that morning.

Some very complex Download tests had been planned for the morning ahead and they would actually be conducted upon not only the small creatures inside the hidden enclosure but also upon some robotic frames that Professor Heisner kept in a long built-in wall cabinet at one side of the hidden smaller room. Although the animals and robotic frames were a far cry from an actual human body, they had been utilized successfully for many years by the Professor to test his work as human bodies were not easy to secure for the purpose of scientific experiments. The animals and robotic frames however, allowed Professor Heisner to conduct live experiments without the complexity of human beings which in his mind was absolutely necessary in order to ensure that the Downloads and bodily enhancements were actually safe and fit for actual human consumption.

Live experimentation upon human beings was quite frankly, totally out of the question and Professor Heisner fully understood and appreciated that fact as such experiments could never actually happen, not in a state endorsed clinic that had actually been granted special licenses by the government to operate. Prior to the formation of Restructure, throughout the Professor's research years, he'd actually managed to find a few human volunteers among his personal friends, social contacts and associates that he'd managed to convince to participate in his experiments but that participation was not common or usual and such volunteers didn't come along every day.

In the past, some of those human volunteers had actually allowed the Professor to experiment upon their bodies which fortunately for Professor Heisner had helped him to prepare for the opening of Restructure but that had actually taken him years. The work that Restructure was expected to perform was not simple or straightforward from a scientific or a technological perspective and it had required years and years of tireless dedication and devotion but Professor Heisner had diligently put in the hours and committed to his goals and now, he stood on the brink of actual realization and that reality absolutely thrilled him.

Meanwhile, on the other side of the Restructure building, Talitha had by now arrived outside her consultation room and as she unlocked the door, she took a deep breath and then pushed it gently open as she prepared to step inside the room. Every inch of Talitha felt absolutely thrilled as she quietly rejoiced internally and silently accepted that this large space was all really for her and that now she would operate and function inside it as a professional every single working day. The responsibility that Talitha had been given was indeed huge but she welcomed it with very open arms as she internally stepped up towards it and prepared to carry the weight of that honor upon her shoulders every working day. Seven very real human clients had already been allocated to Talitha and as she sat down behind her desk and switched on the Restructure system, she prepared to browse through each of their client profiles in preparation for her briefing with Professor Heisner later that afternoon.

Regarding Talitha's actual client list, she had played absolutely no part whatsoever in the selection of her first group of clients as Professor Heisner had selected each one himself and in many ways that lack of involvement was a relief to Talitha as it had given her a start that would perhaps be slightly easier. Due to the fact that this was Restructure's very first client intake, Professor Heisner had carefully selected each client, in order to ensure that the newly formed corporate entity would hit the ground running and to minimize any potential problems during the company's corporate launch and Talitha could fully appreciate why he'd actually done so.

The input from Professor Heisner had comforted Talitha somewhat as he'd sought to reduce any potential complexities that might actually hamper Talitha's ability to deliver and he'd kept her initial client list relatively simple until her skills and experience were slightly more established. To actually jump in at the deep end initially and actually be responsible for the selection of her own clients herself, would have really been a difficult task for Talitha and definitely a step too far out of her comfort zone and she'd accepted that instinctively and automatically. Once the clinic had grown, established itself and Talitha had fully settled in, Professor Heisner had reassured her that the quite stringent monitoring and selection process of potential clients would be less necessary and then she would actually be responsible for the selection of her own client intake herself. For the first six months however, Professor Heisner had committed himself to vetting Talitha's clients and simplifying her workload as much as he possibly could and that safety net suited Talitha right down to the ground.

"Now this is a real career." Talitha murmured as she touched the screen directly in front of her and waited for the client profile that she wanted to inspect to appear.

An unread email suddenly popped up on Talitha's screen and she immediately opened it and as she began to read it, she quickly realized that it was in fact, actually from Moses. Professor Heisner's Laboratory Assistant Moses, Talitha had actually met now many times and he had been identified as the person that Talitha should seek assistance from with regards to any systems problems, or if there were any technical problems with the actual Downloads themselves. In terms of his appearance, Moses very much reminded Talitha of the Professor himself as he had a very ruffled, crumpled and untidy exterior and that alone made Talitha smile every time she actually saw him.

Perhaps, Talitha quietly speculated, his untidy

appearance was the result of some kind of internal admiration for Professor Heisner, or perhaps that was just how scientific brainiac males were brainy and messy. Perhaps, Moses tried to mimic everything that the Professor did, due to his scientific admiration for him and perhaps that even extended to his very messy appearance, if so Moses had definitely succeeded as in Talitha's opinion, he was just as, if not even more messy looking than the Professor himself. In Talitha's opinion, it just wasn't humanly possible to be that messy looking unintentionally, she quietly concluded as she inspected the contents of the email and a deliberate effort really had to have gone into that look that Moses seemed to so proudly carry around with him each day.

Nothing particularly urgent was actually inside the email itself, just some system instructions and it didn't contain any kind of socially engaging message at all but that was to be expected really as Moses wasn't really someone that made an effort to be socially engaging. Whenever Talitha had met Moses in the past, he'd seemed to be quite laid back but not a man of many words and he just didn't say anything really that didn't need to actually be said, so the lack of social content in his email made perfect sense, considering the kind of person Moses actually was. In that one way, Moses did actually differ slightly from Professor

Heisner, who despite his messy appearance was actually quite socially astute which was probably due to his varied life experiences, Talitha quietly concluded. Moses was just very quiet and he seemed to be quite socially awkward and at times, he even came across as rather odd but that wasn't something that particularly worried Talitha as she didn't really have much to do with him on a daily basis when it came to the actual performance of her job.

"Someone around here has to be the odd one." Talitha muttered as she smiled. "And I guess that job was assigned to Moses."

A gentle smile lingered upon Talitha's lips as she remembered the very first time that she'd actually met Moses in person, she'd noticed his awkward demeanor even then and he certainly hadn't changed, despite the fact that she'd now actually met many times. Regardless of his social awkwardness however, Moses had seemed helpful enough professionally as he'd offered to assist Talitha several times in any way that he possibly could.

"Any problems Talitha, you just give me a shout." Moses had politely offered. "I do all the systems stuff around here. I'm kind of like the tech guy in a lab coat."

Besides that quite helpful, friendly remark Moses hadn't really said much else to Talitha that day, or any other day for that matter. The offer of assistance that day however had been appreciatively received as Talitha had silently absorbed his chaotic ruffled hair and very creased shirt that had sat just under the white lab coat he'd worn which had seemed to be desperately shouting out for some attention from a comb and an iron, two factors that Moses had seemed to be totally ignorant off. Quite possibly, Talitha quietly decided, Moses didn't actually do any ironing inside his home, or if he did he was absolutely terrible at it as with that shirt, ironing definitely wasn't one of his strengths.

Perhaps physical appearance and tidiness just weren't much of a priority for scientific men, Talitha quietly mused as she silently likened Moses to the Professor and noticed the similarities between them both. Both men looked very chaotic, extremely disorganized and as if they had just crawled out of bed and seemed to show very little concern towards the issue of their own personal grooming. In many ways that actually amused Talitha as she'd come from an environment that was so very different and where most of the men that she met every working day, cared perhaps just a tad too much about their physical appearance. If either man had worked inside some the beauty clinics that Talitha had worked for, they'd never be able to get away with presenting such a rough, disheveled appearance at work every day and that Talitha knew for an absolute fact.

Regardless of how messy the two men actually looked, Talitha quietly accepted, those two very messy looking men would now be the two men that she would spend most of her working days with and that was something that really, she would just have to get used to. Another realization suddenly struck Talitha as she began to review her work diary inside the Restructure system as she analyzed her working week ahead, now her working days were definitely not going to be as fast paced as they'd been in some of the beauty salons and cosmetic surgeries that she'd worked for but that for now, was perfectly fine. The more moderate pace of her workload actually suited Talitha right down to the ground as the work she would now be involved in was much more complex, a lot more involved and required higher levels of care. Once Talitha's experience and skills increased, her workload would almost certainly increase but for now, Talitha was just happy to appreciate the uniqueness of her position and paddle around inside the shallow end of being a professional consultant as her role would definitely present her with some very interesting challenges in the future and that was not only extremely exciting but also very motivating.

INVITATIONS TO RESTRUCTURE

Meanwhile on the other side of the Restructure building, towards the very rear of the structure, the Professor diligently and attentively began to prepare for his experiments that day which would predominantly be performed upon some mice and a squirrel that sat inside some white plastic and wire cages within the hidden enclosure itself. The secret hidden enclosure was concealed just behind a wall inside the actual laboratory and it was quite heavily populated by small mammals of various kinds that were kept locked away inside it, purely for the purpose of Professor Heisner's experiments. Not all the creatures stored there would be utilized that day but a few mice and a squirrel were definitely required which meant, the remainder would remain inside their cages undisturbed, for the time being at least.

All in all, there were at least one hundred species housed inside the hidden enclosure which was concealed from view by the panel like wall that not only hid the enclosure's existence but also the Professor's test subject collection. Most people that entered inside the Professor's laboratory didn't even know that the hidden enclosure actually existed as the wall sufficiently disguised it's presence and the area was completely sealed off whenever it was occupied by Professor Heisner himself. A dark grey security panel masked the enclosure's existence and blended in with the rest of the walls inside the laboratory which protected the area from any unwanted attention and from any prying eyes.

Some robotic human shaped frames were also stored inside the hidden enclosure which were kept in a built-in wall cupboard and both the wall cupboard and enclosure were kept locked whenever the Professor wasn't present, or even when he was present, just as a precaution. Only two people on the face of the earth actually had any access to the hidden enclosure itself, or actually knew it was there, Professor Heisner and Moses and hence they were the only two people that knew about the creatures that resided within it.

Due to the confidential nature of Professor Heisner's work, he always kept the grey security panel closed, just in case anyone unexpectedly visited his laboratory which was rare as Yucala and Talitha usually only attended when they had been personally invited to do so. Neither woman actually knew about the hidden enclosure's existence, or would ever dream of visiting the laboratory alone and uninvited and therefore they were totally oblivious to any of the creatures hidden and housed inside it.

For Professor Heisner, the enclosure was an essential core operations area where he performed some of the background research work that supported the core functions of Restructure's services and it was the only place inside the building where such experiments could actually be performed. Some information about Restructure's operations hadn't actually been shared with either Yucala or Talitha and that was due to the fact that Professor Heisner had felt that very intricate scientific information might make them feel slightly awkward.

In Professor Heisner's opinion, women were not always very supportive of live experimentation upon real animal test subjects and he'd decided that they would perhaps not be in favor of what they might deem as cruel, unnecessary clinical trials. At times, the obvious contradiction amongst the female gender actually amused Professor Heisner as women usually benefited the most from cosmetic procedures and almost all cosmetic procedures had actually required some form of animal experimentation, prior to their actual realization but for some reason, women were usually horrified by the whole notion of such experiments actually occurring.

Humanity and human beings now demanded absolute perfection from every aspect of their lives and the world of science had done its very best to step up to those demands, in order to enable human progress but that progression had come at a price which had to be paid by someone or something and animals had to some extent footed that bill. Science generally was not as concerned with human affections towards the animal world or it's subjects and that was something that Professor Heisner not only fully accepted but was actually, very accustomed to.

The hard reality was that human demands for perfection had been placed upon the scientific community and if the general population actually wanted these advancements from science and from life, a sacrifice definitely had to be made in order to provide them and animals were usually the ones to make that sacrifice as human beings certainly would not. Medical and cosmetic scientific advancements had to be tested on someone, or something before they could actually benefit the world at large and be administered to real human beings and that meant, experiments usually had to be performed on animals, plants and robotic forms before such procedures could actually benefit human beings themselves.

"We better make a start Moses." Professor Heisner instructed as he headed towards his work bench. "We'll be working with some mice, some frames and a squirrel today."

Moses immediately nodded his head in response. "Yes Sir." He replied as he walked towards some of the cages that lined one of the walls inside the hidden enclosure.

A strong cup of black coffee had been collected en-route and Professor Heisner placed it gently down on top of the long worktop bench which ran along one of the enclosure's walls as he prepared to begin. Technically although the Restructure system was now actually live, there were still a couple of tasks that remained to be completed and those tasks had to be performed that very same morning, so that the system would be ready for incoming clients that afternoon which meant, there was a lot to be done before lunchtime.

Directly opposite the Professor's long worktop bench, at least one hundred and twenty white plastic cages with wire fronts lined the wall which were all piled up on top of each other and sat in neat rows. Inside each cage there was a small creature and along another wall in the enclosure there was a long grey wall cabinet that discreetly housed the human like robotic frames which Professor Heisner and one of his colleagues had initially started to build many years ago. Although the hidden enclosure was slightly smaller than Professor Heisner's main laboratory, it was actually quite large and very well equipped which allowed him to conduct the experiments he needed to on a daily basis and so it adequately suited and fulfilled all the Professor's scientific needs.

Over three decades ago, the robotic frames had been built by Professor Heisner and his colleague Professor Latimer, during their junior years when they'd been placed at the same research center together where they had worked as junior scientists but now their work was far more sophisticated and the frames had been adapted accordingly. Each robotic frame inside the cabinet looked extremely realistic and almost human but they all had missing body parts and some had no actual skin overlay over parts of their robotic structures and so it was obvious that they weren't actually human to anyone that actually saw them. Due to Latimer's decision to specialize in robotic science, he'd not joined Professor Heisner in his venture at Restructure but he had provided the Professor with five robotic frames which were now significantly enhanced, to enable Professor Heisner to conduct his experiments freely upon them and realize his goals more effectively.

Absolutely no ethical issues at all lurked inside Professor Heisner's mind and he was extremely comfortable when it came to the performance of tests on live animals and robotic frames, no matter how human the robotic frames might actually look. Some live experimentation definitely had to be performed upon non human entities as opposed to live experimentation on human forms which could possibly result in physical deformities via a system that might yield sporadic, inconsistent and chaotic results and Professor Heisner felt at peace with that scientific reality.

Cosmetic procedures were on the increase and as human beings placed increasing demands on cosmetic surgeons and sought to perfect their physical forms, the results could at times be disastrous. Each surgical procedure involved the insertion of very sharp objects and false materials into actual human flesh and nothing about those procedures was natural and the impact of those procedures at times, could be extremely negative. In Professor Heisner's mind, his clinic's existence was therefore totally justified as it was a necessary provision to replace an inferior method of bodily enhancement that quite often butchered human skin and inflicted more damage upon human flesh than it actually avoided and prevented.

Once Professor Heisner felt satisfied that he was actually ready to proceed with the experiments that he'd planned that morning and that all his preparation work had been performed, he turned to face the animal cages and then began to inspect them slightly more closely. A thoughtful expression crossed the Professor's face as he quietly observed just how messy and dirty some of the cages appeared to be as he glanced at each one. Each cage seemed to be littered and decorated with bits of uneaten food and lumps of excrement and they really looked like they all needed to be cleaned out immediately.

"You have been very busy this weekend haven't you?" Professor Heisner asked as he stood up and then walked towards some of the cages. He glanced down at the floor and quickly noticed that some bits of straw and sawdust lay scattered across the ground and then gently shook his head as he turned to face Moses. "Moses can you feed the animals please and clean out their cages?"

"Yes Professor Heisner." Moses replied as he nodded his head. "I'll start doing that straight away."

"They really seem to do quite a lot of things in such a tiny space don't they?" Professor Heisner asked as he peered inside one of the cages and quietly began to inspect it's interior.

"They do Professor Heisner." Moses agreed. "They're very busy little things."

For the next few minutes, nothing but silence accompanied Moses as he quietly began his rather laborious task of cleaning out all the animals' cages and feeding the cage occupants. The animals inside the cages suddenly seemed to sense that they were just about to get fed as Moses opened up some of the wire cage doors and dipped his hand inside the cage interiors and a commotion of squeals and scratches rapidly began to emanate from each one as Professor Heisner stood and watched him for a few minutes.

"You've really gone and done it now Moses, now they all know it's time to get fed." Professor Heisner teased. "And the noise won't stop until their feeding trays are full."

An empty cage lay on the ground right next the rows of cages and Moses quickly picked it up as he prepared to empty each cage out one at a time in order to clean each creature's home out. Once Moses had the empty cage inside his hands, he began to open up one of the cages directly in front of him and then attempted to catch the squirrel inside it which he'd planned to transfer into the empty cage. Despite his efforts to try and capture the small creature however, the occupant of the cage he'd opened was having absolutely none of it as animal began to rapidly dart around it's cage and avoid his clutch and Professor Heisner smiled as he watched.

Much to Moses's relief however, just a few minutes later, he finally managed to catch the squirrel and it was then quickly transferred to the empty cage, so that he could then actually start to clean out the cage that it had just occupied. A few more animal cages were then cleaned out relatively quickly as Moses began to make his way along the lines of cages as he continued to perform his tasks for that particular Monday morning.

Upon Professor Heisner's face there was a very amused smile as he returned to his work bench and his experiments as he left Moses to complete with the rather laborious task he'd assigned to him. The cleaning of cages task that the Professor had allocated to Moses that morning would definitely take him a while but it was a very necessary one and it had to be performed at least once every few days, in order to ensure that the animals were kept in a decent, clean environment. Once seated, the Professor quickly began to interact with Restructure as he began to access some of the functionalities inside of it that would enable him to conduct the experiments he wished to perform that day.

Quite unexpectedly and rather suddenly however, when Moses arrived at the tenth cage, just as he was about to clean the cage out and fed the creature that lived inside it which was a mouse, the mouse actually managed to escape. Somehow, the mouse had actually managed to slip in-between Moses's hand and the two cages when he'd tried to transfer it and as it silently dropped down onto the floor, Moses frantically tried to stretch out his hands in order to catch it.

Rather interestingly and much to Professor Heisner's amusement, the mouse somehow managed to actually avoid being captured by Moses as he lunged forward to grab it and the mouse ducked just below his hand. The Professor began to chuckle as he started to watch a fiasco unfold as the mouse scurried rapidly across the floor until it found a hiding place where it quickly attempted to conceal it's body from view.

A hot pursuit rapidly began as Moses frantically began to chase the mouse around the inside of the hidden enclosure which amused Professor Heisner no end as he silently watched Moses's quite strategic but completely useless efforts. Several objects positioned on the floor, seemed to provide the perfect hiding place for the small mammal as it darted in and out of each one and the tiny creature almost appeared to silently, very cheekily, mock Moses and rejoice in his inability to capture it. Somehow, it almost seemed to Professor Heisner as he watched as if the creature wanted to taunt Moses and it had definitely managed to frustrate him as Moses gave off an angry sigh and then shook his head in annoyance.

"I don't know Moses, it seems to me like that mouse might be a bit too fast for you." Professor Heisner teased. "You'll have to be a bit faster if you want to catch that one. It's really giving you a run for your money and your test tubes."

Moses nodded in agreement. "I know, how can something so small be so fast Professor Heisner?" He asked. "And it's very smart, look at how it's hiding from me."

"It'll get tired soon and then you might actually be able to catch it Moses, there's really nowhere else that it can go, there's no holes in the floorboards, or in any of the walls." Professor Heisner quickly pointed out as he grinned.

Approximately ten minutes more passed by as Professor Heisner continued to watch Moses with an amused expression on his face as Moses pursued the mouse and chased the tiny creature all around the hidden enclosure. Somehow, quite interestingly, the animal actually managed to avoid Moses and capture several times as it scurried rapidly across the grey shiny floor and kept just out of his reach. On several occasions, the small brown creature even actually stopped for a split second and then looked at Moses as if it knew that Moses was actually it's enemy, just before it quickly darted underneath another piece of furniture or equipment and hid from him again.

"This is definitely going to take a while." Moses finally admitted as he stopped and just stared at the shiny black stool legs that the mouse had just hidden behind.

"Quite possibly all morning." Professor Heisner agreed. "You're just not fast enough really Moses. I'd just carry on with your tasks and let it run around until it's tired and then you might just be able to catch it."

"Absolutely not Professor Heisner, I refuse to be defeated by such a tiny, inferior creature." Moses replied as he stubbornly shook his head. "I can't be defeated by a mouse that would be totally unacceptable."

Professor Heisner laughed. "I know Moses, if anyone finds out, you'll never live it down. Don't worry though, I won't tell anyone." He teased.

Regardless of Moses's sheer determination however, the mouse continued to cheekily evade capture as it mockingly peeked out at him and then darted in and out of various hiding places whenever he actually lunged forward and attempted to grab it. Very frustratingly and quite annoyingly for Moses, the second he actually drew close enough to almost catch the creature, it would suddenly dart out of one hiding place and then scurry off in another direction completely as it found hiding place after hiding place which it utilized effectively as it managed to totally avoid Moses's grasp.

"I better get on with some work Moses because you'll be trying to catch that mouse all day." Professor Heisner concluded as he gently shook his head, grinned and then rose to his feet. "That mouse sure doesn't want to go back inside any of those cages."

For the purposes of Professor Heisner's first experiment that morning, he required a squirrel and so he crossed the room as he approached the occupied animal cages and then plucked the required cage from one of the rows as he prepared to make a start. The creature inside the cage began to frantically scurry around the interior of the cage as it was rapidly whisked across the room but the cage door remained tightly locked, so unlike the mouse, there was no possible means of escape. Inside the squirrel's paw like hands, it clutched onto a small nut and in some respects, the creature almost looked human as it darted around the cage, obviously alarmed by the sudden movement.

Once Professor Heisner had returned to his workbench, the occupied cage was then quickly placed upon it as he sat back down and then touched the wafer thin screen directly in front of him which immediately lit up. A grid suddenly appeared on the screen directly in front of the Professor as the cage dropped down below the surface of the worktop as a rectangular hole suddenly appeared.

"Specimen 25." A female voice suddenly announced.

Professor Heisner smiled as he touched the screen in front of him again and entered some commands. "Specimen 25 is now ready for modification Restructure. Prepare experiment number 350." He instructed.

"Download sequence 350 is ready for implementation." The female voice rapidly confirmed as Restructure responded to his request. "Specimen 25 is now being scanned."

"Don't worry this won't hurt Mr. Squirrel. Restructure's just measuring you and checking your bodily parameters and then I'll be giving you a bodily enhancement." Professor Heisner reassured the creature as he glanced down inside the rectangular hole. "You do eat rather well, so your weight has probably changed since last week."

"Scan complete." Restructure confirmed. "Download sequence 350 has been initialized."

"Have you managed to catch that mouse yet Moses?" Professor Heisner teased as he turned to face Moses with an amused expression on his face as he quietly observed that the chase with the mouse definitely seemed far from over and that it looked as if it still had a very long way to go.

Moses shook his head.

"Right. I better get ready for my next experiment." Professor Heisner muttered as he suddenly rose to his feet and then strode across the room towards the grey wall cabinet as he prepared to open it up. "Unlike you Moses, my tasks seem to be going according to plan this morning." He teased.

Five robotic frames sat inside the cabinet, hung up upon the wall and as Professor Heisner rolled the cabinet door open, he cast his eyes thoughtfully over each one as he internally considered which one he required that morning. A quick glance was cast back towards Moses as his assistance would actually be required to move the robotic frame around the room that Professor Heisner wanted to utilize but he didn't want to distract Moses from catching the mouse just yet as it seemed to have become a very personal mission.

For a split second, Moses stopped chasing the mouse and then paused as he stared at the interior of the cabinet and the robotic frames it contained but not a word was spoken. The Professor's actions had distracted Moses momentarily from his pursuit and the mouse but once Professor Heisner closed the cabinet door, Moses quickly refocused himself and then glanced back down at the floor as he began to search for the tiny, elusive creature once again. Almost immediately Moses frustratingly realized however that the mouse was now actually nowhere to be seen and that it had hidden from sight completely.

"I'll tell you what Moses, if you actually manage to catch that mouse by lunchtime, I'll give you a larger lab space." Professor Heisner teased. "Since your own lab space is actually quite small."

"Thank you very much Professor Heisner." Moses replied. "I'm definitely going to catch it very soon. I've analyzed all its weaknesses and I've even blocked some of its hiding places."

"Well Moses, you can't possibly let a tiny mouse like that beat you, so you better keep trying." Professor Heisner teased. "You have a great mind and a huge physical presence and that mouse, well it's just a tiny, little thing. How can such a tiny creature be smarter and faster than you?"

"I know, it's very annoying and extremely frustrating." Moses agreed as he suddenly lunged forward and then tried to grab the mouse again as it stuck it's tiny head out from around the corner of the cage that it had hidden behind.

Quite unfortunately however, just a few seconds later, Moses actually landed flat on his face upon the ground as he attempted to stretch forward just a little too far as he attempted to grab the mouse again, much to Professor Heisner's amusement and Moses's absolute horror. Rather mockingly, the mouse then actually ran across the tips of Moses's fingers as it rapidly scurried across the ground just in front of him as it seemed to rejoice in his frustration and his fall. Failure seemed to quietly taunt Moses as he silently picked himself up of the floor and then prepared to pursue the creature that had evaded his grasp once again.

"You'll never be a mouse catcher Moses." Professor Heisner observed playfully as he watched. "It's a good thing you're a scientist really."

On the other side of the Restructure building, Talitha sat quietly inside her consultation room as she reviewed some of the client profiles that had been allocated to her by Professor Heisner. According to Professor Heisner, the first client intake comprised of seven clients that had now been formally invited to attend the clinic as actual clients and their initial consultations had already been planned, agreed and confirmed, all of which would take place that very same week. Time that morning seemed to go by very quickly as each minute literally flew out of Talitha's consultation room window as she waited for the afternoon to begin when her first client consultation was due to occur and her first human client would actually arrive.

Lunchtime silently came and then went in a flash as it rapidly deserted Talitha and as she headed back to the building, she internally prepared for her meeting with Professor Heisner that afternoon which was due to happen just before her first client consultation. Although Professor

Heisner had a laboratory and an office, Talitha rarely met him inside his laboratory and because their meeting that afternoon had been scheduled to occur inside his office as she returned from lunch, she made her way directly towards it.

When Talitha arrived outside Professor Heisner's office which was situated on the opposite side of the building from her actual consultation room, she knocked on the door and then patiently waited for him to invite her inside but no response was immediately forthcoming. Another few minutes was spent as Talitha just stood outside the door and continued to wait as she quietly deliberated as to where Professor Heisner might actually be and why he might possibly be delayed. Just a few minutes later however, the Professor turned up with a slightly flustered expression upon his face as he glanced at Talitha apologetically and then quickly unlocked his office door and pushed it open.

"I almost thought you'd forgotten about me Professor Heisner." Talitha teased.

"Apologies Talitha, I had to conduct some experiments inside my laboratory this morning and well to be perfectly honest, I got a bit carried away." Professor Heisner quickly confessed. "Time it appears can actually be our enemy and it's not always our friend."

"That's okay Professor Heisner, I completely understand." Talitha replied as she smiled.

"Please come in." Professor Heisner invited as he politely held the door open for her. "And take a seat."

"Thanks." Talitha replied as she stepped inside the room and then headed towards one of the large leather, dark grey chairs that sat right next to Professor Heisner's desk. She smiled as she began to quietly observe her surroundings, unlike the Professor's rather chaotic appearance, his office at least seemed to be quite well organized and very tidy, perhaps the cleaner kept it in order, she quietly concluded as she sat down. "I do have a client consultation scheduled for three this afternoon Professor Heisner with Dean, so I'll have to keep an eye on the time." Talitha politely reminded him.

"Don't worry Talitha, I'm aware of that so our meeting won't take very long." Professor Heisner immediately confirmed as he sat down behind his desk and then faced her. "Right, let's look at who you have to actually see this week." He said as he touched the wafer thin screen directly in front of him. "No one too tricky I hope."

Talitha smiled in response. "Yes, hopefully not." She agreed.

"Some of your client's requirements will perhaps be quite complex and even slightly unusual at times but don't let that put you off." Professor Heisner quickly reassured her. "Just give them what they want and what they've paid for as that's the service we're ultimately here to provide and what they choose to do with that provision is quite frankly, none of our business."

"Of course Professor Heisner." Talitha replied.

"Ah yes, I see you have an appointment with Dean this afternoon, I did update his client notes again on Friday." Professor Heisner explained. "You might not have had a chance to read them yet but they were actually quite detailed as I wanted to make sure that you hit the ground running and had a great start to your first face to face client consultation."

"Yes, I've actually seen them." Talitha quickly confirmed. "And I read through them very thoroughly this morning, several times.

"Great that's what I like to hear, a thorough approach and a very positive, proactive attitude." Professor Heisner boomed as he smiled at Talitha. "That means there's less work for me to do."

Talitha smiled. "Is there anything in particular I really should or shouldn't do during each of my client briefings?" She enquired. "I really want my clients to feel comfortable."

"I would just advise you to listen to your clients very carefully and try to listen out for the things they don't say as well as what they directly express to you as not everything that we think is verbally communicated. At times, you might have to read between the lines as sometimes what people don't say is just as important, or even more important than what they do say and you'll have to be sensitive to that in order to establish exactly what they need and what they really want." Professor Heisner advised. "Some people don't really know what they want or need themselves Talitha and in those situations, you'll have to learn to exercise your own judgment."

Talitha nodded her head. "Right Professor Heisner. I'll try my best." She replied.

"It's human nature really to be slightly unsure and indecisive. There's no absolute certainty I've found when it comes to the issue of human beings, their internal desires, motives and overall objectives in life." Professor Heisner advised. "So, you'll have to be quite mindful of those very human complications."

"Yes, I understand." Talitha agreed.

"For instance, someone might decide that they want much larger breasts but then they might discover that their back is aching as their body is not used to the weight of their breast enlargement." Professor Heisner explained as he began to elaborate. "Such situations are bound to arise but you have to be equipped to handle them and sometimes, you really have to think ahead for your clients and make useful recommendations for them. For example, if a client requests a very large breast enlargement, you could then recommend a back strengthening Download to accompany it and so forth."

Talitha nodded.

"Rather unfortunately, unlike science, human beings are not very precise at times Talitha, so you'll also have to take that into account and try to be as precise for your clients as you can possibly be." Professor Heisner advised as he glanced at Talitha's face. "That way, you can satisfy their requests as quickly as possible and keep them reasonably happy."

"Yes Professor Heisner." Talitha agreed.

Just as Professor Heisner had promised, the meeting between the two ended at around quarter to three and as Talitha made her way back towards her consultation room, she prepared slightly nervously for her first client consultation which was due to commence in just fifteen minutes time. A combination of nerves and excitement began to rapidly surge around Talitha's mind and body as she entered back inside the room and then sat down beside her desk as she prepared to skim through Dean's notes again as she waited for him to arrive. Eager anticipation filled Talitha's core but she also noticed that there was a lump of nervousness that sat at the very bottom of her stomach which was almost like a small rock of undigested food and it appeared to be unmovable.

DOWNLOADABLE

Several Download procedures had actually been requested by Dean as Talitha could see from the Restructure system but as Talitha was well aware, not all of those procedures could actually happen in one day, or even during Dean's first or second consultation. Very precise instructions had been provided to Talitha by Professor Heisner and according to those instructions, only one actual Download could be performed for each client during any given client session and no client was exempt from that very strict rule. Professor Heisner had made that absolutely clear to Talitha on several different occasions now and so that was one rule that hung very clearly inside her mind as she prepared to meet Dean for the very first time.

"People's bodies and minds need time to digest the physical changes we make to their appearance Talitha." Professor Heisner had advised during one of his briefings. "Your clients will need time to adjust, not just physically but also emotionally and mentally as every change you make will have an impact upon the rest of their lives and their world and they'll need to be able to cope with the rippling effects of those changes."

Despite the fact that Professor Heisner often seemed rather messy, very disorganized and at times, even quite absent minded, his explanations, logic and sensible approach on that particular issue had made absolute sense to Talitha and she totally agreed with his reasoning. Regardless of his external chaos, Professor Heisner definitely seemed to understand human beings, the world they lived in, their social networks and the impact that his work could potentially have upon each of his client's lives. The majority of people and their bodies did not usually live in a fixed state of isolation, surrounded by just the waters of solitude and most people usually had families, partners, friends, work colleagues, associates and various other acquaintances that they interacted with and hence any changes that they made to themselves would definitely be noticed by someone.

"We want people to enjoy their physical modifications." Professor Heisner had explained. "Not to be traumatized by them as our clients are spending a lot of money to improve their physical assets and that should be an enjoyable experience for them and a very pleasant purchase. A Download can take just five minutes to enhance a client's body but the impact of those changes can last an entire lifetime."

The physical changes that Talitha made to each of her clients would not only require a period of adjustment from them but also from those around them and that was in Talitha's opinion, really just common sense. Whether or not the people in her client's social circles actually accepted the changes that Talitha made to their bodies was another issue entirely and not one that she could possibly have any kind of control over, or actually even attempt to predict. Inside Talitha's mind however, there was absolutely no doubt at all as she waited for Dean to arrive that the acceptance of others was definitely going to be an issue that would present at least a few of her clients with some very real problems.

When three on the dot arrived, so too did Dean as a gentle knock suddenly sounded at Talitha's consultation room door and she quickly rose to her feet and then crossed the room to open it. Once Talitha arrived in front of the door, she hesitated for a few seconds, just before she actually opened it as she quickly smoothed down her uniform dress, adorned her face with a warm cheerful smile and internally prepared to begin Dean's actual consultation. Three in the afternoon had finally definitely arrived and so too, just as expected had Dean.

Some sugary remnants from the smooth, milky, piping hot latte that Talitha had just consumed which had been provided to her courtesy of the coffee machine inside her consultation room, coated her lips and as she quickly licked the last few drops away, she placed her hand upon her consultation room door and then pulled it open. The coffee machine definitely worked extremely well, she quietly concluded as the caramel latte that she'd just drunk had been, absolutely divine but further interactions with the coffee machine could definitely wait whereas Dean, her first ever human client, certainly could not.

"You must be Dean, it's lovely to meet you. I'm Talitha, your Bodily Enhancements Consultant." Talitha immediately stated as soon as she opened the door as she greeted Dean with a friendly tone and a very warm smile. "Please come in and take a seat." She invited as she stepped back from the door in order to provide Dean with enough space to enter the room.

"Thanks." Dean replied as he nodded his head and then stepped inside the room.

Talitha turned to face Yucala and smiled appreciatively. "Thank you very much Yucala." She whispered.

Yucala smiled as she quietly accepted that now she'd performed her duties, she was free to return to her desk and the reception area. "If you need anything else Talitha, you know where to find me." She offered politely.

"Yes thank you Yucala, I better go and make a start." Talitha replied as she nodded her head appreciatively and then began to close her consultation room door.

"Good luck." Yucala whispered as she prepared to depart.

"Thanks, I definitely need it." Talitha whispered back as she inhaled deeply. "It's a very, very big day for me."

Nothing but silence filled Talitha's consultation room as she closed the door and then quickly made her way back towards her desk. A slightly nervous glance was cast across Talitha's desk towards Dean as she sat back down, who had already made himself comfortable on one of the chair's situated right next to Talitha's desk. Two client chairs had been provided by Professor Heisner and placed inside Talitha's consultation room exclusively for clients and they were much fancier than Talitha's own chair and made out of black and white leather and Dean now occupied one of the two. The third chair that Talitha usually occupied herself was made from a dark grey leather but that was more built for comfort rather than style and was much more compact.

In terms of Dean's build and appearance, he was relatively slight and quite slim in comparison to most other men and his height could be described as neither tall nor short and fell somewhere rather politely in-between. Due to the fact that Talitha had already seen Dean's profile images inside the Restructure system, she'd already had a rough idea what he actually looked like and so his presence in reality didn't really surprise her but was more or less as she'd expected.

"Would you like a cup of tea or coffee Dean, or perhaps something cold to drink?" Talitha offered.

"Yes that would be great, can I have a cup of coffee please?" Dean asked. "I usually have it white with two sugars."

"Sure. That'll be no problem at all. There's definitely some sugar and there's definitely some milk." Talitha immediately reassured him as she quickly stood up and then crossed the room as she headed towards the coffee machine. She began to prepare the cup of coffee quietly as she internally prepared to begin Dean's actual consultation and then returned to her desk and placed it gently down in front of him. "Will you need anything else before we start Dean?" Talitha asked politely as she sat back down and then faced him.

"No, not that I can think off Talitha." Dean immediately confirmed. "Thank you for the coffee." He said as he glanced at the cup in front of him enthusiastically and then eagerly picked it up as he prepared to actually drink it.

"Great, let's make a start then as your Bodily Enhancements Consultant, I'm here to ensure that your experience with Restructure is a very pleasant one." Talitha explained as she smiled. "So, if you have any questions about the Download procedures, or any of the Downloads themselves, please feel free to ask me and the only thing that I ask from you Dean, is that you try your best to be as honest with me as you possibly can."

"I'll try my best to do that Talitha." Dean replied as he nodded his head in agreement.

"Good, then we should get along just fine." Talitha quickly reassured him as she smiled. "There are some very important questions that I have to ask you first Dean and they are, why are you actually here and what do you hope to achieve? Why are the Download procedures actually required?" She enquired.

"I would say that ever since the accident seven years ago, I've really struggled to get back into the swing of life generally." Dean began to explain as he gently shook his head. "I've tried so many times but the accident totally destroyed my confidence and that's manifest itself in various ways. I don't really live anymore, now I just exist."

"I completely understand Dean and now that you're here, well that's a huge step back into a fuller life and the outside world. I can see from the system that you've actually requested four Download procedures, are you very sure about every single one?" Talitha asked as she glanced at Dean's request list on the screen on top of her desk. "It's just that reversals can be rather tricky as the whole process is very complex and extremely difficult to implement, so I need to make you aware of that before you make any final decisions. Any changes that you decide to make to your body must be considered very carefully as going back with regards to certain Downloads, is not even actually an option."

"I'm very sure Talitha." Dean insisted as he enthusiastically nodded his head. "In fact, I'm absolutely certain."

"Good. I just don't want you to have any regrets Dean as I've seen so many people make changes to their bodies which they've later regretted and it's part of my job to check these things." Talitha explained as she quietly considered Professor Heisner's advice and her own past experiences from the various cosmetic surgeries she'd worked inside.

"I know." Dean replied. "But really, I've given this a lot of thought and these are the changes that I really want to make."

Talitha nodded.

Essentially, the reversals process that Professor Heisner had outlined to Talitha during her training period had sounded extremely complex, rather tedious and very awkward and therefore Talitha was anxious to try and avoid such complications arising in the first place with regards to any of her clients' bodies.

"In some instances, the bodily changes requested by a client might have a negative or detrimental impact upon their life." Professor

Heisner had warned Talitha during her training period. "We want our clients to be happy, both in the short and long term and sometimes, the things they seek to change might not actually provide them with the perfection, happiness and enjoyment that they'd originally hoped it would." He'd continued. "At times, there may even be some very undesirable consequences, so it's extremely important that our clients fully understand all the implications of their choices, before any changes are made to their actual physicality. Part of your job will be to make sure that they understand that it's not as easy to reverse procedures once they've been implemented as it is to make those changes in the first place."

Each of the four requests that Dean had made sat upon Talitha's screen as she quietly reviewed his procedure request list, none of them applied to any facial adjustments at all which meant, Dean could at least hide any adjusted parts of his body, if he was unhappy with the results. A few more seconds was spent deep in thought as Talitha quietly considered which procedure from the four she should actually recommend that Dean should receive first.

- Chest Enhancement
- Arm Sculptor
- Leg Contour

- Penis Enlargement

Predominantly, the list rather discreetly expressed Dean's desire to have a much more athletic frame and a more buff looking appearance without enduring the agony of having to attend an actual gym, all except the penis enlargement which was of course very personal and sexual in nature. Such changes however, could not be taken lightly by either Dean or Talitha herself and she fully understood the implications of each change but she was slightly unsure that Dean actually did. In so many ways, it really motivated Talitha to be providing her clients with life changing technological bodily enhancements but giving people a deeper sense of satisfaction about their personal physical appearance also had some very serious implications in the longer term and Talitha fully appreciated that fact.

"How's your cup of coffee Dean?" Talitha asked as she glanced at Dean's face as she attempted to divert their conversation towards something slightly lighter as she could sense that the mood inside the room was becoming rather heavy and she had no desire at all to make Dean feel any more nervous than she could see he already was. "Do you need any more sugar or more milk?" She enquired.

"No thanks, it's absolutely perfect." Dean quickly clarified as he nodded his head, smiled and then sipped on the cup of coffee inside one of his hands. "This is actually the best cup of coffee I've had in a very long time."

"I think we should start with your Chest Enhancement first Dean and then we'll look at another item on your request list next week." Talitha suggested as she smiled and touched the screen in front of her. "That physical change will be the one that has the least impact on your general physicality and you can always cover up your chest afterwards, if you're not entirely happy with the changes but you're only allowed to have one procedure per consultation, so the others will have to wait until a later date."

"Thanks Talitha that's a great idea." Dean agreed.

Once the plan of action had been agreed, Talitha quickly loaded up some chest images onto her screen for Dean's perusal and then turned her screen to face him. The vast array of images on offer actually stunned Talitha as she began to admire the huge range of chests available to Dean as the two started to browse through each of the images in front of them. Every chest enhancement appeared to be vastly different in terms of their shape, size and muscular dispersion and the images actually quite intrigued her as she glanced at some of them thoughtfully and quietly considered what some might look on Dean's actual body.

"Wow, I had no idea that male chests could be so complicated." Dean said as he glanced at the screen. "There's literally hundreds here to choose from and they're all very different."

"There's actually over a thousand Dean but I can try to narrow down the range for you and that should help. If you can show me some that you definitely don't want and I'll get rid of chests like those first." Talitha suggested. "And then if you can show me some that you do like, I'll narrow down the range again, so that there'll be far less chests to choose from and the ones that are left will be more aligned with your actual preferences."

"Now that's another great idea." Dean agreed.

"Take as long as you want to choose one as there's no actual rush and I want you to be completely happy with the shape, size and structure of your chosen chest enhancement." Talitha clarified. "After all, you'll have to live with that chest and wear it on your body every single day, so I want you to be very sure about it."

"I guess it is kind of like buying a new suit in some ways." Dean joked as he smiled. "Just with this suit, you can't actually take it off."

"Exactly. Once you've chosen about five chests that you really like then I can show you what your body might actually look like with those particular chest enhancements and that should help you make a final decision." Talitha offered as she quietly considered Bryson's chest for a moment which she lovingly caressed most nights, it was perhaps something that they both took for granted as it was so deliciously, naturally, very well shaped and she'd never even considered before what it might be like if it wasn't.

"It's kind of like giving yourself a designer body." Dean said as he smiled.

"Yes and a painless physical upgrade." Talitha agreed.

"Are you ever tempted to try it out yourself Talitha?" Dean asked. "Not that you'd need to of course." He quickly added. "I mean, you look absolutely great."

"Fortunately, I've never felt a need to but you never know, perhaps one day I might actually find myself in a situation where I would feel a need to consider it." Talitha replied. "It's just like cosmetic surgery really, just minus the nasty scalpels and scars."

"Very true, very true." Dean agreed.

Approximately thirty minutes later and once Dean had finally chosen and decided upon the actual chest enhancement that he wanted, Talitha quietly led him into the small adjoining room where the actual Download procedure itself would be implemented. In the very center of the much smaller procedure room which was about the size of a small lounge, there was a transparent capsule and Talitha immediately encouraged Dean to lie down inside it as she lifted up the lid and then held it open for him.

"You'll have to walk up these steps Dean and then you have to lie down inside here." Talitha instructed.

"Right, I'll do that." Dean immediately replied as he quickly began to mount the small steps at the very front of the transparent capsule and then lay down inside the body like container.

When Talitha felt satisfied that Dean was reasonably comfortable and in the correct position, she pulled the capsule lid back down over his body and then quietly left the room. In order to activate the actual procedure itself, Talitha wanted to return to her desk and although the system screen was not actually totally necessary as there was a remote facility that she could utilize and various voice commands, she felt quite reluctant about orchestrating the Download procedure that way. Essentially, this was Talitha's first ever procedure and being that she was in very unfamiliar territory and because it was her first client consultation and Dean's, she wanted to make sure that absolutely everything went according to plan.

Much to Dean's relief, once he was left alone, the actual Download procedure itself only seemed to take a few minutes and he felt absolutely no pain at all as he lay quietly inside the capsule and waited patiently for the bodily changes to occur. In just a matter of minutes, his shirt began to tighten which very clearly indicated that his bodily enhancement had definitely began and that soon, he would have the chest that he'd always dreamed off. An expression of sheer delight rapidly began to spread out across Dean's face as he gently ran his finger across his chest and started to physically feel his new chest through the material of his shirt as his chest now definitely felt much buffer and much more physically appealing.

"Right Dean that's your chest enhancement done." Talitha suddenly announced as she began to lift up the capsule lid and politely notified Dean that the first Download procedure was indeed actually complete.

Interestingly for Talitha, her body seemed to quickly fill up with nervous anticipation and it began to tingle as she stood next to the capsule and just looked at Dean's face. The moment between them both was huge as not only had he been given a whole new chest through a ground breaking scientific method but Talitha had also performed her very first ever actual Download procedure upon a real human client and a very real human body.

Internally, Talitha almost wished that she could take a peek at Dean's actual chest, just to see the physical transformation but she resisted the urge to entertain her curiosity as it silently tickled her thoughts. Nerves teased the surface of Talitha's skin as she smiled at Dean, glanced down at his chest and internally hoped that everything had gone according to plan, it certainly looked like they had as his chest certainly looked much buffer.

Just a few seconds later, Dean sat up and Talitha watched him quietly as he dismounted the contraption and smiled as his feet came back into direct contact with solid ground. From what Talitha could see, Dean didn't appear to be disturbed or distressed from his experience inside the capsule and actually looked quite comfortable and very relaxed.

"I can't believe it was so quick." Dean said as he faced Talitha.

"Yes it really was and how do you feel now Dean?" Talitha enquired.

"Like I'm in heaven." Dean replied. "I can even go swimming now and to the beach with this chest."

Talitha grinned.

"You really don't know what it's like Talitha, it can be quite embarrassing for us men at times, to be all puny and to be surrounded by lots of buff, chunky looking men that aren't scared to show off their assets." Dean explained.

"Trust me Dean, we women face exactly the same issues every single day and they usually they revolve around the prettiness of our faces and the size of our body parts." Talitha explained as she began to lead Dean back towards her consultation room. "It can be a lot of pressure at times to be a woman and we don't even have to go to a beach or swimming pool to be judged."

"Yeah, I guess you're right." Dean agreed as he followed her out of the room. "It's just well, it seems to be a lot more acceptable when women feel embarrassed about such things but it's not the same for men. Women are allowed to feel insecure about their physical appearance and to express that without any fear and women actually encourage each other and tell each other how good they look but for men that would be absolutely unthinkable."

"You know Dean, I think you definitely have a point." Talitha replied thoughtfully as she walked back towards her desk. "I've just never really thought about it before I guess. Well, you look absolutely great and that chest enhancement really suits you, so I think today, you've definitely made a great choice."

Dean grinned.

Inside the passageways of Talitha's mind, there were now some very curious questions which began to prick her thoughts as they dangled down unanswered like a ripe cherry on stalk just waiting to be plucked and eaten. A quick glance was cast towards her screen as Talitha sat back down and then faced Dean as she prepared to arrange his next appointment. The questions that Talitha dared not ask related to Dean's actual Download experience and continued to silently distract her as Talitha quietly considered whether or not she should present them to Dean for further clarity. Due to Dean's quite relaxed nature, it did seem somehow acceptable to present those questions to him as he really was quite approachable but Talitha felt slightly nervous about actually doing so as they were purely questions that she wanted answers to and they were not actually, professionally required.

A few minutes silence passed by as Talitha continued to internally deliberate over whether or not she should actually ask Dean the questions that tugged away inside her mind and that gnawed away at her curiosity which it seemed could not be easily dismissed. After just a few minutes more, Talitha finally caved in to her curiosity as she fully surrendered to her internal ambitions to seek out answers and squashed her internal fears as she assertively decided that she should ask Dean whatever she wanted to about the Download procedures as it was a first time for them both. Some dusty particles from the curious silence between them both seemed to have gathered inside Talitha's throat and now obstructed her speech and so she coughed slightly to clear her airwaves as she glanced at Dean's face and then smiled.

"How was the Download itself Dean?" Talitha enquired softly. "Did it feel strange? Did you actually feel anything at all?"

"You know Talitha, it was actually quite a strange sensation." Dean began to explain as he smiled. "I could actually feel my body parts growing internally and they kind of tingled for a few minutes." He quickly clarified as he began to elaborate. "In some ways, it was almost a bit of a turn on. I felt a kind of warm, tingling sensation inside my body that was actually, really quite sensual and almost like a woman's touch."

"Wow, it sounds like it was actually quite enjoyable." Talitha observed.

"It really was Talitha." Dean rapidly confirmed as he grinned. "You should try it sometime." He teased playfully.

Talitha giggled. "You never know Dean, one day, perhaps I will." She replied.

Much to Talitha's delight, Dean's experience seemed to have been a very pleasant one and that gave her a tremendous sense of satisfaction as the fears inside her mind were briskly swept away by his enthusiastic reassurances. A sudden wave of relief washed over Talitha's body much like the wave from an ocean washing up against the grains of sand on a beach in order to refresh and cleanse each grain it embraced and she felt very pleasantly relaxed as she internally accepted that Dean's experience had been actually quite enjoyable. Inwardly, Talitha had harbored some worries that perhaps the Download experience might be unpleasant, awkward or slightly uncomfortable for her clients but Dean's joyful reassurances had quickly dismissed those concerns which had now been totally rebutted. In reality it seemed, Professor Heisner had in fact created the ultimate replacement to painful operations and surgical procedures, a painless, scar-free bodily enhancement procedure and that comforting thought appeased Talitha's mind as her thoughts slipped into a gentle equilibrium of peace.

Another appointment had to be quickly arranged for Dean, Talitha quietly decided as she suddenly noticed that the minutes of the afternoon had rapidly slipped away and that time had really escaped from her grasp. Somehow, it was almost as if a greedy boisterous wind had grabbed each minute from the day and then lifted them out of Talitha's reach and cast each one into an abyss of spent time, never to return again.

"When should I see you again Dean?" Talitha asked. "How's next Monday, at around the same time?" She suggested.

"I can't do Monday afternoon next week but the Monday morning would definitely work for me." Dean replied. "At around eleven."

"Right. I've put that in my diary, Monday at eleven." Talitha quickly confirmed as she suddenly rose to her feet. "In the meantime Dean, if you have any problems or concerns, please make a note of them and then we can discuss them at your next appointment." She advised. "And if something is really worrying you, you can even drop me an email about it."

"I'll make sure I do that." Dean immediately agreed as he quickly stood up.

"It's been a huge day for us both really Dean." Talitha said as she crossed the room and then opened up her consultation room door. "Totally life changing."

"Actually, I felt quite nervous about my appointment today before I arrived but it really wasn't horrible at all." Dean replied.

"Well Dean, now that you have a great new buff chest, your life has been changed forever." Talitha said as she smiled. "And that's something really different to take home with you from work today instead of just the usual shopping, weary bones and tiredness."

"True, very true." Dean immediately agreed as he enthusiastically nodded his head.

Upon Talitha's face there was a very satisfied smile as she politely escorted Dean back along the crisp, white corridor that led towards the reception area. In terms of Talitha's day, so far it had been almost perfect and her very first ever Download procedure had now been successfully performed absolutely meticulously. The actual physical impact of the Download would obviously be felt more by Dean but his appointment had kick started Talitha's career and her future as a Bodily Enhancements Consultant and so it had been immensely important for them both. Essentially, it had been a professional ice breaker for Talitha as Dean's procedure had broken her into the world of cosmetic procedures that she would now be expected to perform upon each of her clients every single working day and that for Talitha felt extremely significant.

Achievement seemed to gently wrap it's warm arms around Talitha as she bade farewell to Dean inside the reception area and then quickly returned to her consultation room, so that she could write up his notes. In some ways, Dean's session had broken Talitha's professional virginity and that thought amused her slightly as she walked as she'd never ever actually performed such an elaborate cosmetic procedure before on anyone's body in her entire life. Any barriers of doubt had now been gently removed from Talitha's mind as she silently accepted that throughout that afternoon, she'd performed a job that initially, she'd been slightly unsure that she could actually really do.

The suggestion that Dean had made to Talitha about trying the Download procedures herself wasn't something that Talitha had ever considered before but his suggestion amused her slightly as she stepped back inside her consultation room and then returned to her desk. Client notes however, definitely had to be written up and submitted that day before Talitha could actually go home, so Dean's playful suggestion wasn't something that Talitha could dwell upon for very long as several tasks had to be completed before her working day completely evaporated and disappeared into nothing. Once Talitha had returned to her desk, she immediately touched the screen on top of it as she prepared to write up Dean's notes, the hours of her working day definitely did not actually belong to her and Talitha was mindful of that reality and fact, they belonged to Professor Heisner and Restructure.

Later that evening, when Talitha arrived at home, she felt completely worn out but extremely happy as her first ever client consultation had in her opinion, gone amazingly well. Fortunately, Talitha did not actually have to start cooking that evening as Bryson greeted her just outside the front door with not just a kiss but also with a large paper bag that was filled to the absolute brim with takeaway food. A gentle but enthusiastic kiss was quickly planted on Talitha's cheek as soon as she was in close enough proximity to him and Talitha giggled with delight as she accepted Bryson's warm and affectionate embrace.

"I bought some takeaway, to celebrate the success of your first client consultation." Bryson announced triumphantly as he held the full paper bag up in front of Talitha's face. "It's Chinese, from Wantons."

"My favorite." Talitha replied as she smiled. "Bryson, you're such a darling."

"Where would I be without you Talitha?" Bryson asked. "I have to treat you good, otherwise I'll get no nooky."

Talitha giggled. "You're so uncouth sometimes Bryson." She teased as she stepped through the front door of their home and entered inside the hallway.

"Look, it's just common sense really, if you keep the woman in your life happy, there'll be lots of really great, very enjoyable sexual pleasure." Bryson explained. "And if you don't, you'll be absolutely starved, sexually destitute and extremely hungry all the time."

Talitha laughed. "You're absolutely shameless Bryson." She joked.

"I'm a realist Talitha and there's nothing wrong with that." Bryson teased as he entered inside the hallway and then shut the front door behind them both. "Sex is a very real thing and right now, I'm absolutely starved and in desperate need of some nourishment." He whispered seductively as he began to tenderly caress Talitha's neck.

"Let's eat dinner first Bryson then we can make a start on desert." Talitha insisted as she suddenly grabbed the paper bag from Bryson's hands and then began to make her way towards the large combined lounge and dining room.

"Technically Talitha, we could actually do dinner the other way round and have our desert first today." Bryson immediately suggested as he followed Talitha into the huge front room and walked towards the large black marble dining table situated at one end of it. "I mean we are both adults now, so that means, we can swap our meal courses around if we really want to."

"But the food'll get cold Bryson and it's my favorite." Talitha quickly pointed out.

"That's what microwaves are for." Bryson argued playfully as he raised his eyebrows suggestively. "To enable people to eat hot food when they want to and to allow them to do other more important things first."

"I'm starving Bryson." Talitha pleaded. "I really can't wait, I haven't eaten a crumb since lunchtime and I only had a salad roll for lunch today."

"Okay, okay." Bryson replied as he quickly surrendered and plucked a bottle of champagne out of his briefcase. "The food and your stomach win this time. I brought this home with me too, to celebrate."

"You know Bryson, I'm a very lucky woman." Talitha admitted appreciatively as she kissed him seductively on the lips. "And later on tonight, I'll make sure you're a lucky man." She teased as she winked at him.

"How was your first day as a real consultant?" Bryson asked as he sat down next to the dining table and then began to unpack food filled containers from the large paper bag. "Was it all that you hoped and dreamed it would be?"

"It sure was and I met my first real human client." Talitha gushed as she sat down beside him. "I mean seriously, my world and life is so perfect right now and you're definitely a sexy, handsome, very large part of that perfection Bryson."

"It's what you deserve Talitha, you work really hard, so you deserve a great opportunity." Bryson replied. "Life can't be full of hard work and no rewards forever, eventually something great had to happen for you."

"And now, it definitely has." Talitha agreed. "I can't wait until tomorrow Bryson, I mean for the first time ever, I'm actually looking forward to being at work."

Bryson smiled as he opened up the bottle of champagne and then began to fill two glasses. "Here's to your new job and to a much happier, brighter future." He announced as he handed a filled glass of champagne to Talitha and then raised his own glass up in the air. "And here's to us."

Talitha smiled as she joyfully joined his toast. "Yes, here's to us." She agreed. "Life has finally dealt us an ace."

When the Tuesday morning dawned, the weather was warm and welcoming as the morning pleasantly greeted the world and found Talitha still fast asleep inside the large king-size bed that she usually shared with Bryson every night. Due to the fact that Bryson usually left for work about an hour earlier than Talitha did, he'd woken up as usual at six thirty and then quietly departed at around seven as he'd left Talitha alone and she'd continued to slumber, blissfully unaware yet that the morning had actually begun. At seven thirty on the dot however, an alarm suddenly began to beep and as the shrill, sharp loud sounds rapidly filled the room, it immediately urged Talitha to get up as the device rapidly reminded her that it was indeed a working day and that she definitely had work to attend. The alarm seemed absolutely determined and utterly relentless in its mission to wake Talitha up as each sound pierced the air and shot through the room as the noises headed straight into Talitha's two ears and her peaceful night's rest was rather rudely interrupted.

Once awake and out of bed, Talitha headed straight for the shower and then quickly rushed inside it and turned the water on. Time for Talitha on weekday mornings was now rather sparse, due to her recent employment and the sense of urgency that filled her, forced her to not only respect that constraint but also show careful consideration towards it. Approximately, fifteen minutes later, once Talitha had showered, creamed her skin with lotion and then brushed her teeth, she made her way back towards the bedroom and then dressed as she plucked one of the remaining four uniform dresses that had been hung up inside her closet from the rail and then slipped it over her body.

A quick glance was cast into the body length mirror inside Talitha's bedroom as she admired the uniform dress, the bottom was made from a soft stretchy black material whilst the top was formed from a soft white fabric which pleasantly accentuated her curves. In some ways, the uniform was quite corporate looking but it still managed to retain a slight feel of elegance that satisfied Talitha's taste and rather superbly complimented her figure as the dress clung to her physical frame. Once a hair brush had been pulled through Talitha's soft, dark shoulder length black ringlets, she quickly picked up her car keys, phone and work handbag as she prepared to depart.

On the way to work, Talitha thoughtfully considered her day ahead which she was extremely excited about as that morning, just before lunchtime, it had been planned that she would meet Renee, her second client and first ever female client. According to Renee's profile, inside the Restructure system, Renee was a female in her late thirties and from what Talitha had seen, she appeared to have a very athletic looking frame and slim, toned shape. In fact, in terms of her appearance, Renee had actually looked quite masculine and boyish when Talitha had viewed her profile images and apparently that was why Renee had sought out Professor Heisner's clinic in the first place as that was something that she really wanted to change.

Fortunately, the roads were extremely clear as Talitha drove quickly towards work as she made her way towards the building that housed not only Professor Heisner but that was also the corporate home of his clinic Restructure every working day. Approximately thirty minutes later, when Talitha arrived inside her consultation room, she quickly made her way towards her desk and then immediately switched on the Restructure system as she intended to read through Renee's notes several times, before Renee was actually due to arrive, in order to adequately prepare herself for Renee's actual consultation.

From the notes inside the Restructure system, Talitha could very clearly see that only three actual bodily enhancements had been requested by Renee and that there was nothing particularly unusual about any of Renee's requests. In fact, Renee's requests pretty much reminded Talitha of the various cosmetic surgeries that she'd worked inside for many years where such requests were extremely common.

- Nose Reduction & Refinement
- Lip Enhancement
- Breast Enlargement

Quite interestingly for Talitha, the fact that Renee had requested a breast enlargement and because her request had not bothered Talitha in the slightest whilst Dean's request for a penis enlargement the previous day had slightly surprised her, it suddenly struck Talitha how different attitudes could be towards the two genders. Somehow, it seemed perfectly acceptable for a woman to request breast enlargement but for a man to request a penis enlargement, it was seen as something very unusual and even viewed as something slightly awkward.

Perhaps the world was slightly more bias than Talitha had realized, she quietly considered as she waited for Renee to arrive and perhaps even she herself, unknowingly and quite unintentionally, was even more bias than even she'd actually realized. Some introspective examination quietly began as Talitha's thoughts suddenly meandered into her own prejudices more deeply and she became distracted by the reality of her own attitude and the deep seeded discrimination that she held inside herself that she'd been totally unaware of up until that precise moment in time. In some ways, Talitha almost felt shocked by her own personal outlook as she quietly began to inspect and challenge herself and her own perceptions of the world around her.

Just a few minutes later, Talitha was rather abruptly shaken out of her thoughts as her attention was politely demanded by a gentle knock at her consultation room door. Whatever lay inside Talitha's own mind, right or wrong really could not be examined or dealt with right now as she had a client to see and she rapidly rose to her feet as she prepared to meet Renee for the very first time.

"Hi Talitha, your client Renee is here." Yucala announced as the door directly in front of her opened.

Talitha smiled. "Thank you Yucala and it's lovely to meet you Renee, I'm Talitha your Bodily Enhancements Consultant, please come in and take a seat." She replied.

"No problem Talitha. You're very welcome." Yucala said as she smiled and then quickly turned around as she prepared to depart and head back along the corridor towards the reception area.

Due to the fact that Renee's requests all seemed pretty straight forward, Talitha wasn't particularly worried about Renee's consultation that morning as Renee stepped inside the room and then walked towards one of the client chairs beside Talitha's desk. The consultation room door was closed and then Talitha enthusiastically headed back towards her desk as she politely offered Renee a beverage. A pineapple juice was requested which was then quickly prepared as Talitha internally accepted that her second real consultation was just about to actually begin and that now, she really was actually a consultant.

For the first ten minutes of Renee's consultation, Talitha explained the Download procedure process to her, the complexity of reversals and the implications of the bodily changes that she had requested as Talitha dove straight into the main issues with boldness. Once the necessary explanations had been very thoroughly provided, Talitha then leapt into the important questions that she'd been instructed by Professor Heisner to ask each one of her clients.

"Why are you actually here Renee? What do you actually hope to achieve and why are the Downloads actually required?" Talitha enquired as she faced Renee and smiled.

"Well the thing is Talitha, I've always been a bit of Tom Boy though not by choice, purely due to my physical feminine lacking. Over the years, I've tried to hide my physical shortcomings as a woman as at high school, I was teased quite a lot about it, so the Tom Boy disguise and the boyish mask kind of worked for me and helped me to hide what I didn't actually have." Renee explained. "I'd really like to change that now and become more of a feminine woman."

"Just so you know Renee, your requests are not really that unusual. A lot of women ask for breast enlargements and lots of men and women, ask for nose refinements and lip enhancements. I don't know why so many people really hate their noses but lots of people really do." Talitha immediately reassured her as she inwardly appreciated Renee's humble attitude which was extremely refreshing. "So, you're not the only woman that doesn't have an abundant portion of breasts which means, you really don't need to feel ashamed about anything, or hide yourself from anyone. What society expects from us physically as women Renee, is not actually our responsibility in any way, shape or form."

Renee nodded as she listened.

"I've noticed from the system that you've actually requested a very significant increase in terms of your breast enlargement, are you really sure about the size of this change Renee?" Talitha enquired softly as she glanced into Renee's eyes as streams of empathy rapidly began to gather and accumulate inside her being. "As your consultant, I just have to make totally sure as reversals at a later date, can be extremely complex and very tricky."

Strangely and for some inexplicable reason, Talitha's curiosity suddenly provoked her to glance down at Renee's white blouse as she spoke, due to the question that she'd just posed as she began to silently inspect the outline of Renee's breasts through her clothing. No actual curves seemed to be present at all that Talitha could see and Renee did appear to be quite flat chested. In some professions however as Talitha knew, women being quite flat chested was actually considered beneficial and natural, so it wasn't something that was particularly unusual, in Talitha's opinion. Many ballerinas and female athletes tended to have more muscular chests, purely due to their exercise routines which would iron out any plumpness and replace the fat with muscles instead and so the lack of curves in Renee's chest wasn't something that seemed strange to Talitha by any means.

"I'm very sure Talitha." Renee rapidly confirmed as she vigorously nodded her head in response. "I was teased a lot at high school about my physical lacking as I wasn't very blessed and I really want to enjoy and feel the fullness of a being a woman." She explained. "They said I looked like a boy."

"Renee, children and teenagers can be very cruel sometimes but I don't personally believe that having very large breasts makes you more of a woman." Talitha gently reassured her. "Not in my personal opinion anyway."

"I think when there's something that you haven't had and you've been defined by that for so long by other people, you really feel like there's something missing in your life and from your body." Renee explained. "Call it over compensation if you will but it's just something that I really need to do."

"You do know that you'll receive a lot of attention with such large breasts and that some of that attention won't actually be positive, or something that you particularly want?" Talitha enquired.

"Yes." Renee replied.

"In fact, some of that attention could actually be quite negative and even become problematic. A double G cup size is very large, are you sure you wouldn't prefer to try something like a double D first and then you can increase your cup size again, if you're not entirely happy with it?" Talitha gently persuaded as she attempted to find a compromise that perhaps Renee could live with, if only in the short term. "I could perhaps even do the breast enlargement in two stages, at no extra cost of course."

Quite sadly, Renee's remarks and her explanations had highlighted to Talitha the harsh reality and cruelness of the real world as she absorbed Renee's comments thoughtfully. Society really did place such a huge amount of recognition and importance upon various female body parts and those physical features seemed to really define femininity and gender in the world's sight. In essence, Renee had unfortunately been labeled and defined by something that she did not naturally possess and now that had become extremely important to her as that perceived shortcoming was why she was actually there in the first place. Childhood playground taunts had definitely emotionally scarred Renee quite deeply and now it seemed, the only way to heal that pain was for Renee to possess breasts in abundantly sized proportions.

"Look Talitha, this is something that I've wanted for a very long time and I know that there might be some negative consequences to this decision but I really want this." Renee clarified decisively. "I've always been a bit scared of surgical procedures, so this is the perfect solution for me really."

"Yes surgical procedures can be a bit of a nightmare at times, I've worked for a few cosmetic surgeries and there were definitely some horror stories and some very ugly physical scars left behind." Talitha agreed. "I just have to advise you however that a double G is our largest cup size, so you won't be able to increase them any further after that."

"That's fine." Renee replied.

"Right Renee, if you can just make a selection for me please and then I'll get that request processed for you." Talitha instructed as she touched her screen and it rapidly populated with images of breasts. She turned her screen towards Renee and smiled. "Just pick out some that you do like, the ones that you definitely don't and then I'll narrow down the range for you, until we find the breasts that you're the most comfortable with."

Approximately thirty minutes later and once Renee's breast enlargement Download had actually been performed, Talitha stood next to Renee inside the procedure room in front of the long client mirror as they began to inspect the physical results of Professor Heisner's Download procedure. Physically, Renee's body and chest had just been enhanced by the Professor's scientific technology and Talitha was almost in awe as the two women marveled at the two large, very pert, succulent looking breasts that now protruded from Renee's chest area. The very flat chest that had once occupied Renee's upper torso had now completely vanished and it was almost as if her buds had magically blossomed into huge sunflowers through some kind of miraculous occurrence.

"The pancakes are definitely gone now." Renee observed as she giggled and then pushed her shoulder blades together. "I'll really need some new bras now, just to keep these two bazookas in position."

"And you'll never ever get lost with those." Talitha teased. "They'll always point you in the right direction."

Renee giggled. "I know and they'll improve my love life too which is in desperate need of a major transformation." She agreed. "I haven't actually had sex for about three years now, or even gone out on a date, it's just been so embarrassing for me. I felt so inadequate and so incomplete and that put me off really."

"Well now, I think you'll be the envy of the whole city with those physical assets." Talitha playfully reassured Renee.

"Yeah, now I might actually get a sideward glance from some of the men that I actually like." Renee replied as she enthusiastically twisted and turned on the spot and viewed her body from various angles.

"I'd say you'll get more than a sideward glance with that pair. You'll literally be stopping and commanding traffic, very male traffic with drooling, hungry mouths." Talitha joked.

"Thank goodness, I've been accepting the leftovers from the dating pool for so long now but now, I might actually get a chunk of rump, medium rare steak." Renee replied as she started to giggle. "Thank you so much Talitha for all your help." She said as she leant forward and then affectionately hugged her.

"I just want you to be happy Renee." Talitha explained as she glanced at Renee's face and noticed that Renee's eyes seemed to glisten with excitement. "So if I can help you in any way and make you feel slightly happier then I've definitely done my job."

Renee smiled. "Trust me Talitha, you've definitely done your job, I'm very, very happy with these." She immediately confirmed. "Double G happy."

"Good." Talitha replied. "And they look, absolutely fantastic."

When the end of Talitha's second working day arrived, once she'd written up some very extensive client notes about Renee's consultation, taken lunch and then submitted them, Talitha began to prepare to leave work and actually make her way home. A quick glance was cast at her appointment schedule just before she switched of the Restructure system and Talitha rapidly noticed that she still had another five clients to see that week and only three days left in which to do it. Quite fortunately, Talitha's remaining five appointments had however been scattered across the three working days of the week quite proportionately which meant there would actually only be one client appointment during any given morning or afternoon.

The Friday afternoon for that first week had been kept completely free and Talitha immediately assumed that she would be expected to either utilize it to write up client notes, or perhaps even to meet with Professor Heisner, who had arranged all her client appointments that week himself. In many ways, the lightness of Talitha's work schedule that week was actually quite refreshing as Professor Heisner hadn't just dumped a multitude of clients on top of Talitha's lap and then just expected her to get on with things and cope with all their respective issues. A gentle introduction into the Professor's work and the services that Restructure offered had been planned and Talitha had been gently guided into the shallow waters of Restructure's potential and she would it seemed, be allowed to continue to gently paddle along the edges throughout the first few weeks.

Time would definitely change that quite relaxed work schedule, Talitha quietly concluded as she rose to her feet and then picked up her handbag which sat on the floor, right next to her chair and her desk. Quite soon, Talitha would definitely be expected to venture out into the much deeper depths of the pool of Restructure's potential without the rubber ring and safety arm bands in the form of guidance and the daily note supervision that Professor Heisner provided to her each day and soon, she would have to learn to swim in the deep end all by herself. Once Talitha had garnered some real client experience as a consultant, the level of support from Professor Heisner would definitely reduce and eventually be totally stripped away and then she would have to actually function as a Bodily Enhancements Consultant totally independently and then she would either sink or swim.

UPGRADE OPTIONS

Much to Talitha's surprise, just a few minutes later, when she arrived inside the reception area as she headed towards the building's main entrance and the parking lot, she actually found that the reception desk had already been manned by the Night Watchman. Due to the fact that it was just after five thirty, Yucala had already abandoned her desk for the day and her place had now been taken by the male Night Watchman that Professor Heisner employed to guard Restructure's assets every night. Although Talitha had also seen him the day before, seeing his face in Yucala's place every working evening would definitely take her some time to get used to as she was used to seeing Yucala's warm, friendly smile and he definitely didn't smile, or at least not very often.

The male Security Guard that usually manned the building throughout the week was in his early fifties but Talitha didn't know his name yet as she'd only ever seen him on one prior occasion and all they'd ever exchanged was a polite nod as they'd never been formally introduced, or ever attempted to speak to each another. During Talitha's training period, she'd left work at around four thirty but that week, everything had changed and so too had her working hours which now ended at five thirty as per Professor Heisner's instructions and because the night watchman usually arrived at five each day, he was already in position.

An executive decision was quickly made inside Talitha's mind as she gave him a courteous nod as she walked towards the exterior doors, now was definitely not the right time to engage in a polite conversation to actually find out what his name was as now, she was in a rush to get home. Another much more important man awaited Talitha's attention right now and it certainly wasn't the Night Watchman and she really couldn't wait to get home that evening so that she could see Bryson's smiling face.

Only three bays inside the parking lot were occupied by vehicles when Talitha stepped outside which was not unusual as the parking lot was usually quite sparsely occupied by the time she left work. One car belonged to Talitha, a silver salon and a rather old, battered looking vehicle which Talitha definitely knew, belonged to Professor

Heisner and the third car that certainly hadn't been there that lunchtime or morning, Talitha immediately assumed belonged to the Night Watchman. Once the door of Talitha's car had been unlocked, she gave the quite deserted parking lot once last quick glance as she quietly contemplated whether Bryson might actually be at home by the time she arrived, it was quite doubtful but it was a very real possibility.

A warm gentle breeze silently caressed Talitha's skin as she entered inside her vehicle and it was almost as if the pleasant summer evening was calling out to her to embrace its existence as it encouraged her to leave work very firmly behind her, at least for that day. Upon Talitha's face there was a very satisfied smile as she started the engine of her car and began to focus her mind more fully upon the man in her life that she hoped she would see and physically embrace quite soon. Just as Talitha was about to drive off however, something suddenly caught her eye which slightly distracted her and she paused for a moment as a large, mustard colored van suddenly entered inside the parking lot.

Quite strangely, on one side of the mustard yellow van which was a decidedly ugly color for any kind of vehicle, Talitha noticed that there was some very large, bold black lettering which spelt out the name of the company that the van seemed to belong to. The company's name immediately intrigued Talitha as she read the words 'PET SUPPLIES Inc.' over and over again and began to quietly speculate as to why the van might actually be there.

Due to the time that the van had arrived, the premises had already been vacated by some of its usual occupants so Talitha knew, the van could not possibly be making a delivery for any of them and that left only three possibilities. The van had to be making a delivery for either Professor Heisner, Moses or the Night Watchman but neither the Professor or Moses really struck Talitha as the kind of people that would keep pets and as far as she knew, there were no animals on the premises itself but yet, the van full of pet food was definitely there and it was making an actual delivery.

Distraction rapidly set in as Talitha paused and began to watch the van slightly more closely as she internally deliberated over its presence as the whole scenario was slightly strange and quite confusing. Just a few seconds later, a man in his mid-thirties suddenly jumped out of the van and then began to make his way towards the entrance of the building as Talitha watched him quietly. On his way towards the main entrance, he suddenly seemed to notice Talitha's car and her presence and a polite nod and smile was quickly given but despite his polite acknowledgement, Talitha's curiosity remained unsatisfied as no answers had yet actually been provided.

In order to avoid looking nosy, just in case anyone had actually noticed her, Talitha quickly began to play around with the mirrors on her car as if they needed to be adjusted as she silently delayed her departure in an attempt to satisfy her now very curious, curiosity. The mirrors provided a rough but fast, very welcome excuse as she fiddled around with each one and waited to see what would actually happen next.

For almost a minute, the delivery man actually completely disappeared as he entered inside the entrance to the building which immediately confirmed to Talitha that he was definitely expected as he'd been given immediate access to the premises. Curiosity continued to battle away inside Talitha's mind as she kept one eye on the building's entrance and one eye on the time but just a couple of minutes later, she finally decided to cave in to her own personal life which was actually now waiting for her to enjoy it. A serious attempt was made to dismiss her curiosity as Talitha gently shook her head and then started the engine of her car as she suddenly decided that Bryson and her journey home were far more important than a mysterious delivery van. Every second that was spent inside the parking lot would be a second that Talitha would not spend with Bryson that evening and that meant, she really had to leave and totally forget about the very strange van.

"I really have to go." Talitha muttered to herself. "Bryson will definitely be at home by the time I get there."

Suddenly however, just as Talitha was about to depart, all her good intentions were scattered across the ground of the parking lot as she glanced up at the entrance to the building one final time and the man reappeared but this time with the Night Watchman in tow. Some very large sacks were quickly unloaded from the van by the two men as Talitha sat absolutely still for a few minutes and just watched them. No actual answers were forthcoming however, no matter how long Talitha stared at the two men and finally she surrendered as she glanced down at her phone and quickly accepted that now was definitely not the right time to entertain her curiosity any further as time really was rapidly escaping from her grasp.

Irrespective of the intrigue that had been aroused and stirred up inside Talitha, due to the delivery man's presence and that fact that he had delivered some kind of pet supplies to the building for some kind of animals, she had to leave as Bryson would be at home soon and his presence intrigued her a whole lot more than a strange van. The weekday evenings and the weekends usually consisted of time that the couple would spend together, far away from the responsibilities of work and that was time that was really cherished by them both. Their free time was not an employer's time and it was actually their time to do with as they wished when they would not be paid to be at someone else's beck and call, or disposal. During those precious moments the couple could create memories together, perform any tasks which needed to be done that related to their relationship, lives and social networks and in that time, they could simply just be together and bask in each other's companionship, situated far away from the sometimes hectic nature of other people's demands.

"I should ask Professor Heisner about it tomorrow." Talitha muttered as she began to drive out of the parking lot. "There's probably a totally logical explanation."

Approximately twenty minutes drive along the highway and inside Talitha's home, a calm romantic evening with Bryson definitely awaited her and she was absolutely determined to thoroughly enjoy it, regardless of the strange delivery van and the large amount of pet supplies that had been unloaded from it. Whether or not there were any actual animals inside the Restructure building itself, was another issue entirely as there really were so many possible reasons why the van might have actually been there and that was just one possibility.

Perhaps, Talitha quietly deliberated as she drove, the pet supplies were for some fictitious animals and perhaps Professor Heisner wanted to conduct some top secret experiments upon the contents of each sack and perhaps, there were no real animals involved at all. A smile suddenly crossed Talitha's face as she gently shook her head and rapidly dismissed the notion of fictitious animals as that would be way too weird and couldn't possibly be grounded in any kind of reality. Another much more likely explanation had to exist, Talitha quietly considered and it was far more likely that the pet food supplies had been delivered for a member of staff, who because of work had been unable to receive a delivery at home, like the Night Watchman that guarded the building each night.

Suddenly Talitha's phone which was attached to the dashboard in front of her began to ring and as she quickly glanced down at the screen, a joyful smile rapidly spread out across her face as she saw Bryson's name displayed upon it. Due to the fact that Talitha was actually driving, she quickly touched the screen of her phone as she answered his call and placed Bryson on loud speaker.

"Hi Sweetie." Bryson immediately said.

"Hi Hun. I'm still driving, I'm not quite home yet." Talitha quickly explained.

"In that case, let's meet at the Rhinestone Steakhouse for dinner that way, no one actually has to do any cooking tonight." Bryson suggested. "Since you're still out on the road."

"That's a great idea Bryson and it is one of my favorite restaurants. You're full of such good ideas sometimes." Talitha teased. "I mean seriously, sometimes I think I'm in love with a total genius."

"Anything to make our lives just a little bit easier Sweetie and if we eat dinner out, we can save all our energy for something slightly more adventurous later on tonight." Bryson replied. "And something even more delicious."

Talitha giggled. "When will you get there Bryson? I can be there in about fifteen minutes." She confirmed.

"I'll be there in about five." Bryson mentioned. "Don't worry though Talitha, I'll definitely wait for you." He teased.

"You better." Talitha joked. "I'm can't be sitting at a table eating dinner on my own and then actually pay for it that would be very unladylike and socially obscene."

Bryson laughed. "I'll see you soon Sweetie." He quickly reassured her.

Talitha touched the screen of her phone once more as she ended the call and then smiled. "Bryson really is such a darling sometimes and we're actually going to have dinner at Rhinestones, it's actually a good thing that I took my time to leave work today." She acknowledged triumphantly.

Fatigue was not present when Wednesday morning arrived and as it knocked politely upon Talitha's door upon the calendar of life, her alarm sounded out inside her bedroom and she quickly leapt out of bed as she greeted the day with a joyful expression upon her face. The first two days of her real client consultations that week had gone exceptionally well and Talitha just couldn't wait for the rest of the working week to actually happen so that she could confirm to Professor Heisner that he'd definitely employed the right person to serve as a consultant to his clinic.

On the way to work, Talitha stopped off to buy a sausage bap with lashings of brown sauce as she silently rejoiced in her professional achievements so far that week and enthusiastically prepared for the remainder. Unlike the first two days of that week, the Wednesday promised to be slightly busier as Talitha had two client consultations scheduled for to perform that day and that challenge excited her.

At around eleven that morning, it had been planned that Talitha would see a female client called Charmaine for the very first time but her second appointment which would not be until the afternoon, was with a male client called Samson and so her working day was really quite occupied. According to the Restructure system, Charmaine was quite a young woman in her early-twenties and as soon as Talitha actually arrived at work, she began to read through Charmaine's client notes inside the Restructure system, just to ensure that she was sufficiently prepared for Charmaine's arrival.

Fortunately, Professor Heisner had now updated Charmaine's profile and a simulated image had now been provided and as Talitha perused her profile, she became quite deeply engrossed in her particulars as she read each one and began to familiarize herself with Charmaine's situation. The simulated image provided clearly showed that Charmaine was actually quite pretty and reasonably attractive although perhaps not what one might consider to be 'conventionally pretty' or stunningly beautiful but to Talitha, she did possess a certain kind of prettiness and there was definitely something very attractive about her.

Rather unexpectedly, when eleven arrived and Yucala's usual knock sounded at the Talitha's consultation room door, when Talitha opened the door, she actually found not only the two women she expected to see but also a young man on the other side of it. A somewhat nervous expression rapidly crossed Talitha's face as she glanced at the three for a few seconds and then almost completely froze as she really hadn't expected Charmaine to attend her appointment with anyone else in tow and especially not a young man.

"This is your client Charmaine, Talitha." Yucala suddenly announced as she politely attempted to break the silence inside the hallway with her words and a warm smile.

"Yes, thank you very much Yucala." Talitha replied as she rapidly internally shook herself out of her surprised state and then actively attempted to engage with the world once more. She gave the couple directly in front of her a nervous smile as she glanced at them both. "Lovely to meet you Charmaine. I'm Talitha, I'm your Bodily Enhancements Consultant, please come in and take a seat." She invited as she politely stepped back from the door.

The silence inside the corridor had now become slightly awkward but thankfully, Yucala had actually managed to rescue Talitha from her slight hesitation but it definitely felt as if it had been quite noticeable. In terms of Charmaine's rights as a client, Talitha knew technically, she had actually done absolutely nothing wrong as there was nothing specific that stipulated within the client terms and conditions of Restructure that clients had to attend their actual consultations alone. Theoretically that meant, Charmaine could actually attend her sessions with whoever she actually wished to and the lack of clarity on that point also implied that Talitha could not actually object to the male presence that she'd been presented with, even if she'd wanted to.

Internal worries, for some inexplicable reason, suddenly seemed to flood through Talitha's mind as she quietly watched the two enter inside her consultation room and make their way towards the two large chairs beside her desk. Despite her inner turmoil however, Talitha quickly forced herself to actually smile as she knew, she definitely could not afford to allow the nervousness she felt to be visible as that might worry Charmaine. A polite nod and smile was quickly given to Yucala as Talitha inhaled deeply as she silently attempted to disguise her reaction and prepared to face Charmaine and her very unexpected male companion alone.

"Thank you very much Yucala." Talitha muttered again. She literally had to squeeze and force every word out of her mouth as she quite nervously attempted to reassure Yucala that everything was indeed completely fine, even though she wasn't actually sure that it actually really was. "I'll call you if I need anything else."

Yucala immediately nodded in response. "Yes, you know where to find me." She replied.

"I do." Talitha muttered as she began to close her consultation room door.

Regardless of Talitha's discomfort which could not actually be rationally explained, two guests not just one now sat inside her consultation room and

Talitha had to not only actually face them both but also perform an actual consultation. A deep breath was taken as Talitha bravely began to cross the room as she headed back towards her desk and chair as she prepared to make a start. Despite the quite charming, rather pleasant external greeting that Talitha had given the couple, deep down inside of her there was now a definite undercurrent of fear that ran rampant through her veins which she could not possibly actually explain but she tried her very best to disguise it.

From what Talitha could see, Charmaine's male companion appeared to be at least five years older than she was and although his presence had initially startled Talitha, she began to quietly accept that he was actually there and that he would be a part of the actual consultation, whether Talitha expected him to be there or not. A slightly strained smile was plastered across Talitha's face as she faced the couple and prepared to offer them both a beverage as the usual manners that Talitha usually displayed towards each of her clients definitely had to be offered to the couple, regardless of her discomfort and who was or wasn't actually present.

"Would either of you like a hot or cold drink?" Talitha asked. "There's tea, coffee, orange juice, apple juice, pineapple juice, latte, cappuccino and even some hot chocolate."

No words had actually been exchanged between the couple that confirmed any kind of romantic connection existed between the two young people but as Talitha glanced at them both, it quickly became apparent that there definitely was. The young man was certainly not Charmaine's relative, or even a distant family member and there was definitely a romantic relationship between them both and that was immediately apparent as Talitha quietly observed the flirtatious glances the two exchanged and sensual hand touches. They were an actual couple and that was silently confirmed to Talitha several times, before they'd even actually opened their mouths and attempted to answer her question.

"Yes please, could I have a tea please and this is Lachlan?" Charmaine suddenly replied as she courteously began to offer Talitha an explanation for Lachlan's presence. "He's my fiancée." She continued. "And he's paying for my procedures."

"Ah yes, I see." Talitha said as she immediately nodded her head in understanding and then smiled at Lachlan. "Would you like something to drink Lachlan?"

Quite interestingly, Talitha quickly noticed that Charmaine's voice was actually very gentle and that she was softly spoken but extremely concise and precise as in her very brief explanation, she'd told Talitha all that she actually needed to know.

Despite the lack of a personal invitation from either Talitha or Restructure, Lachlan was indeed actually present for a reason and that was because he was Charmaine's financial sponsor and in that respect, his presence now made perfect sense to Talitha as her internal fears began to gently subside. Due to the fact that Lachlan was ultimately footing the bill, he'd obviously decided to actually attend in person and he actually had a right to be there as Talitha began to quietly understand and respect the reason for his attendance.

"A coffee would be great. White with one sugar." Lachlan quickly confirmed as he flashed a charming smile at the two women.

"Could I have some milk and three sugars in my cup of tea please Talitha?" Charmaine asked.

"Certainly Charmaine." Talitha replied as she began to stride across the room towards the coffee machine in an almost militant fashion as super efficiency mode began to kick in.

Rather strangely, although the introduction to Lachlan had been quite pleasant, a small part of Talitha deep down inside actually still felt quite defensive about his presence as she began to quietly prepare the cup of coffee and tea that the two had requested. The presence of a third party somehow, almost felt like an alien experience as up until that point in time, Talitha had only met with clients that were actually privy to the actual

Download procedures themselves but nonetheless, Lachlan's presence was non-negotiable as Talitha certainly couldn't ask him to actually leave.

Once Talitha had finished preparing the hot drinks, she carried them both back towards her desk and then gently placed them down in front of both Charmaine and Lachlan and a polite smile and gentle nod of appreciation was immediately given in response.   Internally, Talitha began to quietly accept that now her work as a consultant would be viewed by a third party, a spectator and a much more remote, detached pair of eyes but something about those eyes still worried Talitha although she couldn't quite put her finger on exactly what that was.   Money was ultimately being spent upon Charmaine's body by Lachlan and therefore he would definitely want to see that the procedures he was paying for were not only legitimate but also performed to his satisfaction and Talitha really couldn't object to that.

Unlike Talitha's other clients so far that week, Charmaine's procedure request list inside Restructure was slightly longer and much more extensive and as Talitha returned to her desk, she quietly read it once more as she prepared to start Charmaine's actual consultation.   The screen in front of Talitha lit up as soon as she touched it as Restructure silently confirmed that it was indeed ready for action.

- Breast Enlargement
- Waist Reduction
- Stomach Flattening
- Lip Enhancement
- Leg Contour

In many ways, Charmaine's list made no actual sense to Talitha as she was a very attractive young woman and the list seemed surprisingly long and Talitha immediately began to question if perhaps, Charmaine suffered from low self esteem. Once the actual list of requests had been completed, Talitha felt that Charmaine would look nothing like her current self and that to some extent worried her slightly.

Perhaps, Talitha began to internally speculate, Lachlan was actually paying to transform Charmaine into what he deemed to be a 'physically perfect' woman in order to satisfy his own ideals of feminine perfection. If that was the indeed the case, Charmaine really didn't seem to mind and appeared to be a willing participant in the realization of Lachlan's desires. Some women as Talitha knew, were actually raised to believe that pleasing a man was their main objective in life and that women should live in subservience to male desires and that their feelings and desires came second to that priority and perhaps, just perhaps, Charmaine was one such woman.

"I've noticed that you've requested quite a few changes Charmaine. Are you both very sure about all the procedures that you've asked for?" Talitha ventured softly as she gently began to probe the couple in order to establish exactly who had decided upon the rather large list of requests between them both. "I have to ask, it's procedure." She quickly clarified.

For a few minutes, nothing but an tense, awkward silence seemed to fill the air as it dangled in-between the three and silence ruled Talitha's consultation room. Despite Talitha's desire to speak and break the awkward tension that seemed to be gathering inside the room, she held her tongue and waited for at least one of the couple to respond to her question as the silence pressed them to provide her with an actual answer. Upon Lachlan's face there was stony stare as Charmaine glanced at him with a nervous expression but he seemed either totally oblivious to her discomfort, or absolutely disinterested in it as his face remained as hard as nails as Talitha patiently waited for a reply.

Tension continued to mount inside Talitha's consultation room and although no words were exchanged, Talitha could sense that Lachlan had interpreted her question in a very negative manner as his eyes oozed with suspicion and his unwavering stare remained focused upon her face. Nothing but malice seemed to be contained within Lachlan's gaze as his face fully reflected what he so obviously felt deep down inside his heart as Talitha silently absorbed his reaction. The stony stare appeared to suddenly deepen and darken as Lachlan's face began to display his internal anger, irritation and agitation as Talitha continued to wait for a response.

Upon Lachlan's brow, it almost seemed as if a thunderous storm had gathered as his angry silence continued to reign inside the room and Talitha internally started to worry. Quite obviously and from what she could see, Lachlan had interpreted her question as an attempt to undermine him and perhaps, Talitha quietly considered, she had pushed the issue slightly too far as her question and tone had been slightly provocative. Every drop of air inside the room seemed to have suddenly vanished as Talitha's throat suddenly began to tighten and she struggled to draw breath and it was almost as if Lachlan's anger had sucked out every drop of air out of the room as Talitha actually physically flinched. The angry silence that surrounded the three was by now almost deafening as tension continued to mount with every second that went by and seemed to grip every particle of air inside the room and then hold it hostage as Talitha felt the dusty bitterness of Lachlan's anger almost choke her.

"We're very sure. This is exactly what we both want." Lachlan suddenly barked as he scowled at Talitha. "We've discussed this many times and we've agreed on the changes that we feel will make our relationship and our lives more enjoyable." He snapped.

Discomfort and disgust rapidly seemed to surround Talitha as she quietly processed Lachlan's response, it wasn't what he'd said to her but how he'd actually said it that worried her but nonetheless, she had to soldier on and finish Charmaine's actual consultation, regardless of Lachlan's attitude. A nervous cough escaped from Talitha's lips as she attempted to clear her throat and dislodge the dust of comfort that seemed to have settled inside it, simply due to the very nasty, angry undertone of Lachlan's voice.

"Okay, no problem." Talitha replied as she gave the couple a slightly strained smile. "I just had to check, it's our procedure."

Suddenly, Talitha had a much deeper understanding of Lachlan and despite the smile on her face and her pleasant verbal reassurances, internally, Talitha almost felt as if she was actually going to vomit. The response from Lachlan had absolutely disgusted her on every possible level imaginable but there was in fact, very little that she could actually do or say about it. Every word that Lachlan had spoken had sounded arrogant, angry and sharp and as his words had cut through the air of the consultation room almost like a knife of denial, he'd actually denied Charmaine the right to speak for herself.

Someone else definitely ruled Charmaine's body and it certainly wasn't Charmaine as the requested procedures were what Lachlan wanted and Charmaine was just a second class citizen, not only in their relationship but also in her own life and with regards to her own actual physicality. The decisions and choices that Lachlan made came first and Charmaine was just a secondary consideration to Lachlan's desires, choices and decisions and that was now, blatantly obvious. From the very brief conversation that the three had just held, Talitha now realized, the extensive procedure request list inside Restructure had ultimately been, Lachlan's request list and not actually Charmaine's request list at all.

"I usually ask all my clients a series of questions about their procedures during our initial consultation to ensure that every client is absolutely certain about the changes that they've requested, before we actually proceed and implement any of them." Talitha explained as she attempted to mask the probing question that she'd posed which had so obviously angered Lachlan as she quickly moved the discussion forward and soldiered on. "Reservals at a later date can be very complicated." She quickly pointed out.

"Yes that's fine Talitha." Charmaine immediately replied as she nodded her head enthusiastically. "We understand, don't we Lachlan? Which procedure will you be doing first Talitha?"

"Well Charmaine, today I'd like to recommend that you actually have the lip enhancement first as that is the smallest physical adjustment on your list and that will give your body and mind time to adjust to the physical changes, before you change something much larger." Talitha advised. "That's how I usually work with all my clients." She mentioned as she glanced at Lachlan's face.

"Right that's a great idea." Charmaine agreed. "That's a very sensible approach, isn't it Lachlan?"

"These are very big physical changes and most cosmetic surgeries would actually make you wait for weeks, sometimes even months before performing such procedures." Talitha explained.

"Yes that's very true." Charmaine replied as she enthusiastically nodded her head in agreement.

Unfortunately for Talitha, the rest of Charmaine's consultation was actually quite tense as Talitha showed the couple a range of lip enhancement options and Lachlan dominated Charmaine's choices and basically dictated what lip enhancements were preferable to him and which weren't. In terms of Charmaine's choices, they were completely ignored and pushed to one side like unwanted items of food on a plate which was something that Talitha almost expected to happen, due to what she'd already seen of Lachlan.

Once the lip enhancement that Lachlan had chosen had been performed the two women returned to Talitha's consultation room and sat back down as Talitha quietly prepared to organize Charmaine's next appointment. Upon Lachlan's face there was now a very triumphant smile which irritated the heck out of Talitha as his domineering attitude grated against her beliefs and began to really annoy her. In response to Lachlan's behavior however, Charmaine was really quite docile and seemed very compliant and Talitha perhaps wondered if she felt in awe of Lachlan's economic dictatorship due to his access to vast amounts of wealth.

From what Talitha had seen so far of Lachlan, it had become increasingly apparent that Lachlan was not only a wealthy young man that was used to getting his own way but that on this occasion, his own way actually involved Charmaine's physical body. Internally, Talitha actually felt quite worried as she rounded of the consultation about Charmaine's lack of input into the decision making process as when it came to the issue of her own body, she seemed to have absolutely no say at all but whether Talitha could intervene and challenge Lachlan's dictatorship was another matter entirely.

"Your lips look totally amazing Charmaine." Lachlan purred as he held onto Charmaine's hand and verbally confirmed his satisfaction with the results of the Download procedure. "Absolutely gorgeous."

"Thanks, I'm glad you like them and you were actually right Lachlan these lips look really nice." Charmaine replied as she smiled.

Annoyance rapidly began to set in as Talitha glanced at Charmaine's face and quietly absorbed Charmaine's positive response, it was becoming increasingly obvious that she was just giving Lachlan whatever he wanted, regardless of her own desires. A nagging question sauntered through Talitha's mind as she quietly considered how Lachlan could possibly know more about Charmaine's face or body than she did as it was almost as if Charmaine doubted herself and her own judgment but her question remained firmly locked behind her lips as Talitha simply smiled and nodded her head.

Regardless of Talitha's personal beliefs, Charmaine it appeared had already decided to bow her head, life and body to Lachlan's demands and desires and that was quickly becoming blatantly obvious. Very soon, Talitha quietly speculated,

Charmaine would simply become a mind that lived inside a body that Lachlan had specifically designed to fulfill his own needs, in order to meet his desires and to satisfy his passions but Talitha was absolutely powerless to intervene in that reality and that really bugged her.

Another appointment for Charmaine was quickly made, just before Talitha rose to her feet as she silently welcomed the opportunity to get rid of Lachlan for an entire week. The smile upon Lachlan's face very clearly indicated that Lachlan was really pleased with the lip enhancement but his happiness absolutely internally disgusted Talitha. Technically, although Lachlan hadn't really actually done anything wrong that day, instinctively Talitha knew that he definitely had and that provoked her to quietly consider whether or not she should actually speak to Professor Heisner about Charmaine and her situation as it worried her profusely. Some further clarity, instructions and guidance definitely had to be sought out and certainly wouldn't hurt, Talitha quietly concluded as she crossed the room and prepared to escort the couple back towards the reception area.

"Right, I'll see you next week Charmaine." Talitha confirmed as she stood in front of her consultation room door.

"Thanks so much for helping us out." Lachlan stated as he stood up.

"No problem." Talitha replied as she quietly observed and digested the huge grin that was plastered across Lachlan's face.

A sarcastic smile spread out across Talitha's face as she quietly absorbed Lachlan's mood and his remark, he seemed to be extremely happy though why exactly Charmaine's lip enhancement would affect his mood that much worried and disturbed Talitha slightly. Part of Talitha still felt slightly annoyed that Charmaine seemed to be such a willing participant to Lachlan's dominant actions and decisions but there was nothing that she could do about it.

Not a word was actually spoken to Lachlan as Talitha attempted to ignore his presence as she silently escorted the two back towards the reception area, she'd now decided just to tolerate his existence even though he made her feel extremely uncomfortable. The choice of romantic partners that Charmaine had made was definitely something that Charmaine would have to live with but fortunately for Talitha, she didn't and therefore she could choose to spend as little time with Lachlan as possible and that was one absolute relief.

An escape from Lachlan's vile, repulsive, distasteful presence suddenly came as the two exited the building and Talitha internally began to relish Lachlan's departure as the physical distance between them both rapidly increased. Despite all

Talitha's good intentions towards her clients which were very sincere, regarding respect towards them or their associates, Lachlan was one person that she'd definitely taken an instant disliking to and there was absolutely no escaping that as absolute disgust continued to linger inside her mind even after he'd left.

Some worried thoughts began to gather and accumulate inside Talitha's mind as she returned to her consultation room as literally everything about Charmaine would actually be changed in just a matter of weeks and that was Lachlan's plan for the woman that he claimed to love. Although Lachlan professed to love Charmaine, he wanted to change almost every single thing about her, simply because he could and that in Talitha's mind was absolutely disgusting. The inherent underlying principles of that desired transformation on Lachlan's part, really shocked and disturbed Talitha as she quietly absorbed the implications of Lachlan's intentions which were definitely far from honorable.

Fortunately and much to Talitha's delight, once Lachlan had cleared her airspace, the rest of her day was actually quite pleasant and passed by very smoothly. When Samson arrived at three on the dot as scheduled, he was full of enthusiasm, amusing stories about his life and a very clear vision regarding his objectives and it rapidly transpired that apparently, Samson was actually a living advertisement for a marketing company which meant, he would need regular Downloads and would probably be a client of Talitha's for a while. The Downloads that Samson would need would vary, Talitha rapidly discovered, according to the needs of his work which required him to change his appearance quite frequently, in order to comply with the requirements of the various advertising campaigns that he would be involved in.

"Two years ago Talitha, I sold my body to Endorsement Marketing plc for five years for $25 million dollars, so whatever their clients want me to be for any given advertising campaign, I become. I'm a living advertisement so that's how it works and every second of my life is filmed in some form for various commercials." Samson explained as he sipped on the glass of apple juice that Talitha had provided to him.

"So what would you like me to do for you today Samson?" Talitha asked as she smiled.

"Well right about now, I actually need a much bigger nose." Samson explained. "I have a commercial for a pharmaceutical company coming up to advertise a cold remedy and my nose isn't really big enough."

Talitha giggled. "That's very unusual Samson, usually most people I see want their noses reduced not enlarged." She teased playfully.

"Well, I'll probably reduce it again later, once the series of commercials is over." Samson quickly clarified. "So it'll just be a temporary huge hooter hire, not a permanent employee."

"Okay but the Professor did explain to you that reinstating your original nose could be quite tricky and rather complex." Talitha advised.

"Yes but that's okay, I'll just pick out another new nose that's smaller. I'm not very attached to my nose really, I've had five surgical procedures on it already and it's still not quite right, so that won't be an issue for me." Samson quickly clarified. "I mean, it's not even the nose that I was born with right now."

"Great, let's make a start then. Do you know what other changes you'll need in the future, or do those just come up as and when the marketing company gives you another series of commercials?" Talitha asked.

"Sometimes, I know about the required changes a few months in advance, due to the actual physical adjustments that I need to make and sometimes, I only get a few weeks' notice but the next one I have to prepare for will involve a chest, arm and leg enlargement as I have to appear in that commercial as a weight lifter." Samson clarified.

"How did you actually get into that kind of work Samson?" Talitha asked as curiosity suddenly pricked her thoughts. "It's very unusual."

"It started when I was a child really, I did a few advertisements and they were hugely popular and then I did a few more as a teenager and for one reason or another, they were hugely successful and I actually became quite well known." Samson explained. "Then when I left school, I was taken on by an advertising agency straight away and they got me lots more commercial work and eventually, I just became the commercials man. I've appeared in over a thousand commercials now and I've advertised almost everything you could possibly think off, from teeth whiteners to penile dysfunction tablets, I've done it all"

"Do you enjoy it?" Talitha asked.

"I guess, everything we do every single day is about selling ourselves really, so it's not actually anything different. You work for an employer, you sell your skills to them every working day, you have a girlfriend, you sell your romantic capabilities to her and provide her with a decent, happy relationship and so on." Samson replied. "Everything in life is about selling an image to those around us and we are in essence a product that we want people to buy with their time, resources, or their emotional commitment. In each commercial, I just portray a lifestyle or an appearance that people might want to aspire to and then that they sometimes buy into."

"I think your right Samson, I've just never really thought about things that way before."   Talitha agreed.

"Most people don't.   People usually live quite blinkered lives and like to pretend that their interactions each day are based on deeply formed emotional attachments when the reality is usually so very different."   Samson explained.   "For example, if you treat your girlfriend like crap and don't provide her with the customer service that you initially seemed to be offering to her and then someone else comes along that sells her a better offer and a superior relationship, eventually you'll get dumped."

"True that is very true."   Talitha replied as she giggled.

Unlike Talitha's first consultation that day, her second appointment with Samson was an absolute refreshment to her weary mind which Lachlan's presence had drained as Samson was friendly, lively, transparent and brutally honest.   A profound thought suddenly struck to Talitha as to how very different life could actually be at times, simply due to the relationships that one chose to participate in and those that you actually didn't.   People, choices and decisions were quite a complex topic as Talitha knew as you were only really able to choose from in life what you were given access to, knew about or sought out but there was one element of control that you could exercise and that was, your own participation.

Rather unfortunately, Charmaine had chosen to participate romantically with Lachlan and that would be a cross that Charmaine would now have to carry for as long as they were both romantically involved. Not all Talitha's clients would be likable, Talitha quietly concluded, or even easy to tolerate, not if Lachlan was anything to go by as he was utterly distasteful, extremely irritating, absolutely vile and totally repulsive and that was something that she'd rapidly discovered and then had to accept for the very first time that day.

Inside Talitha, an intense disliking for Lachlan had already started to form and as it continued to gather, it silently provoked her to consider for a moment why someone lovely and sweet like Charmaine would choose to participate in a relationship with such a vile, condescending, arrogant, patronizing, difficult and distasteful creature. Any future consultations that Lachlan actually attended at the clinic, Talitha could already sense without a shadow of a doubt, would be unpleasant, uncomfortable and very trying as he was extremely difficult and so she really wasn't looking forward to them at all.

All Lachlan seemed to care about was his own desires and sexual ideals, whereas Samson at least appreciated and understood that you had to at least try to make a woman happy or you'd be traded in for someone else that would step up to deliver what you'd promised and failed to provide. Marriage was, at the end of the day, still a legally binding contract and relationships were usually a preamble to that legal romantic commitment between two people that reality had not changed, regardless of the times. Perhaps, just perhaps, Talitha quietly considered, Charmaine's rather subservient attitude towards Lachlan had somehow actually enabled him to become the monster that he now actually was and perhaps, Lachlan wouldn't actually change until Charmaine did.

"Thanks very much for the apple juice Talitha. Now how do I choose my nose?" Samson suddenly asked.

Quite unintentionally, Talitha's mind had taken a slight wander as she'd allowed her thoughts to delve back into the subject of Lachlan and Charmaine and Samson, albeit momentarily had almost been forgotten. The polite interruption on Samson's part brought Talitha swiftly back down to earth with a gentle bump as he gently reminded her that she had an actual consultation to deliver and that his consultation required Talitha to be extremely focused upon his needs, not her dislike for Lachlan.

"Well Samson, I'll show you a range of noses now and then you can select some that you like."

Talitha replied as she touched her screen and it rapidly populated with nose images.

Samson nodded. "Wow, I even get to choose my own nose." He announced enthusiastically. "Usually, you only get to choose from what they can cut from your existing nose. This is absolutely awesome."

"I know, the Downloads that Restructure offer are so advanced compared to cosmetic surgery." Talitha agreed. "And a lot less messy."

"True and there's no ugly scars left behind." Samson agreed as he grinned.

"The wonders of technology." Talitha said as she smiled. "We live in a truly amazing world."

The rest of Talitha's afternoon literally flew by as Talitha spent the remainder of her working day, very attentively focused upon Samson's nose reshape. Once Samson had been given the nose that he'd wanted and once his appointment was over, Talitha politely escorted him back towards the reception area and then bade him farewell. Upon Talitha's face there was a satisfied smile as she walked quietly back towards her consultation room and prepared to write up Samson's notes as she silently welcomed the approach of the end of her working day. Soon, Talitha would make her way home towards Bryson, the love of her life and that was definitely something to look forward to as it lay upon the not too distant horizon of her working day which had by now almost been, fully consumed.

When the Thursday morning arrived, Talitha greeted it extremely appreciatively as she joyfully celebrated the fact that she'd actually managed to get more than half way through her first week at work with real human clients without encountering any huge, unmanageable problems. Just four more client appointments were due to take place and occur throughout the remainder of that week before Talitha's working week would be over and the weekend would arrive but she fervently hoped deep down inside that none of those clients would be anything like Lachlan. Technically, although Lachlan wasn't really actually Talitha's client, indirectly somehow, he actually was simply due to the fact that he was the person footing the bill for Charmaine's procedures. Quite frustratingly and rather annoyingly that small financial detail meant that Lachlan would actually the one that Talitha would ultimately have to answer to, satisfy and please, even more so than Charmaine herself.

Interestingly for Talitha as the Thursday commenced, it brought along with it a very unusual male client called Frank and as both eleven and Frank stepped through Restructure's doors, Talitha welcomed them both enthusiastically. Unlike most of Talitha's other clients, Frank was actually much more senior and in his early seventies and he seemed to possess a very friendly disposition and joyful attitude towards life and the rest of the world. Once Frank was reasonably settled and seated, Talitha offered him a beverage as she began to attentively listen to him as he discussed his objectives and attempted to establish his exact requirements and how she and Restructure could actually meet his needs.

Every client that Talitha had met so far, she'd discovered would present her with a fresh set of challenges and there was absolutely no doubt at all inside Talitha's mind as she listened to Frank speak that he would certainly not be an exception to that discovery. In terms of Frank's approach to Restructure, it seemed that he was definitely there to receive a service from Restructure that the clinic could certainly provide and he had absolutely no qualms at all about discussing that as he explained to Talitha exactly what he wanted from Restructure and from life in general. Absolutely no reservations seemed to exist as Frank openly began to elaborate as to the reason for his attendance at Restructure as he confidently confided in Talitha with a refreshing amount of transparency.

"I just want to be young all my life, so I need the body parts to retain my youth as my natural body is literally, falling apart." Frank explained. "As you can see."

"What exactly would you like to change Frank?" Talitha asked.

"Absolutely everything." Frank replied.

"That could take a while. Weeks, perhaps even months." Talitha quickly pointed out. "And it could be very expensive."

"I really don't mind. It's not like I have much else to do with my time, or my money. I've never had any children, I don't have much family and my financial resources are definitely sufficient as I grew up in a very wealthy home and inherited a lot of wealth." Frank explained.

"Right, so what would you actually like to change first Frank?" Talitha asked.

"My legs, I really need legs that work as I want to run, leap and jump and my legs just won't participate with those physical demands. The mind is very willing but my body is lying on top of the scrapyard of life and refuses to cooperate." Frank explained as he grinned. "Then I'll do my arms and my face because they sure could do with a refresh, to get rid of all the wrinkles."

Talitha giggled. "Some people like wrinkles." She teased playfully.

"My girlfriend Maude doesn't, she's sixty eight and doesn't have a single wrinkle on her face." Frank explained.

"How come?" Talitha asked.

"She said, it's because I had a bad skin routine and because she has a great one. Seriously, what's a skin routine when it's at home and why does it matter?" Frank asked as he shrugged. "Anyway, I have to have better skin than she does and less wrinkles, just to annoy her."

Talitha laughed. "Will Maude mind, if you can jump over fences and she can't?" She teased.

"I doubt that would ever happen, she was an Olympic champion in her younger years, so technically she can still jump over fences whenever she wants to, it's just me that can't." Frank replied.

"Poor you. You picked a life partner that is so fit and healthy." Talitha sympathized as she gently shook her head. "That's such a dilemma."

"Maude is a great lover though, so it definitely has it's upside. She's extremely flexible which can be very handy at times." Frank quickly pointed out as he grinned. "We've been together for over forty years now."

"You never married?" Talitha enquired.

"If it's not broken, I ain't fixing it." Frank replied. "We've always been happy as we are. Neither of us have huge families that would demand a wedding ceremony from us, so we don't have to satisfy other people's expectations as when you decide to have a wedding, you're ultimately spending a lot of money just to tell the world that you are committed to each other. We say that to each other every day when we share our lives together and we're the ones that really count."

"True." Talitha agreed. "I guess weddings are just nice though in that it's nice to make that public commitment to someone you love forever."

"Most marriages nowadays don't even last five years." Frank quickly pointed out as he gently shook his head. "People think they want forever and then get fed up with each other in a day. It's like going to a restaurant and ordering a steak, then halfway through eating it, you decide that you really wanted the veal and then you blame the waiter for not bringing you the veal as if he should have read your mind."

"Yeah, divorces can be really messy." Talitha agreed.

"Yep they can, they can be full of blame, dissatisfaction, disappointment, heartbreak and huge legal bills." Frank said as he smiled. "Weddings cost a lot and divorces can cost even more and then there's a lot of lies and disappointments in-between, it's much cheaper really just to lie to each other and disappoint without the expensive facade of a wedding."

"Such a cynical outlook, for a such a young man." Talitha teased.

"I'm a realist, not an optimist." Frank replied as he grinned.

Talitha giggled. "Right Frank, I have thousands of legs for you to choose from." She mentioned as she turned her screen to face him. "Which would you like to have attached to your body? Pick some out that you like and then I'll narrow down the range based on your selections."

"Right, my legs have to be chunkier than Maude's legs but not more shapely, or she might get jealous and then she might even start to feel slightly inadequate." Frank joked. "And that could really lead to trouble."

"True, women do like to be physically admired and appreciated." She agreed.

"A man can't look better than his female lover, or she'll sack him and dump him." Frank explained. "Trust me, women really don't like men that look better than them."

"I think you could have a valid point there Frank." Talitha agreed. "I mean seriously, women are supposed to be beautiful and men are supposed to be handsome but if a man's too handsome and you're not beautiful enough that could spell trouble."

"Yes and my Maude sure is pretty and I'm not much of a looker really, so that's probably why we're still together. She keeps me on my toes and I keep her happy." Frank concluded. "That's the recipe for romantic bliss and the perfect ingredients for a peaceful relationship."

"True, you seen any legs that you fancy yet?" Talitha asked.

"Lots. Could I just pick all of them and then try out a different pair of legs every week?" Frank enquired.

"I think you should try to focus on one pair for now and if they really don't work well for you then perhaps we can discuss changing them but remember, reversals are extremely complex, so once you give up your own legs, it's very difficult to get them back again." Talitha warned.

"Great that works for me, I really don't want these tired pins back." Frank replied as he grinned. "I think I like those legs and those legs and perhaps even those legs as they look quite good." He said as he pointed towards several images on the screen in front of him.

"Good, I'll just narrow down the leg range based on your preferences and then you can make a final decision." Talitha explained as she began to touch her screen and narrow down the range in alignment with Frank's choices.

"Then I'll have to make an actual leg commitment, it's kind of like a marriage really." Frank deliberated as he grinned. "It's such a hard decision as I'll have to commit to using them every day and then I'll actually have to live with them. It's much harder than picking out a new suit or selecting a new style of haircut."

"Yes, it is more like choosing a permanent lover." Talitha agreed. "You'll have to see them every morning, so I guess it is kind of similar."

Frank grinned. "Yes Maude, I've been faithful to you for most of our relationship but at one point I did start to cheat on you and I was seeing a new pair of legs." He joked. "Eventually, I had to dump them as all they did was run away from me whenever I tried to kiss them."

Talitha giggled.

"Do you Frank Malvern take these legs to be lawfully attached to your body and your lower torso in sickness and in health, for richer, for poorer, for better, or for worse, to love and to cherish, until death do you part?" Frank joked. "I do."

Talitha laughed.

Later the day, when the mid-afternoon graced the earth with its arrival and once Talitha had consumed a very hearty lunch, her sixth client of the week finally arrived at three on the dot, a male called Rodney. Due to the fact that Talitha had just spent a very pleasant morning with Frank, she was extremely hopeful that her final client consultation that day would be just as pleasant and satisfying for all the parties involved and she rose to her feet enthusiastically as soon as she heard Yucala knock on her consultation room door.

According to the Restructure system, Rodney was a quite young man in his late twenties and

Talitha could see that he'd requested several very specific changes, all of which seemed to relate to bodily improvements and that none of the changes he'd requested, actually seemed to relate to his face at all. A young, very handsome, quite tall, athletic looking man was situated on the other side of the door, inside the crisp white corridor alongside Yucala and as Talitha smiled at him for a minute, she began to wonder why Rodney was actually there as he certainly didn't seem to look as if he needed to be.

"You must be Rodney, come in please. I'm Talitha, your Bodily Enhancements Consultant." Talitha immediately invited as she smiled at Rodney and then turned to face Yucala. "Thank you very much Yucala."

"You're very welcome Talitha." Yucala replied. "And if you need anything else, you know where I am."

Once the usual pleasantries had been exchanged between the two women, Yucala quickly departed as she headed off in the direction of the reception area as Talitha closed her consultation room door and internally began to prepare for Rodney's very first client consultation. Technically, Talitha couldn't actually see any physical reason why Rodney would require Restructure's services in the first place but nonetheless, he was there, so he obviously felt dissatisfied about something and her job was not to question why but simply to deliver the services that he'd actually paid for. A beverage was quickly offered to Rodney and then an orange juice was provided to him as Talitha prepared to begin his actual consultation.

"I can see from the Restructure system Rodney that you've actually made three enhancement requests. Can I ask what your overall objective is please?" Talitha enquired as she returned to her seat, sat back down and then faced him.

Regardless of how long or short each client's list was, Talitha had to ask every client the same initial questions during their first consultation, just to ensure that the procedures they'd requested would actually meet their overall objectives and Rodney was no exception. The three procedures that Rodney had asked for sat in bold lettering upon Talitha's screen as she quietly read them over and over again as she patiently waited for Rodney to respond.

- Penis Enlargement
- Chest Enhancement
- Leg Contour

"Look, I'll be brutally honest with you Talitha, I just need to have the largest penis there is on offer as I have to satisfy some very hungry women and that requires a very large piece of equipment."

Rodney explained. "I get paid to deliver a service, much like you do and that service is to satisfy women sexually and it's very hard to deliver that service effectively, if the equipment being used to do so, isn't quite up to scratch."

Talitha nodded her head as she listened. "I see Rodney." She replied.

"It would be like someone ordering a glass of champagne and then you giving them a cup of tea without even a biscuit." Rodney said as he began to elaborate. "Expectations would remain unfulfilled, they'd be disappointed and then they'd start to question the bill. I have very skinny legs that I absolutely hate and my chest isn't quite up to par and this dish of my physical self, is a special that I offer on my menu." He continued.

"Yes, I think I understand Rodney." Talitha replied. "You do seem to know rather a lot about restaurants." She teased.

"I was a trainee chef but it didn't work out for me. I got fired for sleeping with my bosses wife." Rodney explained as he grinned. "The services I provided to my bosses wife worked out for me though, so here I am."

"What a shame." Talitha said as she gently shook her head.

"Yes apparently, you don't sleep with your bosses wife, it's not the done thing." Rodney joked as he winked at Talitha. "I was in rather a tight spot, so I had to find another way to make a living fast and women seemed to love the services I offered to provide."

"Right." Talitha replied.

"So I need a bit of something for my chest, so that women can comfortably rest their heads on it and my legs need to be slightly sturdier and stronger, so that my lower torso has more power to improve my thrust capabilities. I need to be a living sex and love machine." Rodney clarified. "So that's why I'm here."

"Will you need to have any facial Downloads at all?" Talitha asked.

"Nope, look at my face, it's practically perfect. I dealt with that first. I've spent an absolute fortune on facial cosmetic surgery." Rodney explained. "I had a nose job and a few other bits and pieces done."

"You seem very committed." Talitha observed.

"I am very committed." Rodney quickly confirmed. "I love women and women love me and because I get paid to love women, why not do it properly?"

Talitha nodded as she smiled. "Right Rodney, we'll make a start which procedure would you like first?" She asked.

"Definitely the penis enlargement." Rodney immediately clarified. "I need my gear stick to be in perfect working order as that is the most important component when it comes to my machinery."

"Right, you need a larger screw driver inside your tool box?" Talitha teased.

"Exactly." Rodney agreed.

Talitha tried not to giggle as she nodded her head. "Okay Rodney, here are some of the enlargements that we currently have on offer, you can browse through those, choose some that you like and then I'll narrow down the range for you." She explained as she turned her screen towards Rodney which had now been populated by a vast array of images of male sexual organs that were various shapes, sizes and widths.

"This is fantastic Talitha and there's so many to choose from." Rodney replied as he leant towards the screen enthusiastically. "And they're all so different."

"Yes indeed. Some bend to the left, some to the right, some are longer and some are thicker. It really just depends on what you're looking for I guess." Talitha agreed. "Some are thicker at the bottom and others thicker at the top. I'll let you have five or ten minutes just to browse through them all and then if you can pick out about ten for me, I'll narrow down the range so that you can make your final selection."

Rodney quickly nodded his head in agreement. "There really is a lot more to choosing a new penis than I'd actually realized, I might need a bit more time than that to decide. Is that okay?" He asked.

"Yes that's fine. Men's penises can be a very complex issue Rodney, so take as long as you like there's really no rush." Talitha quickly reassured him.

One huge thing amused Talitha as she quietly watched Rodney browse through some of the images on her screen and that was his absolute frankness and honesty. In terms of Rodney's client needs, he hadn't beaten around the bush and as he'd taken a deep dive straight into his motives for being there, he'd actually surprised Talitha as his objectives were really very different from the other clients that she'd met so far that week and not just different but what one might call, extremely different. Rather surprisingly, although Talitha was actually a stranger, Rodney didn't seem to feel intimidated by that fact, or even remotely bothered by it at all and his brazen bold nature amused Talitha ever so slightly.

Suddenly as Talitha glanced at the screen that Rodney's attention and gaze were now fixated upon, it dawned upon her that she'd really led a very sheltered life as she quietly accepted that she'd not really seen a lot of naked men, or naked penises. In fact, when it actually came to the issue of men's penises, Talitha had only actually ever seen three in her entire lifetime and all of those had belonged to the three partners she'd been in actual romantic relationships with but now, much to Talitha's amusement, she was literally surrounded by images of thousands of them, all of which actually belonged to no man at all.

"I think I really like the look of these Talitha." Rodney suddenly confirmed as he turned to face Talitha and then grinned as he broke the silence between them.

"Right Rodney, now I'll need you to pick out a final five for me." Talitha rapidly clarified as she touched the screen again and narrowed down the range of images on display.

Rodney nodded. "Can you give me ten more minutes please? This is very important decision and I have to get it absolutely right." He replied.

"Take as long as you want Rodney, really there's no rush." Talitha immediately reassured him.

"Women don't say that to me very often Talitha. Usually, they tell me to hurry up and get on with things." Rodney joked. "Especially when their husbands are due back."

"Well Rodney, today this is about you not them." Talitha mentioned as she smiled. "So today, you can take your time."

Despite the droplets of embarrassment that Talitha felt gather upon her forehead, due to the rather personal nature of their discussion and

Rodney's procedure that day, Talitha diligently persevered as she prepared to process the final five choices that Rodney had made around ten minutes later. Each of the five chosen penis images were attached to the simulated image of Rodney inside the Restructure system and then shown to him as Talitha attempted to enable him to make the optimal choice that best suited his precise and very unique physical requirements.

Every single client profile had a simulated image inside Restructure and that image could either be displayed naked or clothed as required and the image could actually be replicated and any potential changes attached to it in order to allow clients to preview of their final selections. Very precise body measurements had been taken by Professor Heisner and the Restructure scanner during each client's pre-consultation interview, in order to provide clients with the opportunity to see how each bodily enhancement would look prior to implementation and to give them a chance to analyze their choice.

Once Rodney's consultation was over, Talitha politely escorted him back towards the reception area and she listened to him chat as he made jokes and clowned around as they walked. Regardless of which body part Rodney had actually wanted change that day and no matter how embarrassed Talitha might have felt about that change, there was one small grain of comfort inside Talitha's mind as she walked, she had definitely done her job and provided him with a decent number of options from which to choose from. Technically, Talitha quietly reassured herself as she watched Rodney depart, she really had done all that she could actually do to ensure that he had the best possible chance of making the change that he wanted to make to his body and as his consultant that was her primary objective.

When the Thursday evening gently floated into Talitha's day and five thirty finally arrived, once Rodney's notes had been written up, Talitha welcomed home time with very open arms as she quickly rose to her feet and then switched off the Restructure system. Home and Bryson awaited and as Bryson was the only man in the entire universe that held Talitha's heart gently in his hands as they ventured through the rocky terrain of life together, she couldn't wait to see him. Fortunately that day, Frank had been an utter delight to see and Rodney had been very pleased with his actual Download in the end and he'd left his consultation with a smile on his face and so Talitha had enjoyed a very pleasant, extremely productive working day.

In fact, life couldn't possibly be more perfect, Talitha quietly decided as she headed towards the reception area and then exited the building and now, she would enjoy a perfect evening which she would definitely spend with her favorite person in the entire world, Bryson. A silent vow was made as Talitha entered her vehicle and then started the engine, she would spend as much of that evening as she possibly could inside Bryson's loving arms and then hopefully, her next working day would just as pleasant before the weekend arrived when she would have two whole days to spend exactly as she wished.

Quite fortunately, when it came to the couple's relationship, arguments were not something that were commonplace inside the couple's home as they rarely had anything to argue about as Bryson was very committed to their relationship and so too was Talitha. Since the very first day they'd met, it had always been that way and as Talitha quietly considered the couple's relationship as she drove along the highway towards the home that they both shared, she began to more deeply appreciate Bryson's love and commitment to her which was certainly far more enjoyable than someone like Lachlan's love offerings.

COMPLEX CLIENTS

The Friday morning arrived almost too quickly for Talitha's liking as it suddenly flew into her life and then landed upon the runway of her day as her alarm clock began to beep very loudly inside her bedroom and the morning rudely interrupted her very peaceful night of rest. Each very loud beep from the alarm had a sense of urgency to it that not only disturbed her sleep but that also propelled Talitha to immediately clamber out of bed as it literally forced her to embrace and start the day.

Due to the fact that Talitha had actually slept on the wrong side of midnight the night before as she'd made love to Bryson into the early morning hours, she still felt quite sleepy and slightly groggy and she groaned as she clambered out of bed. Reality had just arrived and that meant, work definitely had to be attended to, irrespective of whether Talitha had just enjoyed a late night of sexual frolics with

Bryson or not. Much to Talitha's amazement and surprise however, somehow Bryson had actually managed to get up and leave earlier that morning she observed as she glanced at the space in their bed that he usually occupied and found it empty.

"Next time there'll be no more sex for Bryson after midnight, not on a weekday at least." Talitha muttered as she stepped inside the bathroom and prepared to take a shower.

Only one client consultation had been scheduled inside Talitha's work diary for that morning and so her workload for the working day ahead had the potential to be quite light and that comforted Talitha slightly as she began to take a shower. Later that afternoon, Talitha was actually due to meet with Professor Heisner for a briefing which she hoped would provide her with the ideal opportunity to present a few issues to him that related to some of her current clients.

Since Talitha's training period had actually ended and since her last face to face meeting with Professor Heisner had occurred, the two had rarely crossed paths in the physical sense and there were definitely issues that Talitha now wanted to raise with him. After each client session, Talitha would write up her notes almost religiously and then submit them but besides that form of communication, the two had not actually exchanged more than a few words all week. Inside

Talitha's mind there were now however, a few pressing issues that she really wished to discuss with him, in a confidential setting and discreet manner that really couldn't be communicated through the note system within Restructure as some issues, Talitha had decided, definitely had to be discussed in person. The note system required absolute professionalism at all times and Talitha actually felt quite uncomfortable about writing anything inside it that fell just outside the scope of her professional duties and obligations but there were some rather personal observations and sensitive issues that she definitely wanted to discuss that fell slightly outside that remit.

Approximately thirty minutes later, once Talitha arrived at work, she headed straight for her consultation room as she prepared quietly for the morning ahead. The one client consultation that Talitha was due to perform that morning was actually with Saskia, who was not an external client intake but actually the daughter of Professor Heisner's personal friend and Talitha felt extremely nervous about it. Due to the fact that Saskia was personally connected to Professor Heisner, or rather one of his friends that worried Talitha as it meant that she had to ensure that Saskia's client consultation went exactly as it should do and there was absolutely no margin of error, or getting it wrong. One thing however went in Talitha's favor and that was the fact that the actual consultation itself would merely be a meeting to discuss Saskia's requirements and so no actual procedures would be performed that day which meant, there would be less room for any possible mistakes on Talitha's part.

Much to Talitha's horror however, once she'd collected her usual morning latte and sat down at her desk, she rapidly discovered as she turned the Restructure system on that a very extensive list of procedure requests had now been input into the system by Professor Heisner. A gasp of shock almost flew out of Talitha's mouth as she reviewed each one in dismay, Saskia wanted to make a lot of changes and that meant, if Saskia or her Download experiences presented any problems to Talitha, those problems would definitely be around for a while. One small grain of comfort remained inside Talitha's mind as she sipped on the hot, milky cup of latte as she faced Saskia's huge list of requests and attempted to comfort herself and that was the fact that during that first week, she'd delivered her first six client's procedures immaculately.

"Saskia is the daughter of my personal friend." Professor Heisner had explained to Talitha throughout one of his briefings. "And I owe him some favors." He'd continued as he'd attempted to justify his position.

Every single detail that the Professor had shared throughout that briefing had told Talitha absolutely everything that she'd needed to know about the Professor's obligation towards Saskia and her father and he'd had left no possible room for any shadow of a doubt. In terms of Professor Heisner's position, there had been no actual choice about this particular client intake as he'd felt personally obligated to accommodate Saskia as a client and therefore that now meant, Talitha was obligated also.

Each minute of that Friday morning seemed to saunter by very slowly as Talitha patiently waited for Saskia to arrive as she quietly reflected upon the lack of information she possessed about her pending client as there were very sparse details inside the Restructure itself. The very long procedure request list and a simulated image was all that there really was and that added a sense of mystery to Talitha's morning and puzzled her slightly as she waited to meet Saskia for the very first time.

A huge weight of pressure seemed to sit idly upon Talitha's shoulders, simply because of the Professor's relationship with Saskia's father and as Talitha waited, she quietly accepted that the burden of pressure would definitely have to be endured, at the very least until all of Saskia's requirements had actually been fulfilled. Every inch of Saskia's profile was inspected and then re-inspected as Talitha waited as she tried to make the most of the information that was available instead of focusing upon what actually wasn't there which would worry her even more. The reality was however, Talitha had absolutely no choice but to participate in Saskia's consultation as refusal just wasn't a viable option, not if Talitha wanted to actually keep her job, simply due to who Saskia actually was.

Fortunately, there were two facts Talitha definitely did know for sure and she contemplated each one thoughtfully as she waited, Saskia would attend her consultation along with her father and she was only nineteen years old as Professor Heisner had already explained both those things to Talitha. At least, Saskia didn't appear to have two heads, so that meant, her consultation couldn't be that tricky or complex, Talitha contemplated quietly as she glanced at Saskia's simulated image on the screen directly in front of her.

Finally, the last few remaining grains and minutes of the early morning slipped silently away as a gentle knock sounded at Talitha's door. A deep breath was taken as Talitha quickly rose to her feet and then crossed the room as she internally prepared to meet Saskia and her father for the very first time. The majority of Talitha's morning had been spent speculating as to exactly what Saskia was actually hoping to achieve at Restructure but now, Talitha would actually find out.

Upon Talitha's face there was a very warm pleasant smile as she gently pulled the door open as she prepared to greet the three people she expected to find on the other side of it. Very faithfully as usual, Yucala had performed her duties meticulously as she had ushered the two from the reception area and delivered them directly to Talitha's consultation room door. Just a few seconds later, Yucala quickly sped off as she left to return to the reception area and attend to other matters as Talitha politely invited the two visitors inside her consultation room.

From what Talitha could see Saskia was actually quite pretty, in terms of her physical appearance and that immediately provoked her to question the number of procedures that Saskia had requested before Saskia's consultation even began. Some refreshments were politely offered to the two as soon as they were seated as Talitha attempted to break the ice and make Saskia and her father feel as comfortable and welcome as she possibly could. Once the requested drinks had been prepared and then served to them both, Talitha quickly sat back down behind her desk as she faced the father and daughter and smiled at them.

Just before Talitha began her actual consultation, a quick double check was performed to see if the Professor had provided any further information to her about Saskia but his silence regarding Saskia strangely continued and nothing further had been added to her Restructure profile at all. Due to the fact that Professor Heisner had remained quite quiet regarding the issue of Saskia that meant, Talitha now had to ask Saskia absolutely everything that she wanted to know about her objectives directly herself and she quietly began to prepare to actually do so.

"What exactly are you hoping to achieve at Restructure Saskia?" Talitha asked softly as she leant towards Saskia in a friendly manner. "And which Download would you actually like to have first as I noticed that you've requested quite a few? Are you really sure that you'll need so many?"

Due to the personal relationship between Professor Heisner and Marcus and Saskia's age, Talitha was anxious to tread very carefully as she verbally tiptoed towards the issue of Saskia's procedures. In terms of Talitha's client list, Saskia was Talitha's youngest client and because of that rather delicate factor, Talitha was quite mindful to display as much sensitivity and empathy towards her as she possibly could and to be very gentle in her approach.

"What do you think Talitha?" Marcus asked as he quickly stepped into the conversation and rapidly prompted Talitha to offer his daughter a professional opinion. "I'm not sure that Saskia actually needs so many physical enhancements. What would you recommend?"

For the very first time that week, an actual client had actually asked Talitha her opinion and it absolutely delighted her as she nodded her head and thoughtfully considered exactly how she should respond. In so many ways, it was actually a very sensitive and tricky issue as if Talitha suggested too many changes, or a change that perhaps wasn't something that Saskia had intended to change, then Saskia might be slightly hurt and offended by Talitha's response.

"Well Marcus, I think that the changes you might wish to make to your own body and face are a very personal decision, so I would have to understand Saskia's personal objectives first, in order to make appropriate recommendations." Talitha advised as she encouraged Saskia to join in and participate in the conversation.

Silence filled Talitha's consultation room for a minute or two as everyone inside the room kept very quiet as both Talitha and Marcus waited expectantly for Saskia to respond but no words were spoken. Essentially, this was Saskia's chance to communicate and explain exactly why she was there and what exactly she hoped to achieve but there seemed to be a slight hesitation on her part as Talitha glanced at her face, smiled and continued to wait as she quietly assumed that perhaps Saskia was slightly unsure or nervous. The last thing on Saskia's mind however, Talitha quickly discovered, was uncertainty and as Saskia suddenly opened her mouth and began to respond, Talitha was surprised and slightly shocked by the words and attitude that flowed out from her lips.

"Daddy, I want absolutely everything." Saskia demanded in a determined tone as she began to shake her head defiantly. "I want to be the most beautiful woman in the world and I want to be absolutely stunning."

Drops of irritation seemed to drip from Saskia's tongue and her voice had been slightly raised and as each angry drop clung to the particles of air inside the consultation room, the angry particles appeared to linger even after she'd spoken. From the words that Saskia had spoken and the attitude that she'd presented, it was immediately apparent to everyone inside the room that Saskia knew exactly why she was there, exactly what she wanted and exactly what she was absolutely determined to receive. Despite her father's rather sensible approach, Saskia was very clearly having none of it as she rapidly dismissed his interference and his suggestion and eagerly embraced the red carpet that Talitha had quite unintentionally, verbally placed down for her to walk upon with her demands.

Suddenly, an invisible blanket of discomfort rapidly seemed to sweep across the room as Talitha glanced at Marcus's face and noticed that he sighed quietly under his breath. This client consultation, Talitha quietly concluded, was definitely not going to be straight forward, or very simple but she gave Saskia a soft pretentious smile as she attempted to externally mask her inner concerns and reassure Saskia that everything was indeed, perfectly fine. Just from that very brief exchange and within a matter of minutes, it had become immediately apparent to Talitha that Saskia was a young woman that was used to getting exactly what she wanted, when she actually wanted it and that Marcus was used to footing the bill as he attempted to satisfy and quench her desires. A sudden realization struck Talitha's mind as she quietly absorbed any droplets of doubt that she might have possessed before that precise moment in time, Professor Heisner's friend's daughter was actually really, a spoilt brat.

"Well, I could put together a package of suggestions for you Saskia and Marcus, if you could specify the kind of budget that you'd like to commit to spending, I'll tailor the package accordingly." Talitha quickly suggested as she attempted to find a compromise and potential solution that they could perhaps all actually live with. "Some procedures are more expensive than others." She pointed out.

"Money really won't be a problem." Saskia replied curtly as she glanced at Talitha's face and then smiled smugly. "My father is extremely wealthy."

The smugness of Saskia's response immediately grated Talitha inside as it rapidly confirmed to her that all reason, logic and common sense had just flown out of her consultation room window. In less than a minute, Saskia had essentially ended the debate and it now appeared that there would be no further negotiations and that she would simply get what she wanted and that Marcus would foot the bill. Upon Marcus's face there was a silent look of defeat as he seemed to internally digest Saskia's response and it became instantly apparent to Talitha that Saskia was definitely the one making all the decisions in their family. A very strange family dynamic seemed to exist between the two which meant that Marcus had absolutely no control over the daughter he'd fathered and raised and in fact, Saskia actually appeared to have more control over Marcus than he had over her and the role reversal really wasn't a positive one.

"Right." Talitha replied as she smiled at Saskia in an attempt to mask her emotions.

Somehow, something somewhere along the line had definitely gone wrong between the two and Marcus's body seemed to fully reflect that reality as he slumped down inside his chair in absolute defeat. A glassy, haunted look seemed to reside inside Marcus's eyes as Talitha watched his posture crumble as he slipped even further down inside his chair but no actual words were spoken as Saskia's victory ruled his mind, heart and tongue and totally humiliated him.

In many ways, Marcus almost reminded Talitha of a withered leaf that clung frantically onto the branch of a tree that it had once thrived on which it was now unable to draw even a drop of nourishment from as it was sucked silently dry and shriveled up wearily as it made its way towards death. Inside Talitha's mind, she considered the relationship between the two to be the veins of the tree which had once provide Marcus with nutrition, vibrancy and life but now instead Saskia literally sapped every ounce of life out of him and the vibrant green leaf that had once represented his heart had now become a very dismal, withered dying brown. Joy it seemed was no longer the crown and the jewel of their family, or their relationship and any joy that had once perhaps existed between a loving father and daughter had very clearly now departed and had abandoned them both a very long time ago.

Regardless of what Talitha had expected to see, now all that clearly remained between the two was a dictatorship of convenience, very clearly dominated by Saskia which catered towards her needs and ultimately her desires. In Marcus's kingdom, the kingdom of his own life, he now occupied a position of servitude and was merely a servant that serviced and obeyed Saskia's demands as she ruled over him like a very dominant queen. A very selfish and extremely demanding queen that cared very little for her subjects.

Perhaps throughout Saskia's younger years, Talitha quietly speculated, it had been different for them both and perhaps at one time, they had actually thrived from each other's love but the retreat from Marcus had been very obvious as Talitha had quietly observed a father being dominated by his very spoilt and very determined, obnoxious daughter. Now Saskia was a daughter, who it seemed was not only dissatisfied with herself but also with all those around her as she sought out satisfaction in the financial rewards that she felt her father was obliged to provide to her.

A very negative precedent had been set between them both and something had definitely happened in the past to provoke that and that something had pushed their relationship down this path of destruction and the negativity between them had flourished but what that something was, Talitha was for now, completely unsure. No matter how many times Talitha studied both their faces however, no answers were forthcoming to her internal questions and due to the professional nature of her relationship with them both, Talitha dared not even ask them directly, or attempt to dig any further in search of the truth. Saskia, Talitha concluded, was like a wild, thorny, rose bush that pricked anyone that she came into close emotional proximity to and her father seemed to be the closest victim as the thorns she bore scratched and clawed away at him as he battled to protect, shield and remain close to the daughter that he so deeply loved.

Once Saskia's consultation ended, Talitha escorted both her visitors back towards the reception area and she almost sighed with relief as she watched them leave the building. Just as Talitha had suspected it might be, Saskia's consultation had in the end been rather tricky and that tricky situation would definitely continue to needle away at her mind for the coming weeks, Talitha concluded as she returned to her consultation room as Saskia had requested more than just a few actual procedures. If Talitha decided to raise the issue with Professor Heisner, she knew it would have to handled with as much tact as she could possibly muster, due to the nature of Professor Heisner's relationship with Marcus and that was a reality that Talitha could definitely not escape, at least not in the short term.

From Talitha's point of view, regardless of Saskia's spoilt behavior and Lachlan's vile, repugnant presence as she collected her handbag and prepared to go for lunch, she decided that her first week with real human clients had gone exceptionally well and that she actually felt quite proud of what she'd managed to achieve. Each client consultation had been conducted precisely, according to Professor Heisner's training and instructions and every client had been attended to and prepared meticulously for the intricate, complex, individual and very specific changes that had either taken place, or that would occur in the very near future inside their bodies.

Quite fortunately, a hearty lunch was not very far away as Talitha was absolutely famished as just about ten minutes drive along the highway there was a small diner that Talitha usually visited most lunchtimes as the food there was quite simply, absolutely delicious. Once Talitha arrived back inside the reception area, she walked briskly towards the building's main entrance with a spring in her step and then exited the building as she made her way towards food and a very well deserved lunch. Some internal waves of joy seemed to lift Talitha's spirits as she walked as her very first really challenging working week had now almost come to an end and later that day, very shortly in fact, she would actually spend a very relaxing, pleasant weekend with Bryson.

Once the mid-afternoon arrived and just before the clock struck three, Talitha made her way towards Professor Heisner's office for their scheduled meeting, just as they'd previously agreed. Due to the fact that Talitha had delivered her client consultations successfully that week, she was actually looking forward to their official gathering as she confidently approached the door of Professor Heisner's office which was situated towards the rear of the building and then gave it a gentle tap.

For a few seconds nothing happened as Talitha just stood inside the corridor and waited for a response but there was none and she began to wonder if perhaps Professor Heisner had actually forgotten about their appointment completely. The Professor as Talitha knew, wasn't always the most organized person on the face of the earth and sometimes, he did seem slightly absent minded and quite forgetful and so that was an actual possibility.

"Just a minute Talitha." Professor Heisner suddenly shouted out.

"Okay." Talitha replied as she welcomed the signs of life from behind the door and the very familiar voice that had just emanated from it.

Another minute or so actually passed by before Professor Heisner actually opened the door but when he did so, he immediately smiled at Talitha and then invited her into his office straight away. Due to the positive reception, Talitha immediately began to relax as a smile was a great start to their meeting and that meant, Professor Heisner was definitely not upset with Talitha and that he hadn't felt disappointed by her performance at work that week.

"Please come in Talitha and take a seat." Professor Heisner offered.

"Thank you." Talitha replied as she stepped inside his office and then crossed the room as she walked towards one of the empty chairs situated beside his desk.

In terms of Professor Heisner's office space, the room was actually much larger than Talitha's consultation room and very well equipped and at one side of the room there was a large black, shiny glossy desk which they both sat next to as Professor Heisner prepared to start their meeting. The rather large desk was much bigger than Talitha's own and as it sat silently, politely in-between them both, Talitha faced Professor

Heisner and just waited patiently for him to proceed.

Scattered around the rest of the room, in a slightly disorganized manner, there were some very elaborate looking pieces of equipment and apparatus that seemed very scientific. None of the pieces of equipment or apparatus were instantly recognizable to Talitha but she began to quietly inspect each one with her eyes as she waited as if somehow that would perhaps give her some kind of clue as to what each piece of equipment actually did. No matter how long Talitha looked at them however, no answers were forthcoming as she quietly accepted that their functions lay just beyond the scope of her knowledge and understanding and that today, when the weekend was just about to start, it really wasn't the best time to find out exactly each item actually did.

"How are your clients Talitha?" Professor Heisner suddenly asked as he peered at her face across his desk over the top of his glasses and silently began to scrutinize every inch of her face.

"Most of my clients are great Professor Heisner. I performed some Download procedures this week for the majority of them and they seemed absolutely delighted with the results." Talitha immediately confirmed as she enthusiastically nodded her head. "Although I do have a couple of concerns that relate to one or two of my clients that

I'd really like to discuss further with you, if you don't mind."

"Sure, go ahead. Concerns are good." Professor Heisner encouraged as he smiled. "It shows me that you take an interest in your clients and ultimately in my clients. I did anticipate that one or two of those clients that I'd assigned to you might present you with a few challenges, so that's absolutely nothing to worry about. If the position was easy Talitha, it wouldn't have required two months training." He quickly pointed out. "People are not a formula and at times, human beings can be very unpredictable."

"Well Professor Heisner, I've noticed that Charmaine seems to be the subservient partner within her romantic relationship and that her partner seems to be quite domineering and since he's the one paying for all her procedures that was slightly worrying." Talitha explained.

Professor Heisner gazed at Talitha's face thoughtfully for a few seconds and then began to nod his head in response. "Yes, I did suspect that their relationship might be a bit of an issue when I initially met them both but I decided that we shouldn't shy away from such problems when they present themselves and that we should face them head on, or rather that you should Talitha. This situation will help to build your experience and counseling skills and I have every confidence in you that you'll find the correct approach."

Talitha nodded.

"If the situation becomes extremely tricky in the future, I'm always here to advise you." Professor Heisner quickly clarified.

"I've also noticed that there's a potentially problematic family dynamic between Saskia and Marcus in that she is rather demanding and he seems to have no control over her financial demands." Talitha explained.

"Ah yes that is a slightly tricky situation and I'm afraid I can't really do much about that problem for now. Saskia is Saskia and she's a highly strung, very determined young woman that Marcus tiptoes around as I'm sure you've noticed, mainly due to their family history which he feels responsible for and quite guilty about. Unfortunately, their problems lie well beyond the scope of my work and such issues can't really be solved by a few physical enhancements, or even by myself." Professor Heisner said as he gently shook his head in frustration. "I accepted that sad reality a long time ago and so you'll just have to cope with Saskia's demands as best you can." He advised. "You can't really fix their family history and they'll have to arrive at a place where they recognize that there is actually a problem and then they'll have to want to fix themselves before anything can really change."

Talitha nodded her agreement. "I understand Professor Heisner and of course you are totally correct." She replied as it suddenly struck her that Professor Heisner had been fully aware of every client's situation, the factors at play and the problems that each would present when he'd actually allocated them to her. "I'll try my best." Talitha promised as she internally accepted that the burden of her client's problems was essentially something that she would now have to actually carry. She was expected to cope with their problems, not Professor Heisner, regardless of the root cause and she had to find outcomes, solutions and compromises that would be satisfactory to all the parties involved.

"Great stuff and next week, since you're doing so well, I'm going to add another client to your list." Professor Heisner announced as he suddenly rose to his feet. "Her name is Rita. I'll flag her details up inside the Restructure system shortly, so that you can review them before you go home tonight."

Talitha smiled and nodded.

"Right, I better get back to work." Professor Heisner boomed cheerfully as he began to walk towards his consultation room door.

Officially for that day it seemed, the meeting between the two was over and so Talitha quickly rose to her feet as she prepared to leave Professor Heisner's office and return to her consultation room to complete the tasks she had to finish before she could actually go home that evening. Despite Talitha's initial worries regarding some of her clients that she'd felt might pose a problem to her, Talitha felt slightly comforted by Professor Heisner's reassurances as she began to walk towards his office door as he'd definitely encouraged her. Some issues had been clarified, addressed and explained throughout their meeting but even more than that, Professor Heisner had actually believed in Talitha herself and her abilities and that revelation strengthened and motivated her internally somehow as it silently began to build her confidence.

In order to validate the Professor's faith in Talitha's abilities however, she absolutely had to deliver and she was extremely determined to step up to his faith in her and do so as she walked towards the door. Essentially that day, Professor Heisner had very clearly illustrated to Talitha that he actually trusted her judgment and her ability to steer her way through the murky waters of uncertainty and handle complex issues and scenarios that related to each of her clients and that really motivated her. The confidence that Professor Heisner had in Talitha suddenly seemed to become contagious as she inwardly grabbed onto the reigns of uncertainty and pushed any nagging doubts very firmly towards the back of her mind as she began to fully embrace his trust in her as a consultant and prepared to steer the horse of opportunity.

"Have you got any plans this weekend Professor Heisner?" Talitha asked cheerfully as the two neared the door.

"Nothing special really. You?" Professor Heisner replied as he pulled the door of his office open and then politely held onto it.

"I'll just be spending some time with Bryson." Talitha explained as she stepped through the door and entered the corridor. "We've got nothing special planned this weekend, we'll probably just relax at home and maybe go out somewhere nice for dinner on Saturday."

"It must be really nice to have that special someone to share your life with." Professor Heisner said as he followed Talitha out of the room.

"It really is Professor Heisner. You should try to find someone that you like." Talitha encouraged him. "Give love another chance."

"I'm afraid I'm far too busy right now Talitha. The clinic's just opened and all the work that involves takes up a lot of my time. Women like attention and they don't really like to compete with anything that consumes too much of your time, or your resources." Professor Heisner explained. "And usually, they feel that the majority of your time and resources should be reallocated to them, almost immediately and that can be very tricky. Perhaps when things are up and running and a bit more settled then I can think about it, if I meet someone nice."

"That is very true Professor Heisner, women do appreciate attention when they're in a relationship with someone." Talitha agreed as she smiled and nodded her head. "Perhaps you're right, it might be better to wait for a while as some women can be very demanding."

"Yes and I really don't have the time for lots of romantic demands right now." Professor Heisner insisted.

Some light discussion was engaged in as the two began to walk along the crisp white corridor that led back towards the reception area as Talitha quietly considered whether or not she should ask the Professor about the pet food delivery van that she'd seen on the Tuesday evening. Due to the fact that Talitha's consultation room was situated on the other side of the building that meant, Talitha had to walk back towards the reception area before she could reach the hallway that led towards it and so there was still a minute or so of walking time which Talitha could utilize to present her question to Professor Heisner. The main issue for Talitha now however, was whether she was actually brave enough to ask him her question as it was a rather strange question to ask and had absolutely nothing at all to do with her work and was very unlike their usual verbal discourse.

Another route did actually lead to Talitha's consultation room, if she walked along the corridor in the other direction but that led all the way around the rear perimeter of the building and was much longer and therefore it wasn't the preferred means of return. The much longer route and the corridor that led towards the back of the building was rarely facilitated by anyone besides the Professor himself and certainly not very often by Talitha but it did led to Professor Heisner's laboratory, so he utilized it quite frequently and at least several times on any given working day.

Since the day that Talitha had seen the pet food delivery van, earlier that week, the strangeness of its presence had niggled away at the back of her mind but as yet, she'd not dared to discuss its presence with anyone. Just as the two were about to step inside the reception area however, Talitha bravely took a deep breath as she grabbed boldness by the hand and finally decided to take the plunge in an attempt to satisfy her curiosity. A question was after all just a question Talitha finally decided and an answer, if one was actually provided, might satisfy her curiosity or it might not, it certainly couldn't hurt or make things any worse. Some final grains of courage were quickly plucked from deep down inside her gut as Talitha prepared to entertain her very curious, curiosity and ask the question that had sat locked away behind her lips for most of her working week as she turned to face Professor Heisner and smiled.

"Professor Heisner, I noticed the other day that there was a pet food delivery van inside the parking lot." Talitha mentioned as she glanced at the Professor's face with a slightly puzzled expression. "I couldn't help but wonder if they might have visited the wrong address as there aren't any animals here." She continued.

"Ah yes, the pet food delivery van." Professor Heisner replied as he gave Talitha a gentle smile and then nodded his head as he rapidly sought out an excuse. "That would have been for Moses. He has some pets at home and he doesn't always have the time to pick up food for them as he works very long hours you know. So sometimes, he orders food for his pets and they deliver it here for him instead." He explained as he internally decided that the actual truth was definitely not a viable response at that precise moment in time as women tended to be quite squeamish.

Perhaps there would never be a right time to divulge that information to Talitha, Professor Heisner considered thoughtfully as he paused for a moment next to her inside the reception. What happened inside the hidden enclosure in his laboratory wasn't particularly something that he wanted to divulge to another living soul and perhaps, just perhaps, his laboratory creatures would remain a secret from the rest of the world forever.

"Right, it was a delivery for Moses." Talitha replied as she nodded her head and immediately accepted his explanation. "That possibility did actually cross my mind at the time as I knew the delivery couldn't possibly be for Yucala as she'd already left for the day."

"Moses absolutely loves animals." Professor Heisner mentioned as he eagerly tried to reinforce his half-truth through a positive affirmation which again was another half-truth. "Right Talitha, you'll have to excuse me I'm afraid. Rather unfortunately, I have to get back to my laboratory now as I have an experiment that I have to complete by the end of today, so I better get a move on." He glanced up at the large clock on the wall just behind the reception desk as he gently shook his head. "The afternoon is almost over and today, time is definitely not my friend as it's slipped away at the blink of an eye and completely disappeared when I least wanted or expected it to."

Talitha nodded her head as she smiled. "I know, isn't time really annoying sometimes, it would be great if you could pause a minute and then make it last for an hour." She agreed. "Or if you could insert a couple more hours here and there as required, or even a day when you wanted to."

"Now that would be very handy." Professor Heisner replied. "Well done Talitha, you've managed to get through your very first week with real human clients and there have been no physical injuries, angry outbursts, or hurricanes of despair."

"Thanks for all your support Professor Heisner, I really couldn't have done it without you." Talitha courteously acknowledged as she watched the Professor turn and then head off back down the hallway from which they'd just come.

On Talitha's way back to her consultation room, she quietly regurgitated and thoughtfully considered Professor Heisner's words as she walked. Due to the fact that their respective destinations were situated on opposite sides of the building, the two naturally had, had to part straight after their meeting to complete their remaining tasks that day, so Talitha was not offended at all by the Professor's rather abrupt departure and completely understood it. Quite strangely however, Professor Heisner had actually attributed the pet food van's presence to Moses and as Talitha quietly considered that explanation further, it actually seemed rather strange.

The thought of Moses actually being responsible for any actual pets was in Talitha's opinion, slightly unbelievable as Moses and his very untidy, rather chaotic and extremely disorganized appearance didn't seem to really correlate very well with the responsibilities that looking after animals actually involved. Pets were a real responsibility and Moses, in Talitha's mind, didn't really come across as someone who was very responsible, especially when it came to the issue of his own physical appearance.

Animals required very intricate levels of care, ample amounts of dedication and a regular decent sized portion of attention and Talitha could not begin to imagine, even for a second, how someone like Moses would cope with such demands, if they were indeed actually placed upon him. The Professor's explanation seemed implausible as Talitha quietly began to dissect it and she was unable to actually digest it as she inspected it slightly more closely and it suddenly dawned upon her that she hadn't actually questioned it at all and that she'd simply accepted the Professor's response at face value.

Due to the fact that home time and the weekend was near as Talitha stepped back inside her consultation room, a triumphant smile spread out across her face as she began to push thoughts of Moses and animals towards the back of her mind. The working week had been a tremendous success and Talitha's meeting with Professor Heisner had gone exceptionally well as he had appreciated her work and her delivery and that was definitely something to celebrate and rejoice in. Despite all Talitha's good intentions which were to focus solely upon Saskia's notes and her pending weekend, thoughts of Moses and the animals gradually began to creep back to the forefront of her mind as she sat back down at her desk and began to work.

Perhaps she was being slightly presumptuous when it came to her analysis of Moses, Talitha quietly considered as she retrieved Saskia's notes which she'd started to write earlier that day and perhaps, just perhaps, underneath that very rough looking external chaos, there really was a very responsible and highly considerate individual. Perhaps Moses's responsibilities outside of work, Talitha internally deliberated, were the reason that he actually looked so untidy and disorganized. Perhaps Moses was so devoted to the many animals that he looked after in his spare time that he even neglected his own appearance as a result.

Interestingly, it suddenly struck Talitha how alike Professor Heisner and Moses actually were, especially when it came to the issue of their very ruffled, crumpled exterior but Professor Heisner had provided Talitha with stable employment and that to Talitha was a significant achievement, regardless of his untidy presentation. Curious thoughts began to cross Talitha's mind as she began to speculate as to whether or not Moses actually had a romantic partner but it was quickly decided that the romantic possibility of Moses actually being in a committed relationship was highly unlikely. Women could be very tolerant towards someone they loved but to tolerate Moses and his very messy attitude towards his own personal presentation and his disheveled appearance every single day would definitely be too much of a romantic cross to carry, Talitha quietly concluded as such a messy appearance was just a huge ask of any woman.

Horror suddenly struck Talitha's mind as she rapidly realized just how blinkered and biased she'd actually become as she began to analyze her own thoughts and question them. The superficial measures of physical perfection within the beauty industry had perhaps had more of an impact upon Talitha's mind than she'd ever imagined as that wasn't how many people really thought and functioned in the actual world outside of it. Romance wasn't an arena that was as narrow minded as the world of beauty and perhaps Moses appealed to his lover in a different way. For some people, an untidy appearance just wouldn't be deemed as very important and perhaps, it would even add to the physical attraction someone felt towards Moses not actually detract from it.

Some people as Talitha knew, absolutely loved and admired intellect in a man which meant, Professor Heisner and Moses with their big brains and scientific prowess would be absolutely adored and sought after by some people that cared far less about cosmetic pleasantries. For all Talitha knew, Moses could actually already be a very happily married man, or he could be engaged as not everyone yearned for the comforts that a perfectly physically formed partner that conformed to society's prescribed standards of beauty and superficial measures provided. Perhaps the two men actually really liked men and perhaps, just perhaps, they were even secret lovers, Talitha quietly deliberated as she began to allow her mind to wander and challenged her own perceptions of the world and her own quite narrow minded thinking.

A quick glance at the time rapidly confirmed that it was almost five thirty as Talitha submitted Saskia's notes and then prepared to depart as work was finally over for that week. Right beside Talitha's desk and chair, her handbag sat on the floor, in its usual spot that it usually occupied every working day and she quickly plucked it from the ground as a huge smile spread out across her face and then shut down the Restructure system. Technically, Talitha could actually keep her handbag inside a drawer in her desk but that just felt so formal and her consultation room, at the end of the day, was all hers to do with as she wished and so her handbag had been allocated a specially designated spot on the ground, right next to her desk and chair for its sole occupation that was within very easy reach.

One thing had become very apparent to Talitha during her afternoon of quiet deliberations and as she walked towards the reception area, she quietly considered the fact that she really didn't actually know very much about either of the two men that she worked with outside of work. Every working day Talitha would engage in some quite personal conversations with Yucala where they'd share some quite intimate personal details about themselves but such conversations were held far less frequently with Professor Heisner and absolutely never ever engaged in with Moses.

In fact, outside the professional capacity that Talitha usually operated, functioned and interacted in alongside the two men, she actually knew absolutely nothing about them at all. When Talitha spoke to either of the two men, their conversations tended to predominantly revolve around work and were usually very functional in nature. On a few occasions, Talitha had ventured into some slightly more personal topics verbally with Professor Heisner but whether he was actually really disclosing the reality of his personal life to Talitha or not, was another matter entirely and not something that she could actually be certain of.

Once Talitha stepped inside the parking lot, she smiled as she walked towards her vehicle as her silver salon glistened in the early evening sunlight as gentle rays bounced of the sides and edges of her car. Although Talitha's internal deliberations about Moses had entertained her for a while that afternoon, she'd definitely allowed her mind to mischievously digress and now, she really had to focus upon the man in her life, Bryson and their weekend. The weekend had now definitely arrived and it would whisk Talitha away from work for some fun and frolics and for some much needed leisure time which she would spend inside Bryson's very devoted loving arms. Each step Talitha took was light as she walked and there was a definite spring in her step as she internally celebrated the end of her very first working week as a real Bodily Enhancements Consultant and looked forward to her weekend.

Thoughts surrounding Moses and Professor Heisner and their respective love lives, or lack of one, were quickly abandoned as Talitha entered her vehicle and then started the engine of her car as she prepared to enjoy her own love life which was very definite, absolutely certain and actually waiting to be enjoyed. Fortunately for Talitha, her workload that week had been relatively simple, easy to cope with and quite straight forward but she definitely knew that the future would bring some very tricky issues to her door and perhaps even invite some extremely complex clients into her consultation room.

"Professor Heisner's put such a lot of trust in me, I just have to try and do my best to deliver." Talitha murmured quietly to herself as she began to roll her car towards the entrance of the parking lot. "I don't want to let anyone down."

Almost everything about Talitha's new job seemed to be absolutely perfect and suited her right down to the ground which meant her shoulders did not feel burdened, or weighed down by the responsibilities that Professor Heisner had allocated to her. One thing did worry Talitha slightly however and that was Saskia's very stubborn attitude and her father's relationship with Professor Heisner. Whatever mistakes Talitha might make with any other client, she certainly could not afford to make with Saskia and she knew it as errors might actually cost Talitha, her actual job.

"How strange." Talitha suddenly muttered as she stopped her car just beside by the entrance to the parking lot. "Where is Moses's car?"

For the first time ever, it actually struck Talitha as she glanced back at the parking lot that was now almost empty, there was no actual vehicle inside it that could possibly belong to Moses. Only two cars now remained and one of those definitely belonged to Professor Heisner, an old battered looking black sedan and the other car to the Night Watchman as it definitely hadn't been there that morning and that meant, Moses had no actual vehicle.

"How on earth does Moses get to work every day?" Talitha muttered to herself as she suddenly began to question his lack of transportation. "And how did he get all those pet food supplies home?"

Unanswered questions rapidly began to pile up inside Talitha's mind as she noticed that for some inexplicable reason, she'd never once actually seen a vehicle that could belong to Moses at all and she'd not even noticed it until that precise moment in time. Despite Talitha's niggling the curiosity, the parking lot certainly didn't seem to want to provide her with an answer and it remained completely silent and sat totally still, no matter how long Talitha stared at it.

"No buses come this far along the highway and a taxi every day would cost him an absolute fortune." Talitha muttered quietly under her breath. "I'll ask Moses on Monday." She announced decisively as she prepared to resume her journey.

Purely due to the very remote location of the Restructure building itself, Talitha already knew that there were quite limited methods of transportation to reach that actual destination as public transport definitely could not be utilized. Taxis were very expensive and even more so during peak times and it was highly unlikely that Moses would be able to afford such a luxury as the huge expense would be hard to justify, unless he had very cheap accommodation and lived on bread and butter.

An incoming text on Talitha's phone suddenly arrived and her phone began to beep as the message demanded her attention and rather abruptly interrupted her thoughts. Thoughts surrounding Moses and his means of transportation were then quickly abandoned as Talitha immediately turned her attention towards the text message and glanced at the screen of her phone which now sat inside the holder on the dashboard of her car.

"That's got to be from Bryson." Talitha muttered happily as a satisfied smile rapidly spread out across her face. "He's definitely thinking about me and by now, he must be on his way home from work. Moses and how he gets to work each day is not really my problem, right now I need to focus on Bryson, the man in my very real personal life and our weekend." She stated decisively as she opened up the message and then began to read it.

'See you soon sweetie. I'm on my way home. Bryson xx.'

A torrent of excitement surged through Talitha's veins as she quietly read the message from Bryson and then began to drive out of the parking lot as the weekend was now actually waiting for her participation. Fortunately, Bryson was already on his way home from work and that meant, Talitha would definitely see him soon and that they could then bask in their glorious weekend together. Their free time on the weekends was a luxury that the couple usually enjoyed spending together and Talitha silently vowed to make their weekend absolutely delightful as she entered onto the highway and then began to speed enthusiastically along it towards her weekend, towards Bryson and towards his very open loving arms.

Approximately twenty minutes later, when Talitha finally arrived at home, she found Bryson already there waiting for her and he'd even started cooking their evening meal. A splendid feast which consisted of several types of seafood, crunchy fries and some soft, very sweet, baby cobs of corn was being prepared as Bryson pandered to Talitha's hunger and she rejoiced in his preemptive efforts to satisfy her stomach. Everything about the couple's evening meal was absolutely heavenly and totally divine and a chilled bottle of wine was served alongside the food which had been brought up especially from Bryson's special wine collection that lived inside the basement earlier that day.

The collection of wines inside the basement came from all over the world and Bryson had literally collected a bottle of local wine almost religiously, from every vacation spot that the two had ever visited together and so the bottles of wine were only opened on very special occasions. Between the couple, cooking wasn't really seen as an issue and was pretty much viewed as a shared responsibility and that meant, they both cooked for each other quite regularly and that also meant, very often they would also actually cook meals together.

Once dinner and the very special bottle of wine had been consumed, the couple made their way towards the sofa inside the lounge as they prepared to relax for the night, in good spirits and fully refreshed just by each other's presence. Their companionship was definitely one of the best things about Talitha's life and the entire world as far as she was concerned and as she sat down upon the cream and gold leather sofa inside the lounge, Bryson knelt down in front of her and then began to tenderly massage her feet.

Talitha started to giggle. "Bryson, now you're really spoiling me." She teased.

"I just want to spoil you today." Bryson explained. "I'm really proud of you and what you've achieved this week."

"You know Bryson, I don't actually spend all day at work on my feet." She teased playfully. "They did give me a chair and a desk."

Bryson chuckled. "Can't a man spoil his fiancée sometimes?" He asked as he plucked a large feather from a nearby vase and then began to tickle Talitha's feet with it.

"That's so ticklish Bryson." Talitha gushed between giggles as she tried her best not to erupt into fits of laughter.

"I can do something even more ticklish than that." Bryson suggested playfully as he winked suggestively.

Talitha grinned. "I'm sure you can." She replied.

"Let's have an early night and then I can tickle you some more in all the naughty places." Bryson said as he suddenly rose to his feet.

Talitha smiled.

"I'll even help you up. That's how nice I am." Bryson teased as he courteously stretched out his hand towards Talitha and then grinned.

"Seriously Bryson, sometimes you're just so kind." Talitha replied as she held his hand and allowed Bryson to pull her to her feet. "I mean really, they broke the mold of compassion when they made you."

"I know Talitha, I just don't know where I would actually be in life, if I wasn't engaged to you." Bryson joked as he began to lead Talitha out of the lounge towards the hallway.

"You might have been a Saint or a Priest, or you might have even been given a noble peace prize or something." Talitha teased as she followed Bryson along the hall towards their bedroom.

"A Priest, only if they gave me good wine." Bryson replied. "No sex and bad wine just wouldn't work well for me at all."

Talitha giggled.

Finally, Talitha considered quietly as the couple headed towards their bedroom, her life was headed down the road of joy towards the city of absolute perfection. Life just really couldn't get any better in Talitha's sight as she had a great loving relationship that was extremely enjoyable and now, she also had the perfect job and career to match it. An adoring smile adorned Talitha's face as she glanced at Bryson's face, he wasn't what some women might consider to be extremely handsome but in her eyes, he was definitely the buffest man in the city of Shuttlesburg.

Over the years, Bryson had been extremely faithful to her and he'd provided her with all the love, attention and devotion that a woman could ever possibly want or need from a partner and that was one thing that Talitha definitely couldn't fault him on. Joy had blessed their relationship, from the very first moment they'd met and there had been no huge troubles, heartbreaking betrayals, weird issues or complex conundrums to face that would have either emotionally drained Talitha, or dragged her heart down into the depths of despair.

Some grey clouds had darkened the skies of the couple's life since they'd been together and their relationship had been tested in various ways but the bond between them both had remained strong and very firmly in place. One example of that in recent times had been when Talitha had been unemployed for a year as she'd been forced to leave the last cosmetic surgery she'd worked for under a dark cloud, due to her male bosses very unwanted sexual advances. Throughout that year, Talitha had spent most of her time at home and it had been an extremely difficult time for her but Bryson had constantly encouraged her although he hardly cared whether she actually went out to work or not as finances had never been a bone of contention between the couple. Money just wasn't an issue that they'd ever argued about and whenever Talitha had been out of work which had happened a few times over the five years since their relationship had actually begun, Bryson had always financially supported her.

Due to the fact that the cosmetic surgeon in question had been rather influential and very powerful in his field when Talitha had notified the relevant bodies about his misconduct, she'd faced a solid wall of rejection afterwards and she'd been unable to find alternative employment in the same industry ever since. For at least a year after those horrible events, Talitha had tried to apply for various positions of employment and she'd been turned down time and time again and it was almost as if somehow, she'd actually been blacklisted. Restructure and Professor Heisner had finally changed all that however as Talitha's life had suddenly, quite unexpectedly, taken a turn for the better when she'd applied for the Bodily Enhancements Consultants role and then been given the position and it had broken the professional heartbreak that Talitha had endured.

In hindsight, it almost felt now as if the negative events had actually been a blessing in disguise as Talitha had moved forward in her career in the same kind of industry as before but with a very different employer and Restructure had almost been like a Godsend to her life. Either Professor Heisner didn't actually know about the difficulties that Talitha had faced or he just didn't care as he'd offered her the position, trained her and then nurtured, supported and encouraged her and she'd begun to achieve.

Deep down inside, Talitha felt immensely grateful to the Professor for the opportunity he'd provided to her as now, Talitha was actually something more than just a cosmetic surgeon's assistant and that had in the end, been a golden lining inside a grey miserable cloud of despair. The appointment to her new position of employment had allowed Talitha to shed the past hurts she'd carried around with her for so long as she'd left them well and truly behind, stepped confidently into the present and embraced a future of real hope and for that opportunity, she was truly grateful.

Quite sadly for Talitha, the weekend seemed to rapidly sprint by and as it silently departed from Talitha's life and evaporated into total nothingness, Monday morning rather rudely showed up on her doorstep way too early and all too eager to take the weekend's place. The day was absolutely determined to commence, whether Talitha embraced it or not as it knocked very loudly upon her door in the form of some very loud beeps that emanated from her alarm clock which sat on the bedside cabinet right next to her bed that urged her to get up and participate in the day.

A gentle groan escaped from Talitha's lips as soon as she opened her eyes and then glanced around at the bedroom that surrounded her as she consciously decided that the calendar of life could at times actually be quite heartless. Slumber and sleepiness was pushed to one side as Talitha literally forced herself to get up as laziness just wasn't an option on a workday and neither was a longer lie-in. Monday morning had definitely arrived whether Talitha liked it or not and that meant, she definitely had to go to work.

Approximately forty minutes later, once Talitha had showered, dressed and then grabbed a cup of coffee, she stepped out of the front door and began to walk towards her vehicle which as usual was parked inside the driveway right next to the home that she shared with Bryson each night. The front garden had two paths and one was quite a short path which led towards the driveway where Talitha's car was usually parked but the other much longer path actually led towards the front gate but it was rarely utilized as the space in the driveway was big enough to accommodate both Bryson and Talitha's vehicles. Along the side of both paths however, there were some very neatly cut emerald green lawns which politely decorated each stony, grey walkway that Bryson tried his best to keep well maintained.

From above Talitha's head, a few rays of sunshine shone down onto the garden and bounced off each blade of grass as Talitha walked along the short path and she admired the garden as it glistened due to the drops of dew that adorned and decorated each shiny green surface. The previous night it appeared, or perhaps even in the very early hours of the morning, the rain had decided that the grass had been in need of some natural refreshment and it had very kindly actually done Bryson's job for him as it had provided the lawns with some much needed nourishment.

Each golden ray made the green mass sparkle as somehow, the sun poked it's head out through some clouds that surrounded it and actually managed to squeeze a few rays through each one. Unfortunately that morning it seemed, the clouds had wanted to wrap themselves around the sun which almost looked as if it was trying to break through them so that it could shine more brightly but the clouds were having none of it as the grey, spongy masses clung onto the sun quite tightly and restricted its ability to shine more freely.

"I really could have spent at least another hour of quality time with my duvet." Talitha muttered as the chilly morning air gently brushed against her cheeks and they began to shine a bright rosy red. "The weekend just seems to go so fast and it's probably going to rain later as those clouds look a bit suspicious." She mumbled as she entered inside her vehicle and then started the engine.

The drive to work was relatively peaceful and straight forward enough but it took Talitha around forty minutes as she stopped off en-route at the diner that she usually visited for lunch each day to pick up a sausage bap for breakfast and had to wait in a queue. Once Talitha arrived at work, she found Yucala's usual cheerful, smiling face inside the reception area and she immediately smiled back as she approached the reception desk and prepared to greet her.

"Good morning Yucala." Talitha said as gave Yucala a polite nod.

"Good morning Talitha." Yucala immediately replied. "How was your weekend?"

"It was great, nothing to strenuous really, I just relaxed at home. How was yours?" Talitha asked.

"Usual stuff really, husband, kids but a bit more cooking and cleaning as his mother came round and she's very judgmental. The house has to be absolutely spick and span whenever she visits, or I never hear the end of it and that can be quite difficult to achieve when you have three rowdy, messy boys." Yucala explained. "They definitely take after their father."

Talitha laughed. "I better go and do some work." She said as she held the wrapped paper bag that contained the sausage bap up in front of her face. "And I have to at least try and eat this while it's still warm.

"I've already had breakfast this morning, I usually get up at six during the week and do breakfast at home for everyone, it's a lot of work but someone has to do it." Yucala explained as she nodded her head and smiled. "Or else no one would eat a decent meal in our house."

"What about your husband, doesn't he help?" Talitha asked.

"Please. Not at all, he won't even step foot inside a kitchen. He's a bit old fashioned really but he's great at DIY and he earns quite a lot of money, so he definitely has his uses." Yucala replied. "The boys are all at school now, so I like to work, it gets me out of the house."

"Men." Talitha joked as she gently shook her head. "And you have to live with four of them Yucala, now that is a lot of work."

Yucala laughed.

"I'll speak to you later on Yucala." Talitha said as she began to walk away from the reception desk towards the corridor that led directly to her consultation room. "Have a good morning."

"You too Talitha, you too." Yucala replied.

Once Talitha stepped inside the crisp white hallway that led towards her consultation room, she held eagerness firmly by the hand as she began to walk briskly along it, enthusiastic to make a start and begin her Monday morning. The week ahead for Talitha promised to be full of interesting clients, lots of Downloads procedures that had to be performed, some complex issues to wrap her mind around and there would even be a brand new female client to see and that excited her.

Just a few minutes later as Talitha stepped inside her consultation room, she found that everything was very quiet which was pretty much as she expected it to be as the only other person who visited it in her absence was a cleaner and that only ever happened after eight during some weekday evenings. Although Talitha had never actually met the cleaner, she always knew when they'd been as her consultation room would be freshly dusted off, vacuumed and all the bins would be emptied and the provision of a cleaner was another thing that Yucala had successfully managed to organize for Professor Heisner that kept his Restructure clinic in order.

"Time for my favorite start to the morning." Talitha muttered as she headed straight for the coffee machine to prepare a milky caramel latte which would accompany her sausage bap. "The morning really can't start without a decent coffee."

Much to Talitha's dismay, by the time she actually managed to sit down at her desk and began to eat her sausage bap with lashings of brown sauce, she rapidly discovered that it was not actually piping hot anymore but just a rather inferior, mediocre lukewarm. The delightful aroma that should have wafted into Talitha's nostrils therefore wasn't as strong, due to the decrease in temperature but the bap was still sufficient enough to fill Talitha's growling stomach and so she quickly began to tuck in. A quick inspection of Rita's profile inside the Restructure system was quietly conducted as Talitha ate but there really wasn't much to see there yet which probably meant that Professor Heisner still hadn't actually had a chance to complete it.

At around eleven, Dean arrived punctually for his consultation and Talitha immediately invited him inside her consultation room and then offered him a refreshment. Strangely on this particular occasion, Talitha rapidly noticed that Dean seemed slightly more nervous about their consultation than the first time they'd met as he sat and fidgeted with his hands as beads of sweat trickled down onto his cheeks from his forehead. The obvious nervousness that Dean displayed made absolutely no sense at all to Talitha as she placed a cup of coffee gently down in front of him and then smiled at him in a reassuring manner as this was their second consultation and she'd have expected him to be less nervous not more nervous than he'd been about his first.

"Are you okay Dean?" Talitha asked as she sat down beside her desk and then smiled at him.

Dean nodded in response. "Yes thanks Talitha but if it's not too much trouble, I'd really like to have a penis enlargement today." He blurted out.

"Sure Dean that's no trouble at all." Talitha replied. "And don't worry, it'll be very much like your first procedure, nothing scary or anything."

"Thanks Talitha. I have been a bit worried about this appointment because I've never really done anything like this before. The most I've ever done in the past is had my teeth polished." Dean admitted.

"Don't worry, I understand Dean, changing our bodies or faces can be a little bit scary at times." Talitha gently reassured him as she immediately sympathized with his obvious display of nerves. "Here would you like one of these?" She offered as she plucked a box of tissues from the top of her desk and then handed him the box.

"Yes please." Dean confirmed as he rapidly nodded his head. "I think nerves definitely got the better of me today."

"Happens to us all sometimes. We can't always be fearless. If you'd prefer Dean, we could always do another procedure today and then do the penis enlargement at your next consultation." Talitha suggested.

Dean quickly shook his head. "No that won't be necessary Talitha. I really need to do this straight away." He insisted. "I've spent a lot of money, so there's absolutely no way I'm backing out now."

"Okay, I'll just load up the image range for your enhancement, so that you can make a selection." Talitha explained.

"Thanks and don't worry Talitha, I'm totally ready for this." Dean replied as he nodded his head.

"Okay Dean, I was just making sure." Talitha clarified. "It's a very big change to make."

"I know, it's absolutely huge." Dean agreed. "It's not every day we change our bits."

Talitha giggled.

A few seconds of silence sat delicately in-between the two as Talitha loaded up the various images of men's penises on the screen directly in front of her as Dean sat quietly and just patiently waited. Despite Talitha's gentle reassurances and comforting words, Dean's forehead and hands continued to gather more drops of sweat as fear crept silently and invisibly around his body and infiltrated his flesh but there wasn't much more that Talitha could actually do or say to reassure him. The procedure itself did involve a very sensitive, personal bodily adjustment and so Talitha could totally understand Dean's nervous state and the beads of sweat that continued to trickle down his brow.

"Here Dean, have a look at these and then you can pick out the ones that you like." Talitha invited as she turned her screen to face him. "Don't worry, you can take your time there's no rush or anything." She gently reassured him as she attempted to ease his obvious discomfort.

"Thanks Talitha." Dean replied as he smiled. "This one's a very unusual shape." He suddenly mentioned as he pointed towards an image on the screen.

"Ah yes that penis is called the Tip Simulator." Talitha explained politely as she smiled. "Apparently from what I've heard, it's structure and shape are supposed to give a woman more pleasure that's why it's slightly thicker at the top."

"I definitely don't want that one." Dean mentioned as he suddenly pointed towards another image and then gently shook his head. "Although it's very long, it's really way too thin. It looks like a pencil."

"You know Dean, shapes and sizes don't really actually make that much of a difference to women." Talitha replied. "I think it's really more about making the most of what you have."

"You only say that Talitha because you're a woman and you've not been equipped with a smaller than average penis. When that happens, the physical challenges you face are not that easy to cope with." Dean explained.

Talitha nodded as she listened. "Take as long as you need Dean, there's really no rush." She reassured him.

Approximately twenty minutes went by as Talitha narrowed down the range several times and assisted Dean as much as she possibly could in his quest to find the ideal penis. Every inch of Dean's face looked taut with tension and his body trembled slightly as he searched as Talitha quietly observed that the procedure had almost transformed Dean into a pile of nerves. Male penises were definitely not something that Talitha had specialized in and due to the quite sheltered life she'd led and the fact that she was a woman, she was certainly not an expert on the topic in any capacity at all and so there was actually very little advice or guidance that she could provide to Dean.

Despite Talitha's own shortcomings regarding her quite limited knowledge of male genitalia, she somehow managed to persevere as she attempted to assist Dean in any way she possibly could and answer his questions about those images which sparked his interest. Yes, Talitha definitely recognized her own limits regarding the subject matter but she was being paid to do a job and that job definitely had to be done, regardless of her own personal limitations. Once the final five penis images had been chosen that Dean seemed to be comfortable with and happy about, Talitha quickly displayed each image upon Dean's simulated naked body image inside the Restructure system in order to allow him to make a final choice.

"Perhaps this will help you make a final decision Dean." Talitha suggested as the screen repopulated with Dean's simulated image and she replicated it five times and then attached his final five choices to each one.

Nothing but silence surrounded them both for at least five minutes as Talitha held her tongue and just watched Dean inspect each image very carefully and extremely thoroughly. Despite the internal desire to speak and break the silence which felt slightly awkward, Talitha kept very quiet as she allowed Dean to focus solely upon his decision without any distractions.

"I think I'd like to go for that one." Dean finally said as he leant towards the screen and then pointed towards the Tip Simulator. He nodded his head decisively as he smiled. "Yeah that one looks great."

"Right, I'll just get that organized for you now." Talitha confirmed as she smiled and then glanced at the time. She rapidly noticed that Dean's appointment was now actually due to end in less than fifteen minutes and that prompted her to process his choice on the Restructure system as quickly as she possibly could. "It should be just a few more seconds Dean, it's processing now."

Dean nodded.

"Right that's all done, if you'd like to follow me please Dean." Talitha instructed as she quickly rose to her feet.

"Okay." Dean replied obediently as he quickly stood up. "You know Talitha, I was actually dreading my appointment today." He mentioned as the two walked towards the smaller adjoining room.

"It's really nothing to worry about Dean, it's just a little adjustment." Talitha reassured him as she smiled. "Now, if you'd like to get inside the capsule for me and then lie down please, I'll have that sorted out for you in no time at all."

Dean nodded. "Thanks for making this so easy for me Talitha." He said appreciatively as he walked up the steps and then lay down inside the transparent capsule. "I really appreciate it."

"Are you sure that this is what you really want to do and that the penis you've selected is really the one you want?" Talitha asked Dean as she politely provided him with one final opportunity to change his mind. "As I mentioned before reversals can be extremely difficult, quite tricky and very risky.

"I'm very sure. This is exactly what I want." Dean immediately confirmed as he nodded his head decisively.

"Right, well I better get a move on then. Time is really slipping out of my grasp." Talitha replied as she began to gently lower the capsule lid down over Dean's body. "And there's not a second to waste really as your consultation will soon be over."

"Yes and soon, I'll be physically liberated from the curse of being smaller than average." Dean joked.

Talitha smiled.

"It's going to be a great day." Dean muttered happily as he watched Talitha leave the room.

Quite surprisingly for Dean, the initial nervousness that he'd felt when he'd entered inside Talitha's consultation room that day had now gone and he actually felt quite comfortable about what was just about to happen to his body and that really surprised him. The most awkward and personal request that Dean had made had been handled by Talitha with a lot of sensitivity and a tremendous amount of professionalism and being that Talitha was a female consultant, Dean had worried slightly about this particular request. In terms of Talitha's assistance however, it had been absolutely faultless and her gentle reassurances had been very soothing and comforting to Dean's very worried mind.

Five minutes later, once the Download procedure had been initialized, implemented and performed, Talitha returned to the small adjoining room as she prepared to wrap up Dean's consultation and organize his next appointment. Although it had been Dean's most tricky request, it had gone quite smoothly in the end and the initial embarrassment that Talitha had felt at the outset of Dean's consultation had now gone as she'd quickly realized and accepted that Dean had been even more nervous about it than she'd been.

Two of Talitha's male clients had now actually requested penis enlargements during their consultations and both those experiences had really opened her eyes and enlightened Talitha to just how complex the issue of mens' penises could actually be. Unlike the female anatomy which was frequently publicly deliberated and dissected at every turn, the male anatomy was far less frequently or openly discussed but it had really highlighted to Talitha that very often men had their own physical insecurities to worry about that quite often women knew absolutely nothing about.

"How was it Dean?" Talitha enquired as she lifted up the lid of the capsule and smiled at him.

Dean immediately smiled in response and enthusiastically nodded his head as he sat back up. "It was absolutely fine Talitha." He replied. "And everything seems to be in the right place." Dean joked as he climbed back down the steps. "At least I think it is."

"Well, I hope it is Dean." Talitha teased playfully as she smiled. "Or there'll be no nighttime nooky for you."

"I can gladly confirm that the baton of sexual pleasure, is definitely dangling much further down now, very happily indeed." Dean clarified playfully.

Talitha giggled. "I should really make your next appointment for you now Dean before you leave." She insisted as she began to walk back towards her consultation room. "And I just hope that it gives you as much enjoyment in the bedroom as you hoped it would."

"Me too. It's certainly long overdue." Dean agreed. "I just can't wait to unleash this beast but first I have to actually find a lady that's willing."

"Now that can be the trickiest part." Talitha replied.

"Yes, it really can." Dean agreed. "Romance isn't easy and some women really aren't easy either."

"You have to find one that you like and then wine and dine them." Talitha recommended. "A splash of charm, a solid portion of patience and a dash of adoring devotion usually does the trick."

"Thanks, I'll try that." Dean replied.

The smile on Dean's face as Talitha escorted him back to the reception area once his consultation ended, soothed Talitha's mind as it silently reassured her that Dean felt very happy about what had just taken place as he certainly looked much happier than when he'd initially arrived. Whether or not the huge penis enlargement that Dean had requested would actually bring him the pleasure he sought, was not a question that Talitha could answer yet but it had already provided Dean with some positive gifts, a portion of hope and a cup of confidence and those gifts, he'd desperately needed.

"I'll see you next week Dean." Talitha said as she turned to face Dean and bade him farewell. "And good luck out there."

"Thanks so much Talitha." Dean replied as he smiled.

On her way back towards her consultation room, Talitha quietly contemplated Dean's consultation that morning as she began to speculate what she might actually do if Bryson had been in the same physical position as Dean. The issue had never been one that the couple had ever had to worry about as in terms of Bryson's manhood, he was reasonably well endowed but it could so easily have been very different and then perhaps Bryson would have sought out some assistance like Dean had. Neither one of the couple that Talitha knew off had ever considered cosmetic procedures or artificial physical enhancements but if they had been less physically blessed, perhaps they might have, Talitha concluded as she stepped back inside her consultation room.

Some notes were written up for Dean as Talitha kept an eye on the time which that day definitely wasn't on her side as she still had lunch to take and then another client consultation in the afternoon and she'd spent slightly longer with Dean than she'd originally planned. Lunch would have to be very brief that day, Talitha decided and a takeaway lunch would definitely have to happen as a sit down lunch that day was a luxury that she could definitely not afford.

Fortunately enough as the morning totally disappeared and quickly evaporated into nothing, Talitha actually managed to complete Dean's notes and then submit them just as lunchtime arrived. The afternoon was now definitely threatening to show up but thankfully, Talitha would still have time for a quick lunch before Rita was actually due to appear. Hunger began to angrily rumble away inside Talitha's stomach as she made her way towards the diner that she usually visited each day in order to collect a sandwich for lunch. Once a salami and cheese sandwich had been purchased which had been wrapped up inside a brown paper bag, Talitha quickly returned to work with her purchase clasped inside one of her hands as she prepared to satisfy her hunger and fill her now almost empty stomach.

At exactly three on the dot, Rita showed up and was immediately escorted to Talitha's consultation room by Yucala and as a gentle tap sounded at Talitha's consultation room door, Talitha quickly rose to her feet as she prepared to begin Rita's first consultation. Upon Talitha's face there was a warm, friendly smile as she opened the door and greeted the woman for the first time that she would now be committed to servicing as a client. Unlike some of Talitha's other female clients, Talitha rapidly discovered that Rita was definitely very different in that she was absolutely stunning, well maintained and immaculately presented and for a moment, Talitha actually wondered why she was even there in the first place.

"Please come in Rita and I'm Talitha, your Bodily Enhancements Consultant." Talitha invited as she politely held open her consultation room door and then stepped out of the way to allow Rita enough space to enter inside the room.

Once Rita's consultation begun, Talitha quickly discovered that Rita was very assertive, direct and straight to the point as she quickly explained exactly why she was there and what she hoped to actually achieve. A verbal dive was taken fearlessly straight into the issues that Rita faced with a splash of hilarity and a charming smile and it seemed, there was absolutely no beating around the bush with Rita at all.

"Look, I'm gonna be very honest with you Talitha. I sleep with very rich married men to extract as much money from them as I possibly can. They are rich and I am beautiful and their sexual gratification which comes at a cost is a lubricant to the achievement of my financial desires." Rita explained. "At times, I will need to change my appearance just to facilitate my goals and although some would regard what I do as slightly unethical, I don't see it that way. I wouldn't call it blackmail exactly, it's just a very feminine method of redistributing wealth. I target very rich, powerful men to extract very large sums of money from them and at times, I even usher in their downfall."

"Okay Rita I understand, so you'll be quite a regular client then?" Talitha asked.

"Definitely." Rita quickly confirmed as she nodded her head vigorously in response. "I have a lot of work to do."

Talitha smiled. "What kind of changes would you like me to implement first as I haven't been given any information about any of your requests." She asked.

"Actually, I have quite a few physical changes that I'll need straight away, or as soon as possible. First I'll need a lip enhancement, then a breast enlargement, a nose reshape and I'll also need to flatten my stomach." Rita explained. "Those are the most pressing and urgent issues."

"Are you aware Rita that you're only actually permitted to have one Download procedure per consultation?" Talitha asked.

"Yes that was explained to me." Rita replied. "So the changes will have to be gradual."

"Right." Talitha agreed.

"Great, I have a new male target that I'm planning to meet in a few weeks time, so I'll need my face to be ready for that." Rita explained. "He's very rich."

"Right Rita, I'll just load some lip images up for you now, so that you can make your selection." Talitha said as she gently touched the screen in front of her.

"You know Talitha, I didn't really choose this lifestyle, somehow I just ended up doing what I do.

I dropped out of high school because my father used to beat my mother senseless, so I had to find a way to make a living and this was the only way I could find." Rita explained.

"Rita, how you make a living is really none of my business." Talitha immediately reassured her. "Whatever you choose to do with your own life is really up to you."

"I know, it's just well, some people can be so judgmental." Rita said.

"I'm not here to judge you Rita, I'm just here to provide you with the services that you've paid for." Talitha quickly pointed out as she turned her screen towards Rita.

Rita nodded.

"Here you go Rita, if you can just make some selections for me please and then I'll narrow down the range based on your preferences." Talitha instructed. "Show me some you do like, the ones that you definitely don't and I can make a start from those."

"There's so many lips to choose from. I never even knew that lips could come in so many different shapes, shades and sizes." Rita observed as she giggled and pointed towards an image on the screen. "Definitely not those ones please Talitha, they look all huge and rubbery, it would look like someone had glued them onto your face."

"Yes, Restructure does have a very vast range." Talitha agreed as she smiled. "But take your time Rita, there's absolutely no rush."

For approximately ten minutes more, Talitha went through the various lip enhancement images with Rita until she'd identified the five that she felt the most drawn to. Once Rita was happy with her final five choices, Talitha courteously displayed each one as she attached them to Rita's simulated facial image inside the Restructure system. Due to the very complex nature of the decisions that each client faced, Talitha didn't envy her clients at all as essentially, each of her clients were making decisions that would last for an entire lifetime and that meant, they had to be really sure and absolutely certain. Lips were even more tricky than body parts, Talitha quietly contemplated as she watched Rita inspect each of the five images as lips were stuck smack bang on the lower third of your face and so there was absolutely no getting it wrong and if you didn't like how they looked, you couldn't even wear clothes over them to hide them.

"Those lips look absolutely fantastic." Rita confirmed with excitement as she pointed towards one of the simulated facial images.

"Yes, they do look lip smackingly good." Talitha agreed. "You seem to have very good taste in lips Rita and I think they'll all really suit you, it'll be a very hard decision to choose from those five."

"I could always just close my eyes and then pick one out randomly." Rita suggested. "That might be quicker and a whole lot easier."

"That would be a bit of gamble but it's a gamble that you really can't lose as they all look absolutely stunning." Talitha quickly pointed out. "There's no rush though, so please take your time."

Approximately fifteen minutes later, once Rita had made her final choice and once the actual Download itself had been performed, the two women stood inside the adjoining procedure room in front of the tall body length client mirror and stared at Rita's reflection in awe. The lip enhancement really suited Rita's face and both women immediately noticed it as a huge smile of satisfaction adorned Rita's face and Talitha began to nod her head in approval as she appreciated Rita's final selection.

"Your lips and face look absolutely great Rita." Talitha said as she verbally confirmed her inner sentiments.

"Yes and now I'm ready to kiss a few frogs." Rita joked. "For very large sums of money of course."

"You take care out there and mind how you go." Talitha replied. "Some frogs can be really nasty and they even bite back."

Rita nodded. "I know but don't worry Talitha, there's a couple of guys that kind of look out for me and sometimes they help me out, if things get a little bit too rough." She explained.

"When would you like to have your next consultation?" Talitha asked as she began to lead Rita back towards her consultation room. "Next week?"

"Yes please and I'll need to have either the breast enlargement or the nose reshape next. I have to get ready for my next client." Rita quickly clarified as she followed Talitha into her consultation room.

"What day and time would you like to return?" Talitha asked as she sat back down beside her desk and then touched the screen directly in front of her.

"I can do either Monday, Tuesday or Friday afternoon next week." Rita replied. "At about four."

"I could see you on the Tuesday afternoon at around four." Talitha suggested.

Rita immediately nodded her head in response. "That'll be perfect." She agreed.

"Right that's all booked in, well we're all done here for today Rita, so I can see you back to the reception area now." Talitha offered as she rose to her feet.

Despite the fact that the two women were completely different in terms of their careers, their outlook on life and even their attitude towards other people, Talitha still felt an empathetic warmth towards Rita as the two women walked towards the reception area. Life, in Talitha's opinion, wasn't always as simple as people wanted it to be and at times, people could end up in very negative cycles and Rita in her mind was a perfect example of that.

"What do you think you might have been Rita, if you'd done something else with your life?" Talitha asked as the two women walked along the crisp, white corridor towards the reception area. "If life had been different?"

"You know Talitha, I think I might have actually created my own jewelry line. When I was a kid in school, I used to make bracelets, earrings and necklaces and people really loved them." Rita replied. "I even sold a few and then life happened and I ended up doing something completely different."

"That's really nice, do you still make stuff?" Talitha asked as the two women entered the reception area.

"Not really, I haven't even thought about making jewelry for years. Now, I just buy it, or someone else buys it for me and then I just wear it." Rita explained as she smiled. "Life happens and things change I guess."

"True I guess, well I'll see you next Tuesday Rita." Talitha clarified as the two women stood inside the reception area. "Have a good week."

"Thanks and you have a good week too Talitha." Rita replied as she began to walk towards the smoked glass doors.

Some ribbons of sadness seemed to gently wrap themselves around Talitha's body as she watched Rita depart and then turned as she prepared to make her way back towards her consultation room. Perhaps life wasn't always what one made it, Talitha quietly considered as she began to walk back along the crisp white corridor and perhaps some part of a person's life was actually determined right from the very start. Although Talitha had never achieved much academically herself, she had managed to find a career that she was interested in at least and she'd pursued work in that area and that was how she'd ended up working in beauty salons and cosmetic surgeries for many years. Naturally, Talitha just always seemed to have a knack for that kind of work and throughout her high school years, she'd spent many of her break periods with her school friends faces doing their makeup and plucking their eyebrows, just for a bit of extra pocket money.

The lifestyle that Rita had pursued was certainly very different in comparison to Talitha's own life but then Talitha's childhood had been pretty run of the mill and she'd grown up in a very settled, firm foundation that had provided her with a stable home, a decent education and a quite ethical approach to life. Life wasn't always predictable and sometimes the hand you were dealt could be cruel and heartless and Talitha had experienced that in recent years when she'd gone through her own challenges but she'd been fortunate, she'd had Bryson to lean on whereas Rita it seemed had, had absolutely no one.

INFINITE DESIRES

At exactly seven thirty on the Tuesday morning, the day arrived on Talitha's doorstep with a noisy bump as her alarm clock suddenly began to beep rather loudly and urged Talitha to get up, greet the world and actually join the day. Approximately forty minutes later, once Talitha had showered and dressed, she left the house and then walked towards her car which was parked in its usual spot inside the driveway with a spring in her step and a joyful smile plastered across her face. Life was really improving for Talitha and she was actually achieving lots of very positive things at work which ultimately validated her capabilities and that drove her very happily forward as she prepared for the drive towards the corporate home of Restructure and her day of work ahead.

The morning was very bright and deliciously warm as rays of sunshine playfully caressed

Talitha's skin and gently tickled her pores as she headed towards her car. Bryson had promised Talitha the night before that the couple would go away for the weekend on the Friday and have a short weekend break from the city and so Talitha couldn't wait for that to actually happen as the couple hadn't been away together anywhere nice for quite a while. Another few days sat rather annoyingly in-between the short get away that Bryson had planned and the Tuesday morning, so Talitha tried to allow the warmth of the morning to pleasantly distract her from the wait ahead that had to be endured before the couple could actually go anywhere.

Every inch of Talitha's soul felt utterly content as she unlocked her car door and then entered inside her vehicle as the hotel had already been chosen and booked and the weekend promised to be tons of fun with barrow loads of amusing entertainment on offer for the couple to enjoy which she hoped would provide them both with buckets full of laughter. Fortunately for Talitha, the love of her life absolutely always kept his promises to her and he was definitely a man of his word and that particular promise had already almost been fulfilled as he'd made their reservations immediately and that was one thing that Talitha could never fault Bryson on.

Due to the clear roads, the drive to work was quite fast and seemed short and en-route, Talitha made her usual stop off for breakfast which she hungrily consumed straight away as she was way too hungry to wait. When Talitha arrived inside the Restructure parking lot, she found two vehicles already parked inside it which she immediately recognized and she smiled as she glanced at Professor Heisner's rather battered looking antique and Yucala's much more modern burgundy family salon. The parking space that Talitha had been allocated was very quickly occupied as she parked her car and then made her way towards the main entrance of the building as she internally prepared for the working day ahead which involved meeting Renee for her second consultation.

Each step that Talitha took towards the entrance of the building was light as she silently rejoiced in her parking space and the fact that she now actually had one at all. In all her working years, Talitha had absolutely never ever been given her own actual parking space and so it was definitely a first, alongside the huge consultation room that she'd been allocated which she could now utilize to see her very own clients. Life had definitely changed and certainly for the better, Talitha quietly concluded as she stepped inside the reception and then walked towards the warm, friendly smile that greeted her from just behind the reception desk. Since there was still a few minutes to spare that morning before Talitha was actually due to sit down at her desk, she decided to converse with Yucala albeit very briefly, in order to tell Yucala all about her exciting plans for the following weekend.

"Good morning Yucala." Talitha announced enthusiastically as she approached Yucala's reception desk and greeted her. "How was your evening?"

"Good morning Talitha. My evening was rather tiring actually, I had to fix Jonas's cadet uniform as he split the jumper at the seams during his last cadet meeting and I won't be able to buy him another one in time for their next gathering, so it had to be sewn up." Yucala replied. "And that wasn't the only thing I had to sort out. At the weekend, we'll be visiting a nature reserve, so I had to plan and organize that too. I had to make the bookings, sort out all the boys clothes for the outing and so on."

"Wow that sounds really adventurous, my weekend will be pretty busy too because this weekend, Bryson is taking me away on a trip to an island resort for the whole weekend." Talitha explained. "I'll be back by Monday though, we're coming back on Sunday evening."

"Enjoy the romance while it lasts Talitha, once you have kids, all that great romantic stuff just jumps straight out the window of love."   Yucala teased as she gently shook her head.   "Like a relationship on a suicide mission."

"Still Yucala, the nature reserve sounds like it'll be fun."   Talitha quickly reassured her as she smiled. "I mean, how bad could it be?"

"With my three boys and my husband, who's like another big kid at times, it could be a total nightmare."   Yucala quickly pointed out.   "The nature reserve has not met my three boys yet and once it has, it'll probably never be the same again. They're like a whirlwind of trouble, in the nicest possibly way of course."

Yucala immediately nodded her head in agreement and then quickly touched the screen directly in front of her to answer a phone call as she suddenly noticed that a call had come in. "Good morning, Restructure Inc. how can I help you today?"   She asked as she smiled at Talitha giggled. "A nature reserve that's so very different from here isn't it?" She observed. "I mean, what we do here is very artificial, whereas a nature reserve is all about untouched, wild places and the preservation of wildlife with dignity and respect. Here at Restructure, we replace the natural things with something artificial, something pretentious and something superficial whereas there, they fight to keep what's natural alive for as long as possible."

"True, it's kind of the opposite I guess." Yucala agreed.

"I better get a move on and start doing some work Yucala." Talitha said as she prepared to depart. "I'll speak to you later."

A warm feeling of comfort seemed to gently wrap itself around Talitha's body as she walked towards her consultation room as she silently rejoiced in the morning, life was great, love and work was great and finally life had dealt her a winning hand and an ace instead of a joker. Although Talitha worked in an environment where money determined how cosmetically perfect you could look and where bodily enhancements provided a quick fix to human desires, the physical ambitions of humanity were essentially how she made a living and that was just the commercial reality of the world that surrounded her and she'd accepted that long ago.

Some people would spend very large sums of money in an attempt to live up to physical ideals and perceptions of perfection that they often aspired to but Talitha knew, they also did that in the halls of academia where large sums would be spent to attain knowledge and to become experts in a particular field. Society demanded perfection and competence in so many ways from those within it and those ideals were definitely something that people strove to live up to and spent large sums to actually achieve, so Restructure's work wasn't really that different from the mainstream in Talitha's sight.

Philosophical deliberations and thoughts dangled down inside Talitha's mind like ripe red cherries on a stalk that just waited to be plucked, eaten and fully digested as she approached the door of her consultation room and then plucked her office key card from the quite large, black leather handbag that she'd brought to work that day. A smile crossed Talitha's face as she unlocked the door and then stepped inside her consultation room, internal deliberations about how the world functioned definitely had to be totally abandoned for now as it was definitely time for work and that required her to be very focused, at least until lunchtime.

When eleven arrived, so too did Renee, very punctually indeed as she attended her appointment dressed in a gold blouse and black skirt which she'd accessorized with not only a gold bracelet but also with a beautiful, joyful smile. Gratitude and excitement seemed to bubble away inside Renee as she sat down and Talitha smiled as she glanced at her face as she sensed her internal happiness.

Upon Renee's shoulder, she carried a very large handbag which had black and white patterns that ran across it and once she sat down, she placed it gently on her lap as she faced Talitha.

Flames of passion seemed to dance through Renee's eyes and excitement seemed to ooze from her every pore as Talitha sat down at her desk, faced her and then touched the screen as she prepared to make a start on Renee's actual consultation.

"Look what I bought Talitha." Renee announced triumphantly as she quickly plucked some lingerie items from her bag and then proudly held some bras up in the air.

"Wow, they look absolutely amazing Renee." Talitha replied as she smiled and nodded her head enthusiastically. "How did your partner feel about the change that you've made to your body?" She ventured to ask. "Are they comfortable with it?"

"Actually Talitha, I don't have a long term partner." Renee replied as she solemnly shook her head. "I haven't dated anyone for a while, so I did hope that the breast enlargement would change things for me and it certainly has."

"Really?" Talitha enquired. "Why? What happened?"

"Well, I was approached by several men in a romantic capacity and they even flirted with me which is totally awesome as things like that don't usually happen to me." Renee gushed as she placed the bras back inside her handbag. "I couldn't possibly have asked for anything more and because of the breast enlargement, I feel much more confident now about dating and I even went out on a few actual dates which I really, really enjoyed."

"And the breast enlargement helped to make that happen?" Talitha asked as she glanced at Renee's eyes which seemed to sparkle with excitement.

"Yes definitely. In the past I've always felt physically inadequate and that caused a lot of problems for me. I've really struggled with my body and that made it difficult for me to sustain a positive romantic relationship successfully in the longer term but now, I feel like I actually can and that romance is something that I can actually try to do." Renee explained as she nodded her head enthusiastically. "I've always wanted to have very large breasts." She continued. "It's always been my dream."

"Well now, you definitely do." Talitha quickly pointed out as she smiled.

Renee laughed. "Yes these two babies are unapologetically huge." She joked.

A smile crossed Talitha's face as she glanced at the two huge bumps that now very eagerly protruded from the front of Renee's body. In terms of Renee's original physical frame, it was a physically ambitious change but Talitha couldn't fault Renee for actually wanting it, or for yearning to realize the fulfillment of her deepest desires. When it came to Talitha's own physicality, Renee's predicament had confirmed to Talitha just how lucky she actually was as her very reasonable and quite manageable breasts which were a cup size D, sat quietly and humbly upon her chest.

Over the years, Talitha's two nicely shaped physical assets had served her quite well, especially when it came to the issue of sexual confidence and being comfortable with her own nakedness in front of someone else and they'd definitely helped her attract the kind of partners that she'd wanted. The inferiority complex that had very clearly built up inside Renee and her internal struggles, due to the size of her breasts, was not something that Talitha had ever had to deal with or face but Talitha could definitely identify with her desire to be more in terms of her own professional aspirations and her career.

"What would you like to focus on today Renee?" Talitha asked as she touched the screen directly in front of her and then turned to face Renee and smiled. "Would you like your nose reshaped, or would you prefer your lip enhancement today?"

"I think I'd like to go for the lip enhancement today please Talitha." Renee replied as she giggled. "I'd really like to have kissable lips right about now as technically, the two most lethal weapons in the battle of female seduction and attraction are already in place."

The frankness of Renee's response prompted Talitha to smile as she quietly appreciated how simple and straight forward Renee was as a client in that she knew exactly what she wanted and exactly what she wanted to achieve and there was absolutely nothing pretentious about her. In terms of Renee's confidence, there had been a definite improvement since Renee had first stepped through Talitha's consultation room door and since they'd first met and that really encouraged and motivated Talitha. An internal change had occurred, not just an external physical change and she was certainly not the same shadow of a woman that Talitha had first encountered. Somehow, it appeared the bodily enhancement had enhanced not just her physical form but also her attitude towards herself, her life, the world around her and the part that she now played in it and that really encouraged Talitha.

"Sure Renee, I'll sort that out for you right now." Talitha replied as she touched the screen directly in front of her again and it rapidly populated with images of lips. "Take your time Renee." Talitha reassured her as she turned the screen towards Renee. "There's absolutely no rush and it is a very big decision as they'll be your lips forever and you'll have wear them every single day for the rest of your life."

Approximately twenty minutes was spent as the two women browsed, perused, wandered and visually explored the many images of lips in front of them until Renee found the five images of lips that appealed to her slightly more than others and enthusiastically selected them. The chosen lip images were then attached to her simulated facial image as Talitha attempted to illustrate exactly how they would appear upon Renee's face before she made a final selection.

"I think some of these lips might actually make my face look a little bit fake." Renee observed as she stared at the screen thoughtfully. "And they'd probably be a bit too big for my face."

"Some people don't mind if their faces and bodies look a bit fake." Talitha quickly pointed out as she smiled. "I guess it just depends on what you're actually trying to achieve."

Some further internal deliberations were entered into by Renee as Talitha sat quietly and just watched her study each image from the final five images in front of her. A slightly confused expression suddenly crossed Renee's face as she began to struggle and pick from the final five but Talitha could definitely understand that as it was such a huge decision as lips were a very essential part of one's face. Internal deliberations regarding her client's choices weren't something that Talitha felt she should try to interfere with as she would not be the one that would have to live with any subsequent decision that her clients made and so she held her tongue and patiently waited for a final decision to be reached.

"I think I'd like to go for these lips please Talitha." Renee suddenly announced decisively as she pointed towards one of the five images on the screen.

"Right, I'll just process that change for you now." Talitha confirmed as she touched the screen once again and commanded Restructure to implement the chosen lip enhancement.

Once the actual Download procedure had been performed, approximately fifteen minutes later, the two women stood beside each other in front of the long client mirror inside the procedure room which was actually about the size of a small lounge. Upon Renee's face there was a huge smile as she internally rejoiced in her physical transformation and the joy and pleasure that Restructure had brought into her life so far.

"I just can't wait to enjoy these lips and thank you so much Talitha for another extremely delicious, ultra perfect bodily enhancement." Renee gushed as she admired her reflection. "Restructure has been such a positive experience for me and it's really changed my life."

An internal wave of hope gently washed over Renee's body and lingered just under the surface of her skin and her body began to tingle with excitement as she smiled and internally began to accept another element of the physical beauty that Restructure had delivered to her. The breasts and lips had definitely been worth every penny and Renee had already reaped some of the rewards in the form of some very attentive male adoration which made a pleasant change from being completely ignored and going totally unnoticed.

"They really do compliment the rest of your face Renee." Talitha said as she enthusiastically expressed her admiration. "But are you totally satisfied with the results?"

"Definitely Talitha and welcome to the world new lips." Renee gushed with excitement as she giggled. "You have now just been born and you look absolutely amazing."

For at least fifteen minutes more, once the two women had returned to Talitha's consultation room, they discussed Renee's lips, planned her next appointment and her nose reshape which was actually due to be her final procedure. Happiness and joy seemed to ooze from every ounce of Renee's being as she very overtly expressed her satisfaction regarding her new facial enhancement and Talitha felt extremely encouraged. Once Renee's consultation came to an end, Talitha quickly rose to her feet as she prepared to escort Renee towards the reception area and the two women began to discuss some of Renee's recent dates as they walked which Renee was extremely open about.

Rather sadly, Talitha knew as she walked Renee along the crisp white corridor, she would only actually see Renee on two more occasions, once for her final Download procedure and then once again for a client closure session. Quite unexpectedly, Renee had in a very short space of time actually become one of Talitha's favorite clients as she was very easy to speak to, extremely transparent and always seemed to be in good spirits which lightened Talitha's workload each week.

"You know Renee, you looked really great before all the changes were made." Talitha gently reassured her as the two women stepped inside the reception area. "I just wanted you to know that."

"Thanks Talitha, you're very sweet and thanks so much for not judging me." Renee replied as she smiled. "I've spent so much of my life hiding away from the world and from the people inside it and so many years have just been totally wasted hiding my body and face from everyone else. Now however, thanks to you that's all changed and it's been so refreshing to actually be able to do something about that and I really appreciate how straight forward and simple you've made all this for me."

"I'll see you next week Renee." Talitha said as she prepared to leave Renee and the reception area and return to her consultation room. "You have a good week."

"I definitely will." Renee whispered as she grinned.

Talitha laughed as she began to gently shake her head. "Don't have too much fun out there, or it could get messy." She advised.

"I know." Renee agreed as she giggled and then stepped through one of the smoked glass doors.

Joy and appreciation silently seemed to dance across Talitha's heart as she watched Renee depart and then began to make her way back towards her consultation room as she graciously accepted Renee's unexpected compliments and praise which had surprised her. Most of Talitha's clients tended to actually focus upon what they wanted from her, not what she actually provided to them and it was utterly refreshing that someone other than Professor Heisner had actually noticed some of the things that she did for people.

A deep sense of satisfaction now seemed to invisibly hold Talitha firmly by the hand as she basked in the knowledge that someone definitely appreciated the warmth, empathy and attentiveness that she'd shown towards each of her clients. Not everyone in life that Talitha would come across would appreciate the small things that she did for them as in the larger scheme of things when it came to other people's lives, perhaps to them those things meant very little and Talitha fully appreciated that fact. Sometimes however, the encouragement and understanding that you extended towards someone else's life and their situation actually did mean something to them and in Renee's instance that certainly seemed to be the case.

Some of the issues that Renee had faced when she'd initially arrived had been issues that Talitha could really identify with as it was essentially a very human wish to be desired and deemed desirable by those you desired and to want to be wanted by those you admired. Feelings of inadequacy and rejection weren't emotional clothes that human beings wore very comfortably and the very human desires that drove one to want to be wanted and accepted weren't necessarily gender specific and applied in equal measure to both men and women. How such issues were handled or expressed by either gender did at times, differ slightly but that did not detract from their actual existence.

Since the first moment that Renee had crossed the threshold of Talitha's consultation room door, Talitha had made an additional effort to be as understanding and as supportive as she possibly could be towards as she'd sensed her internal emotional pain and that emotional investment that she'd made, Renee had now not only noticed but also acknowledged. Initially, when Renee had first stepped into Talitha's life and her consultation room, she'd carried with her some very deep internal wounds that she'd accumulated throughout her journey through life and underneath her brave exterior there had been some obvious injuries caused by the emotional pain that had been inflicted upon her.

The years of Renee's struggle against human rejection and ridicule had definitely taken their toll upon her and the damage that had been inflicted by other people had resulted in deep, invisible scars that had lay hidden inside of her. Invisible to the naked human eye Renee's scars, quite possibly, would never ever have been fully addressed and would have remained unresolved without ever being given a chance to heal, if it had not been for Professor Heisner's clinic Restructure and that reality encouraged Talitha as she stepped back inside her consultation room.

Sadly, the issue of Renee's deep internal scars highlighted to Talitha just how wounded human beings could actually really be underneath their brave exterior as they wandered through the mountains of life and struggled at times to clamber over the rocky terrain and obstacles that life often presented to them. So often those deep pains created by human rejection and inflicted upon them by other people would create deep wounds that would simply lie below the surface of their existence, hidden and invisible, never to be addressed, confronted, or ever fully resolved. Not many people lived a life free from such internal pains as in some capacity, most people had wanted something in life at one time or another and then pursued it with all their being and had then been either shunned or totally rejected, so in some ways Renee's trials were not that unusual. Due to Renee's physical attributes however, she had definitely suffered more than most and Talitha could definitely appreciate and understand that as Renee's physicality had exasperated her very human desires.

Deeply engrained within the human psyche there was definitely an internal desire to be loved, desired, accepted and wanted by other human beings and it was one of the deepest human instincts present in every race, gender and culture that existed upon the face of the earth. The intrinsic need to belong to something, somewhere, somehow and to be accepted, validated and appreciated was a desire that existed inside every human mind and heart and that need was always present, even though it was rarely discussed, or ever acknowledged. No amount of intellectual or technological advancement would ever really change the intrinsic nature of human beings as those primal instincts created a hunger within the human appetite to conform to the ideals that people felt justified and validated their existence.

Somehow, Professor Heisner with his great scientific mind had finally found a way to satisfy those intrinsic, primal desires in a relatively safe manner and for the very first time, Talitha began to more deeply understand the human issues that Restructure attempted to fulfill within the human psyche. Unlike Professor Heisner, Talitha really didn't have a great scientific mind and nor was she a rocket scientist but she definitely understood human beings and their desire to be appreciated, wanted and loved as that desire also resided within herself.

Now at least Renee held a torch of hope, Talitha quietly concluded as she began to write up Renee's notes and that torch contained a flame of promise that her life could really change and that it was about to actually do so. The negative anxieties that had once cast a shadow of inadequacy across the paths of Renee's life would no longer haunt or frustrate her as now, they would be eradicated from her life completely. Now Renee would actually be the woman that she'd always wanted to be and now, she would enjoy all the things in life that she felt it was her right as a woman to enjoy. Now Renee would be adored, wanted, desired and loved as the torment of ridicule that had once plagued her life with its unsightly, ugly misshaped head would bow down at her feet and worship her. Rejection would no longer be the constant companion that mocked Renee's every step and almost drowned her with painful waves of heartbreak every single day and now, Renee would feel complete.

When the Wednesday morning arrived as Talitha made her way to work, she stopped off at a cake shop as she prepared to start her working day with not only a smile but also with a portion of edible joy. Getting up at seven thirty each weekday morning now no longer felt like such a burdensome endurance test and Talitha's body had over the past couple of months grown quite accustomed to her alarm clock that nosily reminded her to get out of bed every single working day and the donuts were a treat to celebrate the battle she'd won with early morning blues. Upon Talitha's face there was a very pleasant, warm smile as she arrived at work, stepped inside the building and then greeted Yucala with a polite nod and the cardboard box packed full of delicious warm donuts that she'd just purchased.

"Good morning Yucala. Today, I come bearing gifts from afar." Talitha joked as she placed the donut box gently down on top of the reception desk and then opened it up. "I bring edible treasures all the way from the distant cake shop."

Yucala giggled. "Good morning Talitha. What did you bring?" She asked.

"Delicious freshly baked donuts. A whole box of them. Would you like one, or even two?" Talitha offered. "There's ten donuts in there which means, you can definitely have more than one."

"Definitely, what's inside them?" Yucala asked as she nodded her head enthusiastically in response.

"Vanilla cream and raspberry jam." Talitha replied.

"Yummy." Yucala said as she quickly dipped her hand inside the donut box and then plucked a donut out. "Now these delicious weapons of mass destruction will add inches to my waistline and totally obliterate my good intentions and my diet but I just can't resist."

"I know, it's such a lethal combination." Talitha agreed as she smiled. "I'll have to walk around the parking lot at least ten times tonight before I go home, just to get rid of the extra calories."

"Please, you really don't need to Talitha." Yucala insisted. "You have the perfect figure. Now I on the other hand, should really work out but I just don't have the time, there's three boys, a husband that doesn't step foot inside the kitchen and a full time job and that just ain't happening."

"You know Yucala, you should really teach one of your boys how to cook and encourage him to become a chef." Talitha suggested.

"Now that is a great idea." Yucala replied. "Seriously that could actually work. Talitha, you're an absolute genius."

Talitha giggled. "I'll see you later Yucala, I have to go and get ready for my clients, I have to see two today." She explained as she plucked two donuts out of the box and then wrapped them up inside a napkin. "I'll just leave the rest of these here for Moses and Professor Heisner, you never know they might fancy one, or even two."

"Thanks for the donuts Talitha." Yucala called out appreciatively as she watched Talitha walk towards the crisp white hallway that led towards her consultation room. "It's really nice of you."

A few donuts was nothing really, Talitha quietly concluded as she walked towards her consultation room as Yucala really was such an encouragement and she definitely deserved more than a donut. Every working day, Yucala greeted Talitha with a friendly smile and a very pleasant attitude and that warm reception really brightened up Talitha's day and that was definitely something that Talitha appreciated as some of the companies that she'd worked for in the past had been rather cold and she'd actually felt quite isolated.

Once Talitha entered inside her consultation room, she quickly prepared a latte and then switched on the Restructure system as she sat down at her desk and began to prepare for her first consultation that morning which was with Frank. At eleven on the dot, just as planned, Frank arrived and was then quickly shown to her consultation room by Yucala. A smile crossed Talitha's face as she invited Frank inside her consultation room and then offered him a beverage to accompany the donut that Yucala had already offered and given to him which now sat inside one of his hands.

"Would you like something to drink Frank?" Talitha asked. "And did Maude like the legs?"

"She absolutely loved them Talitha." Frank immediately confirmed as he smiled and nodded his head. "And I'd love a coffee please, if it's not too much trouble."

"Sure Frank, it's no trouble at all." Talitha replied as she crossed the room and approached the coffee machine.

"This donut is absolutely delicious." Frank announced as he swallowed a mouthful of the jam and cream filled dough. "Thanks."

"I know tell me about it, they taste far too nice and they'll spend a minute on my lips and an absolute lifetime on my tummy and hips." Talitha replied as she grinned.

"Maude doesn't eat donuts or fried food, she's far too healthy. I have to sneak out to cafes if I want a fry up or a cake." Frank explained.

Talitha grinned. "Which procedure would you like to focus on today Frank?" She asked as she returned to her desk with his cup of coffee inside one of her hands.

"My arms. I'd like to be able to pick Maude up and carry her over the threshold, or perhaps just into the bedroom sometimes." Frank joked as he laughed. "Maybe then we might even tie the knot as she might be so impressed with my agility, she might ask me to marry her."

"Now that would be nice." Talitha replied.

"She'd probably divorce me within a year. Marriage is a contract after all and she'd probably say I'd broken the terms and conditions by not cooking dinner for her often enough, or for failing to wash the dishes properly." He joked. "Maude can be quite tough sometimes."

Talitha laughed. "She sounds like quite a tough cookie." She replied.

"Yes she is but she is very consistent, so I guess that's why we're still together after all this time." Frank explained.

"Consistently tough." Talitha teased.

"Exactly." Frank agreed as he grinned.

After a few more jokes had been shared between the two and Frank had made his choice regarding his procedure, his arm sculptor was meticulously performed as per his final selection and then another appointment was arranged by Talitha for his next consultation. Once Frank's next consultation had been organized, Talitha politely escorted him back towards the reception area as they enthusiastically discussed his brand spanking new, now freshly sculpted much stronger arms.

The huge cheerful smile that usually decorated Frank's face was definitely present as they walked and that really encouraged Talitha as she bade him farewell and then returned to her consultation room. Once Frank's notes had been written up and then submitted, Talitha took a break for lunch as hunger beckoned to her as it urged her to feed the upset growls that rumbled and rattled around inside her now empty stomach. A solitary donut still remained on top of Talitha's desk wrapped up inside a napkin but Talitha resisted the urge to eat it before the consumption of proper food as she controlled herself and prepared for a takeaway lunch from the nearby diner.

Due to the fact that the diner was nearby and less than ten minutes drive away, it was actually quite handy and extremely convenient and because of that Talitha rarely bothered to venture any further away in search of food and a decent lunch. The small venue right on the edge of the highway was very clean, the food was fresh and it actually tasted quite nice and it was quite a regular haunt for the long distance lorry drivers that would usually frequent it's interior as they stopped off each day.

Lunch for Talitha however that particular day would not be a luxurious, relaxing treat and it had to be more of a smash and grab than a delicate culinary meander as Talitha had to prepare for the arrival of her next client Rodney, who was actually due to arrive at three that afternoon. Since Talitha had devoted a bit more time than she'd originally planned to and she'd expended a little more effort writing up Frank's notes that meant now, she really didn't have enough time to accommodate a sit down lunch. A soft bread baton filled with meatballs, cheese and tomato sauce was quickly ordered, paid for and then taken away as Talitha accepted the limitations upon her time and responded to them accordingly.

Initially when Talitha had first started working at Restructure, the lack of choice when it came to lunchtime provisions had slightly worried her as there were only a couple of food outlets nearby and one of the other diners that she'd visited wasn't very nice. Being that Talitha had always worked in the heart of the city, prior to her appointment Restructure, she'd enjoyed access to the vast array of fine eateries, restaurants and sandwich bars that lined the city streets but the local range of eating venues in close proximity to the Restructure

268

building was a far cry from those. In those days, Talitha's main dilemma had been choice rather than scarcity and over the years, she'd actually grown quite accustomed to the huge variety on offer and hence she'd immediately noticed the shortcomings of her current work location.

Despite that one negative aspect regarding Restructure's current location, Talitha knew, she definitely wouldn't trade her current job in for a job in the city again as her working conditions at Restructure were so much better and so too was Talitha's actual job. Fine dining and elegant eateries although they were abundantly scattered across the city streets meant far less to Talitha now as she definitely had something far better than just increased access to fine dining choices.

After lunch had been joyfully consumed and Talitha's stomach had been filled, three in the afternoon rapidly arrived and brought Rodney along with it and Talitha quickly rose to her feet as soon as she heard Yucala's gentle knock at her door as she prepared to welcome him and attend to his requirements. Upon Rodney's procedure list there now only remained two unfulfilled procedure requests and Talitha considered each one thoughtfully as she invited Rodney inside her consultation room and then offered him a beverage.

- Chest Enhancement

- Leg Contour

True to his usual form, Rodney was equipped with a huge cheeky grin and his usual jokes as he sat down and the triumphant smile on his face very quickly said everything to Talitha that she needed to know about his last procedure, even though the matter had not yet actually been discussed. The glass of apple juice that Rodney had requested was gently placed down in front of him and then Talitha returned to her seat as she prepared to begin his second consultation as she quietly concluded that the penis enlargement must have delivered some great results for him as his grin was so huge.

"Right Rodney which area of your body would you like me to focus on today?" Talitha asked.

"I'm not really sure Talitha, what area of my body do you think we should focus on?" Rodney replied suggestively as he winked. "I'm very open to suggestions."

"Well Rodney, I don't think my fiancée would be very happy about me making any personal suggestions to male clients, or focusing in a personal way on any part of a man's body that wasn't actually his." Talitha replied as she smiled. "But from your client request list, I can see that you still have two pending requests that relate to your chest and legs, so which one of these two areas would you like to change today?" She continued as she very politely forced Rodney to focus on the actual reason for his attendance at the clinic that day.

"He's a very lucky man Talitha and if he ever lets you go, you just let me know. I'll be by your side in a flash, ready and willing to nurse your broken heart." Rodney quickly offered as he flashed a charming grin at Talitha. "I think today, I'd like to focus on my chest please."

"Right, I'll just load up the chest options for you now." Talitha replied as she turned to face her screen.

Despite the rather obvious flirtation from Rodney, his sugar coated words meant very little to Talitha at all. At most, his comments could perhaps be considered slightly flattering and as some kind of compliment but at the very least, they could perhaps be deemed as highly inappropriate and words that he'd uttered purely to amuse himself. Due to the fact that Rodney was actually a gigolo, charming women was what he actually did for a living and therefore his charming words meant absolutely nothing to Talitha and each one had simply rolled in one ear and then very quickly out the other as she'd rapidly dismissed them. In Talitha's mind, she was under absolutely no illusions at all, Rodney charmed women, slept with them and was paid by them for doing that and she had absolutely no interest whatsoever in joining his playboy entourage.

"Right Rodney, if you can make some chest selections for me now please and then I'll narrow down the range." Talitha instructed as her screen rapidly populated with chest images and she turned it towards him.

The rest of the Wednesday afternoon literally flew by as Talitha showed Rodney the range of chests available and on offer to him and he made his final selection in what seemed like no time at all. Unlike some of Talitha's other clients, Rodney was definitely much more decisive and seemed to know exactly what he wanted in life and from Restructure and his assertiveness made Talitha's job slightly easier. A thought suddenly struck Talitha's mind and began to amuse her however as she processed Rodney's request that Rodney's wants had really actually been defined by what he felt women and other people ultimately wanted from him and so perhaps he wasn't really that decisive after all. Perhaps, Talitha quietly deliberated, there really wasn't any such thing as a purely independent desire or decision as so much of an individual's world really was defined by other people's influence and the world around them.

Just before Rodney's consultation was due to end, Talitha quickly checked to ensure that he was completely satisfied with his bodily enhancement as she stepped inside the small procedure room which adjoined her consultation room and then lifted up the lid of the transparent capsule. The huge smile that was plastered across Rodney's face pretty much said a lot of what Talitha actually needed to know but she still verbally confirmed that he was actually satisfied, just to ensure that he would feel he'd been attended to sufficiently.

"What do you think of your new chest Rodney?" Talitha asked. "Are you happy with it?"

Rodney stepped down from the capsule and then walked towards the long mirror. "Extremely happy Talitha. Very happy indeed." He replied as he glanced at his reflection and then smiled. "My chest looks jaw droppingly fabulous and the ladies will absolutely love it for sure. There just won't be enough of me to go around. They'll have to form a queue to get their hands on this chunk of beef."

"Do you think you'll ever get married one day Rodney, or perhaps have some kids?" Talitha asked.

"Nope, I'm way to selfish for that." Rodney replied as he laughed.

"Well, at least your honest." Talitha said as she smiled.

"I am actually quite honest really, well to an extent I guess." Rodney quickly agreed. "I really don't believe in lying to women, unless they ask me if they're the only one. On those occasions, a lie of omission then becomes perfectly acceptable in order to protect their feelings."

"Complicated stuff." Talitha replied.

"Not really, it's much more complicated when men pretend that they want something that they really don't want at all." Rodney explained. "Like marriage and kids with someone, or the forever kind of thing."

"True." Talitha agreed. "Okay Rodney that's everything for today, I'll just make your next appointment and then I'll walk you back to the reception area."

"Right and sadly, my next appointment might be my last." Rodney quickly pointed out. "Then I won't ever see you again Talitha."

"You'll have to come back for your client closure consultation Rodney, so technically that will be two appointments but I guess the client closure session will be the final one. Never mind Rodney, you do have a lot of female companions already, so I'm sure I won't be missed." Talitha teased as she began to walk back towards her consultation room.

"Yes but remember what I said Talitha, I was very serious about that if he ever lets you down, I'm just a phone call away and extremely willing to participate." Rodney quickly clarified as he smiled. "I can be a great shoulder to cry on and I also have a great chest now where you can lay your head and sob as much as you want as well as a great piece of equipment to go with it."

"I'll certainly try to remember that Rodney." Talitha replied as she smiled and then gently shook her head.

Later that day, when Talitha arrived home and once she'd eaten dinner with Bryson, she told him all about her day and the very flirtatious male client that she'd spent some of her afternoon with. Due to Rodney's very brazen, utterly shameless and quite scandalous approach, Bryson laughed as Talitha related some of the details to him.

"Never mind, he'll soon be out of your hair." Bryson reassured her. "You only have to see him twice more right?"

"Yes. If I organize a client closure consultation for him, it'll definitely be twice." Talitha quickly clarified. "He's okay anyway, he's harmless enough really. I tend to just ignore the flirting, I think he's like that with everyone, or with every woman at least. He's certainly not the kind of man that I'd be interested in, even if I was actually single. He's really not my cup of tea at all."

"Yes that's because you have good taste and so do I and that's why we choose each other." Bryson announced proudly as he turned Talitha's head towards him and then kissed her tenderly on the lips.

"Very true Bryson." Talitha whispered. "Very true."

A gentle but very pleasant breeze brought the Thursday morning softly into Talitha's life and she eagerly welcomed it with very open arms as she left home and then began her journey towards the building that housed the corporation each day that she was employed to work for. Once Talitha arrived outside the Restructure building, she quickly parked her car and then made her way towards the main entrance as she internally appreciated that her working week was now almost over and that very soon, the weekend and the romantic break that Bryson had planned for the couple would actually begin. Due to the fact that Yucala was engaged in a telephone conversation when Talitha stepped inside the reception area, Talitha simply gave her a polite nod and smile as she walked through the reception area as no words could actually be exchanged.

Unlike Talitha, Yucala's working day actually started at eight in the morning and Talitha felt extremely grateful as she walked along the corridor that led towards her consultation room that her working day actually didn't as that allowed her the freedom to sleep slightly longer if she wished to. Another hour of luxury could be spent in bed each weekday morning before Talitha had to leave for work and that suited her right down to the ground as she really wasn't an early morning person and that extra hour of flexibility which Talitha's later started allowed her, was usually spent in bed fast asleep.

Inside Talitha's consultation room, everything was quiet as she entered the room and then immediately headed for the coffee machine as she prepared to facilitate it. Once Talitha's usual cup of milky latte had been prepared, she then walked towards her desk, sat down and switched on the Restructure system as she prepared to start work for the day. Each sip of latte filled Talitha's body with warmth as she glanced at the system and began to review all of the client consultations that she'd actually performed for her clients to date and a contented smile crossed Talitha's face.

Every client consultation that Talitha had provided seemed to add an invisible portion of pride to her core as she browsed through the profiles and marveled at each one as she inspected the physical transformations that had actually occurred. Each client had essentially provided Talitha with a very real experience of the Restructure system and now she actually felt quite well versed in Restructure's procedures as she'd put into practice all the training that she'd been given by Professor Heisner. The joyful but very serious reality was, it was a huge responsibility to learn about things that had such a large potential impact upon other people's lives and then actually put into practice what you'd learnt and Talitha fully appreciated the weight that she now carried upon her shoulders.

Later that day, it had already been planned that Talitha would see Charmaine and although she was quite looking forward to the day as it was actually Thursday which meant, the weekend was quite near, her afternoon appointment with Charmaine did worry her slightly. Essentially, Charmaine didn't worry Talitha in the slightest but the thought of a potentially negative run in with Lachlan, worried her profusely and that consultation definitely had to happen before the weekend could commence. Regardless of Lachlan however and the very ugly issues that he presented which now loomed upon the horizon of Talitha's day, the day and Charmaine's consultation had to actually be faced and performed before a delicious weekend treat could begin and Talitha quietly accepted that fact as she busied herself with the preparation of some client notes.

Quite unfortunately, it rapidly dawned on Talitha that she had only actually performed one procedure for Charmaine to date which meant, Lachlan would still be around for at least another month as there were another four procedures pending on Charmaine's request list. Perhaps Charmaine would see sense, Talitha hoped and perhaps she would dump Lachlan before all of her procedures had been completed and then Talitha wouldn't have to see the face that filled her with dread ever again.

The awful reality was that Lachlan's presence left a very bitter aftertaste in Talitha's mouth as he was, in Talitha's opinion, absolutely foul and none of the services that Restructure offered to clients could fix Lachlan and change that or his totally obnoxious, very unpleasant presence and attitude. Another remote hope did remain that might save Talitha's day and that was the hope that Lachlan would perhaps be absent and too busy to attend Charmaine's appointment with her and that potential possibility absolutely delighted her.

Much to Talitha's dismay however, when three in the afternoon finally arrived, she quickly discovered as soon as she opened her consultation room door that it had brought along with it both Charmaine and the absolutely disgusting Lachlan. Despite Talitha's intense dislike for Lachlan, she politely greeted the couple with a warm smile and friendly nod as she invited them both inside her consultation room as she internally prepared to start Charmaine's consultation.

Once again it had very rapidly transpired, Lachlan had decided to escort Charmaine to her consultation and supervise her participation in it and it now seemed as if he actually intended to attend as many consultations as he possibly could, even though his attendance irritated Talitha profusely. A strained, fake, pretentious smile was quickly offered to the couple along with a beverage as Talitha attended to them as there was no way that she could refuse to participate, or refuse to accommodate Lachlan's attendance as he had paid for Charmaine's procedures and that meant, he had an economic right to be there.

Upon Lachlan's face there was an extremely disgruntled expression which very clearly indicated the irritation that seemed to bubble just below the surface of his skin as Talitha placed the glass of orange juice and cup of tea down in front of them that they'd requested. The seemingly pleasant words and fake smiles that had been offered in an attempt to mask the internal emotions that Talitha really felt didn't change a thing inside her consultation room and Talitha could immediately sense that this client consultation was certainly not going to be a pretty one. Regardless of Talitha's intense dislike for Lachlan however, Charmaine's consultation still had to happen and had to happen politely as her dislike for Lachlan had absolutely nothing to do with Charmaine at all and so it could not actually be obvious to anyone present.

"Today, we'd like Charmaine to have her breast enlargement." Lachlan suddenly demanded in a defiant tone as he immediately attempted to steer Charmaine's consultation in the direction he wanted it to go from the very outset.

"Sure, no problem?" Talitha courteously replied as she returned to her desk, sat down and then faced the couple. "I'll just load some images of breasts up on my screen for you both to look at now." She quickly clarified in a soft, gentle tone.

The soft tone and Talitha's immediate compliance with Lachlan's request was a mild attempt to appease him and reassure him that she was actually listening to him but in all honesty, she really didn't want to. A gentle sigh almost escaped from Talitha's lips as she touched the screen directly in front of her and it rapidly populated with images of breasts as she wondered what it might be like for a moment, if she had a remote control that could actually mute Lachlan's voice. Rather annoyingly, Lachlan had in just a matter of seconds, offered his input which hadn't even been requested and he'd ultimately taken control of the whole consultation and Charmaine had been virtually made redundant as the manager of her own life and body. Due to Charmaine's silence, it seemed as if Lachlan now actually had Charmaine's permission to dominate the entire process and her actual body without any objections at all and that attitude of subservience worried Talitha profusely.

"Which cup size would you like your breasts to be Charmaine?" Talitha asked as she turned her screen towards the couple as if Charmaine actually had a choice in the matter. "The current range of images is a double D cup size."

"Yes, I think a double D cup would be really nice Talitha." Charmaine immediately agreed as she smiled and nodded her head. She cast a slightly nervous glance at Lachlan as she waited for him to respond. "That's a great suggestion."

"A double D cup size is very manageable." Talitha quickly pointed out.

Prior to that moment in time there had been no actual discussion about the size of breast enlargement that Charmaine wanted to have but Talitha could tell, even before Lachlan opened his mouth or uttered a single word, if he had anything to do with that decision, it would be extremely huge. Internally, Talitha silently braced herself for the discussion that she was sure would now follow which she was certain would be extremely difficult and slightly unpleasant as she cast a nervous glance at Lachlan's face and just waited for him to respond.

"I think a double G cup would be much better Charmaine." Lachlan suddenly interjected as he began to vigorously shake his head. "It's better we do this right the first time round." He insisted. "There's no room in our lives for half measures and those breasts are really quite small, I want you to have the best that money can buy and a double D is not the best that my money can buy."

"A double G cup size might be quite heavy Lachlan." Charmaine muttered quietly.

Lachlan immediately shook his head as he totally dismissed her pleas and adamantly pushed them to one side. "Don't you have something bigger and a bit more bouncy?" He asked as he turned and stared at Talitha's face.

An uncomfortable silence suddenly began to wrap itself around the room as Talitha quietly absorbed Lachlan's demands and the expression of absolute disgust upon his face. Despite Charmaine's pleas that urged Lachlan to logically consider the physical implications of his desires, it seemed he was totally unstoppable. Another decision about Charmaine's body was just about to be made by Lachlan and that made Talitha extremely uncomfortable as she began to squirm around inside her chair.

Once again, Lachlan's feelings of dissatisfaction now ruled Talitha's consultation room as he'd butted in and dictated what he wanted and what he wanted was ultimately what would actually happen. Regardless of Talitha's obvious discomfort, Lachlan it seemed was completely undeterred as his eyes pierced sharply into Talitha's skin and his face remained fixed like a stone statue. Despite the nerves that now rattled around inside Talitha's body as she began to tremble however, she attempted to smile in order to mask her inner sentiments.

After a few more seconds of silence that seemed to last for an absolute eternity, Talitha took a deep breath as she prepared to proceed with her actual consultation which had almost been stopped dead in its tracks by Lachlan's very stubborn and obnoxious attitude. Perhaps women in Lachlan's world didn't have the right to make any kind of decisions that lay outside his sphere of control, Talitha quietly concluded as it certainly seemed that way from where she sat.

"I do think these breasts are really nicely shaped." Charmaine suddenly said as she pointed towards one of the images on the screen.

"Yes they are lovely aren't they." Talitha immediately agreed as she turned to face the image and then nodded her head.

Interestingly, Charmaine had actually pointed towards an image of a nice almond shaped pair of breasts that did not jump straight out of the screen and slap you right in the face with bounciness, unlike some of the other images and they looked slightly more natural. Despite Charmaine's efforts to assert herself however, Talitha very much doubted that her suggestions would be accepted by Lachlan, due to the fact that each of the two breasts hung down slightly lower than some of the more explosive looking very pert breasts on offer. In all likelihood, Talitha quietly speculated, Lachlan would want the breasts that stood upright and to attention like regimented soldiers and Charmaine's choice would be deemed an inferior option to what Lachlan ultimately desired.

"They do look very natural." Charmaine quickly pointed out. "I know they won't naturally be my breasts but those really look like they could be and no one else would actually know that they weren't."

"I think they look absolutely amazing." Talitha agreed as she very discreetly attempted to convince and persuade Lachlan that Charmaine's choice was actually a great one.

For a few seconds, nothing but silence filled the room and as the air seemed to swirl nervously around the two women's heads, they waited anxiously with bated breath for Lachlan to actually respond. Every particle of air seemed to be decorated with sentiments of discomfort as the tension continued to mount and hung over the two women's heads like an angry grey cloud that contained too much water which needed to burst in order to relieve itself, so that it could completely drench everything below it with raindrops of distress. The expression upon Lachlan's face wasn't positive at all and quite clearly, he was not impressed either by Charmaine's selection or by Talitha's supportive attitude towards Charmaine choice.

"I'd like to see the double G image range." Lachlan suddenly barked.

"Can I make a suggestion please?" Talitha asked politely.

"Go ahead." Lachlan snapped.

"Well, I'm not really supposed to do this but I'm going to make an exception for you Charmaine." Talitha explained. "I can give you the double D Download today and then if you want to, you can increase the cup size again in a couple of weeks' time." She offered as she tried to provide the couple with a diplomatic compromise that they could perhaps both live with.

"That sounds absolutely fantastic Talitha." Charmaine immediately agreed as she quickly nodded her head in response. "Doesn't it Lachlan?"

The thunderous expression upon Lachlan's face very clearly communicated to everyone inside the room that he was not amused and that this would definitely not be the end of the discussion. A more moderate double D cup size was definitely not what Lachlan wanted and Talitha had suspected that before Charmaine's consultation had even begun and before he'd actually opened his mouth to verbalize his actual preferences. Deep down inside, Talitha knew that she had taken a huge risk as she'd presented Charmaine with the double D sized breast images in the first place and then she'd even dared to oppose Lachlan through her support of Charmaine's preferences but nonetheless she persevered.

"That way Charmaine, your back and your body will have time to adjust to the heavier weight of your new breasts." Talitha explained as she placed a dash of special emphasis upon the words 'your back' and 'your body' as she spoke.

Between the three, a definite power struggle had now developed that silently surged and chaotically raced around inside the room and their minds just below the surface of their thoughts and words. From the expression upon Lachlan's face, it was immediately apparent to the two women that he was totally unmoved by their subtle attempts to reason with him and like a very stubborn, spoilt child his eyes were filled with absolute resentment and laced with utter contempt as he simply just stared at Talitha and didn't utter a single word.

Nothing but tense silence filled the room as Talitha frustratingly accepted that she was ultimately fighting a losing battle as Lachlan had already paid for what he wanted which meant, he would eventually get exactly what he'd paid for but she vowed to fight it anyway. Someone had to stand up to Lachlan and provide some kind of resistance to his dictatorship and it had become increasingly obvious that, that someone certainly wasn't going to be Charmaine. Although it was Charmaine's body that was actually being changed,

Lachlan was actually the one making all the decisions about Charmaine's physical form and Talitha was very eager to highlight that fact to him as discreetly as she could. Despite Talitha's efforts however, Lachlan's face looked as if it might erupt and explode at any given second as he stared at Talitha's face and flames of hatred danced across his eyes.

Suddenly, it struck Talitha that something was actually wrong with the services that Professor Heisner had created and that Restructure offered to the world but that those problems had very little to do with science and related more to humanity itself. The Restructure clinic offered physical perfection for a price and it was an easy perfection, not an ugly, cumbersome and risky perfection like that offered by cosmetic surgeries and that triggered, fuelled and sponsored the infinite desires and unreasonable demands that most human beings harbored inside themselves that they usually managed to keep under control.

From Lachlan's very hard stare, Talitha could sense that he had actually understood exactly what Talitha's remark had implied but that it had meant absolutely nothing to him. In fact, it seemed as if Talitha's words had zipped straight into Lachlan's ears like a well-aimed arrow which had tried to penetrate the depths of his mind but instead that arrow had reached its destination and then just shot straight through his head as her remarks had not even scratched the surface of his thoughts. Inside the destination of Lachlan's mind there was nothing it seemed but a wall of resistance and the harsh reality was, Lachlan did not actually care what Talitha or anyone else thought about his dominance over Charmaine's life and the very obstinate expression on his face silently communicated those sentiments.

"Look, it won't cost any extra money. When I give you a client closure session I can perform the final Download then." Talitha offered as she attempted to accommodate Lachlan's very demanding attitude. She sighed internally as she quietly decided that Charmaine's appointments were becoming the weekly consultations that she dreaded facing the most, simply due to Lachlan's presence.

Charmaine immediately nodded her head in agreement. "That sounds absolutely great Talitha. Can you really do that for me?" She asked.

"Yes and absolutely no additional costs would be incurred." Talitha insisted.

Both women understood exactly what Talitha had tried to do as somehow, they had silently managed to unite and form some kind of opposition against Lachlan's dictatorship but they also both understood the implications of angering Lachlan further. A few nervous glances were exchanged between the two women as Talitha waited for Lachlan to respond as she quietly concluded that he literally ruled Charmaine's life and their romantic relationship with an iron fist and that their gentle defiance had not gone unnoticed.

When it came to Lachlan's attitude, his attitude towards Talitha was very hostile and towards Charmaine, it was extremely dismissive, totally disrespectful and absolutely condescending but nonetheless both women had attempted to cope and tolerate his behavior, at least in the short term. Both women knew, the challenge that Talitha had made was a bold attempt to find a compromise that Lachlan simply had no interest at all in actually making but it was definitely a step in the right direction for Charmaine.

"Okay, we'll do it that way." Lachlan finally agreed reluctantly. "I'm just agreeing to this because of your back Charmaine." He mentioned as he turned to face her. "I don't want you to be too tired and your body needs time to adjust."

"That's very sweet of you Lachlan." Charmaine immediately reassured him as she internally appreciated Talitha's very noble attempts to resist Lachlan's demands.

"Not those breasts though Charmaine, they really look quite awful and they hang down very low, please pick out another pair." Lachlan insisted in a slightly softer tone.

Once Charmaine and Lachlan had reached an agreement, or rather once Lachlan had chosen the actual pair of breasts that he wanted Charmaine to have, Talitha began to quickly process the couple's request, despite her utter disgust. Although Lachlan had made some kind of effort to actually compromise, the conversation that had been held between the couple had made Talitha cringe inside and a very cold, unfriendly shiver slithered down her spine as she led Charmaine into the adjoining procedure room. The compromise that Lachlan had made had been a very hard push to achieve and Talitha had to silently accept that unfortunately, it wasn't even permanent in nature.

The dictatorship that Lachlan upheld within his city of love made Talitha appreciate Bryson even more as she quietly contemplated further that he had never, ever tried to dictate anything to her about her own body, or how she should actually look. Regardless of the various small issues that the couple had faced over the years, they certainly didn't have the huge mountain of problems that were so obviously present in Charmaine and Lachlan's relationship. Power imbalances between Talitha and Bryson as a couple just did not exist in any capacity at all and their romance simply did not house such negative elements or issues within it.

When Charmaine's consultation finally ended, Talitha almost sighed a huge sigh of relief as she escorted the couple towards the reception area and showed them out, it had been a very tough consultation but Talitha had begun to realize just how tricky dealing with Lachlan would actually be. At least, Talitha had a warm, inviting, loving home and partner to return to each day and two very affectionate arms that waited to greet her, hold her and love her, not the hard, militant harshness of a man like Lachlan, who ruled his lover's heart with kisses of iron and steel hugs and for that Talitha was extremely grateful.

Friday morning and seven thirty practically zoomed into Talitha's life as her alarm clock sounded out and she welcomed it with extremely open arms as she enthusiastically leapt out of bed and eagerly embraced the day. A beautiful loving weekend loomed upon the not too distant horizon which promised to be filled with relaxation, lots of sensual interaction with Bryson and a very enjoyable romantic short break. The working day ahead didn't actually look too dreary but Talitha did have one potentially problematic appointment in the afternoon with Saskia and that would be a slight obstruction to what could be a very beautiful day and a beautiful end to her working week.

Approximately one hour later, when Talitha arrived at work, she quickly parked her car inside the parking lot and then walked towards the building that housed Restructure's corporate affairs every business day with a joyful spring in her step and a very warm smile on her face. A few minutes was spent inside the reception area as Talitha stopped to converse with Yucala and exchanged the usual morning pleasantries that the two women usually engaged in, before Talitha headed towards her consultation room. One very positive thing had come out of Talitha's consultation with Charmaine the day before and throughout that week and that was the idea of officially providing each of her client's with a client closure session and Talitha decided to email her suggestion to Professor Heisner as she walked.

Some very interesting stark differences and strange similarities existed between some of Talitha's clients which really intrigued her and Talitha began to consider them further as she entered inside her consultation room and then made her way towards the coffee machine. Both Charmaine and Saskia were being financially supported by third parties, who were paying for their actual procedures but despite this similarity, they sat on opposite ends of the spectrum when it came to the issue of actual consent. Although the two women's issues differed vastly in nature, their problems were equally as problematic and they had both presented Talitha with more than a few ethical dilemmas, even though she'd now only met them both once or twice. In response to those similar problems and their personal differences, Talitha had tried to tailor her approach towards the two women with precision and care but she'd quickly realized, it was extremely challenging.

Regarding Charmaine, she'd actually given her consent to someone that dominated her, both financially and emotionally, whereas Saskia was a different kettle of fish altogether and she actually dominated the person that she financially demanded things from, who was forced to consent to her demands through some kind of guilt. The financial dependencies that existed between the two women and their financial sponsors was technically, very unhealthy but there wasn't really a lot that Talitha could actually do about it as she was merely their consultant, not their mother, friend, or even their therapist.

Much to Talitha's delight, the first part of her Friday morning literally flew by and the rest of her Friday morning was extremely pleasant as the mid-morning arrived and brought Samson along with it, who leapt into the day with jokes and lively tales as usual. The enthusiasm that Samson displayed and his zest for life immediately lifted Talitha's spirit as she listened to him speak as she eagerly embraced the lightness that he brought to her workload each week. Unlike some of Talitha's other clients that presented her with some very heavy, quite deep, tricky, stressful and complex issues, Samson didn't feature anywhere in that number and he was an absolute pleasure to spend time with.

"Right, what exactly do you want me to change today Samson?" Talitha suddenly asked as she glanced at her screen and rapidly realized that at least fifteen minutes had gone by since Samson had arrived and that she hadn't even actually begun her consultation yet.

"Yes, let's get down to business Talitha. I'll need some new legs today please. I have to prepare my body for the weightlifter commercial as it's coming up real soon." Samson explained. "I also wanted a new chin, purely for my own personal reasons, so that women will find me more attractive but I'll have to keep the nobbly one for now as the legs are an urgent commercial requirement and money always comes first."

"Nothing wrong with that Samson, women can be such a fickle bunch at times and when the money runs dry, some of them run away, sometimes very quickly and with a huge pile of the money in their hands." Talitha said as she smiled. "In fact sometimes, women are the actual reason that the money runs dry in the first place as some women are very high maintenance."

"I know, tell me about it. I have a man saying, not all deserts cost the same and that's exactly what it refers to." Samson agreed. "Still, the woman I'm seeing at the moment, she's very sweet and not financially demanding at all. We've been seeing each other for about a month now and she absolutely hates my chin that's another reason why I have to get rid of it."

"Do you really like her?" Talitha enquired.

"Yes but I actually hate my chin too, so that's one thing that we both totally agree on." Samson replied.

"United in love by the hatred of your chin." Talitha teased as she touched her screen and began to process Samson's request. "That's the foundation for a very strong romance right there, you're practically soul mates, it must be destiny. Samson, this must be the one."

"Seriously Talitha, now you're just playing with me." Samson said as he grinned and then gently shook his head.

Talitha chuckled. "Okay Samson, here are the legs that are available to you, browse through the images at your leisure, pick out some that you like and then I'll narrow down the range." She instructed as she turned her screen towards Samson and smiled.

Fortunately for Talitha, Samson would actually be one of her long term clients and that actually suited her right down to the ground as he brightened up her working week and made it slightly less stressful and a lot more pleasant. A hope lay inside Talitha's mind as she watched

Samson inspect the images on her screen that her joy from his morning appointment would be enough to carry her through the afternoon and her appointment with Saskia later that day which she already knew had the potential to be very rough and extremely uncomfortable.

When three in the afternoon that Friday arrived, Saskia actually didn't but about twenty minutes later, she finally turned up with Marcus in tow and as Talitha showed them into her consultation room, she welcomed them both with a slightly nervous smile.   True to her usual form, Saskia was a petulant brat as usual but Talitha patiently persevered as she endeavored to courteously fulfill her procedure requests, regardless of Saskia's lateness, very demanding attitude and extremely impatient nature.   Once again Saskia's very devoted father had decided to accompany her and as he sat beside her and they faced Talitha, she attempted to reason with the unreasonable as Saskia demanded things from Restructure and Talitha that weren't actually even on offer, or available to anyone.

"I want the largest breasts that I can possibly have." Saskia demanded.

"Saskia, I'm afraid our range only goes up to a double G cup size and we don't actually offer larger breast sizes." Talitha quickly pointed out.   "And these breasts are all a double D which is the most commonly requested size."

"I need the biggest breasts you have. I don't want to be common and like everyone else." Saskia ranted as she stared at her father. "Daddy, you said I could have the biggest and the best breasts available."

A gentle sigh suddenly escaped from Marcus's lips as he immediately surrendered to Saskia's demands and nodded his head in defeat as Talitha watched him quietly. The gentle, soft natured man that had accompanied his very demanding daughter remained completely silent as he simply accepted her demands and agreed to give her exactly what she wanted. Apparently, there didn't seem to be an ounce of fight left inside Marcus and there was zero opposition as his weary shoulders rapidly slumped down on top of his body and the large leather chair quickly became his hiding place as he shrank as far down into the leather surfaces as he could possibly go.

"Is that okay Marcus?" Talitha suddenly asked as she tried to encourage Marcus to contribute to the discussion and ultimately the decision. "After all, you are the one paying for these procedures, so I really need your full agreement and consent." She quickly pointed out.

Once again, Talitha made a conscious effort to try and intervene for one of her clients as she quietly accepted that Marcus had simply allowed Saskia to rule his world, his decisions and his bank balance as she listened to them both in utter disbelief. An uncomfortable silence rapidly filled the room for a few minutes as Talitha glanced at them both and waited for Marcus to respond.

"I'm just a bit worried really Saskia about all the negative male attention that such large breasts might attract." Marcus muttered. "I want you to be happy and I want you to have what you want but I don't want you to become a target for male predators."

Despite Marcus's very noble intentions towards Saskia's welfare, no compromise seemed to be immediately forthcoming as Talitha glanced at her face and met nothing but a stony, stubborn, obstinate stare. The very thoughtful and considerate advice that Marcus had provided was like water running of a very stubborn duck's back as Saskia suddenly began to defiantly shake her head to communicate her immediate rejection of his very wise words. Every shake of Saskia's head rapidly confirmed to Talitha that she did not give a dam what her father thought as she simply shook of his advice and the droplets of wisdom his words contained and fully embraced her immaturity and her own internal desires.

The murky waters of very personal, well established family relationships could be a quite treacherous place to swim and Talitha considered that quietly as she contemplated whether or not she should attempt to intervene further and offer a potential compromise to them both. In reality, their family relationship had absolutely nothing to do with Talitha as an actual consultant and hence she actually felt quite reluctant to do so as to meddle further and jump in-between a very frustrated, tired, weary father and his demanding, extremely spoilt daughter was very risky territory indeed. Another factor that discouraged Talitha even further was the fact that the two were actually personally connected to Professor Heisner himself as that relationship alone could place her in a very difficult position professionally, if her intervention did not go favorably.

Talitha took a deep breath as she finally decided to give it a go and offer some kind of compromise to them both, if only for Marcus's sake. "Might I suggest Saskia that you could perhaps try a double D cup size first and then increase the size later, if you're not entirely happy with the outcome?" She suggested as she attempted appeal to Saskia's deeper sense of reason, if one actually existed. "These are huge physical changes and it wouldn't actually cost anymore money as I could perform a breast enlargement in two stages at no extra cost, if that's the option you both decide to take."

Saskia pouted as she glanced defiantly at her father's face. "I want the double G breasts daddy that's what I want." She insisted. "That's the biggest breasts they have, so that's what I want."

"Yes Saskia." Marcus replied as he wearily nodded his head.

"If my mother was here that's what I would get." Saskia said spitefully.

Marcus sighed.

Unfortunately for Marcus, Saskia's mother Judy had left him around ten years ago to be with another woman as she'd claimed that he'd neglected her and their family due to his work and business. Once Judy had left, Saskia had then blamed Marcus for her departure and that blame had created a deep sense of guilt which had lived inside of him ever since that had literally become like a chain around his neck when it came to the issue of pleasing Saskia. Although almost a decade had gone by since his ex-wife's departure, the invisible heavy cross of guilt that Marcus had carried around with him everywhere he went had not yet disappeared, or been forgiven by Saskia as she'd blamed him day after day for the family breakdown. In fact, every single day since that awful day, Marcus had silently carried the burden of blame upon his weary shoulders as absolutely everyone involved had blamed him and he'd silently accepted responsibility for his failure, Judy had blamed him, Saskia had blamed him and he'd even blamed himself.

Many desperate attempts had been made over the years to try and appease and please Saskia as Marcus had sought to try and financially compensate her for the absence of her mother, who had left both their lives due to his mistakes. Everything that Saskia had wanted had been provided and given to her without any further debates as Marcus had sought to make her as happy as he possibly could but somehow, it never seemed to be enough. In terms of his marriage, Marcus's intentions had been extremely honorable as he'd sought to work hard in order to provide his family and ex-wife with a decent lifestyle and the financial luxury that he felt they'd deserved but somehow, his family and marriage had still collapsed anyway. When Judy had slammed the door on their marriage and had said goodbye to their family as she'd left, Marcus had very sadly had to accept that the very long hours he'd expended on work had finally taken their toll upon those closest to him and that the damage done had in the end, been quite simply irreparable.

At times, Marcus had known deep down inside himself that Saskia had definitely gone to far but her immature and selfish nature had it seemed pushed her to capitalize upon his guilt. On several occasions, once Marcus had realized the impact of his guilt, he'd tried to put his foot down and discipline Saskia but by then it had already been too late as the damage had already been done and he'd struggled to regain control of the situation as he'd already caved into her demands way too many times. Inside Saskia's mind now there seemed to be a feeling of entitlement that had escalated over the years and grown into a monster of demands which Marcus was the first to admit, he could no longer actually control.

Throughout Saskia's younger years, Marcus had humored her and bought her all the latest toys and clothes that had been in fashion and so forth but as she'd grown older and her tastes had grown more expensive, her demands had been more difficult to financially sustain. Now whatever Saskia wanted, Saskia usually got and Marcus had struggled as he'd watched Saskia evolve into a domineering, spoilt ruthless dictator that ruled his world without a care for anything or anyone else besides herself as her sense of entitlement had grown into an absolute monster that devoured everything in its path.

"I want the double G sized breasts." Saskia suddenly demanded again as she started at Talitha angrily. She began to shake her head and then leapt to her feet. "That's what I want and I want them now."

Marcus sighed.

Sadly, the dedication that Marcus himself had applied to the accumulation of financial wealth had resulted in this cycle of negativity that he was ultimately responsible for and now, he really didn't know what to do to actually change it. A marriage that had once been full of joy, happiness and love had been lost as his wife had rejected his lack of attentiveness to it and the daughter that once been the apple of his eye and treasure of his heart had been corrupted by the lack of attention that he'd shown towards those he'd professed to love. In totality, Marcus had failed as a husband and a father due to his failure to identify his family's needs which were not material in nature but were quite simply him and that failure had resulted in their family breakdown and his wife's betrayal and the hands of time could not be turned back and nor could the damage be undone.

Regardless of Talitha's attempts to intervene which Marcus definitely appreciated, her attempts to try to moderate Saskia's demands had fallen upon closed ears as there was absolutely no moving Saskia. A mountain of stubbornness definitely lay inside Saskia's mind that no one could actually climb over, tunnel their way through or scale the heights off and Saskia had completely rejected Talitha's suggestions immediately which it seemed had not impressed her in the slightest. Nothing it appeared, could now change the negative precedents that had been set in motion which Marcus had allowed to fester and grow for a decade like a fungus that had infected their once loving world and their once pure family relationship. One day, Marcus hoped that he actually would be able to overcome his feelings of guilt and learn how to say no to Saskia's incessant demands but today he definitely knew, would not be that day.

Suddenly, Saskia's consultation rapidly began to take a turn for the worse, or more specifically Saskia did as she leapt to her feet and then began to storm around the room as her overt display of stubbornness and anger escalated into a full blown temper tantrum. Some objects around the room were quickly picked up and then banged back down and a horrified expression spread out across Talitha's face as she sat and just watched Saskia in total disbelief. Nothing but hatred, anger and spite seemed to occupy Saskia's eyes as she continued her angry outburst as the horrified audience, Marcus and Talitha were totally silenced by her actions. Quite obviously, Saskia now felt as if Talitha had actually tried to patronize her, undermine her and control her and she was having absolutely none of it as her performance continued.

Surprisingly, Marcus didn't actually seem to be surprised by Saskia's temper tantrum as Talitha glanced at his face but his eyes were cast down to the ground which very clearly indicated that he actually felt ashamed. A sympathetic glance was quickly offered as Talitha quietly concluded that by now, Marcus was probably very used to Saskia's childish angry outbursts as he'd probably seen it a thousand times before. Perhaps temper tantrums in a public place were a regular thing for Saskia, Talitha began to speculate as Saskia actually seemed to be quite good at them and Marcus didn't seem shocked at all by her sudden fit of rage.

"Give her what she wants please Talitha." Marcus suddenly mumbled as he nodded his head at Talitha and urged her to cooperate. "The double G cup size breasts."

Just as Marcus spoke those words of defeat, Saskia triumphantly seized her victory and immediately ceased her display of public humiliation as she flopped back down into the chair that she'd been seated in prior to her angry outburst. Silent sparks of hatred seemed to emanate from Saskia's eyes as she gave Talitha an almost deadly stare and absolutely no apologies were offered from Saskia's mouth as she smugly accepted her victory. No actual embarrassment seemed to be present, Talitha rapidly noticed and Saskia seemed to care very little about the angry outburst she'd just embarked upon in the presence of what was practically, almost a total stranger as Talitha had only ever actually met Saskia once before.

Talitha nodded her head obediently. "Sure." She replied. "Here you are Saskia these are the double G cup size breasts that we currently have available, please select the images that you prefer and then I'll narrow down the range for you." Talitha instructed as she turned her screen towards Saskia.

At one point throughout Saskia's consultation, a small glimmer of hope had been ignited inside Marcus's eyes but as Talitha glanced at his face she could now see very clearly that it had totally disappeared. Despite Talitha's attempts to assist him, Marcus had finally fully caved in and accepted Saskia's demands and now the sparkles of possible salvation which had danced through his eyes, albeit very briefly, were no longer present or anywhere to be found. All that occupied Marcus's eyes now was the rather dull, glassy look that they had contained when he'd first stepped inside the room that day as he'd accepted his defeat and they'd returned to their usual lifeless state.

Quite obviously, Saskia's domineering attitude and childish demands had drained and sucked the life out of Marcus and all his body and spirit now seemed to contain was the weary, worn out, fatigued shell of the man he'd once been. In terms of their family relationship, it was a total mess but only Marcus himself could really actually change that and from what Talitha had observed, he definitely wasn't strong enough or ready to do that yet. Despite her desire to assist and help Marcus, Talitha wasn't prepared to risk her job, just to help Marcus stand up to his own stubborn child that was ultimately the product of his own loins.

Approximately thirty minutes later, Saskia and Marcus finally left Talitha's consultation room and as Talitha escorted them back towards the reception area, she gave an internal sigh of relief. When Talitha returned to her consultation room, she sat back down beside her desk and thought about Saskia as she wrote up her client notes but there was no immediate solution that Talitha could see to the problems that Saskia presented. One day perhaps, Talitha considered thoughtfully, she and Bryson would have a child as they'd actually planned to start a family once they were married and she wondered for a moment what she might actually do, if that child behaved anything like Saskia. The very sad reality was that Saskia was an example of just how wrong parenting could actually go, regardless of laud intentions on the behalf of parents and the devoted commitment Saskia had been given by Marcus her father.

Parenting just wasn't like beauty procedures or science, Talitha quietly considered and there really was no manual that could be fully relied upon that provided precise instructions and relevant practical guidance on how to actually do it correctly. Raising children was not a precise science and most parents usually just tried to do their best with the knowledge and skills that they possessed as they tried to make their children as happy as they possibly could. Diversions from healthy, well balanced, loving family relationships sometimes occurred, no matter what parents did or didn't do as children grew up, became adults and developed their own minds, objectives and characters and at times, things definitely went wrong and Saskia was a prime example of that.

A simple breast enlargement would definitely not actually solve Saskia or Marcus's problems, no matter how much Talitha wanted it to, she quietly acknowledged as she finished writing up Saskia's notes and then submitted them to Professor Heisner. The very stubborn attitude and difficult behavior that was now very deeply engrained in Saskia's character would perhaps take years to change and it had become increasingly obvious as Talitha had watched and listened to them both that Marcus could not handle the extremely difficult young woman that he'd actually given breath and life to.

Once the Restructure system beeped to confirm that Saskia's notes had been saved, updated and submitted successfully, Talitha quickly glanced at the time and then began to prepare to leave work for the day and for the entire weekend. The Friday afternoon had definitely already left the world and now the evening had stepped into its place and that meant, it was actually home time and time to embark upon her romantic weekend break and loving adventure with Bryson. Fortunately enough, Talitha had actually managed to finish and submit Saskia's notes before the last few remaining grains and minutes of the afternoon had totally escaped from her grasp and as each one rapidly slipped away and silently vanished, she rejoiced in the fact that she could definitely leave work on time that day.

The challenging nature of Talitha's workload that week had highlighted to her, the human instincts and infinite desires that lurked within most human minds which could ultimately ensnare people and she contemplated those issues thoughtfully as she made her way home. Sometimes, those infinite human desires drove people to desire deeper levels of satisfaction that paid very little regard to rational human logic and at times, those desires could actually destroy all those around them and Saskia had been a prime example of that. Life certainly wasn't always a fairytale and not everyone actually possessed the great body, great face or the great relationship that they really wanted to and for some people, Taliitha quietly concluded as she arrived outside her home and parked her car inside the driveway, those infinite desires would perhaps always rule them and they would never truly ever be, totally satisfied.

SCIENTIFIC MIRACLES

Once a truly amazing, absolutely marvelous and deliciously enjoyable romantic weekend break had been fully consumed, Monday showed up on Talitha's doorstep way too soon but luckily it brought along with it a warm gentle breeze which pleasantly greeted Talitha cheeks as she stepped out of her home. Each soft wave of heat began to eagerly embrace the exposed parts of Talitha's body as she walked towards her car as she delighted in the waves of warmth that playfully teased her pores, rippled across her arms and lapped gently against her cheeks as the weather caressed every inch of her exposed skin. Due to the romantic short break that Talitha had just enjoyed, her mind and body felt totally refreshed as she entered inside her vehicle and then began to quietly prepare for the drive to work.

Something definitely seemed to be missing however as Talitha started the engine of her car but a smile crossed her face as she suddenly realized that, that something wasn't necessarily a bad thing as it wasn't something that she actually wanted to be present. The missing element that Monday morning was in fact, the silent companionship of nervousness that had accompanied her the previous two Monday mornings which it seemed had now completely abandoned and deserted her. A joyful smile adorned Talitha's face as she quickly pressed the remote to open up the driveway gates and then began to roll her car towards the street as her confidence in her ability to deliver had definitely grown and thankfully now, Monday morning doubts would no longer be something that she would have to wrestle with.

When Talitha arrived outside the Restructure building, she quickly parked her car inside the parking lot and as she stepped out of the vehicle, a soft gentle groan escaped from her lips, it was definitely time to return to reality. A beautifully romantic weekend had been fully enjoyed but now, Talitha had to leave it totally behind as it had fully departed from her life, slightly too soon and Monday morning had stepped in and taken the weekend's place. The time that Talitha had spent with Bryson however had somewhat quenched her thirst for some quality time with him but now that time had drizzled away into nothingness which meant, work had to be attended to and focused upon.

For some strange reason, Talitha quietly considered as she walked towards the entrance of the building, weekends seemed to vanish in a flash but weekdays seemed to hang around for so very long, especially when she had to see clients like Lachlan and Saskia. Perhaps weekends could be amended and they could begin on a Thursday each week instead of a Friday, Talitha deliberated thoughtfully as she entered inside the reception area and that shortcoming in the calendar of life could be changed, now that would be a very positive human advancement and that wouldn't require years of research, or geniuses to formulate.

"Good morning Talitha." Yucala said as she quickly glanced up at Talitha's face and then smiled.

"Good morning Yucala, how was your weekend?" Talitha asked politely as she greeted the Receptionist who was seated as usual behind her desk equipped with a warm, friendly smile.

"It was fun, very messy but a lot of fun and before you go, I actually have some supplies for you that I ordered last week." Yucala mentioned as she opened up a built-in storage cupboard just behind her desk and then pulled out a large cardboard box. "It's nothing exciting really, just some teabags, coffee and sugar. How was your weekend, was it all that you hoped and dreamed it would be?"

Talitha immediately nodded her head in response. "It was absolutely heavenly Yucala, mountains moved in many ways." She replied as she giggled. "Are there any biscuits inside there?"

"Nope. Professor Heisner didn't ask me to order any." Yucala explained as she grinned. "He has to authorize the purchase."

"I think I might need to bring in some biscuits for my clients." Talitha replied. "Give them something to chew on with their cups of tea and coffee."

"I'll suggest it to Professor Heisner when I see him again." Yucala confirmed. "You never know, he might let me order some."

"How are the boys and the man of the house?" Talitha enquired.

"Great but I think they're all boys really, even the man and at times, especially the man." Yucala joked. "I'm trying to convince my ten year old to become a chef like you suggested, so I can get him to step inside the kitchen and give me a hand."

Talitha giggled. "Good luck with that one." She teased.

"Since you're here Talitha, I'll just bring these supplies along to your consultation room right now." Yucala replied as she quickly stood up and then picked up the cardboard box from the top of her desk.

"Do you need a hand with that box?" Talitha offered.

"No that's okay Talitha. It's really quite light, it looks way heavier than it actually is." Yucala quickly clarified as she began to carry the box towards the corridor that led towards Talitha's consultation room.

"Thanks Yucala. At least I have some replenishments now, I was actually starting to run a bit low on latte sachets for the coffee machine." Talitha said appreciatively as she began to follow Yucala. "And I do love to have a latte with my breakfast each day."

Once the two women arrived outside Talitha's consultation room door, Talitha quickly plucked the security key card from her hand bag and then swiped it as she unlocked the door and then she politely held the door open for Yucala as she invited her inside. The large cardboard box inside Yucala's hands was carried very carefully across the room and then gently placed down on top of Talitha's desk as Yucala prepared to unpack the box and place the items inside it where they should be. Some coffee sachets, teabags and hot chocolate sachets were neatly stacked inside the coffee machine and then a carton of fresh milk and some cartons of juice were placed inside the fridge as Yucala busily went about her task and Talitha quietly began to prepare herself for her morning ahead.

"Right, I think that's everything Talitha that I ordered for you." Yucala suddenly announced as she returned to Talitha's desk and then glanced inside the now almost empty cardboard box. "The other few bits and pieces are for Professor Heisner."

"Thanks so much Yucala, you're an absolute angel." Talitha replied as she smiled. "Where would we be without you? We'd be totally lost and our throats would be very dry and parched."

Yucala smiled. "Just doing my job really Talitha, someone's got to look after people's very human physical needs. I had to suggest the tea and coffee supplies to Professor Heisner when he originally hired me and then find an actual supplier as he hadn't even thought about it." She explained as she grinned. "These scientific geniuses, they live in another world completely, one that doesn't really think about human thirst."

"Yes, I know exactly what you mean." Talitha agreed.

"I even suggested that he should purchase the coffee machine for your consultation room." Yucala said as she smiled.

"Yucala I bow down before you and kiss your feet." Talitha replied. "Not your butt, just your feet.

317

Thank you so much though that coffee machine really is a life saver."

Yucala giggled. "I better get a move on." She said as she picked up the cardboard box and then prepared to depart. "Phone calls don't answer themselves, well they do if you put them on voicemail but that's a technicality really. Human responses are much better for business."

"Very true, Yucala very true." Talitha agreed as she watched Yucala depart.

Despite Talitha's absence from work for two days and her lack of interaction with the Restructure system, she quickly discovered as soon as she switched it on and turned her attention towards it, the same could not be said for Professor Heisner. Over the weekend, two new clients had been assigned to Talitha inside the Restructure system and one had even been flagged as an 'Urgent Client Intake' though what exactly that meant, Talitha was slightly unsure..

Several things really excited Talitha about the two new clients that she'd been allocated as she began to study their client profiles and one of those was that Professor Heisner had actually increased her client workload. The increase in her workload discreetly indicated to Talitha that Professor Heisner actually felt quite confident about her professional abilities and that he'd felt, she could now handle an actual increase in her client list and that really encouraged her.

Inside Talitha's work schedule there were just two client consultations scheduled to take place that day as she gave it a quick glance but Talitha already knew that as she'd checked it on the Friday just before she'd left work for the weekend. The first mid-morning appointment was actually with Frank and the afternoon consultation that day would be with Dean, who definitely seemed to prefer to see Talitha on Mondays. Both men were pleasant enough and extremely easy to deal with and so Talitha wasn't particularly worried about the day ahead as she'd met them both twice now and they'd always been very polite, friendly and quite straight forward.

When the mid-morning arrived, so too did Frank, on time as usual and Talitha enthusiastically prepared to greet him with a warm smile as she opened up her consultation room door. In terms of her current client list, Frank was always an absolute joy to see and therefore Talitha felt very relaxed about her morning and his session. Unfortunately however, it quickly became apparent that not all was right in Frank's world that morning as she found not only Frank and Yucala on the other side of the door but also a frown which very worryingly was plastered across Frank's face. The usual jovial smile that Frank usually carried around with him

319

everywhere he went certainly wasn't present and instead in its place was a very worried frown that caused the lines on Frank's forehead to gather like a crumpled piece of paper.

"Good morning Frank." Talitha said as she quickly stepped back from the door and invited him inside. "Please come in and take a seat."

Frank nodded as he stepped inside the room. "Thanks." He mumbled.

"Thanks Yucala." Talitha said as she turned to face her. "I'll let you know if I need anything else."

Yucala nodded and smiled. "Right, you know where to find me." She replied.

"I do. Thank you." Talitha said as she smiled and nodded her head appreciatively.

The worried frown on Frank's face immediately began to worry Talitha as she closed the door of her consultation room and then headed back towards her desk as she internally deliberated over what could have possibly gone wrong in Frank's world and life that past week. Regardless of Talitha's concerns however, she adorned her face with a pleasant smile as she sat back down and then prepared to begin Frank's actual consultation. Frank was definitely upset about something but Talitha getting upset because he was upset Talitha knew, really wouldn't help either of them.

"How are you this morning Frank?" Talitha asked. "How's your week been?"

"To be perfectly honest Talitha, it was rather strange to be frank." Frank replied. "Now there's a first, a man called Frank saying it was strange to be frank." He joked.

Talitha smiled.

"I guess though, it was rather strange to be me this week." Frank said as he began to elaborate. "So in more ways than one that is actually true. I just didn't really feel myself to be quite honest and I experienced some very unusual feelings and sensations that were rather strange."

"Really, what happened Frank?" Talitha enquired.

"Well first and foremost, I wasn't really as close to Maude as I usually am and she said I seemed a bit distant." Frank explained. "And on one occasion, when she actually tried to cuddle me, it was almost as if I feared her which was very strange as Maude is a gentle soul and we even had a bit of a row about it."

"Okay, why do you think that was?" Talitha asked. "Did anything else unusual happen last week?"

"I'm not sure really. Nothing unusual happened last week, except the Download procedure." Frank replied.

"Okay, I'll mention this to Professor Heisner, just in case." Talitha quickly reassured him. "So that he can look into it for you."

Frank nodded his head. "That would be much appreciated." He said.

"Would you like to proceed with your next Download today Frank, or would you like to wait for a week or so and see how things go?" Talitha asked considerately. "Remember, these are huge changes that you're making to your body, so there's bound to be some temporary internal imbalances that occur, so you might have to give your body a little extra time to adjust."

"I understand but I don't think I can wait Talitha. I can't let Maude feel like she's the greatest and the best looking person in our coupling forever. I really need to get rid of these wrinkles on my forehead as soon as possible." Frank quickly clarified.

"Right, a new youthful, revitalized, wrinkle free forehead is coming straight up." Talitha teased playfully as she gently touched the screen directly in front of her. "By the time I'm finished with you Frank, I think you'll be ready for the Mr. Universe competition."

"Talitha as long as I can still beat Maude at dominos and chess that's all that really matters to me, oh and have less wrinkles on my face when we do Maude's Mirror Test competition every morning." Frank joked.

"What's Maude's Mirror Test competition?" Talitha asked.

"Maude makes us stand in front of the mirror every morning and then we have to compare our faces and bodies to see who's aging the quickest. So far, I'm losing. I've been losing for years." Frank explained.

"You actually compare yourselves in the mirror every morning?" Talitha asked as a confused expression rapidly spread out across her face.

"That's Maude's thing, she's very competitive you know, drives me round the bend sometimes." Frank replied. "Every single morning, we have to stand right next to each other totally naked in front of this huge mirror on the wall inside our bedroom and then she compares every single inch of us to see which one of us is aging the worst or the best."

"Hilarious and Maude's winning?" Talitha asked as she giggled.

"Yes and she's won every day for the past ten years, so I'm really looking forward to beating her for a change." Frank explained as he grinned.

"Do you get a trophy or a gold medal if you win?" Talitha asked.

"Nope but the loser has to cook dinner and take the trash out every day, so I take the trash out a lot." Frank explained. "In fact, I've visited the trash bin so often, I practically live inside it, it's almost like a second home now."

Talitha giggled. "Well, look on the bright side Frank, there are definitely worse places you could visit every day." She teased.

"Yes, like an old people's home where your forced to eat sloppy, watery porridge every morning and live with moth balls." Frank quickly agreed. "I think I can live with the trash bin for now, until I beat Maude which will hopefully happen real soon and then I can send her out to the trash bin every day."

Talitha laughed.

"That's what happens I'm afraid when you're in love with an athlete and one that's used to winning Talitha." Frank explained as he gently shook his head. "Never date an athlete."

"You must be a real good cook by now though." Talitha quickly pointed out. "Since you cook dinner every single night."

"For the first couple of years, I actually tried to burn the food every day to put her off but Maude persevered and actually ate those burnt offerings and so in the end, I had to learn how to cook properly because I got fed up of eating burnt food myself." Frank explained. "I mean seriously, Maude does not let you off easily at all."

"Can Maude cook?" Talitha asked.

"Yes, she can make you the darn best meal you'll ever eat in your entire life, she's excellent at almost every single thing she does in life that's why it's so dam annoying sometimes." Frank replied.

"Is there anything she can't do?" Talitha probed.

"She's terrible at two things, dominos and chess." Frank immediately clarified as he grinned. "So that's when I get to win but we don't play chess or dominos very often as Maude absolutely hates to lose. She prefers to play games like charades, jenga, or pin the tail on the donkey because she can win those kind of games much more easily."

Talitha grinned.

Later that afternoon, Talitha met with Dean and as he arrived very punctually at three on the dot, she immediately invited him inside her consultation room. Once Talitha had served Dean the beverage of his choice which as usual was a coffee, the two quickly got straight down to business as Talitha began to discuss the procedures he'd already had as she wanted to know how his life had been impacted by the bodily changes so far.

"How are things going Dean?" Talitha asked as she faced Dean. "How are the new body parts functioning? Are they all you hoped they would be?"

"My chest looks absolutely great." Dean replied. "But to be perfectly honest, I haven't actually taken my new penis out for a test drive yet."

"Okay, so you're not dating anyone at the moment?" Talitha enquired as she smiled. "Are you waiting to meet someone special?"

"I think after the accident, my confidence just zeroed out, so it's taken me a while to approach anyone in a romantic sense." Dean began to explain. "I did meet someone quite recently but we haven't really participated in any intimate physical contact yet."

"Okay, well let me know how things go Dean and if you experience any problems." Talitha advised. "The Downloads are pretty straight forward but sometimes, human beings certainly aren't."

"Isn't that the truth." Dean agreed.

"I can see from your procedure request list Dean that you only have two procedures left to perform. Which one would you like this week, the leg contour of arm sculptor?" Talitha asked.

"I think this week Talitha, I'd really like to sort out my legs." Dean replied as a very serious expression rapidly crossed his face. "I guess that's why I haven't given my new body parts a physical test drive yet." He quickly clarified. "My legs are kind off holding me back a bit."

"Okay Dean, let's look for some legs." Talitha encouraged as she touched the screen directly in front of her and it rapidly populated with male leg images. She turned her screen towards Dean so that he could see it as she prepared to assist him. "What kind of legs would you prefer Dean?"

"I definitely don't want those legs." Dean quickly clarified as he pointed towards a pair of very chunky muscular looking legs. "My body would look really weird and bottom heavy with those legs, they're absolutely huge."

"Some people like weird shaped bodies Dean." Talitha teased playfully as she smiled at him. "And chunky legs. Perhaps this will be easier if you show me some legs that you definitely don't want and then I can narrow down the range that way."

"Yeah I think that might be a good idea." Dean agreed.

Approximately fifteen minutes went by and as the two browsed through the various leg images, they discussed some and laughed at others as they giggled together like two small children. Some leg images were completely rejected by Dean for one reason or another and his decisive nature was quite refreshing for Talitha as she quickly managed to narrow down the many images until they arrived at his final five preferences.

In the end, Dean opted for a quite slim looking, very athletic, rather toned pair of legs which had nicely shaped contours and the calves actually looked as if they had been sculpted to perfection by a master craftsman as Talitha internally admired his choice. The pair of legs, in terms of Dean's actual height and build, were absolutely perfect for him and in Talitha's opinion, would actually match and suit the rest of his physique immaculately.

"What do you think of them Talitha?" Dean asked as he anxiously sought out her opinion.

"I think they'll be absolutely perfect for you Dean." Talitha immediately reassured him as she enthusiastically nodded her head and smiled. "I think you've made a really great choice." She encouraged as she persuaded Dean to trust in his own judgment and decision.

"Do you think the download will cover up my scar?" Dean suddenly asked. "I have a huge scar on one of my legs and it looks really awful."

"I think so." Talitha replied. "The Restructure system instructs your DNA to reconfigure in a different shape and form, according to the Download that you've chosen, so it should do."

"It's just well, the scar on my leg is actually very large and that's why I came here in first place really." Dean began to explain as he lifted his leg up and then rested it on top of Talitha's desk. "It's a very long, deep scar, so it's been very hard to hide it." He continued as he began to roll his trouser leg up to show Talitha exactly what he meant.

Rather strangely, it suddenly struck Talitha that she didn't actually know the answer to Dean's question and the issue that he'd raised which was definitely a very valid one. A quick glance was cast towards Dean's leg which was now exposed and as Talitha gazed at his naked calf, a gasp of horror almost escaped from her lips. Fortunately, Talitha was somehow able to control her mouth in time as she pressed her lips very firmly together to ensure that not a single sound escaped but the very large, deep dark scar that was engraved into Dean's leg had really shocked her. Regardless of whether Talitha knew the answer to Dean's question or not, there was one thing she definitely did know for certain and that was that the long dark, deep twisted scar on Dean's leg was extremely difficult to look at and Talitha literally had to force herself to do so.

"I hope it does Dean." Talitha gently reassured him as she silently rebuked herself for almost wincing at the sight of the scar which had devoured almost half of Dean's actual leg. She smiled and nodded her head to encourage him as her heart began to fill with sadness and dismay. "I really hope it does."

"I hope so too." Dean replied. "It would be really nice to get rid of this."

"If you don't mind me asking Dean, what actually happened?" Talitha enquired softly as she gazed into Dean's eyes and a slightly confused expression crossed her face.

"I had an accident. One day I was out on my motorbike and when I turned a blind corner, I ran straight into the back of a lorry. I wasn't able to stop in time." Dean explained as he shook his head. "I flew straight off my motorbike and landed on top of a spike, a very sharp spike that decided to drive itself, straight into my leg and destroy my calf forever. There was nothing I could do to avoid it, it all happened so fast."

"That's really awful Dean, I'm so sorry." Talitha replied as she gently shook her head.

"That's why accountants shouldn't have motorbikes. I sold my motorbike straight after the accident and haven't been near another one since. Kind of puts you off really. Apparently, the garage that replaced the tyres on my motorbike just before the accident took some shortcuts and put some tyres on it that weren't exactly safe. It was an accident waiting to happen." Dean explained.

"I hope this procedure changes things for you Dean." Talitha said as she rose to her feet. "Let's get your Download sorted out now." She insisted as she began to walk towards the procedure room.

"I do too." Dean replied as he stood up. "If it gets rid of the ugly scar, I'll be able to wear shorts again in the summer and I'll be a lot less self conscious when I'm naked around women. It would totally change my life and I might actually have a love life again."

Talitha nodded and smiled. "Yes, being single for a long period of time can be quite difficult at times and very lonely." She agreed.

Although Talitha hadn't actually provided Dean with a conclusive answer to his most pressing question, he seemed satisfied enough with her response as they walked towards the procedure room together and at least there was now an optimistic smile of hope upon his face. Not a single word was uttered as the two silently prepared themselves for Dean's actual Download procedure as Talitha considered that this particular Download was perhaps the most important procedure that she'd been asked to perform since she'd first stepped through the doors of Restructure.

Every ounce of Talitha's being hoped and prayed as she strode briskly towards the transparent Download capsule in the center of the procedure room that this particular Download would provide Dean with the physical closure and healing that he definitely deserved and ultimately, really actually desperately needed. Such a large scar did not fit comfortably onto such a small part of someone's leg and it had completely devoured the flesh of Dean's calf along with his confidence and now, only scar tissue actually remained.

Inside Talitha's procedure room, it almost seemed as if every particle of air had been sucked out of the space and replaced with nervous tension as Talitha quietly watched Dean enter inside the transparent capsule and then lie down. The emotions inside Talitha's mind and body seemed to somersault within her as a combination of excitement and nerves surged through her veins and spiraled through her thoughts. This was essentially Dean's moment of truth and this consultation would perhaps completely transform his entire life.

Emotional desire seemed to seep out of every single one of Talitha's pores as she internally urged Professor Heisner's Download procedure and Restructure to provide Dean with the solution he so desperately needed as she held her breath and closed the transparent capsule lid down over Dean's body. Professor Heisner's work absolutely had to deliver in this instance, Talitha silently demanded as she made her way back towards her desk to initiate and implement the actual Download procedure itself as when it came to the issue of Dean's legs, there was absolutely no room at all for any kind of failure.

Once Dean's procedure had been performed, approximately ten minutes later, Talitha returned to the procedure room and then lifted up the lid of the capsule as she silently prepared herself for the moment of truth. Every inch of Talitha's being prayed and hoped that the Download had actually covered Dean's scar as she watched him climb out of the capsule and then step back down each of the steps that led back to the ground. Upon each of their faces there was a slightly nervous expression as Dean stood in front of the long client mirror and then leant towards the ground as he prepared to roll back his trouser leg and check if the scar had indeed actually gone as Talitha watched him in total and utter silence.

Much to Talitha's total delight, she rapidly discovered that the scar had indeed completely gone and that Dean's leg had now actually been fully restored to its former glory and she almost jumped with joy. Not only had Dean's question been fully answered and his physical leg restored but Professor Heisner and Restructure had totally delivered and Talitha was totally ecstatic. For Talitha, the moment was almost breathtaking as she quietly observed the beautiful reality of what Professor Heisner's work had the potential to achieve and she began to silently rejoice in what she felt had been the best client consultation that she'd given anyone so far.

Regardless of whatever else Talitha did for various clients throughout her time at the Restructure, moments like this one in her mind not only validated Restructure's existence, Professor Heisner's work but also her employment there in totality. The client consultation for Dean that Talitha had facilitated that day had not just delivered for Dean but also for Talitha herself as it had given her a much more meaningful reason to actually be there and to participate in Professor Heisner's work.

Not a single trace from the scar, or scrap of scar tissue remained on Dean's leg as he smiled and rubbed his leg enthusiastically. Every inch of the skin on his calf looked fresh, healthy and vibrant and as if nothing had actually happened to his leg at all as Talitha stared at his calf and smiled. In some ways, it almost felt as if an actual miracle had been delivered right before Talitha's very eyes that she had somehow been a part of as she silently admired Professor Heisner's work and the physical healing and beauty it had managed to deliver.

A scientific miracle had somehow been delivered that day, Talitha silently accepted and she, by virtue of Professor Heisner's work had definitely been part of the miraculous event that had just taken place. Now Talitha finally fully understood and appreciated Professor Heisner's vision and the purpose behind his work more accurately as she'd seen with her own eyes just how important it could actually, really be.

Suddenly inside Talitha's mind, Restructure's purpose had become so much more important than just the delivery of a few breast enlargements and a few painless nose jobs and suddenly, Restructure's potential had evolved and grown right before her very eyes. In just one consultation, Talitha had now realized that Restructure could actually provide some of its clients with a whole new lease on life and that Restructure had the power to totally liberate them from the painful physical shackles and obstacles that held them back and obstructed their potential happiness.

Total disbelief and absolute excitement seemed to grip both Talitha and Dean's tongues for a few minutes and neither of them uttered a single word as they stood in complete silence as they simply absorbed and basked in the joyful moment that had very unexpectedly been given to them. Something deeply profound had happened that day inside Restructure and as they took some time to silently appreciate and digest that very special event, Talitha's respect for Professor Heisner and his groundbreaking work rapidly began to deepen.

The huge smile upon Dean's face said absolutely everything for Talitha and she felt deeply comforted by the events that had taken place and occurred that day. Essentially, this was the very first time since Talitha had actually joined Restructure that she'd experienced a moment that paid homage to an issue of far greater significance among all the moments of frivolous superficiality and it had absolutely delighted her.

Every inch of Talitha's body suddenly began to feel very warm as joy seemed to dance around her limbs and tease the surface of her skin as her heart almost leapt out of her ribcage in absolute delight. Regardless of what Talitha's other clients sought from Restructure, Dean's problems had found a real permanent solution there which Professor Heisner had ultimately provided to him and her cheeks shone as sheer happiness radiated from them as she graciously accepted that she had definitely been a very positive part of that solution.

"We better go and arrange your next appointment now Dean." Talitha suddenly said in almost whisper as she broke the silence between them both.

"This is totally amazing, thank you so much Talitha." Dean gushed as his words rapidly burst out of his mouth in a flurry. "I just don't know what to say, it's so unbelievable."

"You know Dean, I'm just doing my job really. I'm just happy that I could help you." Talitha replied as she graciously accepted his thanks as she began to led him back towards her consultation room.

"Well Talitha, you're really great at your job." Dean insisted appreciatively as he began to follow her. "I can't believe it, I can actually go swimming again now, I can't wait."

"Will this change your love life Dean?" Talitha asked as she sat back down at her desk and then turned to face him.

"Yes definitely Talitha." Dean confirmed as he sat back down. "I met a woman recently, last weekend in fact but we haven't done anything sexual yet but now, I definitely can.

"Well, I hope she gives you the green light." Talitha encouraged as she smiled. "You can't really take anything out for a test drive, if you're stuck behind a red light at the traffic lights of love."

"It was actually quite strange Talitha, I met her and somehow, I just seemed to really, really like her even though, I'd never seen her before. I think I've fallen in love with a total stranger and fortunately that stranger seems to like me too, so that's even more surprising." Dean explained. "Her name's Chantelle."

"Well Dean, I hope it goes well with Chantelle and that's a very pretty name." Talitha replied as she touched the screen on top of her desk. "When would you like to meet again for your next consultation?"

"Very pretty and nothing like that has ever happened to me before. I've never just met someone and felt like, yes this could be the person that I could spend my life with, so it's definitely a first." Dean explained. "I can do the same time next week."

"Right." Talitha replied as she touched her screen again and inserted Dean's next appointment into her work diary. She rose to her feet as she smiled. "That's all arranged for you now Dean, so I'll see you again at the same time next week. When will you be going out on another date with Chantelle?"

"Actually, I'm seeing her again later this week." Dean replied as he stood up and then began to walk towards the consultation room door. "We're meeting up again on either Thursday or Friday evening, I'm just waiting for her to confirm."

"Go easy on her with the Tip Simulator tiger." Talitha teased as she walked towards her consultation room door and then opened it.

Dean laughed.

When Talitha had escorted Dean to the reception area and then bade him farewell, she quickly returned to her consultation room to write up his notes as she internally rejoiced in the events of the day. Excitement scurried chaotically around the passageways of Talitha's mind as she silently celebrated Dean's leg and the scientific miracle that had taken place right before her very eyes. Interestingly enough, Dean had actually been Talitha's very first human client and in many ways, he'd actually changed Talitha's life and although he'd come to Restructure to have his life changed that change had in the end actually been a mutual experience for Talitha as his consultant. Sadly for Talitha, Dean would actually be leaving her client list fairly soon but the memories of his situation and the work that Talitha had done with him would as far as Talitha was concerned, never leave her heart.

Restructure and Professor Heisner's work certainly couldn't solve all the problems in the world, or even all of the problems in her clients' lives but if Talitha could touch and improve just a few of their lives and make them smile then that really was enough for Talitha. The work that Talitha and Professor Heisner did each day had the potential to bring about very positive changes to her client's world and their existence as Talitha had now seen from Dean's situation and that reality made her job slightly more meaningful and a lot more worthwhile in her sight.

Once Dean's notes had been written up and then submitted, Talitha prepared to leave work for the day as it was five thirty on the dot and the evening had already jumped into Talitha's life. Usually, Talitha liked to submit her client notes on the same day as a client's actual consultation as that meant, there would be one less thing to do the next working day but on some occasions, she'd begun to realize that might not actually be possible. For that day however, quite fortunately, it actually was possible and that comforted Talitha as she walked towards the reception area.

Before Talitha actually left the building that evening, even though she was actually quite eager to go home, she decided to pass by Professor Heisner's office and see him in person as she wanted to relate the details of Dean's session to him. Every working day after five from what Talitha knew, Professor Heisner could be found inside his office as he usually abandoned his hideaway laboratory at five on the dot and then spent time in his office which he utilized to focus on paperwork and the client notes that Talitha submitted to him each working day.

True to his usual form, Professor Heisner was indeed inside his office and as Talitha tapped gently on the door, he immediately called out to her as he invited her to enter the room. Excitement gently bubbled away just below the surface of Talitha's skin as she entered inside the Professor's office, sat down and then faced him as she prepared to relate to him the details surrounding Dean's procedure earlier that afternoon. For at least five minutes, Talitha described every moment of Dean's actual consultation that day to Professor Heisner as he sat quietly and just listened, smiled and nodded his head before he actually began to respond.

"You know Talitha, clients like Dean are one of the main reasons that I started Restructure in the first place." Professor Heisner explained. "My intentions were to help and assist people like Dean that face physical obstacles and those are exactly the kind of people I intended to benefit from my work. Yes, the breast enlargements, nose jobs and penis upgrades pay the bills but those are predominantly artificial cosmetic enhancements that allow the clinic to operate financially, so that we can provide a service to those who could not find solutions elsewhere."

"I just couldn't believe it Professor Heisner, the leg Download actually replaced all of the scar tissue." Talitha gushed. "It was like seeing a miracle happen right before my eyes. Your work is amazing Professor Heisner, absolutely amazing."

"Thank you Talitha. I've found that in order to deliver the good I wish to deliver to humanity, I will also have to endure the many superficial demands from a society that craves unrealistic levels of physical perfection but those superficial demands are not the sole purpose for the creation of Restructure and nor are those demands the main reason, or motive for its existence." He explained. "I call those deviations from my overall objectives, compromises for the purpose of financial sustainability as those compromises are the realities of our world and those compromises actually pay the bills. I'm just glad that today however, you finally had a chance to see and understand the core underlying purpose of Restructure and my work."

"Yes Professor Heisner, now I really do understand." Talitha immediately confirmed as she nodded her head.

"Good. Now you enjoy your evening Talitha. I really have to get on with some work, so you'll have to excuse me I'm afraid." Professor Heisner mentioned as he suddenly rose to his feet and politely dismissed her. "I'll see you tomorrow."

Talitha nodded her head as she began to stand up. "Yes, I'll see you tomorrow Professor Heisner." She immediately agreed.

"And don't worry Talitha, Yucala did actually raise the biscuit issue with me, so I've asked her to order some biscuits next week, along with the other supplies that we usually buy." Professor Heisner suddenly mentioned as he strolled towards the door and then opened it.

Talitha grinned. "Thanks Professor Heisner." She replied.

Just a few minutes later, Talitha left the building and as she entered inside the parking lot and headed towards her vehicle, she thoughtfully regurgitated her conversation with Professor Heisner as she walked and the events of the afternoon. What had initially appeared on the surface like a quite superficial provision of services inside the walls of Restructure had now suddenly changed as the full potential of the Restructure system had been realized and very clearly identified in Talitha's thoughts and that potential had absolutely blown Talitha's mind.

The engine of Talitha's car began to purr as she started it as she prepared to embark upon the usual drive home, she simply couldn't wait to tell Bryson about what had actually happened that day as it had been so absolutely huge. Every inch of Talitha's being continued to silently rejoice as she drove out onto the nearby highway, Bryson would be so proud, she quietly decided with not just Professor Heisner's clinic but also with Talitha herself and her new job.

In essence, Professor Heisner's work now had a very clear purpose, an admirable and heroic purpose which sat upon a much more worthy plane than the various cosmetic surgeries and beauty clinics that Talitha had worked for in the past and that definitely demanded a deeper level of respect from the entire world. Now Talitha fully understood the deeper, more profound motivations that had sparked Professor Heisner's research work and the ethical, benevolent logic behind the actual creation of his clinic. Moments like the one that Talitha had shared with Dean would not happen every day, or even very often but Talitha definitely felt, those kind

343

of moments totally justified the existence of the Restructure and her presence at the clinic itself.

At times and along the way, Talitha would definitely encounter clients that acted irrationally or illogically, purely to fulfill superficial desires like Saskia and perhaps such clients would never truly be satisfied by the services that Restructure provided but they were not the reason for Restructure's existence. Such clients would perhaps always be a constant source of irritation and they would exasperate Talitha as they'd provoke her to question the services that she was attempting to provide to them but in the larger scheme of things, there would also be clients like Dean and those clients would definitely make her job, absolutely worthwhile.

On the Tuesday morning as the day arrived, Talitha's working day was ushered quietly and peacefully into the world and as a mild gentle breeze wound itself around the city, Talitha got up, prepared herself for the day ahead and then began to make her way to work. Regardless of the peacefulness that surrounded Talitha as she drove, she was very much aware that her working day ahead would be extremely busy as she'd agreed to see three clients that day instead of the usual one or two.

An increase in the number of client consultations that were due to occur that day had mainly been because two new clients had now been added to Talitha's client list and also because Professor Heisner had arranged a meeting with her on the Friday afternoon which meant, Talitha's usual mid-afternoon Friday slot had not been available in which to see anyone. Due to her lack of availability on the Friday afternoon, three clients had therefore been squeezed into Talitha's Tuesday to ensure that she saw everyone that week in a timely fashion which would have really worried her but there was one small saving grace that stopped her mood from descending into a panic driven state and that was the clients that she would be seeing. Fortunately, the three clients in question were the least problematic clients on Talitha's current client list and that at least provided Talitha with a drop of reassurance as she parked her car inside the Restructure parking lot that her day would not descend into a hectic, stressful pile of chaos.

Inside the reception area, everything was quiet as Talitha entered the building but that was to be expected really as not many people actually visited the Restructure clinic during the week besides Talitha's clients and the odd delivery person. Occasionally, the odd visitor would show up to see Professor Heisner but those visits absolutely never happened very early in the day and rarely even occurred at all. According to Professor Heisner, when the clinic took on more clients and staff, things at Restructure would definitely change and become much busier but for now the working environment was quite relaxed, very peaceful, extremely calm and rather quiet.

A warm, bright smile as usual greeted Talitha from behind the reception desk as Talitha began to walk through the reception area but due to the fact that Yucala was engaged in a phone conversation, only polite nods of acknowledgement were exchanged as Yucala acknowledged both Talitha's presence and her arrival. Just as Talitha was about to walk towards the corridor that led to her consultation room however, Yucala suddenly motioned to her as she requested that Talitha should wait for her call to end. Upon Talitha's face there was an amused smile as she immediately obediently complied with Yucala's gestures, despite the lack of verbal interaction and waited for her to finish her discussion which lasted for just a few more seconds.

"Today, I have something very special for you Talitha." Yucala mentioned as she touched the screen in front of her to end the phone call and then leant towards the back of her chair where her handbag was situated. She quickly plucked a plastic container out of it and then put the container down on top of her desk and smiled. "Last night Thomas, one of my sons actually made these."

Yucala announced proudly as she opened up the container.

"Are you serious Yucala?" Talitha asked as her eyes began to widen in total disbelief. "You mean, he actually went inside the kitchen and then cooked something. Wow, I'm so proud of him."

Yucala grinned and nodded. "Yes, he really did and he even baked something for everyone. These are Coconut cakes. We ate them last night, straight after dinner with some custard." She explained as she opened up the plastic container. "Go ahead take one, or even two, help yourself."

"Now that's two miracles I've seen in just twenty four hours." Talitha joked as she eagerly plucked one of the delicious looking cakes from the plastic container. "Wow, these look absolutely great and they even have cherries on the top of them."

"I know, it's absolutely amazing." Yucala replied. "I'm going to buy him something special this week, just to encourage him."

"He definitely deserves it." Talitha agreed. "Hopefully he's set a positive example now for his brothers and hopefully, they'll all follow his lead."

"And my husband." Yucala added. "He could do with a nudge in the direction of the kitchen. It's almost like that room's become a forbidden zone to him."

Talitha giggled and then took a bite out of the small round cake. "You know Yucala, this Coconut

Cake is absolutely delicious, tell Thomas I said thank you and that it was totally fantastic. He can come round to my house and cook dinner for me anytime." She teased playfully.

"Yeah, if he gets really good, I could even hire him out to friends on the weekends to cater for their dinner parties." Yucala joked as she began to laugh.

"Right Yucala, I better get a move on and I'll eat the rest of this with my morning latte." Talitha said as she politely excused herself. "I have three clients to see today and I have to write up all their notes, it's going to be very busy."

"I'll see you later on Talitha." Yucala replied as she smiled.

Every working day since Talitha had joined Restructure, Yucala had brightened up her morning and as Talitha walked towards the corridor that led to her consultation room, she thoughtfully appreciated the warmth and friendship that exuded from Yucala's being every time the two women met. In terms of her nature, Yucala seemed to be a very sweet natured person that did whatever she possibly could do to assist Talitha and she certainly made sure that Talitha was fully equipped each week to not only face her clients but also to look after them extremely well.

For Talitha, the rest of her Tuesday morning went by almost in a flash, possibly due to the fact that she was so busy and had three clients to actually meet that day. At exactly eleven, Renee showed up and the two women quickly settled in as her consultation began as Talitha began to prepare some nose images for her perusal. Technically, the nose procedure was actually supposed to be Renee's last procedure but Talitha had invited her back for a client closure session and also a follow up appointment about one month later, purely for counseling purposes and Renee had agreed to attend both.

Initially, Talitha had expected most of her time at work to revolve around actual physical bodily enhancements but once she'd met her first real human clients, she'd rapidly begun to realize, the counseling part of her job would play a much more significant role than she'd initially imagined. In many ways that actually intrigued, challenged and interested Talitha as prior to her employment at Restructure, her work experiences had purely been focused upon the very physical aspects of a client's needs and had not actually delved into any psychological considerations at all.

Once Renee's new nose had been selected and then downloaded via the Restructure system, Talitha decided to spend some time with Renee just discussing her past procedures, in order to ensure that everything so far had gone as Renee had hoped and planned. The Download procedures that Professor Heisner offered did come at a very hefty price and that meant, Talitha had to actually ensure that each client not only got their money's worth but also that the procedures themselves were not problematic in any way, shape or form.

"How's your love life going Renee and how are your new breasts?" Talitha enquired. "And how are the new lips are they as kissable as you hoped they would be?"

"Great and not so great I guess." Renee replied as she smiled. "I kind of dumped someone I'd just started seeing last weekend as for one reason or another, I suddenly felt like I really couldn't stand him anymore."

"That does happen sometimes." Talitha said as she giggled. "You meet someone and think they're amazing then it turns out they're really a jerk."

"Yeah, it was a bit strange really but I've met someone else now, so I'm seeing how that goes." Renee explained. "I'm seeing him again on Thursday and although he's slightly younger than me, he's a total stallion and raring to take me out on a ride."

"That was fast." Talitha replied.

"Well, I was celibate for almost a decade Talitha, so my conveyor belt of love right now is very quick. I've got a lot of years to catch up on. I made an executive decision whilst I have the time and my newly acquired assets, I'm definitely going to make the most of them." Renee insisted. "I can't really be celibate for long periods of time right now as my biological clock is definitely ticking and time is really running out and I already did that for far too long. If I don't settle down soon, I'll miss the flower of fertility altogether."

"Yes, I know what you mean." Talitha agreed. "It's a huge pressure really and most of us face it as women at some point in time."

"And I missed out on so many years." Renee mourned. "So I'm already at a disadvantage."

"I don't think it matters really Renee, you could have spent those years with an complete asshole that made your life a total misery and if you'd had a child with someone like that then you're whole life would have been a complete nightmare." Talitha gently reassured her. "Pardon my French but I'm not sure there's a more polite word to describe an asshole, rather than the word asshole."

Renee giggled.

"Your new nose looks absolutely great, so now you have the luscious lips, the delicate nose and the demobilizing breasts. You'll knock their socks off and bowl them to the ground." Talitha teased playfully. "Those men won't stand a chance, they'll be on their knees begging you for a date instead of you hiding away from them."

"After next week, I probably won't see you again Talitha." Renee suddenly mentioned in a solemn tone.

"Well, you can come back for your follow up appointment in one month's time, if you want to that is. They'll probably put someone else in your client slot that'll be a total headache and absolutely awful." Talitha joked as she gently shook her head. "And then I'll be calling you up and begging you to return."

Renee giggled. "Of course I'll come back for my follow up appointment and I could always send you an email from time to time and let you know how I'm getting on." She suggested. "That way, we don't lose touch completely."

"Sure that would be lovely Renee." Talitha agreed. "And if there's any engagements, or weddings, or even christenings I'd like an invite."

"Definitely Talitha and if I get married, I'll ask you to be one of my bridesmaids, since I wouldn't even be dating anyone if it wasn't for you. You really changed my life and especially my love life." Renee replied as she smiled. "And I really needed that change. Thank you so much."

"Well, Professor Heisner played a huge part in that Renee." Talitha said as she smiled. "His work is amazing."

"Yes, it really is." Renee quickly agreed. "You're both totally amazing and earth shatteringly fabulous."

Talitha smiled.

At around twelve thirty, once Renee had left, Talitha popped out and then quickly returned with a take away lunch as she prepared to have a working lunch and write up Renee's notes. Lunchtime didn't seem to last very long and literally flew by for Talitha and at two that afternoon, Samson very promptly arrived. A warm smile and open arms were quickly extended towards him as Talitha opened up her consultation room door and then politely greeted Samson as she prepared to start his actual consultation. Just a few seconds later, Yucala quickly scurried off, satisfied that she had now completed her human delivery as she returned to the reception desk and Talitha immediately invited Samson inside her consultation room and then offered him a beverage as was usual client practice.

"I really need to sort my arms out this week Talitha." Samson said as soon as he sat down as he jumped straight into his consultation. "My chin will just have to wait until next week."

"Right, for the commercial that you're going to do?" Talitha asked.

"Yes exactly." Samson quickly confirmed.

"Well, I'm sure your girlfriend can wait another week Samson. I mean, she met you with that chin." Talitha encouraged. "If she leaves you in a week over a chin then it really wasn't true love to begin with."

"I'm not sure this relationship will work out Talitha." Samson replied as he suddenly began to frown. "We're already having some major problems and it's only been a month."

"Why, what happened?" Talitha enquired.

"Last week, she said I was flirting with a woman in the street because I was polite to someone else and then she got really angry about it." Samson explained. "And then she actually threw some of my stuff out of her apartment window."

"Oh my goodness. What did you do?" Talitha asked.

"I didn't really want to go near her after that so I didn't call her for a few days." Samson explained. "Then when I did see her, she got even more upset and accused me of cheating. She threw a cup at me and it missed me by inches and I haven't been back since."

"Just how polite were you to this someone else?" Talitha enquired.

"Okay, okay, maybe I was a little bit too charming." Samson admitted as he rapidly began to confess. "She asked me for some directions and I gave her the directions and then I told her that she had a lovely figure and that if she was ever lost again, I'd quite happily provide her with a map to my bedroom and a guided tour in person."

"Wow Samson that was definitely way too much." Talitha advised him. "I mean seriously, you actually said that in front of the woman you're supposed to be seeing?"

"Yes and now, we're not seeing each other anymore." Samson quickly clarified.

"I'm not surprised." Talitha replied.

"The funny thing is, I've never done anything like that ever before. It was really strange, I just felt this sudden urge to kiss and make love to this woman that I'd never even seen before, or spoken a word to." Samson explained. "It was almost like I fell in love with her on the spot."

"Are you normally quite a faithful person?" Talitha asked.

Samson nodded his head. "Yeah, I mean I'm not perfect or anything and I have faltered a few times, like once when my girlfriend was away for like six months due to a family emergency, I did cheat a few times but that was a long time ago." He quickly clarified. "I'm not generally the kind of man that goes out there on the scavenge for women, or for sex."

"Well, just give her some time and perhaps she'll calm down a bit and then she might even forgive you." Talitha advised.

"I don't think so Talitha that relationship is well and truly over. Seriously, she threw a cup at me." Samson replied. "I'm not going back there again."

"Never mind Samson, I'm sure someone else will come along. Here are some arms for you to look at, let me know which ones you like please and then I'll narrow down the range." Talitha instructed as she turned her screen towards him.

"Yeah, I guess it just wasn't meant to be." Samson said as he glanced at the screen that was now populated with images. "Right, let's get down to business, I need some very chunky, hunky arms that look like they could lift a whole ship."

Talitha smiled. "Right are these okay, or you do need something a bit thicker and chunkier?" She asked.

"Definitely a bit chunkier." Samson clarified. "My body needs to look like a tank."

"Right, I'll show you some other arms." Talitha replied as she quickly touched the screen again and it rapidly repopulated with some different arm images. "How are these?" She asked.

"Now that's more like it." Samson boomed. "Now we're talking chunky."

Talitha laughed.

Due to Talitha's very busy work schedule that day, the afternoon disappeared extremely quickly and when four in the afternoon turned up at Talitha's consultation room door, so too did Rita.

An enthusiastic smile adorned Rita's face and she was full of life and energy as she swept into Talitha's consultation room and then quickly sat down. According to Talitha's usual client customs and practices, a beverage was quickly offered to her and the two women exchanged a few pleasantries as Talitha prepared to begin Rita's second consultation. Although when the two women had initially met, Talitha hadn't really felt as if she would be able to relate much to Rita, due to her profession, something about her just seemed really quite likable and her very honest approach to life, the world and herself in a world full of fakery was in Talitha's mind, extremely refreshing.

"What can I do for you today Rita?" Talitha asked as she placed a full cup of latte down on her desk in front of Rita and then sat back down.

"Today, I think I'd like my breast enlargement please Talitha." Rita replied as she smiled. "I'll need my breasts to be as big and bouncy as possible as I have a client that absolutely loves women with huge breasts and I'm working on him at the moment. I have to cater very precisely to his desired dish."

"Okay Rita, well I usually recommend a double D cup size but our range does go up to a double G." Talitha explained.

"I'll definitely need the double G Talitha, I need all guns blazing for this one." Rita insisted.

"Right Rita, I'll just get some breast images up on the screen for you now and then you can pick out the ones that you like and I'll narrow down the range so that we can find your ideal bosom." Talitha said as she touched the screen in front of her.

Strangely and rather interestingly, it suddenly struck Talitha that an obvious trend had emerged in relation to at least three of her female clients, all of whom had independently requested very large breast enlargements. All three women had requested the largest cup size available and all three women had rejected the possibility of a slightly more moderate sized breast increase. Quite strangely, Talitha had suddenly realized that when her female clients went bigger, they really went much bigger and that reality intrigued Talitha as she watched Rita browse through the images on her screen.

During each consultation, Talitha had recommended a more moderate increase to a double D cup size but all three women, Rita, Renee and Saskia had instantly dismissed and discarded her advice and any remnants of caution it contained like coats they had absolutely no desire to wear, or even look at. An uncomfortable feeling of inferiority suddenly began to crawl around Talitha's skin almost like a spider as she glanced at the screen and all the huge breast images it contained which further reinforced her slightly negative thoughts.

Perhaps, Talitha considered glumly as she peeked down at her own breasts which were a reasonable but much more humble D cup, more moderate sized breasts were not seen as desirable anymore. Perhaps the very large, pert, succulent images that now populated her screen were what men really desired and wanted and perhaps, just perhaps, Talitha was the one that was really mistaken.

"Talitha, I think these breasts are really nice." Rita suddenly announced with excitement as she broke the silence between them and pointed eagerly towards an image on the screen. "And this pair look interesting too." She mentioned enthusiastically as she pointed towards another image.

"Right Rita, I'll just narrow down the range for you, based on those preferences." Talitha explained as she touched the screen once again. "And then you can pick out your final five."

A glum expression crossed Talitha's face as she glanced at the very bouncy, peachy round images on her screen again as she began to narrow down the range. Some of the breasts on offer seemed to look quite extravagant and very lavish in comparison to her own natural, lower hanging, almond shaped provisions which always required a bra to keep them upright and pointing in the right direction and in some ways, it almost made Talitha feel slightly inadequate.

Although Bryson had never actually complained about Talitha's breasts, she did begin to wonder for a moment whether he would actually appreciate it if she had an actual breast enlargement herself. Perhaps Bryson didn't really like to say anything, Talitha quietly deliberated but he was a man which meant, he definitely harbored some very human male sexual desires and instincts inside of him, regardless of how much they loved each other and how long they'd been together. Female breasts were just a part of most heterosexual males preferred sexual diet and Talitha absolutely could not deny that fact, or ignore it as it was right in front of her face every single working day.

For the remainder of the afternoon, Talitha quietly decided as she began to process Rita's breast enlargement, she definitely had to focus upon her client's requirements and forget about her own insecurities which had never really been an issue for either her or Bryson. In fact, if Talitha even tried to suggest having a breast enlargement to Bryson, she finally concluded, he'd probably laugh at her. Human beings usually tended to over compensate for something that they felt they lacked, once they had access to it, especially when that perceived shortcoming had impacted negatively upon their lives for a long period of time and almost all three of Talitha's female clients were perfect examples of human beings over compensating for their perceived lacking.

Clients over compensation had absolutely nothing at all to do with Bryson, Talitha, their relationship, or even Talitha's actual breasts and that was something that Talitha herself would definitely have to learn to accept in the long term and not take personally. A gentle smile was plastered across Talitha's face as she forced herself to perk up and attend to Rita's client needs as both women returned to Talitha's consultation room, once Rita's breast procedure had been performed and then sat back down as Talitha began to arrange Rita's next consultation. The end of a very long working day was now definitely in sight and Rita's consultation was the final hurdle before home time and for Talitha that was certainly something to smile about as now, she actually felt quite worn out.

Fortunately, the end of Talitha's long working day finally arrived and as five thirty graced the world with its presence, Talitha gave a weary sigh as some physical signs of fatigue suddenly escaped from her lips. The Restructure system was quickly switched off and her handbag retrieved from its usual spot as she prepared to make her way home. The day had not been very merciful towards Talitha at all and in the end, it had been extremely hectic as she'd attempted to deliver everything related to all three of the clients she'd seen that day, in the very same day.

The drive home for Talitha was very peaceful and quiet however as she made the most of the clear roads and thoughtfully reflected upon the week at work she'd had so far as she drove. Some amazing things had happened already that week but some of her clients, Talitha had also noticed, would soon be leaving the Professor's scientific hands as their requirements had almost been fully met at which point, they would no longer actually require the clinic's services.

Both Talitha's two new clients had already been given appointments that week which been slotted into Talitha's diary and she was due to meet them on the Wednesday afternoon and Thursday morning but the lack of information pricked and aroused Talitha's curiosity as she began to speculate further about each one as she drove. A definite air of mystery surrounded them both but Talitha hadn't discussed either of them with Professor Heisner yet as her week so far had been extremely busy.

Once Talitha's vehicle turned into the familiar streets of her own neighborhood, she rapidly pushed any thoughts of work very firmly from her mind as she prepared to focus on her own real life once more and her very real romance with Bryson. Although Talitha certainly didn't have a pair of double G sized breasts to bring home to Bryson every night, the couple's relationship and the love they shared was a very edible, extremely enjoyable dish that she felt had been crafted from the sweetest recipe on the planet.

A hundred dashes of romance, a portion of dedication, a cup full of charm, a heaped spoonful of devotion and a large splash of chemistry had given them both the perfect dish of love that they could consume and hungrily devour every single night, regardless of the current trends and fashion in breast sizes. Breast cup sizes really didn't matter where Talitha's heart lived and the space that she occupied inside Bryson's heart had never given her any reason to ever doubt that.

When the middle of Talitha's working week arrived, it seemed to plonk itself down inside Talitha's bedroom in a bit of a dismal manner as her alarm suddenly sounded out and she groaned. Another hour of rest was definitely required, Talitha quietly considered as she stretched her hand out from under the duvet and then hit the snooze button but she knew, rather unfortunately, responsibilities and work commitments would not permit that additional hour of rest at all, not in the middle of a working week. Due to the fact that the couple had quite a late night the night before as

Bryson had made love to her into the early hours of the morning, Talitha still felt slightly sluggish as she let out another soft groan and then literally forced herself to clamber out of bed.

Despite Talitha's rather sluggish start to the day however, she managed to arrive outside the Restructure building at about quarter to nine and in plenty of time and as she parked her car inside the parking lot, she began to internally prepare for the working day that lay just ahead of her. The usual two cars that Talitha expected to see every working morning were already parked inside the parking lot and that immediately silently reassured her that everything was right with the world and within Restructure itself as she walked towards the main entrance.

In terms of Talitha's workload that day, she had just two client appointments inside her schedule which was quite a relief as the previous day's three consultations had been rather hectic. The mid-morning appointment was with a new client that she hadn't actually met yet that Professor Heisner had arranged for her and the mid-afternoon appointment was with Charmaine which she fervently hoped Lachlan would not attend.

Quite fortunately that week, Saskia's appointment had been scheduled for the Friday morning which meant, Talitha would see her just before her meeting with Professor Heisner and that suited her perfectly. In terms of Talitha's client list, Saskia was currently one of her trickiest clients and the one that she felt, she would definitely have to discuss the most with Professor Heisner which was actually rather strange as Saskia's father was actually the Professor's personal friend. Despite the two men's personal friendship, Saskia was really proving to be quite handful and Talitha really didn't want to put a foot wrong and so she'd decided to seek further clarity from Professor Heisner on how exactly she should deal with Saskia and her incessant demands.

Just before Talitha began to make her way towards her consultation room, a few pleasantries were exchanged as usual with Yucala and then Talitha parted as she headed towards the crisp white corridor that housed her consultation room. A few curious speculations occupied Talitha's mind as she walked about the new client she was due to see that morning that she knew absolutely nothing about as only a blank profile had been inside the Restructure system when she'd last checked which had been flagged as an 'Urgent Client Intake' and Professor Heisner had provided no further information anywhere else.

Once Talitha arrived inside her consultation room and then switched on the Restructure system, she rapidly discovered that the new client's profile status had now been changed and that instantly intrigued as she sat down and began to inspect it slightly more closely. Inside the Restructure system, the client profile had now actually been marked as 'Highly Confidential' and some of the details inside the profile itself had actually been completed since she'd last checked it, just before she'd left work the previous day.

Suddenly, Professor Heisner's secrecy and the last minute client addition began to make total sense as this client was certainly not a client that he would want to advertise to the rest of the world, simply due to the client's actual identity and his family history. Due to the nature of the Professor's work at the Restructure clinic, Talitha quietly accepted that it was only to be expected that at some point, it would attract some very high profile clients and that some of those clients would want to change their physical identities for extremely unorthodox reasons. Despite that reality however, Talitha hadn't really given those kind of issues much thought and so she'd really been caught off guard and surprised when she'd finally discovered who exactly the 'Urgent Client Intake' profile actually belonged to. In short, the identity of the recent 'Urgent Client Intake' had totally shocked the life out of her and now, not only had she been forced to give such issues a lot more thought but it also suddenly struck her that she would ultimately be responsible for servicing that very sensitive group of client's requirements and needs.

The early part of the morning seemed to literally sped by as Talitha waited nervously for her first client to arrive and at eleven on the dot, when a gentle knock sounded at Talitha's consultation room door, she immediately rose to her feet and then crossed the room as she prepared to open it. On the other side of the door, Talitha immediately found Yucala and a tall, very slim, lean looking man with really dark hair waiting for her and she smiled politely at them both as she prepared to greet and address him. Although the man was not instantly recognizable to Talitha, in terms of his physicality, his name definitely had been and it had rung a hundred bells inside her mind as soon as she'd seen it inside the Restructure system earlier that morning and she knew exactly who he was, or more specifically, who his father was.

"Please come in Sylvester and take a seat. I'm Talitha, your Bodily Enhancements Consultant." Talitha immediately invited as she stepped back from the door and offered the rather slight man directly in front of her a friendly smile and enough space to enter inside the room.

"If you need anything else Talitha, you know where to find me." Yucala said as she smiled and then prepared to depart.

"Yes, thanks Yucala." Talitha replied.

Just a few seconds later, once Talitha had closed the door, crossed the room and returned to her desk, she stood quietly beside it for a moment as she faced the man directly in front of her that was now seated and prepared to offer him a beverage. Interestingly enough, Sylvester actually looked nothing like she'd expected him to but Talitha silently reminded herself that she hadn't actually seen an image of him prior to their actual consultation as his simulated image hadn't actually been attached to his profile inside the Restructure system. According to Sylvester's client notes inside Restructure that Professor Heisner had now prepared, he was just supposed to have an introductory session that day which meant, he wouldn't actually receive any actual procedures at all in that particular client session which suited Talitha perfectly as she knew very little about him as a person.

"Would you like something to drink Sylvester?" Talitha asked.

"Yes please, can I have a coffee?" Sylvester replied.

Talitha immediately nodded her head in response. "How would you like it?" She enquired as she walked towards the coffee machine.

"One sugar please and no milk." Sylvester clarified.

"Right Sylvester. I'll just fix that for you now." Talitha quickly confirmed as she began to prepare his cup of coffee.

"Thanks Talitha." Sylvester replied.

"Sylvester, since you're not due to have any actual procedures today, we'll just be discussing what you will be having in the future." Talitha explained as she returned to her desk with the piping hot cup of coffee inside one of her hands.

"Yes. That's right." Sylvester agreed. "Has Professor Heisner told you why I'm actually here?" He asked.

"Briefly yes but you can tell me too if you like." Talitha encouraged as she sat back down. "That will provide me a bit more clarity regarding your client needs."

"Okay, well I don't need to tell you who my father is." Sylvester began to explain. "I mean, you've probably seen the headlines yourself and you probably recognized my name straight away. Most people do."

"Yes, I did actually." Talitha quickly confirmed.

"My father's crimes have created a lot of problems for me Talitha, purely because I'm a man. My father raped a lot of women and so wherever I go, his horrific legacy of violent sexual crimes follows me around." Sylvester explained.

"How does this affect your life?" Talitha enquired.

"I can't work. I can't run a business and I struggle to have simple friendships and relationships, it's wreaked absolute havoc on every single part of my life." Sylvester quickly clarified. "I've already been given a new identity by the government to assist me but I need a new physical appearance to accompany that name as too many people know who I am now and what I look like and I just can't live my life in peace."

"Yes, I completely understand." Talitha gently reassured him.

"The Professor did promise me that since this is an exceptional situation, I would be able to have all the Download procedures that I need in one consultation." Sylvester explained. "So that when I leave the clinic, after the procedures have been performed, I'll look like a completely different person which would then allow me to restart my life with a new identity and a new physical appearance in place simultaneously."

"Yes, I am aware of that." Talitha immediately confirmed. "Is that something you're completely comfortable with as these physical adjustments do have a huge impact upon not just your body but also your mind?"

"Yes, it's definitely worth the risk to me Talitha." Sylvester immediately confirmed as he enthusiastically nodded his head. "I know it's very risky to perform such a large number of physical adjustments in one day but it's what I really need. There really is no other solution, I can't even live my life right now without being hounded by my father's past."

"This is a very unfortunate situation as you Sylvester are certainly not your father's crimes." Talitha empathized.

"Exactly." Sylvester agreed. "Most people don't have to walk around in life with a big sign on their neck that says, my father is a serial rapist but it's like I do. Everywhere I go, people recognize my name, my father's name, what I look like and so on. It's absolutely inescapable."

"Yes, I can certainly imagine the kind of difficulties your father's horrifying legacy might present." Talitha empathized. "You're constantly living under the shadow of the horrors that he orchestrated."

"I've really struggled to find work as absolutely no one would employ me and even though it's been years since they caught and punished him, people don't forget because his crimes were so horrendous." Sylvester explained as he gently shook his head. "How am I supposed to live, where am I supposed to live, what am I supposed to eat, how am I supposed to survive?"

"So what would you actually like me to do for you Sylvester?" Talitha enquired. "How can I assist you?"

"I need to change every single thing about my appearance, my face, my legs, my arms, my chest, my back and so on. The only thing you can't really change is my voice but I can live with that." He quickly clarified. "But the rest has to go and as soon as possible."

"Do you have a partner?" Talitha asked. "Or any children?"

Sylvester shook his head. "Thankfully no as that would have been even worse." He quickly pointed out. "I mean then I wouldn't have been able to just get up and go to start again somewhere else as my life would have definitely had an impact upon their lives."

Talitha shook her head sadly as she listened to him speak. "Let me know when you'd like to proceed with the actual physical changes so that I can prepare all the required Downloads in advance for you. Would you prefer to choose them yourself, or would you like me to do that for you?" She asked.

Every ounce of Talitha's being empathized with Sylvester's predicament as she waited for him to respond, his life and his father's past was an extremely difficult cross to carry and especially for a male son. Life wasn't always kind as Talitha knew and people weren't always accepting or understanding and quite possibly, she quietly concluded, if Sylvester had been a woman, he might not have actually faced such a crippling backlash for his father's horrific crimes.

"I think if we can go through the various options together and we both make some suggestions, we might just be able to come up with something semi acceptable together." Sylvester suggested.

"Sure between us, we should be able to come up with something suitable." Talitha immediately agreed as she smiled. "When would you like to begin Sylvester? We can start looking at the various options now if you'd like?"

"Yes, now would be good Talitha." Sylvester enthusiastically confirmed as he began to nod his head. "I need to change my whole appearance as soon as I can really but I haven't fixed an actual date yet. I'm waiting for some documentation, so I should have a date in about a week or so.

"Right." Talitha replied.

"You know Talitha, sometimes I really hate who I came from and even who I am. Other people's parents go and join the golf club, if they need something special to do in life with their spare time but my father, well he had to be a serial rapist." Sylvester mourned as he shook his head.

"You really can't blame yourself Sylvester, your father wasn't well and his conduct and behavior really isn't your responsibility." Talitha immediately reassured him. "You can't punish yourself, or hate yourself for his crimes."

"Someone once said to me that I should look on the bright side that at least my father didn't kill any of the women he raped but I feel like, he'd have done the whole world a favor if he'd just killed himself." Sylvester explained as he glanced at Talitha's face. "Can you imagine actually thinking something like that about your own father?"

"Let's start with your legs Sylvester." Talitha said as she touched the screen directly in front of her. "What do you think of these legs?" She asked as she quickly attempted to divert and focus Sylvester's attention once more upon the present and his possible future. "You Sylvester, have a future to plan."

STRATEGIC DEFIANCE

Unusually that Wednesday afternoon, Yucala did not actually knock upon Talitha's consultation room door until at least half an hour after Talitha's mid-afternoon appointment had been due to begin but Talitha wasn't surprised when three arrived and Charmaine didn't.   Earlier that day Talitha had actually received a call from Yucala to notify her that Charmaine would be running slightly and so her late arrival was expected and Talitha had already factored it into her day and adjusted her performance of tasks accordingly.   One huge concern hung inside Talitha's mind however as she crossed her consultation room and prepared to face Charmaine and that was of course, the repugnant, vile, extremely distasteful Lachlan.

According to Charmaine's client profile inside the Restructure system, only three pending requests actually remained but because Talitha had promised Lachlan that Charmaine could have a second breast enlargement procedure that meant, there were really four more outstanding requests. Inside Talitha's mind there was absolutely no uncertainty at all that Lachlan would definitely want to pursue that fourth procedure and there was also no doubt that if it didn't actually happen, all hell would break loose. Some time had been provided to Charmaine however, to allow her to either assert herself against Lachlan's rule, or to give her a chance to find a way to challenge his overbearing demands but Talitha knew, she couldn't delay Lachlan forever.

Much to Talitha's utter delight, when she actually opened her consultation room door, she found only Yucala and Charmaine on the other side of it and her heart almost leapt with joy as she immediately noticed Lachlan's absence and began to silently celebrate it. Once Charmaine had been greeted, seated and provided with a beverage, Talitha enthusiastically dove straight into her consultation which she hoped would be much nicer and a lot more transparent without Lachlan's domineering presence and very controlling influence.

Although Charmaine was actually Talitha's client and although they'd actually met on two prior occasions now, the two women had never actually spent any real time alone together during her consultations which in Talitha's mind was something that was absolutely necessary due to Lachlan's dictatorial attitude. During this consultation however that would actually happen and Talitha hoped as she sat down and faced Charmaine that she would be able to develop a deeper understanding about Charmaine's life which would enable Talitha to provide her with the right kind of support as her consultant. Somehow, Talitha had to actually establish the reality that Charmaine had to cope with and live in every day and that would only achievable if Lachlan was not actually around.

When it came to the issue of Charmaine and Lachlan, a conflict of interest definitely existed but not just one as Lachlan was paying for the procedures and whilst doing so, he was exploiting his position of economic power over Charmaine's life and then to make matters worse, the money that Lachlan spent paid Talitha's salary, so it was a bag full of ethical nightmares. In many ways, Talitha was actually quite worried about Charmaine as she wanted to ensure that any changes she made to Charmaine's body were truly, fully consensual and what she actually wanted to happen and not just a coerced decision by a manipulative, controlling male that had the financial upper hand.

"Right Charmaine which procedure would you like to have today?" Talitha asked as she glanced at the screen directly in front of her. "According to the Restructure system there are still three more requests but as you know, you can only have one actual Download on any given day."

For Talitha because this was her first chance to understand Charmaine as a person, minus Lachlan's overbearing, condescending, extremely sexist input, Talitha wanted to make the most of it and she gave Charmaine a warm smile of encouragement as she encouraged her to make an independent decision. The financial position that Charmaine was currently in was not something that Talitha could actually fix, or do anything about but at least Talitha could encourage her to assert herself whenever the chance arose and now that chance had definitely arisen.

"Lachlan said I should have the second breast enlargement today and that I shouldn't do any other procedures until he's with me." Charmaine began to explain nervously as she glanced at Talitha's face.

"I see." Talitha replied as she observed the nervous expression upon Charmaine's face with absolute disgust. "Well Charmaine, you can just tell Lachlan that I refused to do the second breast enlargement today as I didn't feel that your back was strong enough yet and then you can choose whichever procedure you like."

"I think if I do that Talitha, Lachlan will be very angry." Charmaine quickly pointed out.

"Charmaine, you're a second class citizen in your own life. Don't you worry about Lachlan and his anger. Let me worry about that, that's what I'm here for." Talitha immediately reassured her. "Besides Lachlan's not here to get angry with me today, so he can keep his angry for another day."

Charmaine smiled. "Okay then I'd really like to have my stomach flattened today." She replied. "That's something I've wanted to do for a while. I don't go to the gym because Lachlan doesn't really want me to go there on my own and he always says, he's too embarrassed to go there with me. I've put on quite a lot of weight recently and a lot of that weight seems to like my stomach."

"I know that feeling, every time I eat a donut at lunchtime, I wonder where it will go and then I have to walk around the parking lot ten times before I get in my car to drive home." Talitha joked playfully. "Just to make sure I get rid of it."

Charmaine giggled.

"Right here are lots of choices Charmaine. If you can choose some images for me please that will provide me with some examples of how you would actually like your stomach to look and then I'll be able to narrow down the range based on your

379

preferences." Talitha explained as she turned her screen to face Charmaine. "Take as long as you want Charmaine, there's really no rush as I don't have any other consultations this afternoon."

"Thanks Talitha." Charmaine replied appreciatively as she smiled and nodded her head. "You know, Lachlan's just being Lachlan, he's always been like that. His family are very wealthy and he's their only child. I've known him since high school, we met through one of my friends."

"And that's fine Charmaine but Lachlan doesn't rule my world and he's not the king of my kingdom." Talitha quickly pointed out.

Unlike Renee and Rita, Talitha's attitude differed greatly with regards to Charmaine's breast enlargement but that difference as far as Talitha was concerned was totally justified and not without good reason. Essentially, Talitha felt as if she had to protect Charmaine as her two other female clients were two financially independent, mature women making independent choices whereas Charmaine certainly wasn't. Due to Charmaine's financially dependent position and her romantic situation, neither of which seemed very positive, Talitha felt slightly reluctant about actually participating in her client sessions at all but Professor Heisner had not pulled Charmaine from Talitha's client list, so she really had no choice. Regardless of the difficulties however, Talitha had persevered and she'd tried to manage the situation to the best of her abilities but it grated against every ounce of her being and so too did Lachlan.

"Lachlan just wants the best in life really." Charmaine explained. "For us both."

"What would you do Charmaine, if one day you woke up and suddenly Lachlan wasn't there?" Talitha asked. "How would you live?"

"I'd get a job." Charmaine immediately replied. "Or go to university. You know when I was in school, I really wanted to be a doctor."

"And you never pursued that as a profession, why not?" Talitha asked.

"Lachlan didn't want me to go to university, so I didn't go. He said he'd miss me too much." Charmaine replied. "And I probably wouldn't have done very well anyway."

"I think you should really think about that again Charmaine." Talitha advised as she gently shook her head. "You can even attend university as a day student. No man that loves you would want you to sacrifice your whole life for them."

Clumps of vomit seemed to rattle around inside the bottom of Talitha's stomach as it rapidly began to turn over as she considered Charmaine's sickening explanations which very clearly indicated that Charmaine had been totally and utterly brainwashed. Quite obviously, Charmaine had been controlled by Lachlan for years and it really bothered Talitha that no one had done anything about it, or challenged Lachlan about his controlling behavior.

"The university I applied to and got accepted by was quite far away and that's why Lachlan didn't want me to go." Charmaine explained.

"Have you managed to find any tummies that you actually like the look off yet?" Talitha asked.

"Yes, I really like these Talitha." Charmaine replied enthusiastically as she pointed towards some of the images on the screen.

"Right, I'll just narrow down the range for you now." Talitha said as she touched the screen once more and the images began to change.

Another hour rapidly sped by as Talitha spent slightly longer with Charmaine than her allocated appointment slot. The additional time spent, in Talitha's opinion, would definitely be worth it and was absolutely necessary as to have time with Charmaine alone without Lachlan being present was an occurrence that she was unsure would ever actually happen again. Once Charmaine's client consultation ended, Talitha escorted her back to the reception area and then returned to her consultation room to write up some notes but her stomach continued to turn over and over as Talitha quietly regurgitated the details of the discussion that the two women had engaged in.

DOWNLOADABLE

For Charmaine, the journey home from Restructure was absolutely nerve wracking as she prepared to face Lachlan and let him know that the second breast enlargement had not yet actually been performed. Due to an urgent business meeting that involved the family business which he officially worked for, Lachlan had been unable to attend her consultation that day but as she entered into the home that the couple shared each day and made her way towards the kitchen, she readied herself for his return which she knew would definitely happen shortly.

Some efforts were quickly made to appease Lachlan before he even arrived as Charmaine set the large mahogany dining table inside the kitchen for dinner and then began to cook one of his favorite dishes. The culinary peace offering was an attempt to keep Lachlan calm and an attempt to avoid the potentially angry reaction to what had taken place inside Restructure earlier that day as Charmaine knew, there was a potential storm brewing inside Lachlan's mind. Huge explosive issues now loomed just upon the horizon between the couple that evening and silently awaited detonation as soon as Lachlan arrived home as he would definitely carry out an inspection of Charmaine's breasts and expect to see much larger results.

The reality was as Charmaine waited inside the kitchen that there was absolutely nothing that Charmaine could do now to avoid his scrutiny, his questions, or even his potentially angry response, simply due to the fact that the second breast enlargement hadn't yet been performed. An angry confrontation was almost inevitable as Lachlan was absolutely going to hit the roof as in Lachlan's world, the word compromise just didn't exist and the double D cup sized breasts were a mountain away from what he wanted and what he'd ultimately paid for.

Another issue that worried Charmaine was what might happen if Lachlan actually discovered that Charmaine herself had opposed him and gone against his very precise demands. Technically, it was Charmaine's body but financially, Lachlan had paid for exactly what he had wanted to happen to it and a double D cup size wasn't what he'd wanted to happen and they both knew it. A thorny, prickly bed of romance existed between the two that was by now very well defined with established parameters and they both understood exactly where those boundaries lay. Lachlan had access to all the wealth in their relationship and that ultimately meant, Lachlan called all the shots.

Gradually over the years, since they'd first met, Lachlan had become worse and his controlling behavior had now even extended to Charmaine's own body and she definitely realized it but there was very little that she could actually do about it. Several times, Charmaine had actually asked herself how their relationship had ended up that way but there seemed to be no logical explanation and somehow it had just happened, quite gradually and very discreetly and now, there was very little she could do to change it.

At one point in time Charmaine had hoped that Lachlan would change as not all men that were wealthy were as domineering as Lachlan but he had a certain kind of mentality, especially when it came to the women in his life and that seemed to be absolutely unchangeable. Despite his weaknesses and his failure as a lover however, Charmaine had faithfully stood by his side over the years as she'd continued to hope and wish that things could be different and that Lachlan could be different but her wishes had fallen on infertile ground and had breed nothing but weeds of indifference that Lachlan had either ripped to shreds, or just ignored completely.

Just one thing stood between the couple and their potential happiness as far as Charmaine was concerned and that was Lachlan's dictatorial tendencies and Lachlan himself. Despite the fact that Charmaine loved Lachlan dearly, she absolutely abhorred his behavior and his demeaning attitude towards their relationship and her as it definitely put a strain on her and their relationship. Somehow over the years, Charmaine had managed to find a way to cope with Lachlan however as she'd carried the burden of his harshness upon her shoulders and lived for the most part in submission to his rule but it was definitely far from the ideal situation and a million miles away from the type of relationship that she wanted to have.

Regardless of all the difficulties that Lachlan's attitude towards Charmaine presented, she'd managed to find a way to appease Lachlan and found a way to sustain some kind of peace within the imbalanced equilibrium of control that leant more heavily in Lachlan's favor. At times however, Charmaine felt as if she was walking on eggshells as she delicately tiptoed across his world, eggshells which she had to avoid crushing each day as each step she took could invoke Lachlan's anger and his temper might flare and an explosion of rage would be set off like an explosive firework. An unpredictable temper seemed to constantly bubble away just below the surface of Lachlan's skin like hot lava that just waited to erupt inside the fiery heart of a live volcano and if the wrong word was said, the wrong look given, or the wrong attitude presented, an angry eruption would be triggered and provoked.

Suddenly, the front door banged shut and Charmaine almost winced as she was abruptly shaken out of her thoughts and her mind was alerted to Lachlan's arrival. The kitchen where Charmaine had chosen to wait for him was quiet as she nervously waited for him to walk along the hallway towards her and the kitchen. Both parties were fully aware of where she'd been that day and what she'd been supposed to do when she'd arrived at her actual destination and both parties knew exactly what Lachlan expected to see when he arrived home.

A nervous silence filled the kitchen as Lachlan entered inside the room, drew closer to Charmaine and then kissed her on the cheek. In a matter of just seconds, a quick glance was cast down at Charmaine's breasts as Lachlan stepped back and began his inspection as he attempted to analyze the results of the procedures that Charmaine's body had undergone that afternoon. An expression of total disgust, distaste and dissatisfaction rapidly crossed his face as Charmaine silently braced herself for the wrath that was sure to follow.

"That's not what I paid for Charmaine." Lachlan barked angrily. "They are not what I paid for." He shouted as he suddenly snapped and a whirlpool of anger began to swirl around inside of him.

Anger seemed to seep out of Lachlan's every pore as Charmaine watched him quietly and hardly dared to even breathe as he pointed towards her breasts in an accusing manner, breasts which he obviously felt were totally inadequate and completely offensive in his sight. Every part of Charmaine's body began to tremble with fear as she tried to swallow nervously but her throat grated as fear rapidly dehydrated her airwaves. A strange dryness which felt like the sands of a desert under a hot burning sun had gripped Charmaine's throat and her throat now felt extremely parched as she struggled to breathe and fought to lubricate it but saliva seemed to be in very short supply and not even a single drop was present.

Every word that Lachlan had spoken had pounded into Charmaine's ears almost like an iron fist as she quickly glanced nervously around the kitchen in an attempt to find some kind of distraction that could perhaps provide an escape from Lachlan's angry tongue. A monstrous argument was definitely heading Charmaine's way and as it loomed upon the not too distant horizon, she desperately scanned the room for something and anything that could perhaps distract Lachlan before it managed to fully arrive. Despite all her good intentions however, her search was absolutely pointless and as Lachlan's eyes burnt into her skin like hot piercing rods, she quietly accepted that there really was nowhere else to run and no possible distraction she could find that might soothe his anger. Nothing on the face of the planet would calm Lachlan down now and that meant, Charmaine simply had to face him and accept his wrath.

"Lachlan, at the clinic today they said that my back wasn't quite ready for the second breast enlargement." Charmaine began to explain. "They felt that the weight would be too heavy for me right now. They want to give my back a bit more time to adjust." She pleaded.

Eyes full of angry accusations rapidly searched Charmaine's face as she carefully tried to avoid the angry confrontation that she knew was due to follow.   Deep down inside herself, Charmaine actually knew, she had really actually defied Lachlan that day and that his anger was now a direct result and consequence of her defiance. Anger seemed to seep from every part of Lachlan's body and face as Charmaine nervously attempted to soothe the burning flames that had been stirred up inside of him and pour soothing words upon Lachlan's fiery temper.

"I think they'll do it the next time I go there." Charmaine quickly tried to reassure him as she rapidly clutched inside her mind for some calming words and some straw like excuses. "I've made dinner, it's your favorite."

Not even the remotest grain of truth was present in Charmaine's remarks but Lachlan suddenly seemed to accept her gentle reassurances as he glanced at her sharply and then sat down beside the dining table as he prepared to eat the meal that Charmaine had prepared for him earlier that day. The anger that had seethed inside of Lachlan and that had threatened to spill out of his pores and erupt into a full scale physical confrontation, suddenly seemed to subside as he appeared to calm down slightly. A filled plate of food was quickly placed gently down in front of Lachlan as Charmaine served him the beautifully prepared marinated medium rare steak that she'd cooked for him just before he'd been due to arrive home with a nervous smile upon her face.

"They're just making sure I don't suffer from back ache." Charmaine insisted. "It's really nothing to worry about. It's just a health precaution they take."

"As long as that's all it is." Lachlan muttered.

Fortunately for Charmaine, the soft, gentle words that she spoke and the beautifully prepared evening meal, somehow began to soothe Lachlan's anger like a cold liquid that ran down the back of a red hot, raw sore throat as he began to relax. Hunger suddenly seemed to overtake Lachlan's mind and body as he glanced down at the appetizing plate of food in front of him and then completely abandoned any further explorations of what had actually happened earlier that day. The couple both knew that nothing could, or would be sorted out that evening with regards to Charmaine's breasts and Lachlan finally seemed to accept that as he suddenly shifted his focus towards his stomach.

Once Lachlan started to eat, a gentle sigh escaped from Charmaine's lips as she internally contemplated just how close she'd come that day to an aggressive confrontation and a very ugly, angry argument. Good food and a humble attitude had saved Charmaine but as she sat down opposite Lachlan with her plate of food as she prepared to eat, she hoped that her face would not betray her guilt as she had actually lied to him that day.

A delicate peace now existed between the two which could so easily have become a war zone that evening, if Lachlan had not actually calmed down. In fact, the romantic harmony that existed between them both was purely maintained by Charmaine's humble submission to Lachlan's rule and any departure from that she knew, would definitely provoke Lachlan's anger. If Lachlan actually ever suspected, or realized that Charmaine had actually opposed him then their relationship would rapidly sink into the realms of a nightmarish hell that she was unsure she could actually endure, cope with or exist in and that was a fact that Charmaine's love for Lachlan could definitely not change.

When the Thursday morning danced into Talitha's life, she greeted the warm bright day with very open arms and bags of enthusiasm as she eagerly leapt straight out of bed as soon as her alarm sounded as the weekend was officially now, almost on its way. According to Talitha's work schedule for that day, only two client appointments had been arranged and the first client consultation in the morning was with a female client that she hadn't actually met yet called Cassandra which Professor Heisner had organized and so that intrigued Talitha as she quickly showered, dressed and then prepared to leave home. The second client meeting in the afternoon was with Rodney, who Talitha had already seen twice and so she wasn't particularly worried about it as he was quite straight forward really and just a bit of a flirt.

From what Talitha knew, when she'd checked Cassandra's profile inside the Restructure system just before she'd left work on the Wednesday evening, Cassandra was the daughter of a very famous model and actress but that was all she knew as her system profile was incomplete. A simulated image of Cassandra had been live on the system however and that had clearly shown that she was a young woman in her early twenties with a rather drab and quite plain looking appearance.

Since Talitha was due to meet with Cassandra first that day as soon as she arrived at Restructure, she headed straight for her consultation room in order to prepare for the consultation ahead and to see if Professor Heisner had actually added any further details to the Restructure system. To some degree, Talitha almost felt as if she'd been left slightly in the lurch however as nothing further had been added and uncertainty began to quietly gnaw away inside of her as she drank her usual latte and waited patiently for Cassandra to arrive.

At eleven on the dot and as the mid-morning arrived, so too did Cassandra and Talitha immediately invited her inside her consultation room and then offered her a beverage as was usual client practice. In terms of Cassandra's appearance, she looked even more plain in real life and that struck Talitha as slightly odd as her famous mother was strikingly beautiful and actually very well known for her good looks. Some pleasantries were politely exchanged between the two women for a few minutes as Talitha courteously tried to make Cassandra feel as comfortable as she possibly could before she began to discuss her actual requirements.

"What exactly would you like to achieve from your client sessions Cassandra?" Talitha asked as she sat at her desk, faced Cassandra and smiled.

"Talitha, I just really want to look beautiful." Cassandra explained. "I have a very beautiful mother and a very beautiful name but as you can see, I'm just a Plain Jane."

"Well Cassandra, everyone has their own opinion and you're attractive in your own way." Talitha immediately reassured her.

"Yes but I'm not that's the whole problem." Cassandra replied. "I look absolutely awful and how on earth do you live up to a legacy of beauty when you look like I do? People expect me to look absolutely gorgeous when they find out who my mother is and I'm definitely not."

"But people always put other people down Cassandra that's how they make themselves feel good." Talitha quickly pointed out. "Lots of people have procedures, your mother probably had some too, not many people are just naturally beautiful."

"At school, they would always ask me if the good looks in my family skipped a generation." Cassandra mentioned. "It was absolutely awful and so embarrassing."

"Children can be extremely cruel and heartless at times." Talitha empathized. "They don't always display empathy and compassion towards others. I'll tell you what, let's start with a few procedures and we'll see how you go with those. Sometimes, when you change one thing, it can bring out the beauty in something else, so you might not need to change absolutely everything that you might think you need to."

"That sounds like a great plan." Cassandra immediately agreed.

"What would you like to start with?" Talitha asked.

"Definitely my nose, then my lips and after that my legs." Cassandra replied. "Oh and and I can't possibly forget about my breasts."

"Right, we'll start with those but you can only have one download procedure per session. Did Professor Heisner explain that to you?" Talitha asked.

Cassandra nodded.

"We just do that as a precaution as these bodily changes are huge and so they can have a huge impact upon your life." Talitha explained. "So we like to take things step by step."

"Yes that's okay, I totally understand." Cassandra agreed as she smiled.

"Right, we'll start with your nose today." Talitha said as she touched the screen in front of her. "And I'll put your other requests into the Restructure system, so that I can work on those at your future sessions."

"Thanks so much Talitha." Cassandra replied. "This has been so awful for me."

Meanwhile on the other side of the Restructure building, inside Professor Heisner's laboratory and more precisely, inside the hidden enclosure, the rest of Restructure's staff and residents had definitely woken up as the animals scratched away noisily inside their cages. The morning had been spent by the Professor engaged in a variety of experiments and each one had been conducted meticulously as Moses had attended to each of the caged creatures' needs. Just as the morning neared lunchtime however, Professor Heisner suddenly decided to abandon his laboratory and return to his office as he left Moses alone inside the hidden enclosure as he had some paperwork to complete that day that required his attention.

Once most of Moses's tasks inside the hidden enclosure had been performed, according to Professor Heisner's very precise instructions and as lunchtime approached, Moses made his way towards one of the cages that contained a small grey squirrel and then plucked it from the row. The small creature suddenly began to make some squeaking noises as Moses headed towards the door and he quickly plucked a bag of nuts from a storage cupboard on his way out and then unlatched the cage door and placed some nuts inside the animal's cage as he tried to quieten it down. Due to the fact that the Professor's experimental work with animals was highly confidential, Moses had to ensure that the squirrel was quiet as he carried it out of the building, in order to avoid attracting any unnecessary attention from anyone else.

Some of the animals inside the other cages contained within the hidden enclosure suddenly began to jump around as Moses approached the door and he glanced back at them as the noise temporarily distracted him from his task. Quite strangely, it was almost as if the tiny animals could sense that one of them was about to be set free and as if each one wanted to join in and be freed themselves.

"Not today my friends, not today." Moses muttered softly as he shook his head and acknowledged their restlessness. "Unfortunately, I have very precise instructions today and you are not included." He politely clarified as he stepped out of the hidden enclosure and then shut the security panel behind him.

Approximately ten minutes later, Moses arrived at the large waste site situated just on the other side of one of the hills that the Restructure building sat directly in front off. The squirrel inside the cage that Moses carried was due to be released that day, so Moses quickly knelt down towards the ground as he prepared to open up the cage and actually release the creature. For a few minutes, once Moses had opened up the cage, nothing actually happened as the squirrel remained very firmly inside it and just chewed upon one of the nuts that Moses had provided and it almost seemed as if the squirrel was totally oblivious to the fact that it was actually being set free.

"Perhaps you're just used to being inside a cage." Moses said as he glanced at the creature's face with a confused expression. "The cage door is open now, you can leave now Mr. Squirrel." He encouraged politely.

Despite Moses's encouragement, the squirrel seemed to totally ignore him as it continued to chew on the nut and didn't even move an inch. The once wild creature seemed to have become so tame and so accustomed to its cage that it appeared to be quite reluctant now to actually leave it. Perhaps it didn't understand what freedom actually was anymore, Moses quietly deliberated, or perhaps it had never actually been wild or free. A hand was gently slipped inside the cage as Moses prepared to physically encourage the squirrel to leave as he really couldn't spend all day at the trash site trying to convince a squirrel to leave it's cage as he had a lot of other tasks to complete that day.

"You're free now." Moses explained as he attempted to physically release the squirrel by hand. "You're really free. No more experiments for you."

Suddenly, the small grey fluffy creature seemed to understand Moses as it leapt forward in a dash and then jumped out of the cage and landed on a pile of junk nearby. One final gentle nod of encouragement was given to the squirrel as Moses shut the now empty cage, stood up and then prepared to depart. Piles of junk surrounded Moses in every direction he looked as he stood quietly and just watched the squirrel for a moment bounce rather energetically across some of the pieces of junk directly in front of him.

"There'll be no more nuts for you I'm afraid." Moses suddenly pointed out to the small creature. "Now Mr. Squirrel, you'll have to find your own food every day."

Nothing but silence greeted Moses as he stood for a few more seconds and just watched the small creature in front of him. The squirrel wasn't paying the slightest bit of attention to Moses however as it continued to nibble away on the same nut that it had been deeply engrossed in eating before it had actually left it's cage. Pieces of junk silently decorated the horizon as Moses glanced at his surroundings and began to speculate as to where the squirrel might actually find a home.

"Perhaps you can find a home somewhere around here Mr. Squirrel and maybe, you might even make some new friends. It's not that bad really, once you get used to it." Moses reassured the creature. He turned and then faced the hill that he'd just come from as he prepared to head back towards the Restructure building. "I'll be going now

Mr. Squirrel, you take care." Moses called out as he began to walk away.

Absolutely nothing but complete and utter silence greeted Moses's well wishes and polite words as he began to walk back towards the hill that lay just in-between the trash site and the Restructure building. Just a few meters away from the foot of the hill there was a very muddy, quite shallow ditch and as Moses approached it, he began to pick his way through the dead animal carcasses and junk it contained as he started to cross it. Further along the ditch there was actually a wooden plank which led across it but Moses had decided not to bother walking that far along the ditch and had opted for the short cut as he'd decided to brave the contents of the ditch filled with death.

The carcass of a dead fox and some dead rats silently decorated the stagnant river of stodgy mud and some of the animal remains were partially submerged in the brown mass that surrounded them. Remains from the creatures that would no longer scurry through the trash heap behind Moses were literally scattered all across the ditch, just on the brink of the trash site, now dead, alone and completely forgotten and Moses gently shook his head as he picked his way through them. Some of the animal remains lay in such close proximity to each other that they even overlapped one another as their carcasses formed small piles and Moses tried to step around each pile, in order to avoid actually touching them.

In the meantime, Talitha had been out having lunch and as she returned to the parking lot, she quickly parked her car inside her usual space and then stepped out of her vehicle. Lunchtime for Talitha had now almost ended which meant, she was due back at her desk as she had an afternoon client consultation to prepare for with the incorrigible Rodney. Quite unusually, Talitha had actually decided to eat lunch inside the diner that day and had opted for a nice pasta dish that she'd found on the lunch menu which had filled her empty, growling stomach sufficiently and given her a break from her consultation room.

Just as Talitha stepped out of her vehicle however, she suddenly noticed Moses on top of one of the nearby hills that the Restructure building was neatly nestled against and his presence immediately aroused her curiosity as she began to stare at him. The other side of the hill wasn't somewhere that Talitha had ever visited before and as far as she knew, there was nothing particularly interesting there but the fact that Moses had been there that lunchtime intrigued her as she watched him walk down the hill and then head towards the main entrance of the building. Perhaps, Talitha began to speculate as she watched him quietly, there was a lunch venue on the other side of the hill and a lunch venue that she knew absolutely nothing about.

Approximately three minutes later as Moses arrived at the foot of the hill and then began to walk towards the front of the building and the edge of the parking lot, Talitha quickly decided to join him, just so she could ask him what he'd actually been up to as her curiosity had definitely been pricked and aroused. The door of her vehicle was quickly locked and then Talitha rushed towards Moses as she prepared to address him and question him further about the hill and where he'd just been but there was a slight lump of nervousness inside her throat as she approached him.

Due to who Moses was as a person and because he really wasn't the most forthcoming of chaps although he would interact with people when you were in his presence, he simply wasn't the type to seek any kind of companionship from, or someone to hold a frivolous conversation with that served no actual technical purpose. At times, Moses seemed to be slightly detached and quite oblivious to the presence of other people around him as he conducted his daily affairs and went about his tasks quite quietly, in a somewhat mechanical manner. If you actually wanted to speak to Moses, you really had to make an effort to do so as he definitely wouldn't as he really wasn't the most sociable chap on the face of the earth and that was something that Talitha already knew.

"Been anywhere nice for lunch Moses?" Talitha asked as soon as she neared him.

"Nowhere special really." Moses replied as he was unexpectedly interrupted from his usual solitude. He glanced at Talitha's face curiously as she began to walk along beside him. "I don't usually go anywhere at lunchtime."

"It's just, well I noticed that you came from the other side of that hill? Is there a diner or coffee shop over there?" Talitha pressed as she sought out an answer to her question in a rather determined fashion.

Moses gently shook his head as they walked towards the entrance of the building. "No, not that I know off." He replied.

"Oh, I thought perhaps there was." Talitha explained as she attempted to justify her rather inquisitive question. She felt slightly taken back by his very short, rather abrupt answer which lacked any real kind of explanation as to exactly what lay on the other side of the hill but she decided to persevere nonetheless as she smiled at Moses. "What exactly is over there?" Talitha enquired as she attempted to satisfy at least one of the questions that now occupied her very enquiring mind.

"Nothing much really, it's just a dump site." Moses quickly clarified. "How was your lunch today?" He asked.

"It was really nice Moses, one day you should come along to the diner with me for lunch, the food there is absolutely fantastic." Talitha offered.

"Perhaps one day I will." Moses replied. He paused for a moment just in front of the main entrance and then turned to face her. "I really have to go now Talitha."

"Sure." Talitha said as she nodded her head.

"I have lots of things to do today for Professor Heisner." Moses explained as he politely excused himself from Talitha's presence.

"I understand Moses." Talitha quickly reassured him. "And let me know when you'd like to go for lunch."

Moses smiled and nodded. "I'll do that and thank you very much for inviting me." He replied.

All Moses left Talitha with as he walked away was a very puzzled expression and even more unanswered questions as she watched him enter inside the building as he left Talitha outside alone. At times there definitely seemed to be a very strange coldness and formality about Moses that was totally detached from life, the world and the people around him as Talitha quietly accepted that she really didn't understand him at all. Sometimes, Moses could actually be quite engaging but at other times, he was extremely odd and although that oddness sometimes made Talitha laugh, at other times it was totally baffling and this was one of those totally baffling occasions.

Quite clearly, Talitha concluded as she began to walk towards the two smoked glass doors directly in front of her, she had approached Moses in quite a social manner and he'd been completely out of his depth. His rather hesitant and slightly reluctant attempts to tread on what seemed to be the unfamiliar waters of social interactions hadn't gone very well but Talitha silently vowed to persevere and make more of an effort in the future, regardless of Moses's rather abrupt departure. Perhaps Moses was actually being evasive, Talitha quietly considered as she stepped inside the reception area and perhaps, just perhaps, he'd actually being doing something really strange on the other side of the hill that lunchtime.

Unlike the slightly cold, rather frosty reception that Moses had displayed towards Talitha, she immediately found a warm smile, very friendly face and pleasant attitude waiting for her inside the reception area as she walked towards Yucala's desk and greeted her with a polite nod. The two women watched quietly as Moses entered into the corridor on Talitha's right that led directly towards Professor Heisner's office and laboratory and began to walk along it, until he silently vanished from sight.

"He's a strange one that one." Yucala suddenly said as she gently shook her head. "Runs hot and cold at times. Very strange."

"He's probably just got a lot to do." Talitha replied as she attempted to justify Moses's quite distant attitude. "You know these scientific types, they're usually involved in very high level brain activities. It's probably quite tiring sometimes." She whispered playfully. "We can't always expect pleasantries from the brainiacs in our midst and Professor Heisner probably keeps him on his toes inside that lab of his."

Yucala giggled. "True." She agreed. "It's beyond me really, sometimes I get a smile, sometimes I don't, it's like buying a lottery ticket."

"Yeah, Moses certainly isn't the most talkative man I've come across, far from it." Talitha agreed as she laughed. "What do you think that cage he was carrying was for?" She asked. "It looked like an animal cage."

Yucala shrugged. "I'm not sure. Perhaps he has pets." She suggested.

"Yes, perhaps." Talitha agreed. "Right, I better get back to work as interesting as Moses and his mystery cage are, work still needs to be done."

"Yes, me too. I've got a dozen calls to make, Professor Heisner wants me to purchase some scientific supplies this afternoon." Yucala said as she smiled.

"I'll see you later Yucala." Talitha replied as she bade Yucala farewell.

Interestingly enough as Talitha made her way back towards her consultation room, she quickly realized, she was actually no closer to finding out what Moses had been doing that lunchtime, or what was on the other side of the hill. The mystery began to intrigue and fascinate Talitha as she stepped back inside her consultation room and wondered what on earth had actually been going on. Inside one of Moses's hands there had definitely been an empty white plastic box that looked like some kind of animal cage and his slightly abrupt, rather evasive responses to Talitha's questions had definitely provoked her to question the strangeness of it all even more.

"Time to focus on work." Talitha muttered as she quietly began to scold herself and gently shook her head. "Moses and his rather strange peculiarities don't pay my bills and that's one thing I definitely know for sure."

On the other side of the Restructure building, towards the very rear of the structure, the Professor waited patiently inside the hidden enclosure in his laboratory for Moses to return as he prepared for a busy afternoon ahead and some experiments. Several very complex experiments had been planned for that afternoon which the Professor would actually conduct upon another squirrel that he had very carefully selected the previous week and two of the robotic frames and so he was quite anxious to make a start.

The squirrel that Moses had been instructed to set free that day had not been deemed appropriate for further experimentation, due to its weight, size and general health and hence it had been released into the wild. Another live specimen and suitable substitute had already been ordered from the Professor's supplier and so the cage that it occupied had been required and intentionally emptied in preparation for the next animal's arrival as the replacement squirrel was due to be delivered the following morning. At times, Professor Heisner did actually wonder if the animals that he released back into the wild would actually survive as they had been born and bred into captivity but it wasn't something that he was overly concerned about as he really had no further use for them besides the experiments that he performed upon them.

Due to the fact that the robotic frames were actually quite heavy and pretty bulky, Professor Heisner actually required hands on assistance from Moses that afternoon as the robotic frames had to be in position before his work could actually begin. At times, much to Professor Heisner's frustration, his work and experiments could be extremely complex which meant quite often, they definitely required four hands and arms instead of just two.

One thing provided Professor Heisner with a slight comfort as he waited however and that was the fact that, his planned afternoon of experiments would not be interrupted once they actually began. The laboratory and the hidden enclosure it housed were only accessible via a retina security coded door and there was only one human being on the planet that could open that Professor Heisner himself. Usually, whenever Professor Heisner was inside his laboratory alongside Moses both the security coded door and the security wall panel for the hidden enclosure would be locked, to avoid any unnecessary disruptions but there were rarely any as no one really visited his laboratory unless they had been expressly invited.

At times, when the Professor had to actually travel, or attend an appointment outside the city which was extremely rare, he would actually change the security settings in order to allow Moses access to both areas in his absence. Someone had to ensure that the animals would be watered and fed when the Professor was absent and he knew that Moses was definitely totally reliable in that respect. Moses had actually been granted access to the most confidential aspects of Professor Heisner's work, purely because the Professor knew, he could definitely trust him one hundred percent but that trust had not been extended to Restructure's other staff members and Professor Heisner was unsure that it ever actually would be.

Despite Professor Heisner's silence as he waited, some noises emanated from the small cages nearby as the animals inside them went about their daily affairs and he began to watch their movements as he continued to wait for Moses. The creatures it seemed, cared very little about whether Moses was actually present or absent, or even if the Professor himself was actually there and that fascinated him. Animals just didn't seem to care very much about human beings at all, Professor Heisner quietly concluded and they didn't actually seem to notice if people turned up, didn't appear, or even if they went missing for months as long as they were fed and watered each day.

Just a few seconds later, Professor Heisner suddenly rose to his feet and then began to walk towards some of the animal cages as he crossed the hidden enclosure and began to inspect them slightly more closely. The animals inside the cages seemed to sense a human presence and began to clamber around their cages quite energetically as they responded to his close proximity to them.

Trays full of food and clean water lay inside each of the cages as Professor Heisner quickly scanned their interior and then nodded his head in satisfaction as Moses had definitely done his job that day when it came to the issue of animal maintenance. Perhaps, Professor Heisner considered thoughtfully, he could ask Moses to put some toys inside their cages as when they rattled around their cages it could be a distraction at times, especially when he was working. On occasions, Professor Heisner had actually considered and entertained the notion of placing some of the animals inside cages together but in the end, he'd felt that doing so would present him with problems such as breeding and overcrowding issues.

Baby animals were the last thing that Professor Heisner wanted on his hands and most animals tended to give birth to a whole litter of offspring, not just one or two and he had absolutely no desire whatsoever to have to cope with those kind of issues. An undesirable consequence of such actions would be that perhaps his laboratory would then become totally overrun with small test subjects and then it would be an absolute nightmare to work in which simply wouldn't do. A potential nightmare could then result from such actions as his laboratory would be filled with noisy, squabbling test subjects as he tried to work and that was a road that he definitely had absolutely no desire to go down and that was one thing, Professor Heisner was extremely certain about.

Suddenly, a small grey squirrel that had been the subject of some of his experiments the previous week attracted his attention and Professor Heisner sauntered towards the cage it lived in and then picked the cage up. Due to the experiments that had been performed upon the animal, the squirrel now had a buffed up chest area that formed two individual bumps which protruded from its body and the Professor smiled as he began to inspect it slightly more closely.

"You look absolutely great." Professor Heisner quietly reassured the creature. "You'll definitely be the hottest squirrel in town now, for a while at least. You guys don't seem to last very long out there, from what I've seen."

The Professor held up the occupied cage in front of his face as he began to admire his work and inspect the squirrel slightly more closely but just as he did so, Moses suddenly entered inside the hidden enclosure and interrupted his discussion with the creature. A smile crossed Professor Heisner's face as he immediately turned to face Moses just before he strode back across the room towards his workbench.

"Moses, it's great that you could make it. I'm going to run a few tests on this creature this afternoon and then later today, you can take it to the usual place and set it free." Professor Heisner instructed as he placed the occupied cage down on top of his workbench and then sat back down beside it.

"Yes Professor Heisner." Moses quickly agreed.

"And once you've done that you can put some more clean water inside the cages for the night." Professor Heisner instructed as he began to prepare for his planned experiments. "This afternoon though, I'll need you to assist me with the robotic frames."

Moses immediately nodded his head obediently in compliance as he took a step backwards. "Yes Professor Heisner." He replied.

Unfortunately however, just as Moses stepped back towards the animal cages, he actually bumped into a piece of equipment, in the form of a metal trolley that always carried a large sack of pet food on top of it and it clattered very noisily as it collided with the ground. An apologetic glance was rapidly cast towards the Professor as Moses quickly bent down and then began to pick up the metal trolley and the sack of food although now some of the contents of the sack had rather messily scattered across the floor.

Professor Heisner glanced at Moses as he gently shook his head. "I don't know Moses, you'll never be a ballet dancer with that clumsy approach." He teased. "It's a good thing you're a scientist really."

413

For Talitha, the Thursday afternoon was going along swimmingly and Cassandra's client notes had already been submitted as she waited patiently for Rodney, her second client of the day, to actually arrive. According to the Restructure system and what they'd agreed during his last consultation, he was actually due to have his leg contour that day and so Talitha began to browse through some images of male legs that she felt Rodney might be interested in as she waited.

True to his usual form when Rodney did turn up, he was full of energy, life and jokes and Talitha smiled as she listened to him speak as she prepared the leg Download for him that he'd just chosen. Whether or not Rodney would ever settle down with one woman and get married was another question entirely but Talitha very much doubted that he ever actually would as he seemed to thoroughly enjoy the lifestyle that he lived. Not one single regret or doubt had ever been expressed to Talitha about his choice in lifestyle during his consultations and so Talitha didn't even bother to discuss the matter any further with him as that issue fell way outside the scope of her role as his consultant.

Later that afternoon, once Rodney's leg procedure had been performed, a few more jokes were shared between the two as Talitha organized his next appointment which she thought might actually be a client closure session but Rodney it seemed had other ideas. Apparently, Rodney had decided that he still required at least one more physical adjustment and so another appointment was quickly made for the following week as Talitha sought to fulfill his request which on this occasion actually related to his ears.

"Since I'm here and since I'm doing this, I might as well get everything I want done in one go." Rodney explained. "So, if I can do my ears next week and then the week after I might even do my feet."

"Sure Rodney, it's really up to you." Talitha replied. "You can be our client for as long as you need our services."

"Not that there's anything hugely wrong with my ears or my feet but I just want to make the most of the clinic's services really, since I'm here." Rodney explained. "I wish I'd found out about Restructure earlier, it would have saved me from a lot of headache I went through at those cosmetic surgeries."

"Well Rodney, Restructure didn't actually open it's doors that long ago, so it probably wouldn't have made much of a difference." Talitha quickly pointed out. "I know exactly what you mean though, I've worked for some of them myself. They can be a total nightmare at times."

"Yeah and don't forget to let me know if you ever become single again Talitha. I provide a very special service too." Rodney mentioned suggestively as he winked.

"How are things going in life generally Rodney?" Talitha asked. "Are there any problems or any changes that you're not quite comfortable with due to the Downloads that you've received so far?"

"Not that I know of." Rodney replied. "I've seen some of my female clients as usual and I've given them their usual servicing. It's not emotional at all for me, so whether they approve of the physical changes to my body or not makes very little difference to me. I'm just making them happy and they pay me for doing that."

"Do you have an actual girlfriend or lover?" Talitha asked.

"No, why are you interested in the vacancy Talitha? I can stop being a client right now, if there's a professional conflict of interest." Rodney quickly suggested. "Eliminate the conflict."

Talitha laughed. "Rodney trust me, I'm very happy where I am right now in terms of romance." She explained. "I just have to ask these things as part of my job, it forms part of our client counseling service."

"Wow, you even counsel me Talitha, this is such a turn on." Rodney flirted playfully.

"Right Rodney, I'll see you next week." Talitha quickly clarified as she suddenly rose to her feet as she prepared to escort Rodney back towards the reception area.

"Definitely, I wouldn't dare miss my appointment with you and stand you up Talitha." Rodney joked as he grinned. He quickly stood up and then joined her. "I'm coming where you're going, don't leave me here alone."

Talitha smiled as she gently shook her head. "You're really something else Rodney." She teased as she walked towards her consultation room door.

"At least I'm unique." Rodney replied.

"Yes, you're certainly unique Rodney." Talitha agreed as she pulled open her consultation room door.

The Friday morning seemed to saunter into the city of Shuttlesburg quite enthusiastically as warm, bright sunshine silently wrapped itself around the Restructure building and the city streets and as the city began to wake up, so too did Professor Heisner. For a change, Professor Heisner had actually gone home the night before which was a quite rare occurrence, especially during the week when he usually opted to stay on the premises and inside the Restructure building where he'd actually created a makeshift bedroom away from home. Inside the Professor's office, a small adjoining room which housed only a single bed and closet had been created that was only accessible to him and that was where he usually spent most of his nights, it wasn't luxurious by any means but it was certainly big enough for him to sleep in and sufficient for most of his daily needs.

Besides the Professor and Moses, no one else that worked for Restructure actually knew about the small bedroom but the Night Watchman knew that Professor Heisner usually stayed on the premises though he had no idea where he actually slept. When the Professor had originally renovated the building, he'd actually ensured that he'd created a suitable space in order to accommodate his personal needs as due to his devotion to his work, he liked to sleep on the premises as often as he possibly could. At least once or twice a week however, Professor Heisner would actually return to his real home, just to ensure that everything inside his domestic residence was completely fine and so the Thursday night that week had been allocated to that very specific purpose.

Once he was fully awake, Professor Heisner quickly began to prepare himself for the morning ahead as he fully intended to reach the Restructure building by seven that morning and his early arrival had been intricately planned the night before. In no time at all, Professor Heisner had readied himself as he quickly grabbed some breakfast, showered, dressed and then began to make his way outside.

The short twenty minute drive around the outskirts of the city suited him perfectly in terms of distance and location as he lived in a quiet gated community just on the outer rims of Shuttlesburg which meant, the Professor could travel around the outskirts and avoid the busy city center completely throughout his journey. His home was far enough away from work to provide him with a peaceful break but close enough to it so that he did not have to drive through the heart of the city center as Professor Heisner absolutely hated being stuck in heavy traffic.

Nothing but silence accompanied Professor Heisner as he drove to work and thoughtfully deliberated over the order of the experiments that he had to perform that day, Moses's assistance would definitely be required as some of his plans were very complex. Once he arrived outside the Restructure building, Professor Heisner quickly parked his car and then vacated his vehicle as he began to make his way towards the entrance of the building and prepared to start work. Every step the Professor took that morning seemed to be unusually gentle as he strode towards the entrance of the Restructure building and it was almost as if a sense of inner peace had flooded out from his body and carpeted the ground under his feet as he walked.

A quick glance down at his wristwatch rapidly confirmed that it was just before seven and

419

Professor Heisner smiled as he silently congratulated himself on his achievement. In terms of his timekeeping, Professor Heisner wasn't always a very punctual person as that required decent sized portions of discipline and organization and at times, his life could be a bundle of chaos as could he. Intelligent chaos, hard working chaos but still chaos clothed in human skin and Professor Heisner was the first one to admit it as he really didn't believe in lying to himself.

Inside the reception area, everything was extremely quiet as Professor Heisner stepped inside the building and as he glanced at the reception desk that was usually occupied by Yucala but which now only contained the slightly less visually pleasing form of the Night Watchman, he smiled. Some polite silent nods were exchanged between the two men as they quietly acknowledged each other's presence before Professor Heisner headed directly towards the corridor on the right hand side of the reception desk that led to his laboratory.

Upon Professor Heisner's face there was a very satisfied smile as he walked as he quietly began to consider the Receptionist and the Bodily Enhancements Consultant that he'd hired to assist him. Both women had served him well and they were extremely competent, highly efficient and very thorough which were all personal qualities that he really admired and appreciated. The dedication and devotion they'd both shown to his work, Restructure and their jobs, really endorsed Professor Heisner's judgment in human beings and indirectly confirmed to him that in these two instances, his judgment had not let him down. Social skills and human relationships weren't something that Professor Heisner was particularly great at and sometimes, his judgment could be slightly below par but with regards to those two positions and people, he was extremely happy about the decisions he'd actually made so far.

At around quarter to nine that Friday morning, Talitha arrived at work and as she walked towards her consultation room, she silently rejoiced in the fact that it was a Friday and almost the weekend. Only one client consultation actually remained before the entire working week would be over but rather unfortunately, not everything about that day was going to be great as that morning consultation was actually with Saskia, who had begun to fill Talitha's Fridays with dread. In the afternoon, Talitha had a meeting scheduled with Professor Heisner which promised to be slightly more pleasant but the hurdle of Saskia definitely had to be jumped over before either the pleasantness or the weekend could actually begin.

Just below the surface of Talitha's skin there seemed to be a delicate combination of nerves and excitement that silently bubbled away and mingled together as she stepped inside her consultation room and then made her way towards her desk. The Restructure system was quickly switched on just before Talitha headed towards the coffee machine to collect her usual hot, milky latte as she prepared to begin her final working morning of that working week.

Fortunately for Talitha, the Friday morning literally sped by and as Saskia arrived at around eleven thirty, half an hour after her consultation had been due to begin, she still managed to bring her rather nasty attitude along with her as well as her poor father Marcus. Once again Saskia's father had been dragged along to authorize the large sums of money that Saskia wanted him to expend but there was one small blessing that day, Saskia's appointment that Friday had been made in the morning which meant, Talitha could get rid of Saskia even earlier in the day and enjoy more of her Friday. Usually, Talitha saw Saskia on a Friday afternoon but the change really suited Talitha as it meant her Friday afternoon would be both Saskia and stress free.

The truth quite sadly was that Saskia had a very nasty attitude and Talitha simply couldn't deny that reality, regardless of who her father was actually friends with. Unlike the amazing transformation that had taken place upon Dean's leg, a man that Talitha had felt definitely deserved a decent break, Saskia was certainly far less deserving in her sight and one hundred percent less appreciative. True to Saskia's usual form, she was a pile of stress with an aggravated cherry on top and the cherry on this occasion presented itself in the form of another temper tantrum which seemed to be about how many procedures Saskia could actually have in one consultation.

"I want my procedures more quickly Daddy." Saskia ranted as she stood up and then began to storm around the room. She slammed a book down on the meeting table on the other side of the room. "I can't wait, it's taking so long."

Due to Saskia's anger, the whole room seemed to shake with fear as the loudness of her voice seemed to fill every particle of air inside it. Anger and rage seemed to seep out of her lips and every pore of her skin as her face turned crimson as Talitha watched. Much to Talitha's absolute horror the tantrum continued for at least another fifteen minutes and Marcus did absolutely nothing to stop it. Somehow, it was almost as if Saskia was a child living inside an adult body and as if she was still only two years old and as Talitha watched and listened to her, she was tempted to just sit and watch her until she either became tired or bored.

Eventually however, Talitha rose to her feet as she prepared to make an effort to try and calm

Saskia down as Saskia showed absolutely no signs of stopping and Talitha had decided that the sooner Saskia calmed down and had her procedure, the sooner she could actually get rid of her for the day. A soft, very gentle approach was made as Talitha crossed the room and then gently placed her hand on Saskia's arm as Talitha attempted to appeal to a more humane side of Saskia's nature which she wasn't even sure actually existed.

"I'm tired of waiting Talitha." Saskia moaned. "It's been weeks and I want to look more beautiful."

Patience certainly wasn't Saskia strength and as she pouted like a spoilt child that had been refused a bar of candy, Talitha felt frustrated and irritated by her attitude. Regardless of the fact that Saskia had the body of an adult and the physical attributes of a young woman, she still continued to behave emotionally and psychologically like a two year old as she resumed her angry strop around the room. From Saskia's behavior, it was immediately apparent to Talitha that Saskia was used to getting exactly what she wanted when she wanted it and neither Talitha nor Professor Heisner were going to get in the way.

A horrifying realization rapidly struck Talitha like a cold slab of meat being slapped across her cheek as she glanced at Saskia's face, until all of Saskia's requests had actually been fulfilled these angry outbursts would probably occur at every consultation. Gratification of Saskia's desires however, on this particular occasion was complex as clients were only actually allowed one Download procedure per consultation and that meant, it was highly unlikely that Professor Heisner would deviate from that rule and so Saskia might not actually get what she wanted.

More than just a few things really irritated Talitha about Saskia but due to the fact that her father was Professor Heisner's personal friend that friendship dictated there was very little that Talitha could actually say or do about any of them. Somehow, it was almost as if instead of skin all Saskia had was just a layer of stubbornness that adorned her bones which seemed to be as natural to her as the flesh she lived in every single day and Talitha had already learnt to accept that reality. When it came to Saskia, her body and her decisions, she was absolutely immovable and totally unstoppable and Marcus it seemed, was simply carted around to foot the bill and to satisfy her very expensive tastes and desires. In order to avoid childish outbursts, complex angry arguments and distressing temper tantrums, Saskia had to be given exactly what she demanded, when she wanted it and that it seemed was absolutely non-negotiable.

"Look Saskia, I'm meeting with Professor Heisner later this afternoon, so I'll mention it to him then." Talitha replied as she attempted to bring an end to the angry outburst. "Let's focus on your lip enhancement for today, since that's what you came here for and I'll let you know what Professor Heisner decides."

Much like Saskia's skin which as far as Talitha was concerned had been formed from very stubborn leather, her mind seemed to be formed from a rock of stone that could not be dissolved, eroded, penetrated, or even reduced by the gentle waters of persuasion. In fact, if Talitha even dared to try and interfere with Saskia's agenda, she'd quickly learnt that her advice would be interpreted by Saskia as an obstruction and that it would be treated with absolute contempt. Somehow however, Talitha's response on this occasion seemed to calm Saskia down as she nodded her head and then sat back down as she prepared to select the lip enhancement that she wanted.

Once the lip enhancement had been chosen and performed, Saskia seemed to be quite happy with it and as she left the Restructure building with a triumphant smile on her face, Talitha silently joined in Saskia's celebration, grateful to see the back of her for at least another week. Due to the fact that Talitha had agreed to discuss the issue of more than one procedure per client session with Professor Heisner later that afternoon, the consultation towards the end had been relatively calm and peaceful but Saskia was an absolute nightmare for Talitha and she insisted on being a nightmare every single week.

Unusually for Talitha, her meeting that Friday afternoon with Professor Heisner had been arranged to take place inside her own consultation room rather than Professor Heisner's office and as two thirty arrived, so too did the Professor, very punctually indeed which was also quite unusual. A polite smile was offered to the Professor as Talitha opened the door of her consultation room and then quickly invited him inside and the small boardroom meeting table was then utilized for the purposes of their meeting as Professor Heisner strode briskly towards it.

The laptop that Professor Heisner had brought along with him was quickly opened up as soon as he sat down and Talitha immediately joined him as she sat down at the meeting table directly opposite him. A discussion rapidly began as Professor Heisner started to touch on some of the points that he'd wanted to raise and the large, wafer thin screen on the wall just above the boardroom table suddenly lit up as Professor Heisner began to review some client profiles inside the Restructure system.

"Let's have a look at exactly who you're seeing at the moment Talitha and what they've actually requested." Professor Heisner suggested.

Talitha nodded. "Sure, at the moment I actually have ten clients." She replied.

"Make that eleven, by next week, you'll actually have eleven as I've taken on another client but you won't see all of your clients every week and some of them should actually start to drop of your client list quite soon." Professor Heisner explained.

"Yes that's right, a few clients have almost reached the end of their procedure request lists but a couple do seem to be long term." Talitha quickly clarified.

"Yes and those long terms clients, you'll probably only see once a month, or once a fortnight, once they've achieved their initial goals." Professor Heisner pointed out.

"True." Talitha agreed as she nodded her head.

Approximately one hour passed by as the Professor's briefing continued and each of Talitha's clients were discussed at length as the various issues that they presented were addressed, until they arrived at Saskia's profile. A frustrated look suddenly crossed the Professor's face and there was a slight pause as he sighed and then began to shake his head as he inspected Saskia's profile slightly more closely but no words were actually spoken. All Talitha could do was silently sympathize with the Professor as the hesitation on his part was very understandable as it was a very awkward situation and Talitha could empathize with not only his predicament but also her own.

Disapproval was written all over Professor Heisner's face as Talitha quietly absorbed what the Professor so obviously felt inside but that disapproval it appeared, could not actually be verbally expressed to anyone. Inside the Professor there appeared to be an obvious conflict of emotions, due to his long term friendship with Marcus which denoted deep sentiments of attachment and respect that could not be easily pushed aside, regardless of how unreasonable Saskia's demands were. Being that Saskia was a spoilt brat, she on the other hand seemed to care very little about the men's friendship and the pressure that her demands placed upon it.

"Is everything okay with Saskia's requests Professor Heisner?" Talitha finally asked as she sought to break the rather awkward silence that had filled the room. "It's just that she's asking to have more than one procedure per client session and I said I'd speak to you about it as it's not generally allowed?"

Nothing but silence continued to greet Talitha as she watched Professor Heisner's face cloud over as he gently shook his head again. The obvious hesitation and discomfort that Professor Heisner expressed, silently stated absolutely everything that Talitha actually needed to know,

Professor Heisner was very unhappy about Saskia but there was not a lot that he could actually do about it in his current position.

"Should I say it's against our policy?" Talitha enquired.

"It's very difficult Talitha." Professor Heisner finally muttered. "It's a very delicate situation and Saskia is really hard to handle, even for her father."

"Yes, I did notice that." Talitha agreed.

"That's due to the past really." Professor Heisner clarified. "Their family history is actually quite fractured and there's not much that I or anyone else can do to change or fix that."

"I thought it might be." Talitha said as she nodded her head.

"My hands are tied really Talitha." Professor Heisner confirmed. "There's not much that I can actually do about it, Marcus won't do anything about it at all and I have very little control over Saskia's demands." He explained. "You just have to try and manage the situation the best way you can and just tell her that I'm considering her request."

"Right." Talitha quickly reassured him. "I'll try my best."

From what Professor Heisner had said and more importantly, what he hadn't actually said, Talitha knew the situation with Saskia would continue to be a tricky one. A minefield of demands had to be stepped delicately across and managed somehow during each of Saskia's consultations by Talitha as neither Marcus or Professor Heisner had any control over Saskia's demands and her father actually seemed to enable her by striving to satisfy her in whatever way he possibly could. The dynamics of their relationship had definitely gone wrong somewhere along the line and there was now a very clear lack of appropriate boundaries which Marcus seemed to be unable to set for one reason or another.

Something very negative and a much deeper issue had defined their relationship at some point in time and that something had made Marcus weak and unable to control the daughter that he'd actually given life to. Whatever deep, dark issues lurked in the shadows of Saskia's family history however, Talitha rapidly realized, enlightenment would definitely not happen that day as Professor Heisner suddenly stood up as he prepared to leave her consultation room. Whatever that mysterious issue was that lurked just below the surface of their family history would definitely not be addressed yet and perhaps never actually would be.

"Right that's all for today, I'll see you on Monday Talitha." Professor Heisner said as he began to walk towards the door.

"Thanks for all your assistance Professor Heisner, our meeting today was very insightful and extremely helpful." Talitha replied as she quickly rose to her feet and then began to walk back towards her desk.

"Don't worry Talitha, I don't expect you to have all the answers, this is a first time for you and me both." Professor Heisner politely reassured her. "So if we can put our brains together at times, we should be able to muddle our way through it somehow and perhaps, just perhaps, solve some of our client's quite complex problems."

"I'll try my best Professor Heisner." Talitha encouraged him.

"That is all you really can do Talitha." Professor Heisner advised as he opened Talitha's consultation room door and then stepped out of the room.

Some client notes were diligently written up and then submitted as Talitha made the most of what remained of her Friday afternoon. Time meandered by quite gently as Talitha waited for the afternoon to depart and the evening to begin as that was when the weekend would begin and Talitha couldn't wait to embrace and explore it. When five thirty finally arrived, Talitha gleefully switched off the Restructure system and then joyfully leapt to her feet as she internally began to prepare for the pleasant weekend ahead that she'd planned with Bryson which now silently beckoned to her as it invited her to join it.

Friday evening had finally stepped into Talitha's life and chased the working week away and its arrival was extremely welcome as Talitha very enthusiastically grabbed the first few leisurely minutes of the weekend and happily rushed towards the reception area. The whole weekend would be spent inside Bryson's arms and situated very far away from her client's problems and that was definitely something that Talitha could not wait to actually enjoy as some of her client's problems were very complex in nature.

For Talitha, the drive home that Friday evening was extremely quiet as she thoughtfully considered her own life, her own situation and where she actually worked as she drove. The deep dissatisfaction that drove her clients through Restructure's doors suddenly struck her as she quietly considered her own body and her own physical blessings. Life could have been very different and as Talitha drove along the highway, her mind began to wander and meander thoughtfully as she quietly considered what she might have done, if she had been less physically blessed than she actually was.

Despite the fact that Talitha had worked for several beauty salons and cosmetic surgeries for a number of years now, it wasn't really something that she'd actually ever given much thought to as she'd always felt reasonably content when it came to the issue of her own physical form. Some of Talitha's clients situations however had recently challenged her to actually consider that possible eventuality as her life could have so easily been so very different. Questions and deliberations sauntered gently across Talitha's mind as she drove home towards Bryson as she began to reflect more deeply on what she might have done if she'd not been satisfied, or comfortable with her own physicality. A physical body definitely had to be comfortable enough to live with and inside and although Talitha had always had that comfort, some of her clients definitely hadn't.

Technically, it really was a problem that could be faced by anyone as physical attributes were not always inherited and could not be naturally manufactured and that meant, it so easily could have been Talitha seated in that uncomfortable seat of dissatisfaction as one of Professor Heisner's clients. Society definitely placed a tremendous amount of pressure upon women and even men which denoted that they had to be desirable and attractive at all times and that they had to have certain body parts in the right place which had to be a particular size or shape to be deemed physically attractive. Perhaps, Talitha quietly considered, if she'd been less blessed or less satisfied with her own appearance, she might not have even met or dated Bryson as she would have perhaps lacked the confidence to date anyone like Renee had.

Thoughts continued to flow through Talitha's mind almost like a bubbling stream as she drove towards her home as Talitha began to silently appreciate for the very first time that the physical blessings in life which she naturally had perhaps at times, she'd taken slightly for granted. Some of the very negative experiences that Talitha's clients had endured in life had simply arisen due to their natural physical attributes, something which they had absolutely no control over at all and in many ways, Restructure had actually been an eye opening experience for Talitha, in a very personal way.

Sometimes, Talitha realized thoughtfully, it seemed as if the pain and frustration of others served as a reminder that life really wasn't that simple or straight forward for everyone and now Talitha fully appreciated that fact and that reality. A grateful smile adorned Talitha's face as she arrived outside the two black garden gates that politely and faithfully guarded the driveway of the couple's home each day and then plucked the gate remote from the dashboard of her car.

"Thank goodness it's the weekend." Talitha murmured as she pressed the remote and then carefully began to drive her car through the garden gates into the driveway. "And thank goodness, I'm home."

Inside Talitha's mind, she now definitely possessed a much deeper appreciation for her own life which had gathered, formed and developed within her as she'd worked on each of her client's issues and attempted to provide solutions for them, in order to alleviate the issues they faced and in some instances, the pain and discomfort they'd felt as a result. Restructure had highlighted to her just how important society's perceptions and demands for physical perfection could actually be and the tremendous misery that could be caused to someone's life, if it was deemed that they did not meet an acceptable standard of physical human beauty. The work that Talitha performed at Restructure for each of her clients had definitely provoked her to reflect further upon some of their very negative experiences in life and as she'd engaged with her clients, she'd essentially learnt more about life and about herself.

BEDROOM ANTICS

On the Friday evening, Dean finally plucked up the courage to take his newly enlarged penis for an actual test drive as he'd managed to somehow find a willing female participant that would actually allow him to do so. The woman in question that would be providing Dean with this marvelous opportunity, he'd met quite recently and her name was Chantelle. Due to Chantelle's interest in Dean and her very willing attitude, he'd invited her to his home that Friday evening and much to Dean's surprise, she'd actually agreed to come along.

A mixture of excitement and nerves filled every inch of Dean's mind and body as he began to prepare for Chantelle's arrival and for her to be the first ever recipient of the physical return in the form of sexual pleasure that he expected to deliver from his recent investment. The enhanced male physical assets that Dean now possessed had to be depreciated somewhere and Chantelle seemed to be ready and willing to accept a physical love deposit from him which encouraged him immensely. An immediate attraction had been present between the two that it seemed was mutual and in terms of her age, Chantelle was in her mid-thirties just like Dean although unlike Dean, she actually had two children under her belt from a difficult marriage that she'd endured for ten years and a rather messy divorce.

From what Dean had been told, it really hadn't been a good marriage but then Dean knew, not all marriages were and that marriages rarely materialized into what people had often hoped they would be. Regardless of that romantic catastrophe however and the responsibility of two children from a failed marriage, Dean didn't let anything put him off as Chantelle seemed really interested in him and Dean really liked her.

Dinner had been ordered from a local Chinese restaurant that delivered and once Chantelle arrived, it was immediately consumed by them both and then Dean had very proudly stripped off in front of her. Due to his recent procedures, Dean was now actually quite eager to display his new physical assets to an appropriate female audience and Chantelle was definitely an appropriate female audience. A few giggles escaped from Chantelle's mouth as she sat and just watched him and Dean basked in her admiration as she overtly began to express her appreciation of his now very masculine, athletic looking form.

"Dean, it's…it's….so huge." Chantelle exclaimed as her eyes opened wide with surprise. "Where are you going to put all that?"

"All the more love to love you with Chantelle." Dean joked as he gently pulled Chantelle to her feet and then pressed his body seductively against her.

Just a few seconds later, the black leather sofa inside Dean's lounge rapidly became a clothes horse as Dean began to enthusiastically remove Chantelle's clothes and then casually strew each item across it. Much to Dean's utter delight, Chantelle participated very willingly with his sexual advances as she physically surrendered to him immediately and began to comply as excited giggles emanated from her lips.

Uncontrollable surges of passion quickly gripped Dean's body as he frantically began to caress and kiss Chantelle's flesh and as their two bodies began to merge, they quickly became one as she gave herself to him and they embraced their nakedness. Sexual arousal stirred deep inside the two as the excitement that bubbled away just under the surface of their skin like hot lava, suddenly physically united them in their quest for sexual pleasure and satisfaction. Blood pumped rapidly through their veins and rushed around both their bodies as they fully succumbed to the sexual urges inside of them and the sexual gratification that they both knew, loomed on the horizon of their desires.

"Put it inside me Dean." Chantelle quietly murmured as she whispered in Dean's ear. She began to pant with excitement as she continued. "I want to feel you inside me."

Every breath that Chantelle took gently caressed Dean's face as she spoke and her warm breath was hot, heavy and laden with passion as he felt it brush against his cheek which created surges of excitement inside his own body that flowed through his veins as his skin tingled in delight. Just a few seconds later, Dean could control his passion no more as his body began to throb with desire and he rapidly slipped himself inside Chantelle's body as he began to penetrate her. Due to Dean's now enlarged penis size, his entrance was initially gentle and careful as he internally played with the notion of full penetration but held himself back from actually physically doing so.

Partial penetration was steadily maintained for a few minutes as Dean dipped himself in and out of Chantelle's body but resisted the desire to plunge himself more deeply inside of her. The desire to fully penetrate Chantelle finally overcame Dean however and as he suddenly pushed himself deep inside of her, he began to lose control. A very deep, hopeful breath was taken as Dean waited for Chantelle to enjoy and appreciate the fullness of his physical offering and accept the extent of what his body wanted her to enjoy but to Dean's dismay, no joyful sounds were actually forthcoming.

Suddenly and much to Dean's absolute horror, instead of screams of pleasure, a scream of pain emanated from Chantelle's mouth as her body began to spasm in response and an almost choking tightness rapidly gripped him from within. Upon Dean's face there was now a look of severe distress as he quietly accepted the reality that he had just actually physically hurt Chantelle and he quickly began to withdraw himself, very carefully. The scream had in part almost traumatized Dean but he quickly attempted to stroke Chantelle's head in an attempt to comfort her somehow as his body began to tremble. Fear began to scurry around inside Dean's mind as he quietly accepted that if he continued, he would only be inflicting more pain upon Chantelle which would be in direct opposition to what he'd actually hoped to achieve that night.

"I'm so sorry Chantelle." Dean muttered apologetically. "I'm really sorry, I didn't mean to hurt you."

A storm of confusion suddenly seemed to whirl around inside Dean's mind as he quietly began to consider what exactly he should actually do next as he really had absolutely no idea as the evening had not gone as he'd originally planned. The waters of discomfort rapidly seemed to rise up between the two and separate them as it forced them to become two solitary islands and drowned any familiarity, attraction and desire that had once existed between them. Between the couple now there was just an awkward emotional distance which grew larger by the second and as those waters of discomfort quickly became fathoms deep, their solitary islands were forced further and further apart. All that silently crashed against each individual shore of their respective islands was the murky waves of despair that ruthlessly separated them and maintained the distance between them as Dean quickly realized, the waves of pleasure that he'd hoped for had now completely vanished as the tide of passion had turned.

No further words were exchanged as Chantelle suddenly began to dress and as she plucked her dress, bra and knickers from the nearby sofa, she slipped each item back over her physical frame as she prepared to depart and leave Dean's apartment and all Dean could do was watch. The words that Dean needed to say in order to comfort Chantelle, or convince her to stay, seemed to elude his mind and mouth as he began to search frantically inside himself as he stood in all his nakedness, frozen to the spot.

Questions without any answers flooded through Dean's thoughts as regret sank heavily further down inside of him but no answers were forthcoming and Chantelle was definitely leaving. Whatever Dean was supposed to do or say now seemed to be just beyond the grasp of his mind and as comforting words silently evaded him, he could offer Chantelle no further solace as he silently began to mourn. Nothing had prepared Dean for this as quite simply, this had never actually happened to him ever before as his body had never physically hurt anyone and especially not a woman that he'd been very passionately, sexually intertwined with.

The very hurt expression upon Chantelle's face told Dean absolutely everything that he needed to know without any actual words being spoken as she prepared to depart and Dean quietly began to accept, his romantic evening with Chantelle had no possible chance of redemption. A tornado of destruction had hit their potentially passionate moment just before it had fully materialized and now the debris of Chantelle's hurt emotions lay scattered across his lounge and the city of love they'd hoped to find refuge, comfort, pleasure and solace in had been completely destroyed.

Despite Dean's internal desire to comfort Chantelle, it was almost as if he was completely frozen to the spot and unable to move as he quietly watched her prepare to leave, totally unable to respond. An amazingly beautiful, exciting and passionate night had been planned but now, it was well and truly over and Dean's hopes had been dashed down into the murky depths of the lake of broken hearts and his heart had immediately sunk like a very heavy brick formed from nothing but pain and rejection. The main concerns that now occupied Dean's mind, differed vastly from the romantic, sexual and sensual pleasures that had initially tantalized his thoughts at the beginning of that Friday evening as a sense of loss suddenly gripped his spirit.

Several very negative questions that Dean dared not even ask began to suddenly plague his thoughts and rapidly began to consume him as each one sat inside his body like a heavy weight and completely paralyzed him as they tied his feet to the floor. Once Chantelle actually left, Dean knew, it would be highly unlikely that he would ever see her again and perhaps that evening would be all there ever was between them both. No words however were actually spoken as Dean continued to watch Chantelle in complete silence as he dared not ask her anything and so his words were held firmly back just behind his lips as Chantelle began to walk towards the door of his lounge.

"I'll call you." Chantelle suddenly said as she paused just beside the entrance to the lounge.

"Soon." She politely reassured him as she stepped out into the short hallway outside the lounge and then headed towards the apartment's exterior door.

"She won't call me." Dean muttered as he gently shook his head. "I wouldn't call me."

Upon Dean's face there was an expression of profound sadness as he watched Chantelle leave and silently accepted her departure. Deep down inside Dean felt absolutely powerless to stop Chantelle from going and he could tell from her comment and her tone that the call she'd promised to give him would never actually happen. A meaningless promise had been made which would not be honored and her empty words were perhaps just an attempt to avoid any further unpleasantness.

One last effort had to be made, Dean quietly decided as he suddenly decisively shook of his paralysis and then grabbed a nearby towel which he wrapped quickly around his waist. If Dean let Chantelle just walk away and leave now without saying a single word, or making a single effort to show her that he actually cared, she really would never call him again.

Fortunately, the towel was actually large enough to sufficiently cover the part of Dean's body that had caused such deep offense and Dean felt grateful that at least he could hide it under the material as he began to rush out of his lounge and followed Chantelle. Once Dean arrived at the door of his apartment, he quickly opened it and then stepped out into the hallway as he began to plead with Chantelle.

"Chantelle, I'm really sorry. I truly am." Dean pleaded. "Please come back. We can talk about this."

Regardless of his efforts however, it was already too late as Chantelle had already walked along the hall that led towards the main exterior door of Dean's apartment block and now she was just about to actually open the exterior door. Absolutely no intention existed inside Chantelle's mind it seemed to actually return and she was just about to step out of the actual building and out of Dean's life.

"I'll call you Dean." Chantelle promised again as she opened the exterior door.

Sadly for Dean, the humiliation continued but one small mercy remained, the poorly lit corridor was actually empty which meant, no one nearby was present to witness his embarrassment and his romantic failure. Besides Dean and Chantelle, the only other signs of life was a light which flickered on and off just above his head and that was at least one small comfort to him. One final sympathetic glance and smile was given by Chantelle as she turned to face Dean for a split second and then nodded her head just before the exterior door of his apartment building banged shut behind her. Unlike the smiles that Dean had seen on Chantelle's face earlier that evening, this smile was different and it was strained, tainted and overshadowed by brushstrokes of tension, pain and hurt.

The loud bang of the exterior door as it closed directly in front of him, stung Dean's heart as he began to quietly accept the almost deafening lonely rejection that he now faced. Chantelle had not just stepped out of the door but she had also effectively walked out of his whole life. Both the door of Dean's apartment block and the door of Chantelle's heart had now been closed to him and there was absolutely nothing at all that he could actually do about it. All that remained now was an empty, deserted hallway much like his deserted heart and a very firmly closed exterior door that would never be opened by Chantelle's hands ever again.

Nothing but silence surrounded Dean and the flickering light which very annoyingly insisted on keeping him company as it indecisively continued to flicker on and off just above his head. For a few minutes, it was almost as if Dean was rooted to the spot and completely frozen as he stood and just waited for Chantelle to return but his wishes, Dean finally accepted, were like a small particle of air lost in an immense sky with no probability of actually being found. Chantelle would not return, Dean's wish would not materialize and be granted and his hopes for a night filled with romantic passion had already been well and truly dashed, drowned and absolutely trashed.

"This is not good, not good at all." Dean exclaimed in absolute horror as he suddenly began to shake his head in total disbelief. He forced himself to walk back towards the door of his apartment but his legs almost felt like jelly and as he walked they began to wobble. "Not only did this cost me money but now, it's also cost me a woman that I really liked. Bigger isn't always better."

When the Saturday evening arrived, Renee bravely decided to throw caution to the wind and explore her new physical assets with Simon as she made an assertive executive decision about her own body and the new fixtures that she'd recently purchased. The physical upgrades that had been made to Renee's physical portfolio and body had to be explored and sampled by someone and Simon had been a very willing volunteer and he'd offered to be the first explorer to climb up and venture into Renee's summits of sexual pleasure. Sexual passions had been contained inside Renee's physical form for so very long and they had never ever actually been realized and that unrealized passion had stung Renee's heart like an angry wasp for years.

One very persistent application for Renee's vacancy had been received from Simon, who was an eager young man that had applied for the role of a temporary lover and he'd managed to convince Renee that he was indeed the most suitable applicant with which to indulge in a one night stand. Although temporary fast food fixes weren't really Renee's usual approach to dating, love and relationships and it wasn't her style to engage in casual, sexual fumbling with male strangers, for some inexplicable reason, Renee did feel very drawn to Simon. Between the two an attraction had been formed and definitely existed which almost felt magnetic and as Simon had pulled her towards him, Renee had felt encouraged and confident enough to stop paddling around in the pool of passion and take a leap of desire into the deep end.

Due to the fact that Renee had absolutely no plans for the weekend, Saturday evening and night had been allocated to the exploration and pursuit of unbridled passion as Renee had sought to fully immerse herself in Simon's expressions of physical adoration. A very short black, tight fitting dress that sent very obvious silent signals of sensuality had been selected and then slipped on as Renee had prepared for her night ahead and then inspected in the long body length mirror inside her bedroom. Every inch of Renee's body now looked sexualized and visually appealing as her outfit complimented the very pert pair of breasts that she now possessed which poked cheekily out of the top of the dress that clung to her frame invitingly as it beautifully accentuated her curves and her now very voluptuous figure.

Once dressed, Renee smiled with satisfaction as she prepared to depart and picked up her handbag. One final glance was cast into the mirror as Renee admired the two pert, round mounds of feminine sexuality that yearned to be touched, appreciated, admired and adored as Renee adamantly decided that tonight, her body would not be denied the right to be physically worshipped. Every penny of expenditure that Renee had spent upon her body and face, would be celebrated as her physical form would be shown off to another human being, a very attractive, eager male human being.

In terms of the intended recipient of Renee's gift, Simon was a much younger male in his late twenties and he'd approached Renee in a bar one night and then he'd not let her out of his sight all evening. Regardless of the ten year age gap that very clearly existed between the two and that sat very discreetly in-between them both, Renee had welcomed his interest in her and had absolutely no doubts or worries inside her mind as she'd encouraged him to proceed and given Simon a greenlight.

DOWNLOADABLE

Dim lights and a sea of faces greeted Renee as she stepped inside the bar that the two had agreed to meet inside that Saturday evening as Renee began to search for Simon's face within the sea of strangers that now surrounded her. Fortunately, just a few minutes later, Renee actually managed to spot Simon sat on top of a bar stool right next to the bar and then quickly began to make her way over towards him. A few drinks were quickly ordered and then consumed before the two left the bar as they opted for a more discreet location to accommodate the rest of their evening which of course had been the main plan all along. Inside Renee's apartment, the two would physically explore and physically consummate their sexual interest in each other and then spend the night together as that had already been discussed and agreed prior to their actual meeting that evening.

Flames of delight and passion danced through Renee's eyes as she invited Simon boldly inside her apartment door and he immediately leapt at her invitation and as he entered inside her home, Renee delighted in the very charming smile upon his face. For Renee, the Saturday night actually represented a huge change in her life as the insecurities that had once haunted her existence had now been ripped out of her thoughts, discarded and then stamped upon as she'd silently rebelled and protested against the ugly shadows of inferiority that had once ruled her existence and controlled her life. Much to Renee's utter delight, she had discovered that she could now fully embrace, enjoy, celebrate and participate in her femininity like never before and that she could now fully experience being a sexually active, very attractive, heterosexual woman and she couldn't wait to enjoy that discovery and to explore that realization.

Every second between the two that evening seemed almost magical for Renee as she celebrated the beauty of her new breasts and very proudly displayed her naked body to Simon as she confidently stripped off in front of him as soon as they stepped inside her lounge. For the very first time ever in Renee's entire life, Renee actually enjoyed being naked in front of another living human being, a very attractive male human being and that in Renee's mind had definitely been worth every penny that she'd spent. The sexual liberation that Renee felt, absolutely thrilled her as she internally basked in it and reveled every second of it. Frantic sexual passion seemed to rule Renee's mind as Simon almost jumped on top of her and began to caress her naked flesh as Renee eagerly accepted and immediately surrendered to his passionate appreciation, physical adoration and sexual hunger.

"This is so hot." Simon murmured in Renee's ear as he pulled her towards him. "And so are you."

Opportunity that night had knocked at the door of Simon's life and he grabbed it with both hands, appreciatively and hungrily as he took full advantage of Renee's willingness and dove straight into her pool of sexual allure. Although Simon was slightly unsure as to why he'd actually been presented with such a wonderful opportunity, he did feel extremely horny and he really wasn't one to question a gift of sexual pleasure that had literally been handed to him on a plate.

From Simon's point of view, Renee's age and her maturity was actually seen as something positive and it really excited him as he'd wanted to experience a sexual encounter with a woman that was slightly more mature than himself for quite a while now. The fact that Renee was so physically blessed had been an additional turn on and she more than met Simon's criteria in terms of an attractive older woman and even actually exceeded it.

A smile of gratitude had crossed Simon's face when Renee had very seductively stripped of for him and he'd savored every delicious mouthful of the visual treat that she'd provided to him. Sexual excitement and intense arousal had begun to surge through Simon's veins and flow through his fingertips as he'd pulled her towards him and then had began to frantically physically explore every inch of her flesh with his lips, hands and tongue.

Delighted moans emanated from Renee's mouth and floated into Simon's ears as he eagerly slipped his hand in-between Renee's legs and a warm wetness welcomed him as he prepared to penetrate and mount her physically. Just a few seconds later, Simon quickly removed his trousers and then began to push himself inside Renee's body as he very passionately penetrated Renee and prepared to take them both to the peak of the sexual mountain they'd started to climb.

No words were spoken between the two as they quickly became lost in their erotic, extremely adult night of passion as Renee totally surrendered her body to Simon and allowed him to do whatever he wished to do as she basked in his physical adoration. Essentially, Renee had now just been liberated from the curse of her fears and her inferiority complex and she savored every moment of that intoxicating, exciting, thrilling sexual liberation that Simon provided to her very enthusiastically as she silently rejoiced in every delicious second. Finally, Renee had managed to step out of the shadows that she'd existed in for so very long and finally, Renee could now enjoy the fullness of being a physically attractive, sexually desired and passionately adored woman and

Restructure as far as Renee was concerned had been worth every single penny.

The Sunday for Samson was full of exciting sexual prospects as he'd made an arrangement to meet up with Victoria, the woman that he'd mischievously flirted with that had essentially cost him his previous relationship, or more specifically that his attraction to her had. A very pleasant afternoon rapidly commenced as Samson met Victoria, who was completely oblivious to all the trouble she'd caused for Samson regarding his previous romantic attachment and Samson wined, dined and charmed her, very seductively.

Once the afternoon had been consumed, the evening slipped into its place as the two sauntered delicately into their evening meal together which was accompanied by several cocktails and a bottle of champagne. When their evening meal ended, the two then began to make their way back to Samson's apartment where he intended to fully explore the potential of his seductive romantic advances. Inside Samson there was now a very hungry urge to physically consummate his romantic interest in Victoria as long as she was willing to do so which it seemed, she definitely was and that willingness absolutely delighted him. Hot passion and titillating erotic enjoyment rapidly followed and continued throughout the whole Sunday night which was filled with a physical sexual intimacy that

Samson both thoroughly explored and enjoyed as he physically comforted himself for his recent romantic loss and managed to regain an extremely pleasant sexual victory.

After the weekend had been gloriously consumed by Talitha, unfortunately and inevitably, Monday morning quietly showed up and stepped into her life as the next working week began but surprisingly that morning, she woke up at least twenty minutes before her usual alarm call. In a matter of just minutes, Talitha leapt out of bed and then made her way towards the bathroom as she prepared to get ready to leave for work. A refreshing shower was quickly taken and then a cup of coffee thirstily consumed as Talitha readied herself to leave the house, in order to start her very busy working week.

Outside the front door of Talitha's home, the morning air was quite pleasant but light and breezy as she stepped out of the front door and then made her way towards her vehicle which was parked in its usual spot inside the driveway. Fortunately, the drive to work was quite fast and peaceful as the roads were quite clear and as Talitha drove, she began to internally deliberate about the pending client consultations that she was due to perform that coming working week. Every client on Talitha's current client list had various physical adjustments that had to be performed that week, except for one and then there was also the addition of a new client that had been added to her list the previous Friday which she knew absolutely nothing about and that really intrigued her.

At least twenty physical changes had now been performed by Talitha and she'd definitely exceeded her own expectations, in terms of the things that had been achieved since she'd first stepped through Restructure's doors. A gentle smile crossed Talitha's face as she drove as she began to appreciate the happiness that she'd brought to some of her clients lives as just to see each of those physical changes manifest themselves in real client's bodies had been an amazing experience in itself. For the very first time, now Talitha finally understood why so many cosmetic surgeons tried to provide human beings with an alternative, improved physicality as sometimes, it really wasn't about purely superficial things and that physical resculpting could be totally life changing in so many ways.

Every physical change that Talitha had performed and each client that she'd helped to achieve their physical ambitions had motivated Talitha, all except Saskia and Lachlan, who were the two obvious exceptions that were extremely demotivating and really quite annoying. For the first time in Talitha's entire life however, she had witnessed science and technology defy the

457

practical challenges and difficulties of cosmetic surgery as she'd performed a variety of physical transformations without any of the usual horrors like ugly scars and damage caused by the insertion of very sharp surgical instruments into human flesh. Each working day as Talitha performed scientific miracles, she changed not only people's lives but also their inner being as Professor Heisner's work healed their deep emotional wounds and as that comforting realization nestled into her thoughts, she rejoiced in not only his work but also the opportunity that she'd been given when she'd been recruited.

When Talitha arrived in the parking lot she found it almost empty as usual apart from the two cars that she expected to be present which belonged to Yucala and Professor Heisner. Once Talitha had parked her vehicle, she quickly stepped out of it, locked the door and then enthusiastically began to make her way towards the main entrance of the Restructure building as she quietly considered her work for Restructure to date. In terms of Talitha's clients and the various procedures that she had performed, it was actually impossible to tell yet whether or not each client would actually enjoy their upgraded physical forms. Perhaps some clients would, Talitha quietly concluded as she stepped inside the reception area and perhaps in the longer term, some of the improvements they'd requested would cause them more problems than they actually solved as the outcomes of Talitha's work was absolutely unpredictable.

Just inside the reception area, Talitha found a huge beaming smile pleasantly waiting for her and as she walked towards Yucala's desk, she rapidly began to focus upon Yucala's very warm, friendly reaction which was a direct response to her arrival. Regardless of whether the sun shone outside, or the rain poured down from the skies in a torrent there was at least one thing it seemed that Talitha could always be certain about, Yucala would always great her with a warm friendly smile every working day that shone almost like the rays of the sun itself. The usual pleasantries were very happily exchanged between the two women and they also shared a few jokes before Talitha headed of towards her consultation room to start work as that day, she really had a lot to do as it was the beginning of a very busy week.

For the first time ever that Monday morning, Talitha had to perform a client closure session and as Renee showed up for her appointment at eleven, Talitha quickly invited her inside her consultation room a she greeted her politely. Upon Renee's face there was an expression of sheer joy and her eyes were filled with excitement as she sat down and Talitha offered her a beverage. Once the usual pleasantries had been exchanged between the two women, Talitha dived straight into the purpose of her consultation which was predominantly to ensure that everything inside Renee's world post procedures was fine as dissatisfied clients were the last thing that either Talitha or Professor Heisner wanted.

"How have things been Renee?" Talitha asked. "How is your body coping with the breast enlargement as your breasts are much heavier now?"

"My breasts are a little on the heavy side now Talitha, so I do get backache sometimes." Renee replied. "It's definitely worth it though, these boobs are absolutely gorgeous."

"I tell you what Renee, if you like I can give you a back strengthening Download, at no extra cost and that should ease and hopefully eradicate any problems with your back." Talitha quickly suggested as she smiled. "You do have a slender frame so it's to be expected really. Large breasts can be very heavy."

"Thank you so much Talitha that would be absolutely wonderful." Renee quickly agreed as she enthusiastically nodded her head.

"And how's your love life been, now that you've had time to adjust to the physical changes?" Talitha enquired.

"My sex life this past week has been absolutely off the radar and my orgasms hit the highest points on the Richter scale. So I think it's definitely been worth it, my orgasms were like an earthquake." Renee explained.

"Well Renee, I'm very glad to hear that you're enjoying both your body and your orgasms now." Talitha teased.

"Seriously Talitha, I had at least three with Simon in one night and they were all absolutely fantastic." Renee began to elaborate. "He might be slightly younger than I am but he really knows what he's doing."

Talitha giggled. "Well if he's a bit younger than you, I'm sure he has lots of energy and that means, he'll be able to help you catch up on all the years of orgasms that you've missed out on." She quickly pointed out.

"I probably won't be seeing Simon again." Renee said as she gently shook her head.

"Really, not even after three orgasms in one night?" Talitha asked. "Why ever not?"

"I don't think he's that serious about me really, he hasn't called me since then, so I don't think it'll be a long term relationship." Renee explained. "I think he thought that I'd be this really experienced lover because I'm slightly older than him and I wasn't. I'm practically almost like a virgin due to my lack of sexual experience, so that might have put him off me slightly."

"That's his loss Renee not yours because you look absolutely terrific and you're a lovely person." Talitha quickly reassured Renee as she suddenly rose to her feet. "Right, let's go to the procedure room and I'll process the back strengthening treatment for you now."

"I think I'll have to look for someone a bit closer to my own age Talitha, if I want something a bit more serious." Renee concluded as she quickly stood up and then began to walk towards the procedure room. "Someone a bit more mature."

"There might be less than three earthquakes in one night." Talitha teased.

"I know, I could perhaps just experiment for a few months and enjoy lots of earthquakes and then settle down a little bit later on in the year." Renee began to deliberate thoughtfully. "That would give me a chance to really discover myself sexually and it would also allow me to enjoy multiple earthquakes in one night for a while."

"Whatever you choose to do Renee, just make sure it's something that you really want to do as at times, we allow other people's expectations to define our lives and then we end up totally miserable as a result." Talitha advised as she smiled.

"This will be our last consultation won't it Talitha?" Renee asked. "I mean, there's nothing left to actually do to my body now."

"It sure will but I'd like to do a follow up appointment in about a month's time, if that's okay with you?" Talitha replied.

"Sure Talitha that would be absolutely lovely." Renee immediately agreed.

"Right, you know what to do Renee, lie down inside here and think of earthquakes and in no time at all, I'll have your back strong enough to flaunt those weapons of mass attraction." Talitha joked as she held open the lid of the transparent capsule.

Renee giggled.

Later that day, when three in the afternoon arrived so too did Dean as he physically showed up for his consultation, punctually as usual but without his usual smile. A beverage was immediately offered to Dean as Talitha showed him into her consultation room and internally considered thoughtfully what could have possibly gone wrong. Technically, all Dean's procedures had now almost been performed which meant, all that really actually remained was his arm procedure, a client closure appointment and then perhaps a follow up appointment, if he actually wanted one.

During their last briefing, Professor Heisner had suggested and recommended to Talitha that she should offer all her clients with a follow up appointment about one month after their client closure sessions, just to ensure that everything was in order and completely fine. Due to Dean's pending departure from Talitha's client list that implied that she really only had three opportunities left in which to make sure that Dean was fully satisfied and totally happy with his procedures and so she was anxious to ensure that day that everything inside Dean's world and life was perfectly fine.

"It'll be your final procedure today Dean." Talitha mentioned as she placed a fresh cup of coffee down on her desk in front of him and then sat down. "Isn't that exciting?"

"Yes it is but I guess I'll kind of miss coming here every week." Dean replied as he picked up the cup of coffee and began to sip it. "You make a great cup of coffee Talitha and good coffee these days is hard to find."

"Well technically, the coffee machine does." Talitha teased. "Once you've had your client closure consultation next week, I can make another follow up appointment for you in about a month's time, so then you can come back for that and then you can even have another cup of coffee and perhaps even some biscuits." She continued. "Yucala ordered some biscuits this week and they look like they might taste rather nice."

"Yes and hopefully by then my love life will be amazingly great and will have improved because right now, it's truly awful." Dean mourned.

"Why, what happened Dean? Did something go wrong?" Talitha asked.

For a few seconds nothing but total silence greeted Talitha as she quietly observed Dean's downcast expression and his facial signs of total and utter defeat. The unanswered question that Talitha had asked continued to linger and hang around in the air as it silently demanded an answer and she attempted to gently reinforce it as she glanced directly into Dean's eyes and patiently waited for him to respond. In her heart of hearts, Talitha knew, there was no way on earth that she could actually assist Dean unless he opened to her and told her exactly what had actually happened but it was a very sensitive issue, so she totally understood his initial hesitation to elaborate further.

"Absolutely everything went wrong." Dean finally replied as he sighed in defeat and answered the question which had given him a verbal nudge to discuss his disastrous love life in more detail. He began to shake his head sadly in frustration as he began to discuss his recent very awful night of passion, or rather his night of failed passion. "My potentially grand re-entrance into the heterosexual dating world in order to provide sexual pleasure to the abundant supply of attractive, single, eligible females was a complete and utter disaster and it was a million miles away from the breathtaking experience it should have been." Dean explained as he began to dig deep within himself and tried to find the courage to provide Talitha with information about the ugly reality that he'd spent most of his weekend trying to hide away from.

"Okay, so the newly enhanced penis didn't go well?" Talitha asked.

Dean immediately shook his head in response. "It really didn't Talitha, it was a complete and utter disaster." He rapidly clarified.

"That's okay Dean, these are new procedures and there will be times when things go wrong." Talitha quickly reassured him. "That's what these consultations are actually for, to allow you to discuss any problems that arise with me so that we can find a solution together."

"I guess my sexual ambitions kind of fell flat on their face at the very first hurdle." Dean explained.

"What actually happened Dean?" Talitha enquired as she nodded her head and encouraged Dean to speak. "I expected you to be over the moon today really, not sad."

"You and me both, I expected fireworks but instead my love life disintegrated into nothing, before it had even officially restarted again. It's been out of action and dormant for a while now, ever since the accident really." Dean explained.

"I know this is quite a sensitive issue Dean but that's okay, you can discuss it with me that's why I'm here." Talitha encouraged as she glanced at Dean's downcast expression and internally contemplated what could have possibly gone wrong with Dean's sexual journey of exploration and re-assimilation.

"Talitha, I got dumped by someone in the worst way possible last week and technically, we weren't even in a relationship yet." Dean explained as he began to shake his head. "We'd only just met really."

"Please tell me a bit more Dean, I know it's a bit personal but I can't actually help you, if you don't tell me exactly what happened." Talitha urged sympathetically as she tried to persuade Dean to divulge further details to her about the romantic disappointment that he'd so obviously experienced. "You can talk to me about this Dean, you really can."

"At first everything was going really well, I invited Chantelle to my home and she actually came and then we ate dinner together." Dean explained as he glanced at Talitha's face. "Then I stripped off in front of her as you do as I was quite eager to show her what I had to offer."

Talitha nodded and smiled. "Then what happened?" She asked.

"Then we kissed and things became very intimate and once she was naked, I penetrated her and at first that was all fine." Dean explained. "But then I got a bit carried away and put myself all the way inside her and she actually screamed in pain and I was absolutely horrified."

"That sounds awful." Talitha replied. "What happened next?"

"She put her clothes back on and then rushed out of my apartment. I tried to run after her but it was too late, she'd already reached the front door of the building." Dean mourned. "She's never coming back although she said she'd call me but that's never going to happen. I was just too big for her and I got carried away and I actually hurt her. What if this happens again?" He asked as he glanced at Talitha's face. "She actually screamed Talitha because of me because I hurt her."

"Okay Dean, don't panic, there has to be a solution to this problem and we'll try to find it today." Talitha gently reassured him as she suddenly rose to her feet.

Dean nodded.

Penis enlargements it seemed were slightly more complex and far trickier than Talitha had initially imagined, she considered thoughtfully as she began to pace the interior of her consultation room and there clearly was a negative downside to having a very large piece of male sexual equipment. In part, Talitha actually felt quite relieved that at least Dean had managed to open up to her and that he had now provided her with a quite detailed, lengthy explanation but in some ways, she also felt quite frustrated as she was really under equipped to assist him with this very male problem. Regardless of Talitha's experience, or lack of it when it came to the male anatomy, she had been thrust into the heart of this very male issue and now, she fully understood, it was her responsibility to find an actual solution to her client's problem, whether it related to the male anatomy or not.

"You know Dean, no matter what life throws at you sometimes, you just have to find a way to get through it all." Talitha suddenly said as she attempted to reassure Dean that regardless of the silence that had just sat between them both, she was extremely committed to helping him resolve the issue.

Between the two, a few more minutes of silence delicately lingered as Talitha continued to pace her consultation room as she sought deep within herself for some possible solutions and the right words to say that might comfort Dean and that might perhaps even solve his dilemma. A very solemn expression now sat on Dean's face which Talitha was certainly not used to and she wanted to eradicate it completely and to restore Dean's usual cheerful smile that usually greeted life, the world and everyone in it with optimism and enthusiasm.

"Sometimes you know Dean, hope is all we really have." Talitha suddenly said as she turned and faced him. "Hope that there's a solution to the problems that strangle our lives with a noose of frustration, hope that we can love again when our hearts are broken and the hope that we can succeed in life when we've been trampled down into a gutter of defeat."

"Hope doesn't marry you though Talitha, or give you any children." Dean replied.

"Is there any way you can possibly manage this at all Dean? Talitha enquired. "Perhaps you could just insert yourself a little bit, so that you don't hurt anyone." She suggested.

"That really wouldn't work Talitha. I'd probably get carried away and I'm not really sure that I'd be able to uphold a promise like that to anyone, not even myself. It would be impossible to do that every single time." Dean immediately clarified as he shook his head glumly in response.

"You're probably right Dean that's not really a realistic solution, in the longer term." Talitha agreed.

A minefield of complexities surrounded Dean's current predicament and one of the largest issues was that Talitha was not actually a man herself and hence it was slightly difficult for her to fully understand his position, or suggest a solution that might actually resolve it. Regardless of that rather tricky complexity however, Talitha was absolutely committed to finding a solution and the confession that Dean had made seemed to be very logical as he'd admitted to his inability to partially penetrate his partner consistently in the longer term. Usually lovers did get carried away as Talitha was well aware in the heat of the moment when passions had begun to stir and flare up inside of them. Despite Talitha's desire to resolve Dean's predicament however, no answers were not immediately forthcoming.

"You know Dean, she might even come back." Talitha encouraged. "I've found that relationships can be quite tricky at times and at one point or another there will be obstacles to overcome and those obstacles can either tear you apart or bring you closer together."

Dean quickly shook his head. "I think we can quite safely conclude that this obstacle definitely tore us apart. It was far too early and there really wasn't a deep emotional attachment between us both. She won't come back now." He insisted.

"Perhaps someone else might actually enjoy your large penis." Talitha suggested.

"Maybe but I doubt it. I think it's far too big to be pleasant really and I did really like her." Dean mourned. "I don't think she'll give me a second chance now."

Silence once more filled the room as Talitha began to pace around her consultation room again thoughtfully, there was only really one solution to Dean's predicament but it was an expensive one and deep down inside herself, Talitha feared that it would not be financially viable. Despite the cost however, it was the only real solution that Talitha could actually think off and therefore she definitely had to suggest it to Dean, she quietly concluded as she returned to her desk and then sat back down. The wounds from his recent heartbreak had already cut into Dean's heart and the pain now decorated his face like an ugly scar in the form of a grieving frown and his confidence which had only just been reinstated, now lay on the ground once more in a helpless heap totally obliterated, utterly shattered, absolutely destroyed and heartbreakingly defeated.

"I could perhaps give you another enhancement Dean." Talitha offered as she turned to face him and smiled. "Reversals can be extremely tricky but I could replace your first bodily enhancement with a second enhancement that would offer you a slightly smaller and more compact penis, it would be quite similar to the one that you already have really, just not as huge."

Inside Dean's eyes, a spark of hope suddenly seemed to ignite as his downcast expression rapidly began to melt away as Talitha spoke each word but although Talitha's solution was a realistic and viable one, it was an expensive one and she was uncertain that Dean could actually afford it. Now unfortunately, the only issue that stood between Dean's misery and happiness was the price as solutions definitely cost money.

"Can you really do that Talitha? Would it be expensive?" Dean asked as he glanced at Talitha's face. "I'm not sure I'd be able to afford it, the Downloads are very expensive and I'm not the richest man in town by any stretch of the imagination. The enhancements I've had so far have already cost me an absolute fortune." He explained. "And my savings are almost totally depleted now. I'm just an accountant for a small corporate entity, so my means don't always stretch as far as I'd like them too."

"I'll tell you what I'll do Dean, I'll find some suitable replacements for you so that when you attend your client closure session next week I can perhaps do the Download during that session." Talitha suggested. "And in the meantime, I'll speak to Professor Heisner about it and see if he'll allow me to do the procedure at no extra cost, or for a much smaller amount."

"Can you actually do that Talitha?" Dean asked. "That would be really great because I can't really afford to do any more of these procedures at full price, they've cost me an arm and a leg already."

"I'll try my best Dean." Talitha quickly reassured him. "I promise. Right, let's get your new arms sorted out and hopefully these arms will serve you better than the arm and the leg they cost you." She teased.

Dean grinned.

In her heart of hearts, Talitha hoped that Professor Heisner would authorize the second penile adjustment at no extra cost as the first enlargement hadn't gone well at all and now Dean was faced with a second obstruction which would not only hamper his love life but perhaps even completely crucify it. The scar that had almost engulfed Dean's entire calf had almost disabled him as it had stopped him from having any kind of romantic involvement with anyone else and now, a second obstruction faced him which he had actually requested and paid for himself. Deep down inside herself, Talitha now feared that the second obstruction might perhaps romantically demobilize him even more than the first one had.

Once Dean's appointment ended, Talitha politely escorted him back towards the main reception area as she prepared to say farewell and get on with the rest of her day. A slightly solemn expression still adorned Dean's face as Talitha turned to face him to say goodbye but at least now there was a small glimmer of hope present inside his eyes as Talitha internally empathized with his tricky situation and his very difficult circumstances. All in all, Dean really seemed like quite a nice guy, in Talitha's opinion and he appeared to be very sincere and really genuine and she definitely felt that he deserved to have something nice happen for him that might change and improve his life. Due to the motorbike accident and the crippling scar that it had left behind which had virtually robbed Dean of a love life, he'd had to endure years of romantic suffering and those years, Talitha appreciated, must have been extremely difficult for him.

"Right Dean, don't you worry about a thing just yet, I'll speak to Professor Heisner as I promised and I'll see you next week." Talitha cheerfully reassured him.

Dean nodded as he prepared to depart. "Thank you so much for understanding Talitha. There's no one else really that I could speak to about any of this." He explained quietly. "It's been very difficult for me really."

"That's what I'm here for Dean. You can speak to me about anything at all related to your procedures and the impact those changes have upon your life is very important to me." Talitha replied. "That's my job."

"I'll see you next week Talitha." Dean said as he smiled appreciatively and pulled open one of the exterior doors inside the reception area.

"You sure will and I'll be right here waiting for you, so you better be on time because cups of coffee go cold really quickly and they don't like to be kept waiting." Talitha teased. "By then, I'll even have some biscuits to go with your cup of coffee."

Dean grinned as he stepped through the doors. "Thanks Talitha and I'll definitely be on time." He promised. "You can't keep a good cup of coffee waiting."

Talitha laughed.

When the Tuesday morning flew into the runway of Talitha's life and landed very firmly upon her doorstep, she prepared for the day ahead in a quite relaxed manner as her two client appointments that day, she already knew in advance, would be relatively stress free. The two clients that Talitha was scheduled to spend her Tuesday with were Rita and Rodney and since she'd met them both more than once before, she knew exactly what to expect from each of them and exactly what they would expect from her. In terms of their client needs, they were both quite straight forward in that, there were no huge emotional issues or complexities that involved third parties which meant, Talitha's workload that day would actually be quite light.

DOWNLOADABLE

The early part of Tuesday morning literally flew by for Talitha as she arrived at work, prepared herself enthusiastically for her first consultation and then met with Rita at around eleven. A nose reshape was performed and then Rita's notes were written up and actually completed just as lunch time approached. Once Talitha had submitted Rita's notes, she quickly left her consultation room and then headed out towards the parking lot as she began to make her way towards her favorite diner nearby. Quite unusually that day, Talitha opted for a cold lunch and a prawn cocktail sandwich that was decorated generously with a bright pink island dressing and once she'd collected her order, she quickly returned to work and her desk, so that she could prepare for the afternoon ahead.

Approximately one hour after Talitha had eaten lunch, Rodney arrived as scheduled at three on the dot and Talitha courteously performed the ear enhancement Download that he'd requested. During his client consultation, Rodney enthusiastically entertained Talitha with his usual charm, flattery and flirtatious remarks which she'd learned to humor and tolerate but not to encourage. Once Rodney's ear enhancement had been performed, the two sat back down beside Talitha's desk and then faced each other as she prepared to make his next appointment.

477

"Would you like to see the penis enlargement that you gave me the very first week I was here in person Talitha?" Rodney asked cheekily.

"Certainly not Rodney." Talitha immediately replied.

"Come on Talitha, aren't you just a little bit curious?" Rodney teased. "I would be."

"Rodney please, I'm not curious at all about things that are really none of my business." Talitha explained. "I do lots of penis enlargements for male clients, so I really don't have the time to be curious about men's penises."

"It's virtually perfect Talitha." Rodney insisted as he grinned. "You're really missing out. I'll tell you what I can do, I can take a picture of it and then email you the photo, so that you can see it for yourself."

"Trust me Rodney, my partner has a great penis that I'm perfectly satisfied with and I look at it almost every day." Talitha politely reminded him. "So I'm really not missing out at all. Plus I was the one that processed the penis Download for you in the first place, so technically, I've already seen it."

"You see Talitha, you said 'almost every day' which means, you are missing out sometimes." Rodney quickly pointed out. "If you were mine, you'd be seeing my rod of goodness every single day."

Talitha shook her head. "You really are something else Rodney." She replied. "Right, how's next Wednesday afternoon for you, at around the same time for your client closure session?"

"Sure, Wednesday afternoon will be great." Rodney confirmed as he grinned.

"Good that's everything for today then Rodney. I'll see you back to the reception area now." Talitha explained as she quickly rose to her feet.

Upon Rodney's face there was a huge, cheeky smile as he stood up and then joined Talitha as she walked towards her consultation room door though what exactly had provoked that smile, Talitha was blissfully ignorant to and she really didn't actually want to know. Once Rodney had been escorted back to the reception area, Talitha made her way quickly back towards her consultation room as she prepared to write up his notes and then actually submit them before she went home that day. All in all, Talitha's working day had been fairly pleasant, very productive and relatively peaceful but her working day was still not quite over.

For the purposes of Talitha's notes, she usually completely ignored the very flirtatious, suggestive remarks that Rodney made during his appointments as to include them in her communications with Professor Heisner would serve absolutely no purpose at all. The client note system inside Restructure was generally focused upon consultation procedures, reactions to those procedures and any concerns that Talitha might have about client's lives and tended to be far less about a client's personal comments. In terms of Talitha's training, Professor Heisner had trained her very precisely about what exactly should go inside her client notes every working day and Rodney's flirtatious remarks definitely did not form or fulfill any part of those requirements.

At exactly five thirty on the dot, Talitha switched off her system, picked up her handbag and then rose to her feet as she joyfully prepared to go home for the evening. Everything that she'd planned to do that working day had now been done and Rodney's client notes had already been submitted and that meant, technically Talitha was already prepared for her next working day when it did actually arrive. A very satisfied smile spread out across Talitha's face as she headed towards the reception area and then left the Restructure building for the day as appreciation began to set in that her working day was now actually over.

On her way home, Talitha thoughtfully began to consider just how much her confidence and levels of competence had increased since the very first day that she'd met her first client as she drove and she was quite surprised by how quickly she'd grown accustomed to Restructure and the Professor's work. Long gone were the days where

Talitha would actually feel nervous before a client consultation began and now her daily meetings with clients and the implementation of the very complex, scientific procedures she worked with every day, seemed almost as natural to her as driving her car.

Some very positive feedback had been given to Professor Heisner by some of Talitha's clients about her work which had confirmed her ability to deliver and he had even complimented her about her achievements several times himself. Thankfully now, Talitha was definitely just more than an assistant that made cups of tea and that cleaned people's skin in preparation for surgical procedures as now, Talitha actually performed those procedures upon her own clients every working day herself. Later that evening Bryson had actually promised to take Talitha for a meal at one of their favorite restaurants and that was definitely something for Talitha to get excited about as it was a very expensive restaurant and a rare treat for them both and that promise lifted Talitha's spirits as she drove towards home, Bryson and towards the couple's dinner date.

Pleasantly for Frank, when the Wednesday morning arrived, he found that the weather was actually quite nice as he woke up at around eight and then glanced out of the bedroom window. The day ahead was a step out of Frank's usual weekday routine and was slightly unusual in the sense that it actually involved a visit to Restructure which was one of the few places that he'd visited in recent times without Maude in tow, simply because he didn't actually want her to know that he was going there. In terms of Frank's recent procedures, he'd actually told Maude that his doctor had recently prescribed an exercise routine that he had to participate in each week and that was the usual excuse that he facilitated when he slipped out to visit Restructure.

A quick shower was taken and a light breakfast was rapidly eaten which for Frank wasn't particularly enjoyable as it was one of Maude's 'healthy breakfasts' which composed of muesli that tasted a bit like sawdust and some rather sour grapefruit. Once breakfast had been consumed, the usual 'Mirror Test' was then performed as Maude fussed around Frank as per their usual routine which of course Frank lost and he quickly accepted his defeat, humbly and quietly.

Rather strangely in recent times, Frank had noticed that he felt less and less physically attracted to Maude and sometimes, he'd even felt as if he actually disliked and feared her but nothing about the couple's life had changed, except Frank's attendance at the Restructure clinic. Despite the rather strange feelings and the reduction in the level of attraction that Frank felt towards Maude, he'd soldiered on nonetheless as he'd tried to disguise his emotional responses as much as he possibly could.   The Mirror Test that morning however, was particularly hard for Frank and when the couple stood beside each other in front of the mirror, he could barely even stand to be naked in front of Maude and in close proximity to her as he quickly rushed her along.   Unusually for Frank, he accepted defeat immediately which was very unlike him as he usually spent at least thirty minutes objecting to Maude's victory and entertaining her debates about various body parts.

The strangeness of Frank's morning however, did not actually end there as when Frank stepped out of the couple's home at around ten that morning and then began to make his way towards the Restructure clinic, he found that his journey was delayed, not by traffic or any another unpredictable eventuality but by himself.   On his way towards Restructure, Frank usually stopped off at a diner to pick up some 'unhealthy breakfast' which was something that he usually did when he wasn't with Maude as she tended to harp on about calories, unhealthy eating and so on and that would usually be enough to put him off such rare treats.   Since Maude wasn't with Frank that day as he always attended Restructure alone, he'd decided to indulge in a bacon bap laced with fat and oil and covered in lashings of greasy brown diner sauce on his way as a greasy, fatty breakfast was something he looked forward to whenever he visited the Restructure clinic and that morning was certainly no exception.

Upon Frank's face there was a huge smile as he approached the counter inside the diner enthusiastically as he prepared to joyfully consume his rather unhealthy breakfast treat without listening to any nagging in his ears. Behind the counter there was a mature woman with dark, jet black hair and a slightly rounded figure that looked to be around five years younger than Frank that greeted him very politely as he neared and for some very strange, inexplicable reason, Frank suddenly felt rather drawn to her.

A breakfast order was quickly placed and then Frank sat down inside the diner which was also unusual for him as he usually just bought his breakfast and then ate it inside the car as he drove. Today however, Frank just couldn't seem to bring himself to leave the premises without first speaking to the mature, attractive woman behind the counter a little more before he actually left. Something compelled Frank to actually sit down and eat his breakfast that day inside the diner as he waited for an opportunity to strike up a conversation with the woman that he suddenly felt very attracted and physically drawn to.

In terms of Frank's relationship with Maude, he'd never actually physically strayed before as Maude had always kept him on his toes and extremely satisfied sexually, due to her very high sex drive and athletic physique. The bedroom wasn't the only place that Maude kept Frank busy however and she also kept him busy in the hallway, the kitchen, the bathroom and even inside the lounge as the couple had virtually made love in every inch of their home and even a few times, actually outside of it.

Very strangely however that particular morning, for the very first time ever, Frank suddenly felt as if he needed something else and that something else had actually presented itself in the form of another woman. An overwhelming urge to kiss her, hold her and make love to her rapidly ran through Frank's body and mind as she approached his table with his plate of food and a cup of coffee and then placed the items he'd ordered gently down on the table in front of him.

"Thank you." Frank said cheerfully as he glanced up at her face and then smiled. "Do you mind if I ask what your name is?"

"No, not at all. I'm Becky." She replied as she smiled. "Enjoy your breakfast Sir."

"Hi Becky, my name's Frank. Do you work here every day?" Frank asked as he quickly dug for more information.

"Yes, I have to really. This is my diner and if I'm not here, things just won't get done, or they won't get done right." Becky quickly clarified.

"Right." Frank replied as he nodded his head. "I'd love to see you again Becky without your apron on." He continued suggestively.

"Well that's a rather cheeky remark." Becky teased as she smiled. "For so early in the morning."

"I can do quite a few things rather well Becky and being cheeky is just one of them. If I we meet again, I can show you some others and I'm quite good at those too." Frank said playfully.

Becky laughed. "Well, if you pop back later today Frank, say at around eight this evening that's when I shut down for the day and then perhaps you can show me exactly what else you're good at." She teased.

"I definitely do that Becky." Frank quickly confirmed as he stretched out a hand towards her and then playfully tugged the edge of her apron. "I can't wait."

"I have to attend to some customers now, I'll see you later Frank." Becky said as she began to turn as she prepared to walk away.

"You sure will Becky." Frank quickly agreed as he picked up his bacon bap and got ready to devour it.

Due to Frank's flirtatious stop off, when he finally arrived outside the Restructure clinic, it was about eleven fifteen which was fifteen minutes after his consultation had been due to start and he quickly parked his vehicle and then made his way towards the front entrance. A slightly confused expression greeted Frank when he was shown to Talitha's consultation room door as Talitha opened it as it was very unlike Frank to be late but as soon as Talitha invited him inside, he immediately apologized for his lateness.

"I'm very sorry I'm late Talitha, I got held up in traffic." Frank explained as he stepped inside Talitha's consultation room.

"That's okay Frank but I was about to start without you." Talitha teased as she smiled. "Please take a seat. Would you like something to drink?"

Frank nodded. "Yes please, can I have a cappuccino?" He asked.

"Certainly and how's your week been Frank?" Talitha enquired as she crossed the room and headed towards the coffee machine.

"It's been a bit strange really." Frank replied. "I'm not really feeling myself at all."

"Why what's been going on?" Talitha asked.

"I'm not sure, I've been having some very strange feelings and it's almost like I'm totally going off Maude." Frank explained.

"That is very strange." Talitha agreed. "I think I should mention it to Professor Heisner again. How different have things been?"

"I just don't like to be close to Maude anymore, not like I used to." Frank began to elaborate as he gently shook his head. "And I've actually felt very attracted to several other women that I don't even know, strangers on the street and things."

"Don't a lot of men feel like that quite often?" Talitha enquired.

"No not really, this is different. This is a very powerful attraction, like love at first sight." Frank explained. "I don't normally want to spend my entire life with a woman that I've only ever seen once before and I've never ever dreamed of cheating on Maude before now but now, I seem to want to and I seem to want to quite often."

"I'll definitely raise this issue with Professor Heisner again." Talitha gently reassured him. "Would you like to proceed with your next procedure today, or would you rather wait until Professor Heisner comes back to me?"

"I should wait Talitha, at least until next week or something." Frank confirmed.

"Okay, I think that's for the best really Frank. These things you're experiencing are slightly strange and perhaps your body is finding it hard to actually adjust to so many rapid changes." Talitha advised as she nodded her head in agreement. "Slowing things down a bit might actually be good for you and perhaps you can start coming in once a fortnight instead of weekly."

"Yes, I think that's probably a good idea." Frank agreed.

"At least until we know exactly what's going on." Talitha clarified.

Frank nodded.

"Is there anything else that you'd like to discuss today Frank?" Talitha asked. "Or perhaps we could just look through some images and then you can pick out the ones that you are interested in, to prepare for your next procedure."

"Yes, let's do that." Frank agreed.

Talitha nodded as she touched the screen in front of her. "Which area of your body would you like to focus on next Frank?" She asked.

"My chest, definitely my chest." Frank quickly clarified. "I need to have a very strong chest that just oozes with manliness."

"Then Maude'll have some real competition." Talitha teased.

"Yep and she won't like that at all. She'll be really pissed off about losing the 'Mirror Test' every day." Frank replied. "And she'll have to cook dinner for me every day and take the trash out."

Talitha grinned.

Once Frank's consultation came to an end, Talitha courteously escorted him back towards the reception area and then returned to her consultation room quite quickly as she wanted to submit his notes to Professor Heisner before lunchtime was due to start. Alongside the usual client notes, Talitha also requested a meeting with Professor Heisner to discuss Frank's strange experiences with him which Frank had now brought to Talitha's attention on at least two separate occasions. The issue had been discussed briefly with the Professor the last time they'd met but since the situation had continued to deteriorate, Talitha wanted to raise it with him again.

The afternoon breezed gently into Talitha's life as she returned from lunch and as she began to prepare for her pending appointment with Samson, her spirits were high as he was always very cheerful, extremely pleasant and an absolute joy to meet. According to Samson, the last time they'd met, he'd discussed a desire to fix his chin that day but due to his commercial obligations and the nature of his work, Talitha couldn't be absolutely certain that he would actually do so as his body really wasn't his own to make any decisions about.

Despite the fact that Samson as a client differed vastly from Charmaine in many ways, the two did have one thing in common and that was the fact that they had both enhanced their bodies due to other people's demands which meant, in Talitha's opinion that their physical bodies were not really their own property. Regarding the issue of actual physical ownership of one's body however, Talitha worried slightly more about Charmaine than she did about Samson as he had actually chosen to relinquish that control for a price very intentionally himself, whereas Charmaine felt obligated to do so, purely due to her emotional attachment to Lachlan.

At approximately ten to three, Yucala called Talitha from the reception desk to notify her that Samson had already arrived and Talitha immediately began to prepare her consultation room for his appointment, even though he'd arrived slightly earlier than planned. Just a few minutes later there was a gentle tap at Talitha's consultation room door and she quickly rose to her feet and then crossed the room as she prepared to open it. A few pleasantries were politely exchanged as Talitha greeted Samson at the door, thanked Yucala for escorting him and then invited Samson inside her consultation room.

Fortunately for Talitha, the negative experiences of Dean and Frank that week didn't seem to extend to Samson and the cheerful grin that usually adorned his face was present as he sat down. An amused smile adorned Talitha's face as she sat and began to listen to Samson speak as he started to fill her in regarding the wild Sunday he'd enjoyed with his new lover.

"I guess someone else did come along." Talitha observed.

"Yes someone really did and funnily enough, it's actually the same woman that I gave directions to

491

but this time, I gave her a personal tour of my bedroom." Samson explained. "I was her tour guide."

"I won't ask how the tour went." Talitha replied.

"Let's just say, it was climatic and that we reached the peaks of all the mountains I showed her around." Samson joked. "I'm seriously in love with this woman Talitha and I think this is one."

"That was fast." Talitha said as she smiled.

"Really it was. I've never felt like this about anyone else." Samson replied as he grinned. "She's really beautiful. Our afternoon together sauntered delicately into the evening and then sprinted into a passion filled night and I have to admit it was absolutely mind blowing. I just can't wait to see her again."

"Okay Samson, what are we doing today? Your chin, or something else perhaps?" Talitha asked.

"I think I'll do my chin today Talitha but next week, I really need to sort out my chest, final preparations for the commercial." Samson clarified.

Talitha nodded as she touched the screen directly in front of her and it immediately populated with images of male chins. "Do you want something quite chiseled, round or pointed?" She asked as she turned her screen to face him.

"I might even need to replace my whole jaw line." Samson mentioned as he glanced at the images directly in front of him.

"Perhaps, let's just focus on your chin for now and your chest and then we'll think about the rest of your jaw line, if your chin doesn't quite align with the rest of your face." Talitha suggested.

"Right that's a good idea." Samson immediately agreed. "I have to be focused."

Approximately thirty minutes later, once Samson's new chin had been implanted, he expressed his sheer delight as he admired it in the long body sized client mirror inside the procedure room.

"I'm so happy Talitha, my ugly chin has well and truly gone." Samson gushed excitedly. "You are an absolute miracle worker."

Talitha smiled as she admired his new chin. "It really looks great Samson." She agreed. "You have great taste in chins."

Just a few minutes later, the two returned to Talitha's consultation room and then sat back down as Talitha prepared to make another client appointment for Samson the following week to sort out his chest. In many ways, Talitha felt very encouraged and motivated by her job on a daily basis and as she glanced at Samson's face, she smiled as the smile on her client's faces post procedure really did mean the world to her as it meant, she'd done her job to their satisfaction. To bring so much joy into people's lives in a manner that enhanced not only their physicalities but that also increased their levels of confidence was an invisible perk of her job that seemed like it was actually a gift to Talitha herself. Bringing so much joy into someone's life, definitely felt like it was a gift and it was a gift that not everyone had the skills, knowledge, tools, equipment, position, or ability to deliver and Talitha felt quite fortunate that now she could actually do so.

After Samson departed, Talitha spend the remainder of her afternoon writing up his notes and drinking hot cups of milky caramel latte which she decorated with generous helpings of whipped cream. A gentle peacefulness invisibly seemed to rest upon Talitha's shoulders that afternoon and once Samson's notes had been completed and submitted, just as home time arrived, she prepared to leave the building and start to make her way home for the evening as a warm feeling of satisfaction engulfed her body. The satisfaction from Talitha's final appointment that day, seemed to create an aura of peacefulness around Talitha as she drove and it was almost as if a silent blanket of comfort had fallen onto her body and covered her mind which gently reassured her that on that day, when it came to Samson, she'd definitely delivered.

JEALOUS RIVALS

For Saskia the Wednesday evening held very exciting prospects as she'd actually joined a gym the previous week that she now intended to visit once a week for a work out, or more specifically, to enact the pretention of a work out. Fitness routines weren't really Saskia's bag or her cup of tea as she had absolutely no desire whatsoever to get all sweaty in an attempt to improve her general fitness levels but she was very attracted to the possibility of showing of her new bodily changes to a live audience. Currently, Saskia was actually very single and that meant, she had no boyfriend to show off her newly acquired assets to and because she was in an absolute rush to show them of to anyone she possibly could, the gym in the shorter term had become an ideal venue in which to flaunt her new body.

Gyms as Saskia was well aware, were usually packed full of testosterone filled heterosexual males and the females that usually attended them could justifiably wear quite scanty clothing without any eyebrows being raised and that in Saskia's mind was an opportunity. An intention to facilitate that opportunity and parade herself in front an active male audience was a temptation that Saskia simply could not resist and so the preparations for her gym attendance had been taken very seriously indeed.

A black and gold lycra set which compromised of a short crop top and some skin tight shorts that fitted her almost perfectly had been purchased in advance, specifically for that purpose and she'd slipped the outfit on at home that evening just before she'd headed out to the gym. The very low cut top allowed her cleavage to pop out over the top of it as her breasts almost spilled out over the rather low neckline and the outfit was not only inviting but also extremely seductive. Fitness gyms, Saskia felt, were the perfect place to wear such attire and so the outfit suited Saskia's needs very precisely as it fitted the environment that she would be stepping into.

Rows of sweaty male bodies virtually lined the interior of the gym and the main workout room that was rather large as Saskia arrived which caused her heart to leap with joy as soon as she stepped inside the venue. Once inside the main workout room, Saskia very confidently removed the much looser tracksuit she'd worn over the top of her specially selected much shorter outfit as she prepared to begin to pretend to work out. Hot males, rows of exercise machines and sweaty bodies lined the large expanse as Saskia glanced around the large training room and looked for a central spot and the optimal position for her physical display.

When Saskia had chosen what she felt would be the best position, she quickly headed across the room towards an exercise machine as she held her head and breasts high up in the air and pulled her shoulders blades back as far as she possibly could in order to push her breasts out as far as they could go. Much to Saskia's complete and utter delight, some of the males inside the large training room immediately stopped working out and began to watch her as she walked and she silently basked in their attention which was very clearly focused upon her. In essence, Saskia now had exactly what she wanted as almost everyone inside the training room had not only noticed her breasts but had also focused their attention solely upon her.

The treadmill that Saskia selected as her first exercise prop was quickly mounted and stepped onto as soon as she reached it, in order to maintain the pretention that she had actually attended the gym to work out. Despite the fact that Saskia had never actually stepped onto a treadmill ever before in her entire life, she tackled it fearlessly as she glanced at a few other slightly more serious gym attendees nearby on similar pieces of equipment and then attempted to mimic their movements and actions

Several males situated nearby continued to stare at Saskia as she captured and fully retained their attention and she grinned in absolute delight as they admired her bodily proportions and she began to silently rejoice in her achievement. Every second of the men's attention was silently enjoyed and encouraged as Saskia grabbed her moment by the hands and wiggled her chest around to keep their hot blooded male eyes fixed very firmly on every inch of her body.

Just a few seconds later however, disaster suddenly struck as another very pretty looking female entered inside the gym and completely shattered Saskia's joy as she had even bigger breasts than Saskia did. The enormous pair of breasts that sat very firmly attached to the woman's chest were absolutely huge and Saskia's moment of satisfying fulfillment was silently smashed to absolute pieces as the woman walked through the training room and everyone immediately turned round and stared at her. A stunned expression rapidly crossed Saskia's face as she quietly absorbed just how enormous the woman's breasts actually were and she gasped in shock as she almost slipped of the actual treadmill.

Everyone inside the large training room immediately fell silent as both the men and even the women stopped and just stared at the owner of the huge pair of breasts as she silently weaved her way through the pieces of gym equipment. The males that had been so actively engrossed in their admiration of Saskia's body, rapidly averted their gaze towards this new attraction as they visually abandoned Saskia and fixed their attention upon the other woman and a jealous, envious rage rapidly began to accumulate inside of Saskia as she watched. Every single drop of male attention that Saskia had been gloriously basking in just moments before had now totally gone and Saskia felt absolutely horrified.

Once it had fully sunk into Saskia's mind that her breasts no longer reigned the training room and that her reign for that day was indeed over, due to the arrival of a superior, larger pair of breasts and a much prettier face, Saskia prepared to accept her defeat and abandon the gym for the rest of the day. Internally, Saskia's mind almost began to explode as feelings of jealousy and sentiments of inadequacy began to somersault through her thoughts and silently jolted and knocked her confidence. Dissatisfaction and discontent quickly became Saskia's closest companions as a lump of resentment suddenly stuck inside her throat and she almost gagged in absolute disgust.

Regardless of where Saskia looked as she stepped of the treadmill and prepared to depart, the impact of this new female rival was apparent as the occupants of the gym focused solely upon her. Anger and bitterness seemed to seep out of Saskia's pores as she walked and had already filled her heart, flooded through her veins and now threatened to actually spill out onto the floor around her with every step she took. In fact, it actually appeared that the longer Saskia looked at this new female rival, the more jealous she felt and the worse she felt about herself. Every step that was taken towards the training room exit was filled with absolute contempt and total disgust as Saskia shook her head in total disbelief as she walked.

Inside Saskia's mind, a sapling of displeasure had now very firmly rooted itself to each of her inner thoughts and it had rapidly begun to grow into a fully grown tree of discontent which now threatened to consume and devour every part of her. Seeds of disgust from tree of discontent inside Saskia's body rapidly began to exude from her pores as droplets of sweat began to prick and gather upon her forehead as she walked. Every ounce of joy that had once existed had now been totally pushed out of Saskia's body and mind as the branches from the tree of discontent had silently spread out inside of her and replaced any positive sentiments that it had found in its path.

No matter how hard Saskia tried, the soils of her mind seemed to fertilize and nurture those hate filled seeds almost immediately and by the time she neared the exit of the training room, it was almost as if a whole forest of dissatisfaction resided within her. Each awful branch of discomfort seemed to weave itself tightly around her veins and skin as the happiness she'd felt just moments before was silently squeezed out of her. The next time she met Talitha, Saskia quietly decided, she would definitely have to discuss a larger breast enlargement which would perhaps alleviate the unhappiness that she now felt as that would ensure, she would never be upstaged by another female again, or by another pair of breasts.

On Saskia's way towards the exit, she actually had to walk past the woman that she now viewed as some kind of human object and as she did so there was an angry scowl upon her face. The woman's entrance had triggered Saskia's intense jealousy but she seemed totally oblivious to Saskia's emotional inner turmoil. For a few seconds, Saskia paused as she passed her and then stared into her eyes as the flames of hatred which had been sparked inside her continued to burn her heart and nothing but venom laced her stare.

An urge rapidly gathered inside Saskia to shun her verbally and lash out at the woman with her tongue but she had absolutely no reason to do so and an angry outburst would definitely make Saskia appear childish and out of control. Very unusually, Saskia somehow actually managed to hold her rage inside of her as she quietly restrained herself from expressing the anger that boiled away just under the surface of her skin as she held her head up high and then prepared to exit the gym.

"Fake." Saskia muttered under her breath as she gave the woman a snobbish stare and then turned away.

Absolutely no response to Saskia's utterance was forthcoming as the woman with the huge breasts simply continued to enjoy her exercise regime and a conversation that she was involved in with an athletic, very handsome looking man that was situated on a piece of equipment right next to her. The very handsome looking male it appeared had actually offered to demonstrate to her how to utilize a piece of gym equipment and she seemed totally oblivious to Saskia's obvious expression of jealousy and was very deeply engrossed in her conversation. Not even an ounce of comfort was provided to Saskia as the feelings of disgust inside of her almost spiraled out of control as she resumed her walk and flounced across the remainder of the floor as she headed towards the exit in a stroppy, silent tantrum.

Just as Saskia approached the exit, one final glance was cast back over the interior of the large training room that housed over one hundred pieces of gym equipment inside it as Saskia accepted her defeat in absolute disgust and her departure. Much to Saskia's annoyance, the occupants inside the gym continued to stare at the female that had captured their attention with her huge breasts which seemed to stand to attention very proudly, almost as if they knew they were actually being scrutinized and inspected. Quite simply, the woman possessed the largest pair of breasts that Saskia had ever seen in her entire life and there was simply no denying that fact and as she moved around, her captivated audience inside the gym watched her every movement, expression and breath as she actually, really worked out.

"Next time I come here, I'll have bigger breasts than you do." Saskia muttered under her breath as she gave the woman one last hateful glance and then stepped out of the training room.

The Thursday morning for Talitha was an absolute encouragement and total joy as she arrived at work, settled herself in and then at approximately eleven met with Sylvester, one of her more humble and appreciative male clients. Quite interestingly for Talitha although this was actually Sylvester's second consultation, she'd actually been instructed to wait before performing any procedures by Professor Heisner himself which meant there would be no actual Download procedures performed for him that day. In fact, all of Sylvester's actual Downloads would be performed in one day and the date for actual event had not yet been agreed which meant the two spent most of the morning identifying the various body parts and facial features that he was the most interested in to prepare sufficiently. Due to Sylvester's unique needs, Talitha instead threw herself into the intricate counseling requirements that his consultation required which definitely demanded her attention.

"I just hope that this physical transformation will change my life because my life really needs to be changed." Sylvester said as his client consultation came to an end and he rose to his feet. "Life's been pretty horrible so far."

"It could definitely change things for you Sylvester but it can't change other people's attitudes towards you, so you really will have to keep your real identity to yourself." Talitha explained as she walked him towards her consultation room door.

"True. I can't go through this again." Sylvester agreed. "It's been a never ending nightmare. I struggle to carry on every single day."

"Unfortunately Sylvester, life doesn't always provide us with therapy and sometimes that's a gift we have to learn to give ourselves." Talitha advised as she neared her consultation room door. "Life doesn't come with an answer book to all the questions and challenges that we're presented with and sometimes our journey through life is a very lonely walk."

"I did think about real therapy at one point but I didn't really see the point in the end." Sylvester began to explain as he turned to face her. "Therapy can't change other people's attitudes towards you, it can only change your attitude towards them and your attitude towards yourself. Unfortunately, my father's past has been my cross to carry for many years and nothing can change that or the hatred that his name generates inside people's minds."

Talitha smiled as she stood in front of her consultation room door and paused for a moment. "You know Sylvester, I've realized one thing in life and that is, you can't keep carrying the past around with you forever. Sometimes, you have to pack up the negative events that affect you from your past, place them inside a garbage bag and then throw them in the trash and as you leave them behind and move forward in life, you leave them exactly where you found them." She advised. "At times, some of the things that happen to us in life are so horrible that's the only way that you can really actually survive."

"True." Sylvester replied. "And now, I really should be able to leave them truly behind me because no one will know who I am and my father's shadow and history of abuse will no longer follow me around everywhere I go."

"Yes and try to remember that your mind is the most effective tool, the most powerful weapon and the very best shield that you could ever possibly have." Talitha advised. "It can either destroy you, or it can help you thrive, so you have to learn to control your mind and the thoughts it contains, so that you're not defeated by negativity."

Sylvester nodded in agreement.

"When we discard the horrors that haunt us from the past from our minds, we strip them of their power and their ability to destroy our future, our present and our inner selves." Talitha said. "The past can be such an ugly place to live and sometimes, you actually have to move home, renovate your thoughts and redecorate the walls of your life with the joys of the present."

"Thanks Talitha. I really needed some encouragement and that's great advice." Sylvester replied.

"That's what I'm here for Sylvester." Talitha said as she graciously accepted Sylvester's complimentary remarks and opened up her consultation room door. "Let me take you back down to the reception area and I'll see you next week."

Sylvester nodded.

Later that day, when the mid-afternoon arrived, the time of Charmaine's consultation quickly neared and as Talitha nervously prepared to face not only Charmaine but also possibly Lachlan that prospect almost filled her with dread. The second breast enlargement that Lachlan had demanded had not yet been performed and that meant, Lachlan would be on the warpath and that Talitha would be considered his main foe. If he was indeed actually present, his anger definitely would be too and Talitha had no doubt at all that Lachlan would definitely attend after Talitha's refusal to satisfy his request during Charmaine's last consultation.

Worries rapidly began to scurry through Talitha's mind as she sat inside her consultation room and just waited for the couple to arrive as three in the afternoon approached and Charmaine's appointment slot drew closer. The desires that Lachlan harbored inside himself regarding Charmaine's breast enlargement had only been partially satisfied and Talitha knew, Lachlan really wasn't a patient man. Finally just after three, the couple inevitably arrived and Talitha smiled at them both as she showed them into her consultation room and then politely offered them a beverage, despite the extreme nervousness that surged chaotically around inside of her.

Inside Talitha's consultation room there seemed to be an angry grey cloud of tension that swirled around above their heads which seemed to grow by the second as a sudden quietness swept over the room as Talitha silently observed Lachlan's attendance with absolute dread. Regardless of Lachlan's attendance however, Talitha still had to conduct Charmaine's consultation and prepare the beverage that Charmaine had requested and she began to bravely prepare her cup of tea as she attempted to start Charmaine's actual consultation. Nothing but an angry grunt had emanated from Lachlan's mouth when Talitha had offered him a beverage which reminded Talitha of a swine and in many ways, so too did Lachlan's whole persona.

Principles were great things to have in life and to stand up for, Talitha quietly contemplated but everyone inside her consultation room that day knew the actual reality and whether Talitha liked it or not, she also knew, she would eventually have to fulfill Lachlan's request. Each of Charmaine's procedures had been paid for in full in advance which meant technically, Lachlan's demands could not be refused, or denied to him unless Professor

Heisner intervened and refused to deliver them which it seemed, he had absolutely no intention of doing. Interference in Charmaine's life and Lachlan's plan for it on Talitha's part would not be accepted in the longer term by Lachlan and neither would deliberations, negotiations, or any kind of compromise and if he didn't get what he'd paid for, there'd be hell to pay.

"I had to give Charmaine's back and shoulders a bit more time so that her body could adjust to the weight of her enlarged breasts." Talitha explained bravely as she placed the cup of tea gently down in front of Charmaine and then sat back down at her desk. "How's that working out for your Charmaine?" She asked as she faced the couple and reinforced the lie that she'd encouraged Charmaine to tell.

Some silent glances and nervous smiles were exchanged between the two women but only they understood what they actually meant as between them there was now an unspoken mutual understanding that Lachlan was not privy to, or any part of. The glances and smiles symbolized the fact that Talitha had lied to Lachlan and that Charmaine was not to divulge her knowledge of that lie to him and both women understood the words expressed through their faces, instinctively.

"This cup of tea is absolutely lovely Talitha." Charmaine mentioned as she smiled. "Thanks."

"You're very welcome Charmaine. Right, today I recommend that we perform your waist procedure as that goes hand in hand with your last procedure." Talitha suggested as she smiled.

"That sounds like a great idea Talitha." Charmaine immediately agreed.

Nothing but an expression of absolute disgust greeted Talitha as she glanced at Lachlan's face and then touched the screen directly in front of her as she prepared to offer Charmaine some waist choices. Regardless of his disgust however, Lachlan quickly joined in as he suddenly leant forward towards the screen as it rapidly populated with over a hundred images of female waists and began to peruse the large assortment of choices on offer as he began to discuss some of the images with Charmaine. Another procedure would definitely be performed upon Charmaine's body that day and so Lachlan actively began to participate, in order to ensure that his preferences were expressed as Talitha watched him quietly. Internally, Talitha sighed with relief as she silently celebrated that at least for now, she'd managed to stall Lachlan again and that she'd successfully managed to distract him from his relentless pursuit of the second breast enlargement but deep down Talitha knew, her delay tactics would not be effective forever.

Approximately twenty minutes later, the two women made their way towards the procedure room as Talitha prepared to implement the procedure that once again, Lachlan had ultimately, actually chosen. The lid of the transparent capsule was quickly lifted up as Charmaine began to walk up the small steps situated at the front of it and prepared to climb inside.

"Lachlan is very angry." Charmaine whispered. "I managed to keep the peace for a while Talitha but he's really annoyed about the breast enlargement. He wants what he's paid for." She explained solemnly in a very hushed tone.

"I know, I can tell." Talitha whispered back. "Are you happy with the waist Download that I'm about to implement?"

Charmaine smiled and nodded.

"You'd say if you weren't right?" Talitha whispered as she probed Charmaine further in an attempt to try and extract the truth.

"Sure." Charmaine replied as she nodded her head.

Satisfaction was not forthcoming however as Talitha glanced at Charmaine's face and noticed the pleading tone of her voice and the worrying dimness inside her eyes that said absolutely everything that Talitha needed to actually know. Nothing that Charmaine did whilst at Restructure was actually her own decision and in the longer term, Talitha really was fighting a losing battle and she knew it as no matter what stance she attempted to make, ultimately her opposition to Lachlan's rule was in the end going to be, completely ineffective. In terms of the stance that Talitha had taken, she definitely felt that it had been worth it but it worried her that Charmaine had to live with and cope with Lachlan's anger every day as Talitha opposed him and challenged his rule over Charmaine's life and body from a distance.

An awkward silence began to fill the air as Talitha quietly considered that the answer to her question hadn't really been an answer at all and that Lachlan's dominance was the only answer there really was and that was one factor that Talitha could not actually, really change. Perhaps Charmaine had actually only consented to the procedures at Restructure in order to keep the peace and to avoid angry confrontations at home, Talitha thoughtfully speculated as she prepared to close the capsule lid down over Charmaine's body. Discomfort rapidly began to fill Talitha inside as her stomach silently turned over and she felt a sudden desire to actually vomit as Talitha knew eventually, she would also have to surrender to Lachlan's rule and Lachlan's demands.

"Look Talitha, I've given this a lot of thought and in the long run, Lachlan's actually doing me a favor." Charmaine mentioned in a whisper. "He's paying for me to look very physically beautiful and so really, he has my best interests at heart." She insisted. "Though it might not always seem so."

"I guess so." Talitha accepted slightly reluctantly.

Once Charmaine's waist reduction procedure had been performed and her next appointment made, Talitha began to escort the two back towards the reception area. A huge victorious smile was plastered across Lachlan's face as he internally celebrated his victory as the three walked along the crisp white corridor towards the main entrance of the building but there was absolutely nothing that Talitha could do or say about it.

"You look absolutely amazing Charmaine." Lachlan said as he verbally expressed his appreciation. "There'll be no more wandering eyes now, I promise." He vowed as he kissed Charmaine passionately on the cheek.

Every word that Lachlan spoke absolutely repulsed Talitha although his words seemed to please Charmaine as she smiled in response and Talitha's stomach almost turned in disgust as she watched. Regardless of Talitha's noble efforts, deep down she knew, there was an obvious imbalance of power between the couple that thrived within their relationship and that issue fell very far outside the scope and remit of Talitha's work and that issue would definitely not be solved that day, or even by Talitha herself.

In essence, Talitha had to accept that she wasn't actually Charmaine's mother, she was purely a consultant and that she really couldn't fix all the world's problems, or even all her client's problems and that was just a limitation and constraint of her work that would definitely frustrate her at times. Her job was simply to guide people through the bodily changes that they requested and paid for and that was the commercial reality of the transaction that they entered into with Restructure and ultimately Professor Heisner, whether she liked it or not. Some negative things, Talitha would be able to change for some people but she simply couldn't change everything that was wrong for everyone and Charmaine was a perfect example of that limitation and constraint.

Perhaps, Talitha considered quietly as she left the couple inside the reception area and began to walk back towards her consultation room, Lachlan's incessant demands for physical perfection from Charmaine would ultimately in the end, give her the equality in their relationship that she so desperately needed. Perhaps, in some obscure way, Lachlan had actually given Charmaine that equality in the long run himself by making Charmaine more physically attractive and perhaps, Lachlan would in the end shift the balance of power between them both more in Charmaine's favor. Perhaps, Lachlan's persistent quest to satisfy his own sexual desires coupled with his domination over Charmaine's body had essentially created a noose that would now hang around Lachlan's neck and contribute to his own actual downfall. Perhaps, just perhaps, Lachlan had very unintentionally, actually ended his own rule over Charmaine's life, Talitha quietly concluded as she stepped back inside her consultation room, now that was entirely possible.

"I think after that consultation, I definitely deserve a caramel latte." Talitha muttered as she walked towards the coffee machine.

Deep down inside as Talitha walked towards the coffee machine, she hoped that her theory might actually hold true and that one day, Charmaine would be delivered from the curse of Lachlan and the dictatorship that she currently lived inside. Suddenly, a warm, comforting, friendly thought leapt inside Talitha's mind as she sat back down at her desk with her latte that perhaps by caving into Lachlan's current demands, in the longer term, Talitha herself would actually give Charmaine exactly what she really needed. In the short term, Lachlan had definitely won the battle over Charmaine's body but perhaps, just perhaps, in the longer term, he had really lost the war.

When four thirty arrived, so too did Patrick, Talitha's final and third client of that rather hectic

Thursday and she immediately greeted him and then invited him inside her consultation room. In terms of Patrick's appearance, he was a rather simple looking man and had a slight build and he looked very much like the kind of man that one could perhaps find on any city street. A beverage was politely offered to him as Talitha quietly began to speculate as to why he might have actually attended Restructure and why he might require Professor Heisner's services as there were no visible clues at all.

"How can I assist you today Patrick?" Talitha asked as she gently placed a full cup of coffee down on her desk in front of him. "What are your overall objectives and what would you actually like to achieve at Restructure?"

"This is slightly embarrassing Talitha but I was a very famous child actor and I wanted to get back into the business but as you can see, my looks aren't what they were and it's really quite hard out there." Patrick explained.

"Ah yes, I see. Now that you mention it, I do actually recognize your name Patrick, you were a great actor." Talitha replied. "I've watched some of your movies like Family On Ice."

"Yeah Family On Ice, everyone remembers that film and that's part of the problem. Once people remember who I am, or who I was they're like what happened to you, you were such a cute kid."

Patrick explained. "It's a bit embarrassing really, so I'll need to make a few changes to my face and a few changes to my body. Just to get myself back into the saddle of the horse again and pick myself back up off the ground."

"Sure Patrick that won't be a problem." Talitha quickly reassured him as she smiled. "You can only have one Download procedure request performed on any given consultation session however, did Professor Heisner explain that to you?"

"Yes he did." Patrick immediately clarified.

"Great, if you like Patrick we can make a start today by filling in your list of Download requests on the system as currently, there are none." Talitha suggested. "So that when you're ready to proceed, everything is already mapped out and planned for you."

"That would be absolutely great." Patrick agreed.

"Right, so let's start with your procedure request list. Just go through every physical feature that you would like to change from the tip of your head to the bottom of your toes and tell me roughly when you would like to change each one." Talitha instructed. "Exact dates aren't required, just the order that you would like each procedure in."

"My nose, definitely my nose. My ears, definitely my ears. My arms, definitely my arms."

Patrick replied enthusiastically. "My legs because they are truly awful. My chest because that is really puny looking and my stomach as it really needs a lot more definition."

"Wow Patrick that's quite a list." Talitha teased as she smiled. "So you'll be my client for a while then?"

"Yes. You'll probably be lumbered with me for quite a while Talitha, for your sins." Patrick agreed as he smiled.

"If it's for those Patrick then you'll be coming here forever." Talitha joked.

Patrick grinned.

After Patrick's consultation ended, Talitha escorted him back to the reception area and then returned to her consultation room to write up his notes. The working day felt as if it had been extremely long but Talitha suspected that, that was probably due to the fact that she'd squeezed in three client consultations that day instead of the usual one or two. Fatigue seemed to grip Talitha's body when five thirty finally arrived and as she prepared to make her way home, she wearily plucked her handbag from its usual spot on the ground and then switched of the Restructure system.

Not only had Talitha had three client consultations that day but one had actually been with Charmaine and although Charmaine herself wasn't particularly tiring, Lachlan definitely was and his distasteful presence always seemed to really drain Talitha as it was so vile and so repugnant. A smile crossed Talitha's face as she arrived inside the parking lot and then entered her vehicle as she began to internally rejoice in the fact that at least, she had Bryson to go home to each night and that he was definitely a joy and certainly not, a repugnant nightmare like Lachlan.

On the Friday morning, a quite mild morning greeted Talitha as she stepped out of her home and then began to make her way towards her vehicle which as usual was parked in the driveway. At the end of that working day, a delicious weekend was waiting for Talitha to enjoy and so she began to prepare herself internally for her working day ahead and her journey as she started the engine of her car. In comparison to the previous working day, the Friday would definitely be less cumbersome as Talitha only had two client consultations scheduled for that day and then a meeting with Professor Heisner which had been arranged for the late afternoon but as one of those consultations was with Saskia that did worry Talitha slightly.

Rather unfortunately, Saskia was an obstacle of annoyance that Friday which would have to be endured and overcome before the romantic plans that Bryson had made for the couple for the weekend could begin but Talitha was far less interested in Saskia than she was in Bryson's plans. A romantic boat trip had been organized for the couple by Bryson which sounded absolutely fantastic and that lifted Talitha's spirits as she arrived at work, parked her car and then began to make her way towards the main entrance of the building and the two smoked glass main doors. The day would definitely be a bittersweet day and there was now a conflict of emotions inside Talitha, purely due to Saskia's appointment but she definitely knew, her Friday evening and her whole Saturday would be, absolutely spectacular.

At ten thirty on the dot that Friday morning, Cassandra appeared and her consultation was almost performed at the speed of light as she was shown into Talitha's consultation room, selected a lip enhancement, extremely quickly and was then given the Download procedure that she'd requested. When Cassandra departed and lunchtime arrived, Talitha opted for a quick takeaway lunch that day as she visited the nearby diner as her afternoon schedule was really quite busy but since Cassandra's notes had already been written up and submitted that morning, Talitha now had one less thing to do during her busy afternoon.

Despite Talitha's fairly pleasant morning, at around two thirty, well slightly after as Saskia was absolutely never ever on time, Saskia and Marcus inevitably showed up and Talitha braced herself for what might follow as she invited them inside her consultation room. Upon Talitha's face there was an enthusiastic smile as she greeted them both and inside her heart there was a silent hope that Saskia would be slightly more reasonable that day. In a matter of just minutes however, Talitha's hopes were quickly dashed to the ground and then trampled all over by Saskia's words and her extremely ungracious attitude as she began to make her demands for that particular client session extremely clear.

"I need much bigger breasts Talitha." Saskia demanded impatiently as she began to strop around the consultation room.

"Please, sit down Saskia." Marcus muttered as he quickly tried to calm her down. "We've only just got here."

"Would either of you like a drink?" Talitha offered as she smiled discreetly and sighed internally as this session really wasn't going to be pretty and she could already see that from Saskia's attitude.

"Daddy, I need my body to be absolutely perfect and astoundingly sexy and it isn't yet." Saskia barked as she stared angrily at her father's face.

A very ugly outburst and temper tantrum loomed just upon the horizon of Talitha's working day which she had made an effort to interrupt but it was immediately clear, Saskia was having absolutely none of it. Despite the fact that Saskia's consultation had just started, Talitha already felt quite drained and tired as she sat and listened to Saskia as she began to rant. Regardless of Talitha's inner sentiments however, she kept an optimistic, pretentious smile on her face as she attempted to maintain the illusion that everything was perfectly fine and quietly accepted that Saskia was going to be a prickly thorn in her side for quite a while.

In terms of Saskia's client requests, she would always be the hardest client to please amongst Talitha's current client group and she reminded Talitha of a prickly rose bush which now sat very firmly rooted inside the garden of her life that would needle her with thorns of discontent every time the two met. Apparently, the more one did for Saskia, the more she demanded and the more Saskia was given, the more she wanted and that was becoming increasingly apparent as Talitha thoughtfully prepared to offer Saskia a response.

"These breasts are inferior Talitha and now, I have to carry them around with me everywhere I go." Saskia ranted as she flopped down inside the chair next to her father. "I need bigger breasts daddy and I need them now."

DOWNLOADABLE

For five more minutes, Talitha just sat and listened to Saskia speak as she held her tongue and avoided making any further comments as Talitha had already realized that if she tried to interrupt Saskia in mid-demand mode, it would only anger her even more. An angry outburst from Saskia was the last thing that Talitha wanted on a Friday afternoon and so she listened and waited, before she even attempted to rejoin the conversation, until she felt that Saskia had calmed down a bit.

"I'm not sure we can actually do that for you Saskia." Talitha explained patiently. "I mean, I just don't think that it's even possible because there are no larger breast Downloads available inside the Restructure system."

"That can't possibly be correct Talitha, I saw a woman just the other day with larger breasts than mine and so if that's possible naturally, or through cosmetic surgery then it must be available here." Saskia insisted as she stared at Talitha's face.

"I've already given you the largest cup size that we have available on our system Saskia." Talitha immediately reassured her as she observed the sharpness of Saskia's stare which certainly wasn't pleasant and made her feel very uncomfortable. "I'm not sure what else I can do for you."

"I saw a woman with much larger breasts than mine with my very own eyes." Saskia ranted as she suddenly rose to her feet again and then began to storm angrily around the room. "If it's possible to have those breasts naturally then it must be possible for me to get them here. I want bigger breasts."

Reason seemed to fly straight out of Talitha's consultation room window as Saskia continued to rant and incessantly nag as Talitha just sat and listened. No matter what Talitha said, or how Marcus tried to reason with his daughter, it seemed to make absolutely no difference at all as she stormed around the room in an angry rage and verbally expressed her displeasure and unreasonable demands, very loudly. Regardless of how many times Saskia heaped her complaints on top of Talitha's shoulders however, there really wasn't actually very much that Talitha could do as she couldn't actually provide Saskia with what she wanted as Talitha was just a consultant and she couldn't actually change that system constraint. The capacity of what was on offer to clients inside the Restructure system itself had various limitations which meant, the size of breasts that Saskia had demanded and what she ultimately wanted, wasn't even readily available to anyone as larger breasts than a double G cup size just weren't a provision that Restructure actually provided.

Defeat seemed to rapidly consume Marcus as he gave up his opposition to Saskia's temper tantrum almost immediately and just gave a few silent nods as her angry display continued as Talitha watched quietly and waited for Marcus to respond. Once again, Marcus had failed to put his foot down and curb Saskia's behavior which was extremely embarrassing for them both and she seemed to be doing all of the talking, or more specifically, all of the ranting.

"Saskia, getting upset about this won't actually change anything." Talitha suddenly pointed out. "This is a system limitation and that means, only Professor Heisner can actually do anything about it."

Once Saskia's consultation was over, Talitha silently vowed, she would definitely have to raise this as an issue with Professor Heisner as Saskia couldn't even control herself, or conduct herself in a reasonable manner and that felt extremely uncomfortable. The physical manifestations of anger that Saskia displayed when she was unhappy, or upset were totally unacceptable and extremely uncomfortable for everyone around her and Professor Heisner would definitely have to be notified, regardless of who Saskia actually was or wasn't as Marcus didn't seem to want to do anything about it at all.

"Right." Saskia replied as she flopped back down onto the chair. "So I need to ask Professor Heisner to fix this?"

"Professor Heisner is a very busy man Saskia." Marcus quickly pointed out as he gently shook his head. "I'm sure he won't have time to discuss your breast enlargement with you and if he does, it certainly won't be today."

"Look Saskia, I'll see what I can do. I'll speak to the Professor when I see him next and I'll let him know about your request and if there's anything he can do about it, I'm sure he'll do it." Talitha mumbled in defeat as she quickly surrendered. She had tried to resist Saskia but every attempt she'd made had been dashed to the ground and had then been trampled all over by Saskia's very angry feet and Talitha had become weary just trying to put up a resistance.

The dramatic display seemed to have ceased however and Talitha immediately took the opportunity to provide a voice of reason to Saskia's angry chaos and bring some kind of closure to the situation, for that day at least. Regardless of how Talitha actually felt about Saskia's childish tantrums, it was becoming increasingly apparent to her that if she tried to oppose Saskia, she would be dragged into endless arguments that would never ever actually cease and that was extremely exhausting.

Apparently, Marcus usually just gave Saskia whatever she wanted, whenever she demanded it from him as he attempted to keep the peace and tried to make Saskia happy and it was becoming increasingly obvious now that Professor Heisner really was Talitha's only option. Everyone inside the consultation room had caved in and had complied with Saskia's demands and Saskia had been absolutely victorious that day and Talitha knew, it would probably be just a matter of time before she'd have a larger pair of breasts attached to her body, if that was indeed actually possible.

"I just want to be able to hold my head up high and know that I have the biggest breasts on the planet." Saskia explained. "No woman should be my rival and no other woman should feel superior to me because of what I do not have.

"Talitha's going to do what she can Saskia." Marcus quickly reassured her.

Although Talitha's promise to Saskia was not actually conclusive, it seemed to satisfy Saskia temporarily as she suddenly flashed Talitha a charming smile and then nodded her head in agreement. Some small triumphant glimmers seemed to light up and dance around inside Saskia's eyes which glistened as Talitha silently sat and watched her for a few seconds without saying a word as Saskia seemed to silently celebrate her victory. Marcus was quite simply no match when it came to Saskia and her battle for what she wanted in life and Talitha very much doubted that Professor Heisner would be able to handle Saskia either as in

Saskia's mind the men simply represented a small hurdle that stood in the way of her happiness, who's heads had to be jumped over.

Very fortunately for Talitha, once a plan of action had been agreed that satisfied Saskia to some extent, Saskia quickly began to select some legs for her leg contour procedure as her consultation continued. When Saskia's actual leg Download procedure had been performed and another appointment had been organized, an internal sigh was given as Talitha very happily escorted the two back towards the reception area.

A smile of utter joy and sheer relief spread out across Talitha's face as she watched them depart and then returned to her consultation room, grateful that one of the ugliest parts of her week was now officially over. Somehow, Saskia had managed to tie herself up in knots inside Talitha's hair and now, she could not actually be combed out of it as she continued to weave herself in and out of the many strands and aggravate Talitha further every time the two women met and that was something that Talitha definitely knew, would not change for the foreseeable future.

Four thirty drew near and a smile of delight spread out across Talitha's face as the end of her working day finally showed its face as she enthusiastically began to make her way towards Professor Heisner's office for their planned meeting. Once Talitha arrived outside Professor Heisner's office, she immediately knocked on the door and she was quickly invited inside as that day it seemed, Professor Heisner was actually very well organized and was actually waiting for her arrival.

For a few minutes, Talitha spent some time discussing Saskia and the difficulties she presented as she quickly enlightened the Professor about Saskia's most recent demands and her temper tantrums. Some time was spent on Frank's issues as Talitha touched upon the concerns she had about his procedures and the various side effects that he'd mentioned and described to her but Professor Heisner didn't appear to have an immediate solution to either of the problems that Talitha raised.

"Leave these issues with me Talitha." Professor Heisner instructed as he stood up and then began to pace the room as he rubbed his head thoughtfully. "I'll have to see what I can do. Larger breasts than the current range are an avenue that I just haven't explored yet but it might be possible."

"Saskia is very demanding. What should I say to her?" Talitha asked.

Upon Professor Heisner's face there was a disgruntled expression as he continued to pace his office and somehow, although Saskia wasn't actually even present, she'd managed to make their meeting slightly more awkward as she'd placed them both under a lot of pressure. A blanket of discomfort seemed to suddenly cover the room as an uncomfortable silence swept across it and for a few minutes no words were spoken by anyone at all.

"Talitha, I've decided that I'll actually allow you to apply two, or even three Download procedures to Saskia's body per session from now on and that should keep her reasonably happy for a while." Professor Heisner instructed as he turned and faced her. "If you don't do that Saskia will be with us forever and we don't want that now do we?"

"Will her body be able to cope with so many changes at once?" Talitha asked.

"Talitha, I'm sure Saskia could probably cope with a mountain falling on top of her." Professor Heisner joked. "Don't you worry about Saskia, she's a tough cookie and she can take care of herself. Normally, I wouldn't even accept someone like Saskia as a client but my hands are tied on this one as you know. It's a tricky situation, Saskia is a tricky situation and she's a bit of a handful. She's a very determined young women, extremely strong willed and exceptionally difficult."

"Right Professor Heisner, I'll make sure I do that in future." Talitha replied as she smiled.

"Now you get off home and enjoy your weekend Talitha and don't you worry about Saskia. Saskia really isn't your problem, rather unfortunately, she's actually mine." Professor Heisner gently reassured her. "Just give her exactly what she wants and then she'll no longer be my problem, or yours."

"What about Frank and the side effects he mentioned?" Talitha gently reminded him as she sought further clarification about any possible side effects to the Download procedures.

"You'll really have to leave those issues with me Talitha." Professor Heisner insisted as he began to walk towards his office door. "I don't have any answers yet but I'll look into any possible side effects straight away."

"Professor Heisner, I also wanted to discuss Charmaine with you." Talitha said as she began to stand up. "And Dean."

"Look Talitha, when it comes to Charmaine there's not really a lot that you can actually do, she has to be the one to refuse to participate and without her refusal, you're fighting a losing battle." Professor Heisner advised. "I'll have a look at Dean's notes more thoroughly, once I've fully investigated the side effects as that issue is my top priority right now as those affect everyone."

"Right." Talitha replied as began to walk towards the door. "Okay, I'll see you on Monday Professor Heisner and thank you."

"Don't you worry about anything Talitha, I'll sort everything out." Professor Heisner promised as he held his office door open. "Don't take your client's problems home with you that's my job."

"Enjoy your weekend Professor Heisner." Talitha said gratefully as she stepped out into the corridor.

"You too Talitha, you too." Professor Heisner replied as he began to close his office door.

Every step that Talitha took suddenly felt very light as she walked back along the corridor towards the reception area as Professor Heisner had effectively just liberated Talitha from the burden of having to endure Saskia for a very long period of time. The news had brightened up her mood no end and lifted her spirit as at one point, Talitha had begun to think Saskia would never actually leave her list. Throughout their meeting, Professor Heisner had also voiced the sentiments that Talitha herself had felt deep down inside regarding Saskia and she silently rejoiced in the comfort he had provided to her, alongside his very supportive promises that he would take personal responsibility for sorting Saskia's issues out.

Regardless of the Professor's personal friendship with Marcus that demanded additional levels of care and which also implied that Talitha had to be even more tolerant, helpful and polite towards Saskia than any other client, Saskia was a total pain in the butt but fortunately, Professor Heisner fully understood and appreciated that reality and that was an absolute relief. Now very fortunately however, the complicated burden and responsibility of satisfying Saskia's never ending list of demands and tricky issues had been taken from Talitha's hands and sat very firmly inside Professor Heisner's hands and that was an absolute relief to Talitha's weary mind. A grateful smile adorned Talitha's face as she walked as Saskia was one baton of trouble that she was truly grateful to hand over to someone else and escape from.

Once five thirty arrived, Talitha collected her handbag from the floor right next to her desk and then switched of the Restructure system as she began to make her way joyfully towards the parking lot and prepared for her actual weekend. A romantic boat trip and a deliciously romantic weekend with Bryson awaited and not even a run in with Saskia and her temper tantrums could spoil that.

Just a few minutes later as Talitha sat inside her car and then turned on the engine, the engine began to purr gently like an old friend as it greeted her and prepared to carry her towards her home and she smiled as she silently reminded herself of Professor Heisner wise words. The weekend was to be enjoyed fully with the cheerful, loving face that would be waiting for her at home and Talitha's client's problems had to be left at work until Monday inside the walls of the Restructure building.

On Monday morning, Talitha's work duties would definitely return and so too would she but until they did, the next two days which sat very neatly beside each other every week inside the calendar of life that formed the weekend, were her own to spend exactly as she wished and she fully intended to enjoy every single second of them.

Rather sadly, the weekend was consumed almost too quickly for Talitha's liking as Monday morning rapidly arrived and abruptly plonked itself upon her doorstep and her next working week began. The weekend, despite it's rather brief visit had however, been absolutely heavenly as Bryson had taken Talitha out on the boat trip that he'd promised on the Saturday and then they'd visited her parent's home on the Sunday afternoon.

Due to the fact that Bryson was very responsible and extremely serious regarding his romantic commitment to Talitha, her parents absolutely adored him and they were always very happy to see him. An extremely pleasant Sunday afternoon had been enjoyed by all four which had involved a visit to a strawberry farm just on the outskirts of the city. Fresh strawberries had been required as Talitha's mother had wanted to make strawberry jam and so they'd spent their Sunday afternoon together, just picking and consuming a large amount of strawberries as they'd collected all the fresh and very delicious ingredients. Along the way, the four had probably eaten more strawberries than they'd left the strawberry farm with in the end but they'd paid a bit extra for their consumption and the farm staff hadn't seemed to be particularly bothered by it.

Monday morning didn't seem to care about Talitha's desire to have an extended weekend however as it strode relentlessly into her life almost like a regimented soldier and as she drove to work, she began to internally prepare for her busy working day ahead. Once Talitha arrived outside the Restructure building, she quickly parked her vehicle in its allocated space and then made her way towards the entrance as she prepared to greet Yucala. Much to Talitha's delight, she quickly discovered as soon as she stepped inside the building that not only was there the usual warm smile but also some packets of biscuits which Yucala rather triumphantly presented to her.

"Look Talitha, I managed to get these." Yucala announced as she packed a few packets of biscuits inside the small cardboard box on top of her desk that contained some other supplies.

"Well that's a nice change." Talitha replied as she smiled. "Well done you."

"Yes, it's another victory in the battle to encourage brainy scientists to consider human dietary needs." Yucala joked.

"You might have won the biscuit battle Yucala but you probably haven't won the war just yet." Talitha teased. "I mean seriously, does Moses even eat lunch? I did invite him to the diner once but he didn't really seem that interested."

"If I were you I wouldn't take it personally Talitha, he doesn't seem very sociable." Yucala observed. "I usually bring my lunch in, so I don't go out much but now and again, I do pop out to the diner myself, they have some great meatball Panini's."

"They definitely do but you usually take your lunch before I take mine, so it would be quite hard for us to have lunch together." Talitha mentioned.

"True but one day we should." Yucala suggested. "One Friday perhaps I can take my lunch slightly later than usual and you could take your lunch slightly earlier and then we can go there together."

"Should we invite Moses?" Talitha asked.

"I wouldn't bother, he doesn't really seem like the type that would enjoy lunch with two ladies." Yucala replied.

"Now, if Moses was a bit more like Rodney, we'd be fighting him off and he'd be at the diner every lunchtime with us." Talitha joked.

"Yes Rodney, he's very charming, always has a compliment to offer the ladies, I did notice." Yucala agreed.

"Did he flirt with you?" Talitha asked.

"Not really flirt but he is very charming whenever I show him to your consultation room." Yucala replied. "He's a bit of a handful that one."

"Yes, I pity the woman that falls in love with him." Talitha agreed. "He'll probably break her heart."

"Right, since you're here, I'll bring these supplies and these gorgeous biscuits along to your consultation room now. I picked out some luxury brands and they taste absolutely delicious, I've kept a couple of packets for the reception area, just in case I have any visitors, or you're delayed." Yucala explained as she rose to her feet.

"Now that was a very wise decision Yucala." Talitha teased.

"Probably not that wise for my hips though." Yucala joked. "Because if they don't get eaten by someone else then I'll have to eat them myself, or they'll go all soggy and be wasted."

"You will." Talitha agreed as she began to walk towards the corridor that led to her consultation room beside Yucala. "You can't let them rot as that would be a total tragedy and an absolute waste of perfectly yummy biscuits."

Yucala laughed.

When Samson arrived at eleven on the dot that Monday morning as a gentle knock sounded at Talitha's consultation room door, she

537

enthusiastically leapt to her feet and then crossed the room as she prepared to greet her very first client of that working week. According to Samson's plan and his advertiser's requirements, he was due to have a chest enhancement that day and as he stepped inside the room, the mood was light as the two exchanged jokes about the upcoming commercial that he was preparing for and his latest sexual conquest that he'd apparently seen again.

Deep down inside, Talitha was really quite intrigued by Samson's profession which seemed very unusual but she didn't actually envy him as making bodily changes every single week seemed to be a bit of a strange responsibility. Regardless of how imperfect Talitha's own body seemed at times, she was quite happy that it was indeed totally her own and that it wasn't actually the property of someone else.

Lunchtime as usual was a solitary affair as Talitha made her way to the diner and then returned to the parking lot as she prepared for the afternoon ahead. Despite the jokes that Talitha had made with Yucala that morning, she'd now actually become accustomed to the reality that lunchtime during her working week at Restructure would never actually be a social activity, or at least, not very often.

Strangely enough, it suddenly struck Talitha as she parked her car inside the parking lot that she rarely even saw Moses most mornings and that he tended to only come out of hibernation in the afternoons which meant, Talitha rarely even had a chance to even invite him for lunch, even if she'd really wanted to. Due to the fact that Professor Heisner always seemed extremely busy, Talitha dared not even ask him and since there was no one else really to ask, she'd had to accept that for the foreseeable future, lunch would continue to be a very solitary, dining experience and one that Talitha did alone.

Something in the air just outside the building suddenly made Talitha feel as if there was a storm brewing as she stepped out of her car with her meatball Panini with lashings of chilli sauce inside her hand, wrapped in a brown paper bag. The weather was mild but very humid and it definitely felt as if there was a storm just upon the horizon but fortunately, Talitha had already bought lunch which meant, she just had to return to the safety of her desk in order to eat it, before the pending storm had a chance to erupt and unleash its windy, rainy claws upon the city. Right above Talitha's head, some huge angry, dark grey clouds hung in the sky that looked extremely full and as if they couldn't wait to burst and drench the ground below them as she locked her car door and then began to walk towards the main entrance of the building.

Just as Talitha walked towards the building however, something very unusual caught her eye and that something very unusual was Moses. Quite strangely, Moses was about a third of the way up the same hill again but this time he was actually going up it, not returning from it and Talitha quickly, rather mischievously decided to actually follow him. Rather unfortunately, just as Talitha began to walk towards the rear of the building and the hill however, the angry grey clouds above her head decided to finally burst and rain suddenly began to pelt down around her as she walked. Despite the fact that Talitha was now at risk of getting totally drenched, she decided to persevere with her mission anyway which was to find out exactly what Moses was doing as his presence on the hill and the box like cage inside his hands, utterly intrigued her and had captured her attention as it had shaken her curiosity.

Due to the fact that Talitha wasn't really supposed to be following Moses, she tried to hide herself as she walked as she maintained a distance of around twenty steps between them, to avoid being spotted. Once Talitha reached the top of the hill, she immediately noticed the huge trash site that lay just on the other side of it that Moses had already mentioned to her which seemed to spread out into the distance for miles and miles. In fact, Talitha could actually see no end to the trash site at all as she gazed out across the seemingly endless sea of junk.

The sight before Talitha eyes, utterly intrigued her as she stopped and just watched the solitary figure of Moses approach the dumping ground which he seemed to be very comfortable with and quite accustomed to. Curiosity finally got the better of Talitha however as she silently surrendered to her desire to see exactly what Moses was up to, despite the rain and she began to walk down the other side of the hill to get a closer look. Inside Moses's hand there was definitely an animal cage and that ignited Talitha's curiosity even more as she began to question why on earth Moses was there and what he could possibly be doing. Something inside the cage seemed to move around as Talitha watched quietly but what exactly it was, she couldn't be sure and asking Moses right now, wasn't really a sensible option.

Just a few seconds later however, Talitha's question was very suddenly silently answered as Moses leant towards the ground and then opened up the cage. A hand was slipped inside the cage and then a small creature was lifted out of it by Moses as Talitha walked down the hill towards him. When Talitha was about fifteen steps away from Moses, she quickly began to search for somewhere to hide as she had absolutely no desire to be spotted by anyone and certainly not by Moses himself.

At the base of the hill, fortunately for Talitha, she managed to find a very run down, hut like structure which looked as if at one time, it might have actually housed a human being and she quickly utilized it as a hiding place to conceal herself from view. Several loose sheets of metal were twisted around the structure in different directions and it looked as if it had been torn apart by both the weather and time but Talitha didn't let that put her off as she made the most of its rather meager provisions and persevered. Overgrown weeds poked out from every available nook and cranny and it looked absolutely uninhabitable but Talitha quickly crouched down behind it as she continued to silently spy on Moses.

Once crouched behind the structure, Talitha quickly found a spot to peek through so that she could continue to watch Moses from a distance as the small creature that had been inside the cage, leapt out of Moses's hand and then landed on the ground. A bright blue circle of light suddenly appeared just in front of Moses's face which he touched with his fingers as the small furry animal which looked like a squirrel, enthusiastically began to scamper off across the piles of junk that surrounded it. Just a few seconds later, the bright blue light actually disappeared and then Moses began to walk back towards the foot of the hill as he headed back towards the Restructure building with the now empty cage inside his hand.

Apparently, Moses had now completed the tasks that he'd actually visited the trash site to perform but due to the fact that Talitha was quite close to the foot of the hill and so too was Moses, she didn't dare move an inch. Drops of rain continued to pelt down from the skies above Talitha's head as she peered out from behind one of the sheets of twisted metal and waited for Moses to disappear from sight but unfortunately, Moses suddenly paused and stopped right next to the dilapidated structure as something seemed to catch his eye. Quite close to the structure itself, there was actually a muddy ditch and as Moses stared at its interior, Talitha actually held her breathe as she watched him as she feared that Moses might actually be able to hear her breathing. Much to Talitha's relief however, just a few seconds later, Moses quickly resumed his journey as he suddenly began to walk towards the hill again and this time, he actually began to walk back up it.

Curious thoughts had been provoked inside Talitha's mind as she watched Moses leave as to what exactly Moses had been doing there, why he'd set free an animal that had been inside a cage and what the bright blue screen like light had been that he'd interacted with but for now, there were no actual answers. A mountain of questions were definitely piling up inside Talitha's mind and they seemed even bigger than the hill that sat silently in-between Talitha and the Restructure building but for now, she had absolutely none of the answers and she certainly wasn't in a position to present any of her questions to Moses.

Unanswered questions still ruled Talitha's thoughts as Moses disappeared over the crest of the hill and so she decided to explore the dump a little bit before she actually returned to the building. The spot that Moses had been standing in when he'd released the creature from the cage was the first place that Talitha inspected but there was nothing of interest to be seen there and the animal that had just been released had long gone. No signs or actual indications existed that explained anything to Talitha's highly inquisitive mind but at least there was one small salvation, Talitha decided as she prepared to depart, she still had her lunch to eat although the paper bag that it was housed inside was in a slightly worse state now, purely due to the rain.

"It's definitely time to eat lunch now." Talitha muttered decisively as she glanced down at the soggy paper bag inside her hand and then gently shook her head. "I haven't even eaten a bite yet and lunchtime is almost over."

Suddenly, just as Talitha prepared to leave the trash site however, a very strange noise attracted her attention which emanated from the muddy ditch nearby that Moses had been staring at and she began to rush towards it. An element of fear filled Talitha's heart and mind as she moved as she was quite unsure what she would actually find there but as she neared the ditch, she began to gasp as shock and horror surged rapidly through her veins. Inside the muddy, now very slippery ditch there was actually a pile of rotten animal carcasses piled up on top of each other and the stench that wafted into her nostrils from the contents of the ditch was absolutely vile and utterly repugnant.

Confusion rapidly began to flood through Talitha's mind as she just stood for a few minutes and stared at the pile of animal remains as the stench of death rapidly began to fill her nostrils. In the rotten depths of that ditch however, there was still nothing to be found besides the rotten carcasses as the mud offered no explanations, no further information and nothing to draw any logical conclusions from as to why the rotten remains were even there in the first place. When Talitha could stand the smell no more, she decided to make her way back towards the hill although the lunch that she carried inside one of her hands was slightly less appetizing now, due to the rotten animal remains that she'd been in such close proximity to.

Much to Talitha's absolute horror however, just as she took a few steps backwards to leave the area, something physically suddenly obstructed her and actually blocked her actual departure. A deep, sharp breath was taken as Talitha quickly turned round to see exactly what that obstruction actually was and she rapidly discovered that it was in fact, actually Moses who now stood directly behind her, rooted to the spot. His sudden appearance alarmed Talitha as he caught her totally off guard and she immediately gasped in shock as Moses wasn't even supposed to know that Talitha was there. Upon Moses's face there was a very strange expression which seemed slightly eerie and as he looked at Talitha and then glanced down at the muddy ditch, he gently shook his head as the rain continued to pelt down on top of both their heads.

"You really shouldn't be here Talitha." Moses insisted. "You're not supposed to see all this."

"What is all this?" Talitha asked. "What exactly is going on here? What is all this for?"

Moses remained silent.

"Why were you carrying that cage Moses? Why are all those animals dead?" Talitha demanded as she pressed Moses for an answer that would make some kind of logical sense.

"Those are the animals that we experiment on, so that people can enjoy the Downloads that Restructure offers." Moses finally admitted.

On Moses's face there appeared to be a totally blank expression as he spoke which surprised Talitha somewhat, due to the shocking nature of his words and his tone sounded extremely calm. No emotions seemed to be present and there was not a single drop of sadness, or even an ounce of remorse. Every word that Moses had spoken had sounded very factual and even quite clinical and that worried Talitha as Moses gently took her arm and then began to lead her back towards the hill.

Nothing but total silence surrounded the two as they began to walk back up the hill as Talitha began to quietly contemplate exactly how she should respond to what she'd just seen. The answers that Moses had provided had shocked her and although Talitha had wanted answers, once they'd been provided, the answers themselves had raised even more questions inside her mind than they had actually satisfied.

Very surprisingly, the muddy rotten ditch filled with animal remains was it appeared, the secret cost of the human enjoyment that Restructure offered to the world and to human beings and that very ugly truth was hard to stomach as the stench that the ditch contained turned Talitha's stomach. This vile reality was the ugly truth of the price that was paid so that human beings could look the way they wanted to and that was the truth behind Talitha's own participation as an actual consultant.

An ugly truth which Talitha herself had been totally oblivious to that provided the salary which she so joyously consumed every month and that fact left a very bitter taste inside her mouth.

Only an awkward, guilty silence surrounded the two as they continued to walk back towards the Restructure building and it was almost as if Moses felt as if he'd provided Talitha with a sufficient explanation, even though in her mind, his answers had been far from adequate. When the two stepped back inside the Restructure building, Moses simply parted silently as he quickly scurried off in the direction of Professor Heisner's laboratory and Talitha quickly followed suit as she made her way rather solemnly back towards her consultation room. Horror and shock had somehow tied Talitha's tongue up in knots and Moses had offered Talitha absolutely no words of comfort at all.

By the time Talitha arrived back at her desk, she'd sadly realized that the meatball Panini she'd purchased was no longer edible and she quickly threw the soggy paper bag inside the bin as she silently accepted that her hunger would not be satisfied just yet. The lack of edible appeal wasn't just due to the fact that it had actually fallen to pieces because of the rain but also due to the foul stench of rotten animal remains that Talitha had been in such close proximity to which had somehow, actually shrunk her stomach and her appetite. In fact, it was almost as if the smell had forced her hunger to curl back up inside her stomach, shrivel up and go into hiding as her body no longer seemed remotely interested in the contents of the brown soggy paper bag.

Some remnants from the ugly aroma continued to haunt Talitha's mind as her thoughts silently regurgitated the foul stench and she almost vomited as she faced her screen and prepared to start work. Questions and worries began to scurry frantically through the passageways of Talitha's mind as touched the screen in front of her as she was totally unsure what to do about what she'd actually seen. Dead animal corpses had been piled up inside that ditch and had lined every inch of it and Moses hadn't even seemed surprised to see them there, or been bothered at all by their presence and that meant, Professor Heisner must also know about the animal remains as Moses worked for him and Moses followed his instructions.

Whatever those two men did with those creatures inside Professor Heisner's laboratory was something that Professor Heisner did not want Talitha to know about and that day, Talitha had definitely seen something that she wasn't supposed to actually see. Another thing that really bothered Talitha about her experience that day was the fact that Moses didn't seem bothered by any of it at all. Not even a strand of hair upon Moses's head or inch of his flesh had flinched at the sight of all those rotten animal remains and he seemed indifferent to their actual presence.

No matter how long Talitha thought about things however, no answers were actually forthcoming and she quickly abandoned the search for logical explanations as she turned her attention back towards her clients and the consultation that she was due to perform for Dean that afternoon. The multitude of questions about the trash site and the dead animals it contained could only really be answered by one of two people, Moses or Professor Heisner and Talitha quietly accepted defeat as she internally acknowledged that reality.

To ask Professor Heisner would be totally out of the question as Talitha had only just managed to secure another position of employment and to put her job in jeopardy right now, simply due to her curiosity and a few dead animal remains, really wasn't a great idea which only really left Moses. Since Moses wasn't really the type of person that one would ask any questions, unless they were purely technical in nature, not if you actually wanted any answers, Talitha doubted that she would actually receive any kind of answers from him. In fact, the only information that Moses had ever provided to Talitha had almost been forced out of him by Talitha's own actual discovery but aside from that she could sense his reluctance to provide any of the answers she sought.

An interruption suddenly rather abruptly disturbed Talitha's internal deliberations as three on the dot arrived and there was a gentle knock upon her consultation room door and she immediately rose to her feet and then crossed the room. Much to Talitha's relief as she opened up the door, she found an actual smile on Dean's face which immediately lightened her mood as the last time the two had met, he'd been rather worried and really quite sad. Today however, Dean actually looked quite excited, refreshed and somewhat invigorated as he strode enthusiastically towards the chair that he usually occupied whenever he attended the Restructure clinic. The joyful smile and bright eyes filled with excitement, it quickly transpired, was due to a date that Dean had been on the previous weekend and he rapidly began to share some of the details with Talitha as she offered him a cup of coffee and some biscuits.

"You know Talitha, I met this gorgeous woman last week and we actually went out on a date over the weekend." Dean explained.

"That's great Dean, I'm really glad you were able to move on." Talitha replied as she placed a piping hot cup of coffee down in front of him.

"Yes to relieve my heartbreak and pain, I sought comfort in the arms of a stranger." Dean joked. "And it definitely worked, though we didn't quite get to the arms, hugs and naked part yet."

"Well, you can only try Dean." Talitha replied. "Every woman is different and every woman likes different things. Fortunately for us all, attraction and sexual chemistry are not set in stone as if they were, we'd all be in trouble and dumped on the romantic trash heap for life."

"There's nothing certain yet but I'm quite hopeful." Dean mentioned as he began to sip his cup of coffee. "Janice is very nice though and she seems to really like me."

"Hopeful of what Dean?" Talitha asked as she sat back down beside her desk.

"Hopeful that she'll accept me." Dean replied.

"You know Dean, acceptance is really a gift that you have to learn to give yourself before you can even hope to expect it from anyone else." Talitha advised. "You're a really great guy and any woman would be lucky to have a guy like you and you have to really believe that."

"Did you manage to speak to Professor Heisner yet about the decrease in my penis size?" Dean asked.

"I did but he hasn't given me an answer yet. I should know by the time you attend your follow up appointment in one month's time. He's got a lot on his plate right now." Talitha explained.

"Okay, I can live with that." Dean accepted as he quickly nodded his head.

"I think he'll authorize it Dean, I don't really see it being an issue." Talitha immediately reassured him. "There's just a lot of other stuff going on right now."

Dean nodded.

When Dean's client closure consultation came to an end, Talitha politely escorted him back to the reception area and then returned to her consultation room to write up his notes. Quite a few things intrigued Talitha about Dean's situation as it had enlightened her as to how illogical human desires could actually be at times. Sometimes, the things that people sought after and yearned for, once received could quite often cause them more problems than they actually fixed, Talitha quietly concluded. Somehow within humanity and life itself it seemed there was a contradiction, a strange paradox and an enigma that existed which hung over the cliffs of life and dangled downwards in a precarious predicament as it taunted and haunted every ounce of the human spirit and that was the unrealized desires that lay inside every human mind. No true equilibrium it seemed actually existed as the cost of one's desires often outweighed the possible advantages and satisfaction given in return. One day perhaps humanity would figure it all out and then perhaps humanity would conquer life itself, Talitha concluded and one day perhaps, just perhaps, humanity would actually win.

Later that evening as Talitha drove home, she quietly contemplated further the dilemma that Dean faced and pondered over his choice which had now created a dark cloud that hung over his love life. Sometimes, what human beings perceived as being the optimal choice for them was actually the very choice that cost them absolutely everything and at times, it could actually cost them all those they cared about and loved. The results of those human choices however, was absolutely impossible to predict as human nature was so impulsive, so complex and so very unpredictable and Professor Heisner had pointed out that fact to Talitha many times. Once Talitha arrived outside her home, she parked her car in the driveway and then made her way towards the front door as she found comfort in one small pleasure present in her own life, Bryson wasn't complex and nor was their relationship and that night she would sleep peacefully in his arms and that at least was beautifully predictable.

Due to the fact that Talitha had signed a very strict confidentiality agreement when she'd joined Restructure, there was no actual discussion with Bryson that evening about the dead animal remains that Talitha had seen earlier that day as she kept that discovery very much to herself. The very prescriptive stipulations and complex instructions inside that agreement related predominantly to technical, scientific matters but also delved into issues that covered intellectual property and hence Talitha dared not breathe a word about what she'd seen to anyone outside the clinic's walls. In fact, the stipulations were so strict that they not only prohibited Talitha from discussing matters that related to the technical operations with anyone outside Restructure but also even with some of the people inside it.

When Tuesday morning arrived, it brought with it a mixture of emotions to Talitha's life as she drove to work as it was the very first week that Talitha would not actually see Renee, since she'd officially started her role as a consultant and that was a sad progression but also a happy one. Partially, Talitha felt joyful as Renee now actually had what she wanted in life from her own body but in part, Talitha also felt slightly sad as she would definitely miss her as Renee had been her first ever female client but now, Renee would no longer even form a part of Talitha's working week.

Once Talitha arrived inside her consultation room, she quickly switched on the Restructure system and then prepared a milky latte as per her usual workday morning routine as she readied herself for the day ahead which involved a consultation in the morning with Frank and then one in the afternoon with Rita. At exactly eleven, Frank arrived and he was quickly shown into Talitha's consultation room but his face was extremely downcast and his usual jovial grin was definitely missing. Despite the usual lack of joy, Talitha quickly offered him a beverage as she prepared to start his actual consultation and once the cup of tea that Frank had requested had been placed down in front of him, Talitha quickly returned to her desk as she began to discuss Frank's week with him.

"How have things been Frank?" Talitha asked.

"Not good, not good at all Talitha." Frank replied. "In fact they've been absolutely terrible."

"Why, what on earth happened Frank?" Talitha enquired.

"I cheated on Maude." Frank whispered. "And I've never done that ever before."

"Oh dear." Talitha remarked. "That's really awful."

"Yes and I really don't think I should have anymore procedures." Frank explained. "I don't think they're good for me. I want to look younger than Maude but I definitely don't want to cheat on her."

"Yes Frank, I understand. I have actually spoken to Professor Heisner about the issues you raised, so I'm just waiting for him to come back to me now." Talitha quickly reassured him.

"Right." Frank replied. "I'll wait."

Talitha nodded her head in agreement. "Should I make another client appointment for you for next week Frank?" She asked. "I should know a bit more by then."

"Yes that'll be dandy." Frank agreed.

"I'm very sorry about all the problems that you seem to be facing Frank as a result of your procedures." Talitha said apologetically as she glanced into his eyes.

"It's really not your fault Talitha." Frank quickly reassured her as he smiled. "These are very new procedures and I knew that when I signed up for them, so there's bound to be some niggling problems at first."

"Yes." Talitha replied. "Restructure is a ground breaking clinic, so I guess we have to expect some complications sometimes, especially at first."

"Definitely." Frank agreed.

The morning continued quietly and when Frank's consultation ended, Talitha politely escorted him back to the reception area and then returned to her consultation room to write up his notes. On this particular occasion, Frank's notes were rather short, simply due to the fact that he'd not had any procedures that day but nonetheless, they still had to be completed and then submitted.

A quick lunch was eaten as Talitha's working day progressed and then at around three that afternoon, Rita arrived. For Rita that day, a stomach flattening procedure had been requested and planned and so once Rita had been offered a beverage and some biscuits, Talitha quickly returned to her desk as she began to facilitate Rita's request and populated her screen with images of some female stomachs. The screen was turned towards Rita so that she could see it and as Rita began to visually wander through the images in front of her, Talitha watched quietly as she waited for Rita to make her choices and decision. Once the range had been narrowed down to just ten images, Talitha quickly utilized Rita's simulated body image inside Restructure to show her exactly how each choice would look and Rita giggled as she glanced at some of the results.

"Oh, I'm not sure about those two." Rita said as she pointed towards two of the images on the screen. "They wouldn't look right at all."

"Well luckily, you have ten to choose from. So one might be just what you're looking for." Talitha replied as she smiled.

"Yes, I think I'd really like to go for that one there please Talitha." Rita confirmed as she pointed towards another one of the images.

"Certainly Rita, I'll just process that request for you now." Talitha quickly clarified as she turned the screen back towards her and then touched it to process Rita's request. "If you'd like to come with me please." She continued as she rose to her feet and prepared to vacate her consultation room.

Inside the small procedure room everything was quiet as the two women entered the room and Talitha led Rita towards the transparent capsule that lay silently waiting in the very center of the space. In a matter of just a few seconds, Rita had positioned herself inside the capsule and had lain down inside it and so Talitha lowered the capsule lid over her body as she prepared for Rita's physical transformation.

Approximately ten minutes later, once Rita's procedure had been performed, the two women stood next to each other inside the procedure room in front of the long client mirror as Rita began to twist and turn and admire her new stomach. The smile of satisfaction upon Rita's face internally encouraged Talitha as she watched Rita appreciate the bodily change that had just been made.

"I think my stomach looks absolutely great Talitha." Rita confirmed appreciatively as she lifted up her top and then showed Talitha her actual stomach. "What do you think?" She asked.

"I think it looks absolutely amazing." Talitha agreed as she overtly expressed her admiration. "It really compliments the rest of your body. It looks very nice and totally natural."

"Yes and I'm very happy with it." Rita announced.

Talitha glanced up at the clock on the wall that ticked away faithfully as it marked the passing of each second as she suddenly realized that the afternoon was rapidly leaving her consultation room. "I should make your next appointment for you now Rita." She insisted. "The afternoon is running away from us and we haven't even discussed your last procedure yet."

Due to the concerns that Frank had raised, more than once now, Talitha was actually quite anxious to discuss any possible side effects with Rita but in a way that wouldn't alarm her and so as the two women made their way back towards her consultation room, she began to discuss some of Rita's past procedures. Now Talitha was actually on the lookout for any side effects, due to Frank's very negative experiences as she worried about what impact the actual procedures themselves might have upon each of her client's lives.

"Have you experienced anything strange recently Rita?" Talitha asked.

"Well now that you ask Talitha, I have been feeling slightly more attracted to some of my clients than usual." Rita replied. "And they're not generally people that I would ever think about in a romantic sense, so that has been slightly strange."

"Okay, I'll mention it to Professor Heisner." Talitha reassured her. "So that he can look into it."

"I just hope I don't marry one of them in the meantime." Rita joked. "That would ruin everything."

"I'll flag it up as a very urgent issue." Talitha replied.

"Yes it really is. I can't be trying to extract their money from them in a heartless fashion and falling in love with them at the same time that really just wouldn't work for me at all." Rita joked. "I've also noticed that my back is slightly strained probably due to the large breast increase."

"I could give you a back strengthening Download to ease any pain in your back during your next consultation." Talitha offered. "That might ease any discomfort."

Rita nodded in agreement. "Sounds great. Put me down for one of those." She replied.

Unfortunately for Talitha, there definitely appeared to be some actual side effects to Professor Heisner's procedures but that was not unusual in the world of beauty as quite often in the past Talitha had faced and had to handle similar problems. In some respects however, these problems were definitely vastly different as the side effects that Talitha had seen in the past had usually been quite visual and had involved skin rashes, not emotional attachments.

Immediately after Rita's client consultation ended, Talitha escorted her back to the reception area and then returned to her consultation room to write up Rita's notes. When Talitha submitted the notes to Professor Heisner, she attentively flagged up the issue of possible side effects again as she raised her concerns with him. The issues that both her clients had raised that day worried Talitha and her drive home that evening was slightly less peaceful than usual as a direct result.

On the Wednesday morning, Talitha had an appointment scheduled with Patrick and as she arrived at work and started her working day, she began to read his notes in preparation for his arrival. Inside Talitha's diary that day, she just had two client consultations and neither was particularly problematic as she would only be seeing Patrick and Rodney and they were not a headache like Saskia was, so Talitha felt quite relaxed about the working day ahead, despite her worries from the previous day.

Much to Talitha's delight, her consultation with Patrick that morning was very straight forward and simple and there were no issues at all as she performed the requested nose reshape that he'd wanted. Once the requested procedure had been implemented, another appointment was then quickly made for Patrick's next consultation, just before he was shown back to the reception area where the two separated.

Inevitably, once lunch had been eaten, the Wednesday afternoon arrived and as it literally sped into Talitha's life, she prepared for Rodney's afternoon consultation. When Rodney arrived in the mid-afternoon, shortly after lunch, Talitha began his consultation enthusiastically which as usual was full of innuendos and flirtatious suggestions on Rodney's part. His procedure request that particular day related to his feet but Talitha quickly concluded that it might not actually be his final request as Rodney implied towards the end of his consultation that he might require some further procedures but he seemed slightly unsure as to exactly what those procedures might actually be.

"I'll just make your client closure consultation appointment for you now Rodney and if you decide that you need another procedure before or on that day, I'll change it accordingly." Talitha explained as she touched the screen directly in front of her to access her client diary. "How does the same time next week suit you? My Wednesday afternoon slot is still available?"

Rodney immediately nodded his head. "That's what I like to see in a woman Talitha, assertiveness and that's a definite date." He replied as he flashed Talitha a cheeky grin.

"You're something else Rodney." Talitha teased as she gently shook her head.

"I can be something else, I can be anything you want me to be." Rodney flirted playfully. "And even more."

"Soon, you won't even be my client anymore Rodney." Talitha quickly pointed out.

"I know and how will you cope then Talitha?" Rodney asked.

"I don't know Rodney." Talitha teased. "I guess I'll just have to find a way to manage somehow."

"I could always call, or email and even come and see you." Rodney offered.

"I don't think that'll be necessary Rodney. I really don't think I'll miss you that much." Talitha replied as she laughed. "Thanks for offering though, it's very kind of you."

"I won't take your rejection personally Talitha, I know your butt lies in the bed of another man and that your heart is definitely in his hands." Rodney joked as he laughed. "He got there first, or you would have been mine."

"Right Rodney, we're all done here for today." Talitha mentioned as she quickly rose to her feet. "I'll see you next week."

Regardless of Rodney's rather suggestive comments and eager advances, Talitha knew that Bryson was her life partner and best friend and that was not something that Rodney could easily undermine as their relationship was by now, very well established and they had committed to each other one hundred percent. The flirtatious comments that Rodney regularly offered therefore went straight in one ear and out of the other as Talitha took them like a pinch of salt and gave them very little regard. Once she'd escorted Rodney to the reception area, Talitha quickly returned to her consultation room and then began to write up Rodney's client notes as there was just an hour left of that working day and Talitha really wanted to leave work on time that evening. A romantic dinner date had been planned with Bryson at one of the couple's favorite restaurants and for Talitha that was definitely worth more to her than just a pinch of salt.

SIDE EFFECTS & REGRETS

Defeat almost buried Talitha when the Thursday morning arrived as Professor Heisner requested an urgent briefing first thing in the morning which immediately clarified to her that were indeed some very serious complications with his procedures and with the Restructure system. During their meeting Professor Heisner began to explain the various issues as he elaborated further and delved into some of the scientific and technical details, some of which Talitha didn't actually understand as she was really quite ignorant regarding the various scientific intricacies that surrounded his work.

Apparently, according to Professor Heisner, there were some negative, unforeseen side effects from the actual Download procedures themselves in that they skewed human emotions which meant, people feared and disliked those that they usually loved and were strangely attracted to people that they did not even know, in a very intense manner. For Talitha, the Professor's explanations provided her with a thin blanket of comfort as she listened to him speak as he confirmed the very strange emotional detachments and attachments that some of her clients had recently formed, experienced and described to her.

Just before their meeting ended and the two separated, Talitha made the most of the opportunity to raise some of her client's issues as she sauntered verbally towards the issue of Dean and the penis reduction that he definitely required. In terms of Talitha's battles when it came to her client list, she'd learned to accept that the battle of the wills between herself and Lachlan had already been lost and she'd silently buried her disgruntled thoughts and discontent inside a grave of defeat with regards to his dominance over Charmaine's life. Although technically, Talitha had already given up the battle with Lachlan, a small glimmer of hope still existed that she could actually help to change Dean's life and more specifically, rectify his love life and so she began to eagerly petition Professor Heisner again on Dean's behalf. Quite fortunately, Professor Heisner quickly agreed to Talitha's request although he did smile ever so slightly when she raised the matter with him.

"Most people usually complain that they're too

small." Professor Heisner joked.

"He did select the size himself but I just don't think that he was really aware of the full implications surrounding his choice. He has been single for a while due to an accident." Talitha quickly pointed out. "It's making it very difficult for him to sustain a sexual relationship."

"Give him a second chance and let him select something a bit smaller at no extra cost." Professor Heisner said as he nodded his head. "Otherwise, he might spend years alone again."

"What should I do about the other problems?" Talitha asked.

"I'm working on a solution at the moment and I should have a fix by Monday. I've been working on it all week with Moses." Professor Heisner explained. "Day and night."

"Right, should I say anything to any of my clients?" Talitha asked.

"Certainly not, not yet at least. In the meantime, don't perform any other procedures and when you meet your clients, just give them some counseling sessions." Professor Heisner instructed. "They'll need it after what they've been through."

"Right Professor Heisner, I'll wait." Talitha confirmed as she rose to her feet. "Is there anything further I should say to Saskia? She is rather impatient and she really doesn't like to wait."

"Nope, not yet. I've been far too busy with the side effects from the Download procedures to even make a start on Saskia's demands." Professor Heisner replied. "You'll probably have to walk along a tightrope of maybe's for another week I'm afraid and try to balance her anger and impatience delicately with promises of possibilities that might not even actually exist."

"That could get quite ugly, there might be another angry outburst." Talitha quickly pointed out.

"I do have a potential solution that might satisfy her but due to the other problems, it's not really a top priority for now." Professor Heisner explained as he gently shook his head. "Saskia will just have to wait, whether she likes it or not."

"What should I say to my clients in the meantime?" Talitha asked.

"You can just tell them that there's been some system problems and that normal services should resume next week." Professor Heisner advised. "We really don't want a panic on our hands."

Talitha nodded.

"Your clients have been through a lot of changes Talitha and this delay will provide you with an extra opportunity to give them with some additional support which will help them come to terms with the physical realities and implications of those changes." Professor Heisner explained.

"See the delays as an opportunity instead of a problem."

"Right." Talitha agreed. "What about Lachlan and Saskia, they can be very demanding and they might kick up a fuss?"

The very demanding, extremely persistent nature that resided inside Saskia's body, would not allow anything to rest for any reason, until she'd actually been given what she wanted and given everything she desired in its entirety and Talitha feared Saskia's reaction to any procedural delays.

"You can give those two clients procedures are usual." Professor Heisner instructed. "I really can't be dealing with temper tantrums when I'm trying to repair the Download system."

"What about the side effects?" Talitha asked.

"Look Talitha, Saskia's way to self absorbed to have a relationship with anyone else as that require giving someone else attention, so she's probably not even dating anyone long term right now and Charmaine, well it might not actually be a bad thing for her to dislike her current partner, for a little while at least." Professor Heisner replied. "That's my unofficial comment of course."

"Okay Professor Heisner." Talitha said as she grinned. "I'll do that. I'll follow your instructions precisely, unofficially of course."

Everything that Professor Heisner had mentioned throughout their meeting suddenly made perfect sense as Talitha made her way back towards her consultation room and reflected upon his explanations as she walked. The experiences of Frank, the incidents that involved Samson and his former lover, the recent discussion that Talitha had held with Rita, Renee's instant attraction to her younger lover and even Dean's love at first sight dating disaster all fitted in to what Professor Heisner had divulged to her exactly and there was no escaping that actual reality. However, a couple of Talitha's clients didn't seem to have experienced any side effects at all, like Saskia but she was currently single and didn't actively seem to be pursuing any kind of romance with anyone as she seemed to be so wrapped up in her own agenda, romance probably wasn't something that was important to her.

Quite strangely, Talitha suddenly realized as she stepped inside her consultation room, Charmaine seemed to be the only one of Talitha's clients that was romantically active that had escaped the impact of any kind of side effects but that wasn't necessarily a good thing. A reduced attraction on Charmaine's part towards Lachlan, in Talitha's opinion, would have been the most positive thing that could ever possibly happen to her. When it came to the issue of Rodney, he just seemed to pursue anything that moved as long as they were female, so Talitha didn't include him in her analysis as he was very flirtatious, so it was very difficult to draw any kind of conclusions from his behavior.

One very positive thing that lifted Talitha's spirits significantly that morning was that Professor Heisner had actually authorized Dean's adjustment procedure and that pleased Talitha no end. The mistake that Dean had made, he would now have a chance to rectify and hope rapidly began to gather and accumulate inside Talitha as she began to appreciate Professor Heisner's generosity. If any of Talitha's clients deserved that second chance, it was definitely Dean, Talitha thoughtfully concluded as he really did seem like a very nice guy.

For the next few days there would be no new clients, Talitha considered thoughtfully as she glanced at her work diary inside Restructure, until the problems with Restructure had been fixed and resolved. Since Talitha's client list had actually increased, she could no longer bask in the flexibility that a smaller list offered, or organize her working day however she wished too and that liberty had now in fact, totally disappeared. Now Talitha's working days were more heavily populated with client consultations in both the mornings and afternoons and one client session a day was no longer a luxury that she could afford.

A mid-morning appointment had been scheduled that day with Sylvester and it had already been agreed with Professor Heisner that this would be his final consultation before all the procedures that he'd actually requested would be performed. Due to the system problems however, there was now a slight worry inside Talitha's mind that Sylvester's procedure plan might be disrupted but she hoped that Professor Heisner would be able to deliver a fix by the Monday as he'd promised which would avoid such negative eventualities from actually arising.

At eleven that morning as expected, Yucala gently tapped on Talitha's consultation room door and Talitha quickly rose to her feet and then crossed the room as she decorated her face with a smile and prepared to greet Sylvester. The two had already met twice now and Talitha was really pleased with how his consultations were progressing as they'd managed to finalize the majority of the body and facial parts that he required for his physical transformation. In terms of Talitha's workload, Sylvester's consultations tended to be totally stress free and involved absolutely no drama at all, unlike Saskia and Charmaine's consultations and for at least one hour and a half that morning, Talitha assisted Sylvester enthusiastically as she counseled him and prepared him for the huge physical changes ahead.

Lunchtime finally arrived and since Sylvester's consultation had already ended and his notes had been written up, Talitha made the most of her lunchtime as she attended the diner and had an actual sit down lunch that day. A very sweet desert was selected and then eaten, in order to prepare for Charmaine's consultation later that afternoon which Talitha knew had the potential to be very bitter, if Lachlan attended which it was very likely he would. In fact, it was highly likely that Lachlan would continue to attend all of Charmaine's consultations until Talitha had given her the second breast enlargement and that was something Talitha now definitely knew for sure.

The negative thoughts that were housed inside Talitha's mind almost consumed her as she returned to her consultation room and then sat down beside her desk as she patiently waited for the couple to arrive. A stream of disconcerting worries flooded through Talitha's mind as she quietly waited for Yucala's gentle knock at her consultation room door, Charmaine's presence didn't bother Talitha in the slightest but Lachlan's presence really bothered her a lot.

Despite the reluctance that had set into Talitha's mind, when Yucala actually knocked on her consultation room door at three that afternoon, Talitha quickly rose to her feet, crossed the room and prepared herself to face not just Charmaine but also the dreaded Lachlan. A door provided an opportunity to enter someone's world, life or domain but it could also protect you from those that should not be allowed to enter your life or world and just for a split second, Talitha was tempted not to open the door as she stood directly in front of it, in order to avoid Lachlan completely.

Unfortunately however, Talitha really didn't have the luxury of choice and that was the one drawback of her current job, she couldn't pick and choose, or discriminate against any of her clients as once Professor Heisner had allocated them to her, she just had to accept them. Regardless of Talitha's best efforts to disguise her emotions as she adorned her face with a fake pretentious smile, she couldn't help but wince as she opened the door and silently observed Lachlan's attendance. The consultation room had no other exits and Charmaine definitely had to be seen that day and so Talitha knew, there was no way at all she could even try to avoid at least an hour's contact with Lachlan, no matter how grim that might be and it would definitely be, absolutely grim.

Both Talitha and Lachlan knew that Talitha really couldn't stand him but she had absolutely no desire to make that obvious to anyone and especially not to Lachlan himself as to do so would place her job in jeopardy and Lachlan certainly wasn't worth that. Once the couple had been settled in and had been offered a beverage, Talitha leapt straight into Charmaine's consultation armed with the fake smile that she saved each week for difficult clients like Lachlan.

"Right Charmaine, according to your procedure plan and your request list, you'll be having your leg contour today." Talitha said as she smiled at the couple and faced them attentively. "Are you ready?" She asked as she encouraged Charmaine to assert herself and make an actual decision.

Nothing but an awkward silence rapidly filled the room which seemed to invisibly wind itself around the three as Talitha inhaled deeply and just watched Lachlan as she waited for him to interrupt which she knew, he definitely would. The weekend was just a day away but unfortunately, Talitha had to get through not just a consultation with Charmaine and Lachlan that day but also an appointment the next day with Saskia and those two consultations definitely had the potential to be the most difficult appointments of her entire working week.

"When will Charmaine have the second breast enlargement?" Lachlan demanded impatiently as he stared at Talitha's face. "I have already paid for it." He snapped as he quickly reminded Talitha that she was actually withholding something that he'd already bought. Lachlan shook his head impatiently, he was not used to waiting for anything and especially not something that he'd already paid for and his patience with regards to Talitha,

Restructure and Professor Heisner was quickly running out. "Do I need to speak to someone else about it?" He demanded.

"I'll be seeing Charmaine again in a week's time." Talitha began to explain softly as she attempted to appease Lachlan's irritation which was immediately obvious and reassure him that the final breast enlargement would definitely actually occur. "I'll perform the second breast enlargement during that appointment."

Upon Lachlan's face there was an angry scowl as Talitha quietly accepted that he was quite simply not going to be satisfied with anything less than what he'd wanted and had actually paid for. The deep seeded resentment and animosity between Lachlan and Talitha was obvious to anyone who observed them both as they interacted although arguments and very overt displays were politely avoided by Talitha. Inside herself, Talitha fully understood the reality, she challenged Lachlan's authority over Charmaine's life as he exerted his power over a woman that he knew was financially weaker than he was and in Lachlan's kingdom and household, he ruled the roost. A female stranger was definitely not going to be allowed to interfere with that and certainly not an actual stranger that he was paying to provide a service to him.

"Oh I can't wait. Isn't it exciting Lachlan?" Charmaine suddenly interjected enthusiastically. "I think my body's almost ready now Talitha."

Somehow, the two women's gentle reassurances seemed to be effective and appease Lachlan slightly as he began to calm down but his stubbornness was definitely a hurdle that Talitha knew had only been overcome temporarily and one she knew, would definitely present itself again. The remainder of Charmaine's consultation fortunately for Talitha however, was relatively peaceful as she helped the couple narrow down their selection and then prepared to implement the desired leg contour procedure as requested.

Quite interestingly, Talitha quietly observed, to some degree there had been some kind of improvement in terms of Lachlan's attitude towards Charmaine as that day he'd actually allowed her to have slightly more input into the choice that had been made. Their conversation had comforted Talitha slightly as she'd listened to their discussion and reflected upon the initial conversation they'd held about the breast enlargement during one of the very first appointments they'd attended together. On this particular occasion Lachlan, much to Talitha's surprise had actually allowed Charmaine to make the final decision regarding one of her preferences and he'd allowed her for once to overrule his preferred choice and that almost stunned Talitha as she'd watched and listened to him.

Approximately thirty minutes later, once Charmaine's leg contour had been performed and another appointment had been made for the following week, Talitha suddenly rose to her feet and smiled at the couple as she prepared to escort them back towards the reception area. The couple immediately began to follow Talitha as she led them towards her consultation room door.

"Your legs look absolutely stunning Charmaine." Lachlan said as he slipped his hand inside Charmaine's hand.

"Thanks Lachlan." Charmaine replied as she smiled.

Lachlan turned to face Talitha as he paused beside the door. "Thanks so much for helping us out." He boomed. "Physical appearance is just such a sensitive issue."

"Yes it is indeed." Talitha agreed as she nodded her head and then opened the door.

Despite the serious nature of Lachlan's words, his tone had sounded rather flippant and the strangeness of his comment lingered in Talitha's mind as she walked them towards the reception area. The comment was clearly very empathetic and serious but it seemed strange that it had originated from Lachlan's mind and mouth as he really wasn't an empathetic person. When the three arrived inside the reception area, Talitha quickly prepared to depart and return to her consultation room but Lachlan wasn't quite ready to leave yet and he quickly clarified his position to Talitha as he turned to face her.

"We'll be back next week for the second breast enlargement." Lachlan insisted as he stared into Talitha's eyes.

"Yes don't worry Lachlan, I haven't forgotten." Talitha immediately reassured him.

Regardless of whether it rained or shone outside, Lachlan was not going to let anyone forget about his wishes, not even for a second, whether they aligned with Charmaine's own desires or not as he verbally reinforced that there would be no escape from his demands. His stare was hard and it very clearly dictated to Talitha that in the longer term, there would be absolutely no compromise at all and that Charmaine's second breast enlargement would definitely happen. Silence began to fill the air as Talitha silently processed Lachlan's remark thoughtfully, at Charmaine's next consultation, Lachlan would definitely be present and that in itself was not something to actually look forward to.

Tension began to fill the air between the three as Talitha waited for the couple to leave and for Lachlan to clear her airspace as she quietly accepted that the second breast enlargement would definitely happen the following week as Lachlan absolutely would not accept anything less.

Inside Lachlan's mind it appeared, he was unwilling to let the matter go and neither woman could remove that issue from between his clamped teeth and very determined thoughts as Lachlan held onto it with a steel grip like a dog with a bone.

"Right, I'll see you both next week then." Talitha confirmed as she encouraged the couple to depart.

A definite storm was brewing and despite Talitha's intense disliking for Lachlan, upsetting him further right now definitely wouldn't help anyone and especially not Charmaine, who actually had to go home with him. Time had definitely run out and next week Talitha would actually have to participate with Lachlan's request whether she actually wanted to or not and that was totally unavoidable. At least, Lachlan had now vacated Talitha's consultation room and she had survived yet another unpleasant encounter with him, she quietly considered as she watched the two leave the building and that was one small mercy as his presence was absolutely repulsive.

On Talitha's way home that evening, she quietly considered Lachlan and Charmaine as she drove, the afternoon had been quite rough for Talitha due to her interactions with Lachlan and the working week still wasn't actually over yet. Unusually, Talitha felt an intense disliking towards this particular man which was very unfamiliar territory for her as she rarely disliked anyone and that contempt it seemed, could not possibly be eradicated as it continued to grow deeper every time the two actually met. The Thursday certainly hadn't been the highlight of her week and as always, Lachlan had been absolutely distasteful and on the Friday, Talitha would see another bag of problems Saskia and her consultation would have to be endured before the weekend could actually be enjoyed.

One silver lining did lighten Talitha's mind however as she made her way home and that was the thought of Bryson as he would definitely provide Talitha with a weekend of comfort and two very loving arms. The weekend of rest in Bryson's loving arms would help Talitha to recover from the discomfort that Saskia's presence usually created and it would eliminate any remnants of upset and chase away the bitter ugly shadows that an encounter with Saskia or Lachlan usually left behind as Bryson's touch soothed and healed Talitha's spirit.

Inevitably, regardless of Talitha's reluctance, Friday and the day of her planned consultation with Saskia finally arrived and as the day sped into Talitha's life, she began to prepare for her working day ahead. The Friday morning for Talitha was actually quite pleasant as she met with Cassandra and discussed her leg contour which could not actually be performed that day due to the system problems but Talitha hoped that the pleasantness from her morning would somehow spill over into her afternoon as Cassandra's consultation came to an end. Despite the delay to her procedure, Cassandra seemed to be in good spirits as she quickly accepted that the system problems had impacted upon her consultation and instead focused upon the next week when she would return.

Lunch was a relatively quick affair as it was purchased from the nearby diner and then consumed at Talitha's desk as she kept an eye on the time and waited anxiously for the mid-afternoon and Saskia to arrive. In terms of time keeping, Saskia wasn't always on time for her appointments and that was one thing that Talitha had by now, grown quite accustomed to. When it came to the bigger picture however, the issues surrounding Saskia's lateness were rather minor, in comparison to the rather huge, far more complex issue of the second breast enlargement that Saskia wanted which wasn't even available on the system and that Talitha couldn't possibly actually give to her.

Two thirty arrived and Saskia failed to appear which meant once again that Saskia was running late, something that happened quite often which Saskia never ever apologized for as she just didn't really respect anyone's time but her own. One thing lightened Talitha's mood however as she waited and that was the fact that Professor Heisner had given her permission to implement more than procedure during Saskia's consultations as that meant, Saskia would leave Talitha's client list more quickly and that was definitely something to look forward to.

Approximately thirty minutes later, at around three, when Saskia did finally arrive with Marcus her father in tow, she was quickly invited into Talitha's consultation room and then given a variety of choices that related to her nose and her waist. Two procedures would be performed in one consultation that day as Talitha began to implement Professor Heisner's instructions and attempted to appease Saskia's very demanding nature. Unlike some of Talitha's other clients, Saskia's choices were made relatively quickly and that was the one positive thing about her, she was very clear about what she actually wanted to look like and what she wanted from Restructure. Deep down inside, Talitha hoped that the procedures would provide Saskia with exactly what she wanted as there was a fear that if they didn't, she'd be back for more and that really would be a very undesirable outcome.

The afternoon literally sped by as Saskia was quickly given her procedures and for a while at least, she seemed to totally forget about the breast enlargement issue as she became preoccupied with her nose and waist and admired the physical outcome of her choices. Fortunately, there were no actual tantrums that afternoon and the lapse in focus regarding the one issue that Talitha actually had absolutely no control over, relieved Talitha as she tended to Saskia's requests meticulously.

For once it seemed, the headache and nagging that Saskia could deliver had taken a day off as she danced around inside the procedure room and admired the results of her procedures and for that one small mercy, Talitha was extremely grateful. When Saskia wanted to be, she could really be a total pain in the butt and so far it seemed, she wanted to be a pain in the butt quite often.

"I look absolutely amazing Talitha." Saskia gushed as she giggled and then hugged Talitha. "Thank you so much."

Quite strangely, just for a moment, Talitha for once actually saw a completely different side to Saskia and it touched her as Saskia's external display of appreciation provoked Talitha to consider further who Saskia really actually was and wasn't. For the most part, Saskia seemed to be a demanding spoilt brat, especially when she interacted with her father but just for that tiny moment, Talitha had seen another side to her completely and that intrigued her. Inside Saskia there was definitely also a much softer side that was perhaps slightly insecure and that harbored some deep seeded feelings of inadequacy and a side that yearned to be attractive, desirable and loved by others. A side that perhaps yearned to be loved by those that did not have a family duty to accept or want her and perhaps, just perhaps, there was actually a little more to Saskia, than she'd originally assumed, Talitha quietly concluded.

"You're welcome Saskia. I'm just doing my job and if you're happy, I'm happy." Talitha replied as she smiled and then glanced up at the small black clock on the wall. "Right, I better make your next appointment for you and then take you back to reception."

Warm sentiments of relief seemed to wrap themselves around Talitha's body as the two women walked back towards her consultation room and then sat down beside her desk once more, Saskia's consultation had now almost ended and for once, it hadn't involved an actual temper tantrum. A deep, provoking thought suddenly struck Talitha as she watched Saskia gush with excitement as she thanked her father for the procedures she'd had that day that perhaps in this confusing world filled with rejection and criticism, Saskia really wasn't that different from any other young woman her age.

Perhaps Saskia just had access to something that many other young women her age didn't, a wealthy father that she could easily manipulate and access to an open source of funds that she could facilitate and perhaps, if they were in her position, other young women would do exactly the same thing. In essence, Saskia just had greater access to material wealth and that enabled her to actually do something about the things which she observed through the eyes of her thoughts that frustrated her about her world and her own physical appearance.

"Next time I see you Saskia, we'll focus on your arms, chin and hips as Professor Heisner has actually given me special permission to implement three procedures during your next consultation." Talitha explained as she rose to her feet. "I've put you in my diary for next Friday afternoon at the same time."

"Thanks Talitha and please don't forget about my breasts." Saskia quickly reminded her as she stood up. "They're very important."

"As if I would Saskia." Talitha immediately reassured her as she thought internally 'as if I ever could' as there was absolutely no way on earth that Saskia would depart from the clinic as a client without having first had the final breast enlargement that she'd demanded, if it was indeed possible and Talitha knew it.

"Just making sure." Saskia said as she smiled at Talitha.

Underneath that sugary, sweet innocent smile, Talitha knew there lay a total contradiction as she quietly observed it with cynicism as if Saskia didn't get what she wanted, she would kick up a fuss and have a major temper tantrum again. The only real remedy to Saskia's tantrums was giving her exactly what she wanted, when she wanted it, if that were indeed actually possible and Talitha fully understood that. Between the two women there was no illusions, misunderstandings and absolutely no ambiguity at all as that smile only existed as long as Saskia was being given exactly what she wanted.

For once however, Saskia was actually leaving the building in a reasonably happy mood and for that rare occurrence, Talitha felt grateful as she escorted the two towards the reception area and then bade them farewell. The dreaded Friday afternoon appointment that Talitha had feared was now technically over and it hadn't been as bad as Talitha had expected it to be and now, Talitha wouldn't actually have to see Saskia for another week and that was definitely something to celebrate and enjoy as Saskia was a bagful of aggravated stress with a cherry on top.

Once Talitha returned to her consultation room, she spent the rest of the afternoon on the completion of Saskia's notes which she wanted to submit that day before she went home for the evening. Unusually that Friday, Professor Heisner had postponed the meeting that he'd arranged with

Talitha for the Friday afternoon earlier that morning but due to the side effect issues, Talitha completely understood why as the Professor was working on those issues day and night. Their meeting had been rescheduled for first thing on the Monday morning, when Professor Heisner hoped that the fix would be ready and Talitha hoped in her heart of hearts as she left the building and began to make her way home that, that would indeed actually be the case.

Seeds of doubt still lay scattered across Talitha's mind as she began to drive home as to whether Professor Heisner would ever be able to satisfy Saskia's breast enlargement demand as it was such a huge ask and not even something that the Restructure system could actually deliver. Hopefully soon however, Professor Heisner would provide the answer to Saskia's question and then she would find out if what she desired could actually be an addition to her current physicality and hopefully soon, Saskia would be out of Talitha's hair for good.

A smile crossed Talitha's face as she began to wonder if she would ever miss Saskia when she finally did leave her client list like she now missed Renee. Between the two women, a deep emotional connection had been formed as Talitha had helped Renee to jump over the various hurdles and predicaments she'd faced that life had presented to

589

her but with Saskia it had been completely different. Since the very first moment that the two women had met, Saskia had been a proverbial pain in the butt but perhaps in some ways, Talitha decided, she might miss that albeit slightly reluctantly.

Quite interestingly, Talitha quietly contemplated as she drove, Saskia in some respects had been her baptism into the world, minds and desires of very wealthy young women and the women that at one point in her own youth, she'd often wished to be.   At some point in the future, Talitha would definitely meet other young female clients that would perhaps be similar in nature to Saskia, so in some ways Saskia had allowed Talitha to look inside the world that they lived in and had helped her to understand the realities of the lifestyle they lived and the pressures that they faced. A brief dip inside Saskia's world had encouraged Talitha to appreciate her own youth slightly more, despite all it's perceived lacking as she'd observed the thorny minefield of stress, she'd been saved from due to her family's more moderate means.   Puberty was really difficult enough without the added burden of having to maintain such a difficult lifestyle and very expensive image all the time.

First thing on Monday morning, once Talitha's weekend had been gloriously consumed and she'd arrived at work, Talitha put on a brave face as she prepared for her meeting with Professor Heisner.

DOWNLOADABLE

Despite the worries and concerns that surrounded Restructure and the procedures it offered to clients, Talitha trusted the Professor to find a solution and as she entered inside his office and sat down, she adorned her face with an optimistic smile as she hoped for the best and a solution. A spark of hope lay inside Talitha's mind that today Professor Heisner would have the remedy for the problems that her clients faced to actually resolve the side effects from the procedures that had thrown their love lives into absolute chaos.

Much to Talitha's delight, she rapidly discovered that Professor Heisner had indeed managed to actually complete the fix and that it was now ready and waiting to be applied to her client's bodies and minds. The weight of failure was gently lifted from Talitha's shoulders as she accepted that despite Professor Heisner's chaotic appearance, when it came to the issue of his work, he was extremely organized and very committed. Miracles of science it seemed, certainly weren't perfect, despite the very precise nature of science itself.

"Good morning Talitha and I have some great news, I've managed to find a solution and a fix." Professor Heisner boomed as he began to pace around the floor of his office. "So you can start performing procedures again for our clients."

"That's great news Professor Heisner." Talitha replied as she smiled.

"There's no way on earth that I could have possibly foreseen these side effects." Professor Heisner explained. "As they relate to people's minds and emotions and are not physical in nature but despite that I've managed to find the source of the problem."

"Well, the clinic is providing people with experimental procedures Professor Heisner, so I think most people will accept that's a risk they signed up for when they agreed to participate really." Talitha immediately reassured him. "The important thing is however, you've identified the problem and then you've fixed it practically straight away."

"Yes and hopefully not too much damage was done." Professor Heisner agreed. "So this week, you'll have to see all of your clients, past and present and you'll have to implement the Download fix." He instructed.

"What should I tell them?" Talitha asked.

"I would just describe it as a safety upgrade that's required to protect their bodies from any potential harm and to protect them from the risk of any possible viruses." Professor Heisner advised.

"What should I say to Saskia about the breast enlargement? I'm seeing her again on Friday." Talitha asked. "She might throw a tantrum again."

"Talitha, Saskia's tantrums and her demands lie outside the scope of your work and Restructure's limitations." Professor Heisner explained. "Just tell her, there's absolutely nothing you can do about it and that the matter is now in my hands. She can't argue with that. I should have an answer for her soon, perhaps even by Friday, it might not even actually be possible as it does exceed the current safety limits. If she pesters you further about it, just send her to me. Now I have to get on with some work, you'll find the fix inside the Restructure system in the Client Repair menu, so you can access it from there."

"Okay, I'll do that Professor Heisner." Talitha confirmed as she rose to her feet.

The two began to walk towards the door of Professor Heisner's office as they started to discuss exactly how the solution should be applied to Talitha's clients and what she had to do that coming week as this was the first major technical complication that Restructure had actually faced. Despite the very negative circumstances, Talitha felt extremely relieved that Professor Heisner had not only faced the issue head on but had also managed to conquer it as she listened to his very precise instructions.

"Don't worry Talitha." Professor Heisner gently reassured her as he paused in front of his office door and turned to face her. "Once Saskia's gone, you probably never have another client like her ever again. She'll be out of your hair soon enough."

"She's a very determined young woman Professor Heisner." Talitha clarified.

"She's stubborn, spoilt and a drama queen." Professor Heisner replied. "I can hardly blame her though, Marcus let it happen. He feels guilty you know, his wife left them both because he was too busy with work and then Saskia began to run rings around him and he just let things got totally out of hand."

"That would explain a lot." Talitha said as she smiled.

"So don't let Saskia worry you." Professor Heisner advised. "She'll soon be gone."

Talitha nodded.

Once Talitha had returned to her consultation room, she began to prepare for her first client consultation that morning which would actually be with Samson. At least an hour remained before Samson was due to arrive and so Talitha sought out a distraction as she waited to avoid her thoughts running round in circles regarding the current problems with Restructure and to occupy her mind. Some simulated images were quickly loaded onto Talitha's screen from inside the Restructure system as she began to review and inspect just how much each of her client's physicalities had actually changed, since the moment they'd first arrived at Restructure.

Surprise began to surge excitedly through Talitha's thoughts as she glanced at each client's images and inspected the huge physical changes that each client had undergone as in most instances, the transformation was indeed profound. An excited gasp escaped from Talitha's lips as she compared each of the before and after images and deep down inside, Talitha actually felt quite proud as she glanced at each one that she had in some small way contributed to those physical transformations. Although Talitha hadn't come into the Bodily Enhancements Consultant's role with bags of experience, she silently congratulated herself that not only had she met Professor Heisner's but in some ways, she'd even managed to exceed them.

Suddenly, a gentle knock at Talitha's consultation room door interrupted her performance review and Talitha quickly rose to her feet as she prepared to start Samson's consultation. A warm, friendly smile adorned Talitha's face as she crossed the room, opened the door and then greeted Samson as Talitha maintained an image of total professionalism, despite all the problems with Restructure and the Downloads.

The system problems with Restructure were essentially Talitha's first real technical challenge as a consultant and how she handled those issues during the coming week was extremely important as she had to resolve those issues not only to Professor Heisner's satisfaction but also in a way that ensured her client's minds and bodies were not negatively impacted. Other challenges had been presented to Talitha as a consultant like Saskia and Lachlan but they were just a nightmare housed in human clothing made from skin and so those challenges were slightly different.

This challenge however, was very different as this was an actual issue with the services that the clinic provided which essentially meant, it was a corporate crisis and that also meant, Talitha had rise to that challenge and actually manage that crisis effectively. Some of her client's relationships had been affected and their emotions, attractions and emotional responses towards loved ones and strangers were now skewed as a result of Restructure's Download services and that was a total crisis. How Talitha handled this very tricky, complex situation was extremely important as if she actually made a mistake that mistake could potentially make or break the clinic's future and quite possibly even ruin some of her current client's lives.

After Samson had been offered and provided with a beverage and some biscuits, Talitha sat back down and then began her consultation which started with a discussion about Samson's last procedure and the procedure he was supposed to have that day. Due to the fact that Samson was very laid back and cheerful, unlike some of Talitha's other clients, his consultation that day was refreshing for Talitha after her morning of worries.

"How's the new chin going Samson?" Talitha asked.

"Women are absolutely loving the new chin." Samson immediately replied as he grinned. "I've been getting a lot of compliments and I've even been offered a few more facial commercials. A great chin definitely helps."

"Great and how about your new lover? Is she in love with your new chin, or is it a bone of contention and did she actually prefer the old one?" Talitha teased.

"She really seems to like it." Samson quickly clarified. "It's a definite winner all round."

"Great, so what would you like to change today?" Talitha asked as she touched her screen.

"My jaw line." Samson quickly confirmed. "It doesn't quite align with this chin."

Quite fortunately, Samson hadn't actually noticed any issues with his Download procedures which meant, Talitha could simply apply the fix alongside his procedure that day but she was slightly worried that it might crucify his new relationship. Attractions to the opposite sex would definitely change, once the fix had been applied to each client's body and mind and so to would her client's emotional attachments to those around them and Professor Heisner had already explained that to her.

Due to the experimental nature of Restructure's services, no client could actually hold the clinic liable for any romantic losses but it had put Professor Heisner in a difficult position as a professional as he'd missed that inherent flaw in the Download procedures and system itself. One thing comforted Talitha however as she applied the fix and Samson's jaw line enhancement to his body and that was the fact that at least now each client would be returned to their natural state as romantic relationships were difficult enough and skewed emotional attachments certainly wouldn't make love any easier. In her heart of hearts however, Talitha hoped as she escorted Samson back to the reception area and then said farewell that Professor Heisner's solution would resolve the problems that now lay right at the foot of Restructure's door as she really did enjoy her job and like working for Professor Heisner.

When the afternoon arrived, Talitha met with Rita and was notified that it would actually be her client closure session and as Professor Heisner had advised, Talitha immediately implemented the Download fix along with the back strengthening Download that Talitha had promised her. The side effects had definitely already affected Rita as her relationships had started to deviate from their usual patterns and so Talitha was now anxious to resolve that issue before Rita officially left her client list.

Due to the second bodily enhancement that Rita had been provided with which had been a breast enlargement that had caused her a bit of physical discomfort, Talitha had promised to provide her with a back strengthening supplement and so Rita had attended that day for that procedure. Unusually, Rita's face wasn't infused with the usual joys of spring as she entered inside Talitha's consultation room and Talitha quickly began to discuss her procedures with her, in order to establish the root cause of her dissatisfaction.

"I guess there really is a bit more to having the most gorgeous breasts on the planet than I'd originally anticipated." Rita explained. You've got to carry them around every day. They look real good but dam, they're so bloody heavy. It's like having two heavy shopping bags pinned to your body all the time."

"Beauty can be a total pain in the butt." Talitha replied.

"I know and a pain in the back." Rita agreed.

"Are you sure about this being your client closure session Rita?" Talitha asked. "I thought you were going to be a quite regular client."

"You know Talitha, I've decided to give the jewelry thing a go." Rita explained. "I need to think about the long term, good looks don't last forever and one day they run out."

Talitha smiled.

Approximately one hour later, once Rita's procedures had been applied, Talitha escorted her back to the reception area as she prepared to say goodbye.   Essentially, when it came to Rita, Talitha's work had now been done and that meant, she would only return once for a discussion about her life post procedures and then perhaps now and again in the future, if she required something additional. In some ways, her departure as a client saddened Talitha slightly as she'd originally thought that Rita would perhaps be quite a regular client and she'd actually started to quite like her and now, she'd virtually said goodbye to three really nice clients in the space of a week.

"You look after yourself out there Rita." Talitha insisted as she stood inside the reception area and faced her.

"I will Talitha and I brought this for you." Rita replied as she suddenly dipped her hand inside her large handbag and then pulled out a bracelet. "It's not like anything great or anything but I made it for you myself."

"You made this Rita?" Talitha asked as she accepted the gift appreciatively.   "It's absolutely gorgeous."

"I tried." Rita said as she nodded.

"You should try more often, it's beautiful and very unusual." Talitha encouraged as she immediately slipped the elegant looking bracelet onto her wrist. "And I'll definitely wear it. Thank you so much."

"I'll see you in a month Talitha." Rita said as she leant towards Talitha and hugged her affectionately. She turned and then began to walk towards the exterior doors. "You never know, I might even bring you a matching necklace and a pair of earrings to go with the bracelet when I come back."

"That would be lovely Rita." Talitha replied. "Really it would."

For Talitha, the Tuesday morning literally flew by as she arrived at work and then met with Patrick at eleven to give him the ear Download procedure which was next on his request list and at the same time she also applied Professor Heisner's fix to his body. In the afternoon, Cassandra attended her appointment and she was provided with the leg contour that she'd been unable to have the previous week that apparently, she'd been really looking forward to. Once the procedure had been performed, Talitha spent some additional time with Cassandra as they began to discuss her request list, reviewed some of the other procedures that she wanted to have and then explored some of her options.

On the Wednesday morning Talitha had agreed to see Frank and as she arrived at work, she prepared enthusiastically for his arrival as she rejoiced in the fact that now, she at least had a fix to offer him which would eliminate the issues between him and Maude that Professor Heisner's Downloads had created. Due to Frank's very negative experiences Talitha had decided to spend slightly more time with him than she'd originally planned as it was extremely important to her that Frank left Restructure that day with all the problems resolved. At eleven on the dot, Frank arrived and once he'd been offered a beverage and some biscuits, he began to discuss his strange attraction to the woman in the diner and the subsequent affair that he'd recently embarked upon with her as Talitha sat and listened.

"Maude will absolutely kill me if she finds out." Frank insisted. "And she'll definitely divorce me."

"I thought you guys weren't married." Talitha replied.

"We're not but she'll definitely sack me for sure." Frank explained. "She'll pack up her bags and she'll go and she'll never come back. She's quite tough like that."

"I did speak to Professor Heisner again about this and I found out there actually was a problem with one of your Downloads Frank. He's prepared a fix and I'm supposed to give it to you today."

Talitha said.

"I've been trying to stay away from the diner but it's very difficult because the breakfast just tastes so dam good and it's very unhealthy." Frank said as he gently shook his head. "It's quite hard to resist."

"Well Frank, you could perhaps go to the diner that I visit each day for lunch, it's just ten minutes along the highway if you drive towards the city and they have a great breakfast, or you could try Snacks cafe that's just before the start of the highway if you're coming from the city." Talitha suggested. "I get my breakfast there most mornings on my way to work."

"You're right Talitha. I'll find another diner to visit for breakfast." Frank agreed. "A bit of oily food and a quick fumble isn't worth Maude."

"Right, let's go and apply this fix Frank." Talitha encouraged as she rose to her feet. "Then you'll be less likely to stray."

Frank nodded as he stood up and joined her. "That'll be great, I'm a lover not a cheater." He replied as he began to follow Talitha towards the procedure room.

"This should fix all the problems that your having Frank." Talitha reassured him as she stood inside the procedure room and waited for him to mount the transparent capsule. "Then you'll be right as rain and so will Maude."

"You know Talitha, this has all been really strange for me." Frank said as he walked up the steps and then lay down inside the body length transparent body capsule. "I've just never cheated on Maude before, my eyes and hands have been devoted to her since the moment we met." He explained. "And I'm sure, if I don't stop soon, she'll actually catch me. I'm not very good at lying."

"I know Frank." Talitha gently reassured him as she began to pull the capsule lid down over his body. "Don't worry, in just a few minutes time, you'll be back to faithfulness, back to Frank and back to being yourself."

"I sure hope so." Frank said. "I really don't have the energy to have two lovers on the go, not when one of them is as lively as Maude is."

"You will." Talitha insisted. "Just give me a few minutes Frank and I'll be right back and so will you."

Once the Download fix had been performed, Talitha made another appointment for Frank as they planned when she would perform his next Download procedure and he seemed in relatively good spirits. Just before Frank left, Talitha warned him to keep an eye on the situation and to let her know immediately if any other regularities occurred. Due to the fact that Frank had been affected so negatively by the actual procedures and because he was in a long term, extremely serious, very committed relationship, Talitha really wanted to ensure that the situation had been rectified and that it did not continue to deteriorate, for the sake of his relationship with Maude. All in all, despite the complexities and the inconvenience that the Downloads had caused however, Frank left in fairly good spirits as he pointed out that science wasn't perfect and that neither was he and Talitha felt extremely grateful that Frank had such an accommodating and tolerant nature.

The Wednesday afternoon was relatively straightforward for Talitha as she met with Rodney, applied the fix procedure to his body and then performed his client closure session. His client closure session had actually been due to occur the week before but Rodney had requested a last minute procedure when he'd shown up and Talitha had therefore rescheduled it to the following week which worked rather well as it allowed her to apply the Professor's fix without any questions being raised. No lengthy additional explanations were offered to Rodney about the fix and it was just attributed to a standard practice for a client closure session and Talitha doubted that he'd even noticed that anything had gone wrong as skewed emotional responses and attractions probably wouldn't have made that much of a difference to Rodney's love life.

Funnily enough, during Rodney's consultation

he actually seemed more worried about leaving Talitha's client list than his actual procedures and as usual there was a stream of flirtatious remarks and suggestive innuendos that emanated from his lips. Once Rodney's consultation ended, Talitha arranged another follow up appointment for him which was not due to actually occur for about a month and then she rose to her feet as she prepared to escort him back to the reception area.

"Don't worry Talitha, this is not the end of us." Rodney insisted as he flashed her a charming smile.

"Okay Rodney. I'll see you in a month's time." Talitha replied as she gently shook her head and then began to walk towards her consultation room door.

"I'll think of another procedure I need by then Talitha, I promise." Rodney quickly reassured her. "Wait for me, keep a weekly space for me on your client list."

Talitha laughed.

A small part of Talitha felt like she might actually miss Rodney as she showed him out of the building, not a lot but just a touch perhaps as he did liven up her week and he was certainly very memorable and at least, he wasn't a bagful of stress. Although Talitha hadn't bonded with Rodney in quite the same way that she had with Dean and Renee, she still wished him the best as

she quietly watched him depart and she hoped that
he would get what he wanted and needed out of life
and perhaps even one day, actually settle down.
When it came to the issue of Rodney, he was
however, very unpredictable and Talitha smiled as
she began to speculate that perhaps Rodney would
actually end up married within the next six months,
it was possible, if Lachlan could let Charmaine
choose her legs and Rita could turn her whole life
around, there was definitely a glimmer of hope for
Rodney.

When the Thursday morning landed upon the
runway of Talitha's life, she rushed to work as she
prepared herself for an extremely busy day. Due to
the fact that the Professor's fix had to be applied to
all of Talitha's clients that week, past and present,
she'd had to arrange eleven consultations and
three of them were actually due to occur on the
Thursday. Despite the fact that Talitha's week had
been very hectic, due to the internal problems at
Restructure, she'd had to arrange for both Dean
and Renee to return for an additional consultation,
so that the fix could be applied to both their bodies
which meant, eleven consultations would actually
take place that week and three of those had been
squeezed into the Thursday.

An entire physical transformation was due to
occur in the morning for Sylvester and when the
mid-morning arrived, fortunately so did he, on time

and ready for his life changing procedures. Since Sylvester hadn't actually had any procedures yet, he hadn't been affected negatively by the strange side effects which meant he did not need the Professor's fix but it was still a huge day for him as it was the day of his overall transformation. All of his procedures had been authorized by Professor Heisner and scheduled by Talitha to occur in one actual consultation and due to Sylvester's unique situation and circumstances, Professor Heisner had made an exception to his very strict rule. One thing still worried Talitha however and that was the sense of guilt that Sylvester felt and carried around with him about his father's past everywhere he went as that was the one thing that Professor Heisner's Download procedures and Restructure definitely couldn't ever change.

"Are you ready to say goodbye to your body and face Sylvester?" Talitha asked as she stood inside her procedure room next to the transparent capsule.

"Yes." Sylvester replied as he nodded. "I just can't believe it Talitha, I'll be saying goodbye to absolutely everything."

"Are you scared?" Talitha asked.

"Nope, it'll be good for me." Sylvester immediately confirmed as he lay down inside the capsule. "It'll give me a much needed rest from my father's horrible past."

"Just make sure, once you've changed your body and face, you don't keep carrying the guilt from his past around on your shoulders every day." Talitha advised. "It's like an invisible coat you wear that you really need to shed. Life is far too warm for that heavy coat of guilt that technically, isn't really even yours to wear."

Sylvester nodded in agreement. "You're very wise Talitha. Thank you so much." He replied.

Approximately forty minutes later, once all the physical changes had been processed and the physical transformation had taken place, Talitha stood beside Sylvester inside the procedure room in front of the mirror as they silently absorbed his new reflection and his new physical appearance. The change was absolutely mind blowing and as Talitha marveled at what Professor Heisner's work had managed to achieve that day, she began to develop a far deeper respect and appreciation for his work as what he'd done for Sylvester was virtually impossible.

"You look totally different now Sylvester." Talitha said as she suddenly broke the silence between them both. "I wouldn't even recognize you if I passed you on the street."

"I know, I'm absolutely astonished." Sylvester replied as he smiled. "I'm a lot more handsome now too. I might even get a proper girlfriend."

"Just don't tell anyone about your father."

Talitha advised. "You really don't want to keep carrying around that negativity from the past. You really can't afford to spend anymore of your life paying for your father's crimes."

"I won't. This is a great chance for me, so I really have to make the most of it." Sylvester agreed.

"Always remember Sylvester, the past is our lesson and our guide, the present lives within us and is our constant companion but the future is our unborn child of hope." Talitha encouraged.

"Thanks Talitha. You've really changed my life, even without the physical changes. You're such an encouragement and you're very wise." Sylvester replied.

Unfortunately however, the pleasantness of Talitha's day didn't last and when the Thursday afternoon arrived, it brought Lachlan along with it as he turned up for Charmaine's consultation just as Talitha had predicted. Every drop of joy from the morning instantly wore off as soon as Talitha opened up her consultation room door and saw his face. Although Talitha really enjoyed seeing Charmaine, any happiness she derived from Charmaine's consultation was usually very quickly negated by Lachlan's presence which was truly ugly and completely vile.

Rather interestingly for Talitha, the Thursday afternoon also brought along with it a huge dilemma as to whether or not she should actually apply Professor Heisner's fix to Charmaine's body and mind at all. The side effects from the Downloads were skewed human emotional responses and irregular feelings of romantic attraction which meant, it could possibly push Charmaine further away from Lachlan which in Talitha's mind would be a very positive thing and not something that should actually be fixed.

Tireless amounts of devotion and undying adoration had resided in Charmaine's heart for so long but Lachlan had taken her loyalty for granted and so Talitha felt it would be poetic justice, if the 'designer woman' that Lachlan had expended such large sums to create, predominantly to satisfy himself, suddenly left him for another man. Some very complex issues now sat at Talitha's door and she had to make some huge decisions very quickly as Charmaine's consultation had to actually begin.

Ribbons of distaste seemed to float around inside Talitha's body as she glanced at Lachlan's face and placed the cup of tea that Charmaine had requested gently down in front of her. His presence provoked an uneasiness inside of her that could not be comforted or reduced, no matter how much Talitha tried to ignore it. Some sweet biscuits were politely offered to both Lachlan and Charmaine in the hope that the sweetness from the biscuits might somehow drive the bitterness from Lachlan's mind and mouth.

Only one small comfort really remained for Talitha and that was the fact that once she had soldiered through this consultation and performed the second breast enlargement, she would probably never have to endure being in close proximity to Lachlan ever again. Although that was a small comfort, it was a very soothing one as every time Talitha had met Lachlan, she'd felt totally drained afterwards, simply due to the stress he invoked and today, Talitha could definitely tell, would not be an exception. Everything about Lachlan's presence absolutely grated Talitha and he was so intimidating and demanding that she found facing him alone totally unnerving and challenging him, extremely difficult.

Small electric currents of hatred suddenly began to run rampant through Talitha's body which caused her muscles to twitch and shiver as she quietly returned to her seat. In essence, this was perhaps Talitha's last chance to take a stand for Charmaine against Lachlan and his desire to change almost every single part of Charmaine's body but how exactly she should try to take that stand, in a way that would not cost Talitha her job, she was unsure.

Stress and tension rapidly began to fill Talitha's mind as she braced herself for Charmaine's actual consultation to begin, refusal and defiance on

Talitha's part would result in a very ugly, harsh confrontation with Lachlan and she knew that would be a truly horrible event that she was extremely eager to avoid. A huge mental battle now loomed just on the horizon regarding Charmaine's second breast enlargement and for a moment, Talitha was actually unsure that she could actually cope with it. Professor Heisner hadn't intervened, Charmaine hadn't refused to participate and that meant, it now had to actually happen that very same day and that now, Talitha was the only obstacle.

Once the second breast enlargement had been chosen and Talitha had prepared the fix to be applied to Charmaine's body on the system, Talitha led Charmaine quietly towards the procedure room as she fully surrendered to Lachlan's rule. Reality seemed to snake and wrap itself around the two women's bodies in an almost suffocating manner as they walked as they silently caved in to Lachlan's demands, this was Lachlan's dictated reality and this was ultimately, Lachlan's victory. The chauvinistic attitude that Lachlan presented to everyone around him had been virtually impossible for Talitha to change and she'd really struggled with him and finally, Lachlan had won.

In many ways, Professor Heisner's silence had frustrated Talitha but internally, she now had to accept that he was absolutely right in that until Charmaine opposed Lachlan herself there really wasn't much anyone else could do to assist her. Every inch of Talitha's mind, body and spirit was totally against it but she knew deep down, she would have to do exactly what Lachlan demanded that day as she really had no justifiable reason to oppose him any further and she'd already delayed the procedure for weeks.

"Are you happy with how you look Charmaine?" Talitha whispered as she stood next to the transparent capsule inside the procedure room. "Is this what you really want?"

Charmaine looked at her thoughtfully and paused for a moment, before she actually began to respond. "Aren't most of the things that we do in life usually done to make other people happy?" She asked. "How much of our lives is actually really spent doing things for ourselves and for our own enjoyment?"

"I'm not sure Charmaine but I'm in a relationship too and my partner has never ever pressured me to make changes to my body, purely and solely for his own sexual gratification." Talitha explained. "He's my best friend and lover but he's not a dictator. Love doesn't mean that you have to become a martyr to someone else's desires Charmaine, or to the love they profess to have for you."

"I guess you just get used to someone and then it's hard to imagine living your life without that person." Charmaine replied in a hushed voice.

"I just don't feel that someone who really loves you would want you to sacrifice every part of your body to satisfy his wants." Talitha replied. "If someone loves you, why would they want to change every single thing about you?" She asked.

"I'm not sure." Charmaine said as she gently shook her head.

An awkward silence began to rapidly fill the room as Talitha quietly considered Charmaine's submission to Lachlan's rule which one day perhaps, she might actually regret. In essence, Charmaine really was a martyr to a man that she loved and adored and her heart and body seemed to be chained by sentiments of love and sexual lust which defied any inklings of common sense and pragmatic logical reason. Due to Lachlan's financial position, Talitha had placed all the blame at his feet but now, she could very clearly see that perhaps Charmaine had also willingly enabled his behavior as she'd participated and basically given him a license to continue by not walking away. Over the years, Charmaine had never challenged Lachlan, she'd never set appropriate boundaries with him and she'd never left him and in some ways, she'd ultimately enabled him to become the dictator that he now was.

"Sometimes, we women have to be strong in a different way Charmaine and sometimes that strength means actually walking away from men like Lachlan, even if it's just for a short period of time." Talitha advised. "We can reject the things that we do not wish to accept through our own participation as it is our own life and we do have a right to choose what we actually do with it."

Charmaine nodded.

"If someone really loves us Charmaine, they'd want to give us the best of themselves, not the worst." Talitha explained.

Approximately ten minutes later, when both Charmaine and Talitha returned to her consultation room, Lachlan grinned at them both triumphantly as he seemed to rejoice in his achievement and Charmaine's now enlarged breasts. A lump of discomfort stuck in Talitha's throat as she glanced at Lachlan's face and observed his silent celebration, the two women had been no match for Lachlan in the battle of wills in the end and he'd simply bulldozed all over them and then come out the other side, absolutely victorious. Just like a hungry dog that clamps onto a bone with its teeth, Lachlan had held onto that second breast enlargement with relentless tenacity and had ensured that it had actually taken place and Talitha had not been allowed, even for a second, to rip that bone out from between his teeth.

"You look absolutely spectacular Charmaine." Lachlan announced as he rose to his feet. "Totally stunning."

Grains of annoyance seemed to chaotically swirl around inside Talitha's mind as she began to seethe inside as she accepted total defeat and glanced at Charmaine's face. Between Talitha and Charmaine there remained at least a hundred unspoken words that they definitely could not say, at least not in front of Lachlan. Everything about Charmaine's body and face now resembled the physical manifestation of what Lachlan had imagined the perfect woman should look like and his vision of feminine perfection had now been fully achieved and actually realized. Deep down inside himself, Lachlan had probably always yearned for Charmaine to be much more than she was in a physical sense, Talitha quietly speculated and now, she definitely was.

"Money very well spent." Lachlan murmured as he leant forward and kissed Charmaine on the cheek.

"Right, I'll just organize your follow up appointment for you Charmaine which will be in about a month's time." Talitha said as she sat back down beside her desk. "Then I'll see you both to reception."

"Sure Talitha that'll be great." Charmaine replied.

Vomit lined Talitha's stomach as her body silently reacted to Lachlan's disgusting victory and once Charmaine's follow up appointment had been arranged, Talitha eagerly leapt to her feet as she prepared to get rid of Lachlan for good. In the end, Talitha had applied Professor Heisner's fix to Charmaine's body but just for a moment, she'd been tempted not to actually do so. The couple began to follow Talitha as she led them towards her consultation room door and then opened it as she accepted that at least Lachlan would not cost Talitha her job, he'd ruined Charmaine's life but at least, he had not been provided with an opportunity to ruin Talitha's life.

"Thanks for all your help." Lachlan said as he turned to face Talitha and paused just in front of the door. "Charmaine looks absolutely stunning now and it's all thanks to you."

"No problem." Talitha replied slightly sarcastically. "And I'll see you again soon Charmaine."

Inside Talitha's mouth there was a very bitter aftertaste as she quietly accepted the sobering reality and the bitter pill of defeat as ultimately she had actually enabled and participated in Lachlan's dictatorship. A huge lump of discomfort seemed to stick in her throat as she silently accepted the part she'd played in Lachlan's dominance with sadness. Once Talitha had led the couple through the door of her consultation room, she walked briskly towards the reception area as she was anxious to rid herself of Lachlan's presence as soon as she possibly could as inside her veins, her blood began to boil as she walked.

Just a few seconds were spent inside the reception area as Talitha stood and watched the couple actually leave the building as a sigh of relief escaped from her lips as she silently appreciated seeing the back of Lachlan for the very last time. Although another follow up appointment had been arranged for Charmaine in one month's time, it was highly unlikely that Lachlan would actually attend as essentially now, Lachlan had what he wanted in its entirety and that was a comforting fact. Now, there was absolutely no reason for him to actually come back to Restructure and that was the only positive remnant and small comfort that remained from the experience of Lachlan that day, his future absence.

No further pleasantries had been exchanged with Lachlan as he'd left as Talitha had kept her farewell towards him abrupt, cold and even slightly dismissive. His final remarks however had borne down heavily upon Talitha's heart as she'd accepted that she'd failed in her struggle as she'd waded through the murky waters of male chauvinism and male dictatorial tendencies for the most part alone.

The conversation between the two women that day continued to linger inside Talitha's mind as she returned to her consultation room and then began to write up Charmaine's notes. Some huge issues had been raised by Talitha and she just hoped that Charmaine would consider each one and think about them very carefully. In Talitha's opinion, Lachlan had really insulted Charmaine as he'd actually treated her very much like something that he didn't want in her current form. Every single body and facial part that Lachlan had wanted had been picked out just like the items on a menu at a restaurant with absolutely no further regard to Charmaine's feelings and that was not only totally insensitive but also extremely arrogant.

Each minute that Talitha had spent with Lachlan had highlighted to her just how fortunate she'd actually been to meet someone like Bryson as she'd definitely been blessed by the companionship of a good man and not a monster. At times, it was easy to sit outside someone else's relationship and judge it but it was quite another thing to actually be strong enough to leave such a negative situation, if you were actually in it and committed to it.

One day perhaps, Talitha hoped, Charmaine would come to her senses and leave the man that had wanted to change every single thing about her and one day perhaps, she'd realize that he'd traded her body in as part of a financial experiment in an attempt to create the female physicality that he truly desired. In some ways, it was almost as if Charmaine had become a 'made to order' lover for

Lachlan as each body part that she'd possessed that he didn't want, he'd simply replaced.

Interestingly, Talitha's deliberations about Charmaine and Lachlan raised a very strange issue inside Talitha's mind as she began to quietly contemplate what might actually happen, if the whole world followed their example and began to modify their bodies according to their current partner's desires. Some of the implications surrounding Talitha's wandering thoughts amused her but others were actually quite frightening as she considered that perhaps then people would have to change their bodies every single time they changed partners. Dating would then simply become a ritual of modifying one's body and adapting it to suit each different partner that a human being became romantically involved with and that would change each time one relationship ended and a new one began. Although it was a very strange thought and it did amuse Talitha slightly in some ways, the implications of that possibility were also extremely frightening.

A warm smile crossed Talitha's face as she waited for Dean to arrive, at least that day, she had some good news for Dean as Professor Heisner had agreed to his adjustment procedure with minimal fuss and Talitha had already prepared an actual Download that week for him. For Talitha, her working day was now almost over and for that

Talitha was truly grateful as she found being in Lachlan's presence for any amount of time, extremely draining as he absolutely repulsed her.

When four that Thursday afternoon arrived, so too did Dean for his special additional consultation which had been arranged that week by Talitha to apply Professor Heisner's fix and the penis adjustment to his body. Due to the fact that Dean had only been due to attend a final follow up consultation, he'd been invited back especially as that wasn't supposed to happen for at least a few more weeks. Since Professor Heisner's fix had to happen that week and because Talitha wanted to make the most of the additional consultation, it made sense therefore for Talitha to utilize the consultation to perform the second penile adjustment procedure at the same time.

"You know Talitha, this penis is not a blessing, it's a curse, it hurts everyone that I want to give pleasure to." Dean explained as he began to sip the cup of coffee that Talitha had just given him.

"Well, I'll be sorting that out for you today Dean, so it will be slightly smaller, not hugely smaller but great things do come in smaller packages sometimes." Talitha encouraged as she glanced into Dean's eyes and rapidly noticed that they seemed to glisten with tears of dismay that appeared to be just waiting to fall.

"Really?" Dean asked. "Professor Heisner said

that you could do it today?"

"Yes Dean. Professor Heisner has approved the additional procedure and at no extra cost." Talitha explained as she smiled. "So I can implement it for you today, unless you'd like to wait until your follow up consultation."

"Certainly not." Dean immediately confirmed as he grinned.

"One thing I will say though Dean, sex is really much better once you've developed a deeper bond of friendship with a woman first." Talitha advised as she touched the screen in front of her. "So don't be in a rush. You're very special Dean and you should find someone special and that takes time."

"I'm just so glad that you're here Talitha and that I'm not facing all of this on my own, it's really complicated." Dean replied. "And you do make such great coffee, a man couldn't ask for more really."

Talitha grinned. "Well, the coffee machine does." She teased.

Sexual chemistry was a very important factor in modern day relationships and Talitha fully understood that but she sought to quench those heated passions inside Dean slightly as she encouraged him that in this situation, taking his time really was the most appropriate thing to do. Exposing himself physically to lovers that would then simply later shun him and break his heart might destroy Dean's confidence in the longer term and Talitha definitely wanted to avoid that possibility and protect him from such negative eventualities.

"Building a deeper emotional connection with women first will protect your heart Dean." Talitha explained. "Regardless of how big, or small your piece of equipment might be."

"I think you're right Talitha." Dean agreed. "I think I just rushed a bit. My confidence has been pretty low since the accident really, due to the physical injuries I suffered. So perhaps, I just got a bit carried away and probably jumped in a bit too quickly."

"Let me tell you a secret Dean, no one really has confidence. Confidence is just like an outfit that we clothe our minds with in order to face the world so that we can achieve things." Talitha advised. "And the people that you might think have lots of confidence, sometimes doubt themselves more than anybody else. What we see on the outside of a person is not always the same as what's on the inside."

"I think you should help me pick out the right penis enlargement this time Talitha." Dean suggested. "Since I got it so wrong last time, I really can't afford to make another mistake like that again."

"Well I can try but I'm not a man Dean, so I

might not be the best person to advise you." Talitha quickly pointed out.

"No but you are a woman and I date women, so I think you'll be the perfect person to assist me." Dean replied.

"Don't worry Dean, I'll try my best." Talitha agreed. "I promise."

Quite interestingly, Talitha suddenly realized what she had perhaps overlooked during Dean's previous consultations and that was that now, Dean had actually begun to doubt himself, his own choices and perhaps even his own decisions. Perhaps that self doubt was due to the romantic disaster that Dean had suffered as a direct result of the penis he'd chosen, Talitha quietly deliberated. His rash decision had it seemed, thrown his judgment into question and now, Dean didn't seem to trust his own choices anymore, or think that his own preferences were totally reliable.

Once Dean had been given the fix that Professor Heisner had provided and the penis adjustment that Talitha had helped him select which was a slightly smaller version of the one he'd originally chosen, the two made their way back into Talitha's consultation room. The second Download procedure in the end had been the one that Talitha had carefully chosen for him earlier that week as she'd actually done a bit of research beforehand into average penis sizes in terms of lengths and widths and then had selected something, slightly bigger than average but not uncomfortably so.

"It feels much better already Talitha." Dean immediately confirmed as he sat back down next to Talitha's desk. "Much more comfortable. Far less luggage."

Talitha smiled at his positive remarks. "Good." She replied.

"Thank you for everything Talitha." Dean said as he smiled. "And don't worry, I'll let you know if I have any problems with this one but I think it'll be fine now."

"Yes, let me know Dean." Talitha encouraged. "That's what I'm here for."

An air of sadness suddenly seemed to fill the room as Talitha rose to her feet and prepared to escort Dean back to the reception area. Silently inside herself, Talitha began to acknowledge the finality of his departure as they walked along the crisp white corridor together as now, Dean's time as a client had well and truly come to an end. The follow up appointment would just be a final goodbye, just a short conversation that would occur on a day when they would leave each other's lives probably forever. Some part of that finality felt quite bitter sweet to Talitha as she watched Dean walk out of the exterior doors and the building as Dean had been Talitha's first ever client and the first client that had opened her eyes to the magnificent capabilities of the Restructure system and Dean had been Talitha's first scientific miracle.

Later that day as Talitha made her way home, she silently began to regurgitate the day's events inside her mind as she drove. Deep down inside herself, Talitha felt the traces of failure line her stomach as the final outcome to Charmaine's consultations should have been more favorable, should have been different and should have swayed more in Charmaine's favor and a sense of defeat weighed heavily on her heart that it actually hadn't. Rather frustratingly, Lachlan's departure had left behind not only a bitter residue of discomfort but also the burden of blame which he'd somehow managed to place very firmly on Talitha's shoulders, purely through his final remarks.

Another working day rapidly began as it silently plonked itself down onto Talitha's doorstep and as she prepared to meet the day and depart from the home that she so lovingly shared with Bryson every night, she began to think about the weekend ahead. The evening and night had departed more abruptly than Talitha had wished but nonetheless she had to attend work in a timely manner as there were responsibilities to be met and those responsibilities required financial satisfaction but fortunately, the weekend was just around the corner. According to Talitha's schedule that Friday, she would actually be meeting Saskia again which was less than an ideal way to end any week but Talitha resigned herself to the fact that Saskia would definitely attend as she'd want to know if her request for a larger breast enlargement was indeed, actually possible.

Despite the potentially tricky Friday afternoon, some joy was rapidly sprinkled over Talitha's working day that morning as eleven arrived and brought Renee along with it. Joy and excitement seemed to radiate from every inch of Renee's face as Talitha invited her inside her consultation room and glanced at her rosy red cheeks which seemed to glow and shine with happiness. The female body that had once been very slender was now full and curvy and had been adorned with a beautiful black dress which was revealing and confident but still quite sophisticated as it accentuated Renee's frame and some shiny red lip gloss decorated Renee's lips which looked plump and loved as they sparkled and glistened. Not only had Renee's physicality changed it appeared but so too had her attitude towards her own body and herself.

"How are things going Renee?" Talitha asked as the two women sat down and faced each other. "Would you like something to drink before we start?"

"Yes please, a cup of tea would be lovely and things are going absolutely great Talitha." Renee replied enthusiastically. "My breasts and my lips are all in perfect working order. I've tried them out a few times now and they were very well received."

Talitha giggled as she glanced into Renee's eyes which sparkled with excitement. "I love the dress Renee." She mentioned. "It really compliments your figure. Don't try those bits out too much though, or they might get worn out."

Thankfully, Renee's procedures had predominantly gone almost completely to plan and she now seemed to have the results that she'd sought from Restructure in the first place and that comforted Talitha as she prepared the cup of tea that Renee had asked for. Inside Talitha there was now a grain of hope as Renee's testimony provided her with a reassurance that most of her other clients would also experience a similar joy and sense of satisfaction, once Professor Heisner's fix had been applied to all their bodies and minds although that might never be the case for Saskia. Regardless of what Talitha and Professor Heisner did for Saskia, Talitha doubted that Saskia would ever be truly satisfied with herself, or with the world around her as she was extremely difficult to please.

For the next twenty minutes or so, Talitha just listened to Renee as she confidently confided in Talitha with regards to several recent romantic liaisons that she'd participated in and for the most part, it seemed as if Renee was really enjoying the blessings that Restructure had brought into her life.

The happiness Renee felt was obvious and it silently encouraged Talitha as she quietly listened to her discuss some of the intricate details of the various romantic experiences and affairs she'd embarked upon, since her last visit to Restructure.

"Honestly Talitha, I feel like a new person." Renee gushed with excitement. "I've never enjoyed my body like this ever before."

Everything on the surface seemed to be absolutely fine as Renee enthusiastically discussed how the men she'd met physically had appreciated her improved body and abundant breasts but one thing did worry Talitha slightly and that was Renee's long term romantic stability. A question sauntered across Talitha's mind as she quietly began to wonder if the various bodily enhancements had unleashed a hunger inside of Renee for sexual fulfillment that she could not actually control. Years of unrealized passion had built up inside of Renee that had never been utilized and now, Renee was living those years out and giving herself what she'd always missed out on and denied to herself but that in the end, Talitha feared, might actually leave Renee feeling quite empty and used.

"Are you happy with your choices Renee?" Talitha suddenly asked.

"Definitely." Renee quickly confirmed. "Restructure is the best thing that's ever happened to me."

Regardless of Talitha's slight reservations, Renee's face looked absolutely radiant and that was a huge change from the woman that Talitha had initially met during Renee's first consultation. The hunger which lay inside her eyes was evident but it was completely understandable as it was attributable to an accumulation of desires that had built up inside of her for many years. A very hungry lust would perhaps rule Renee's world for a while and she would perhaps find it difficult to settle down in the short term but Talitha hoped in the long term, Renee would be able to find some kind of romantic equilibrium and a stable relationship, once the thrill of her newly enhanced, feminine physical assets had worn off.

"One of the dates I went on last weekend was really fantastic Talitha, we visited a restaurant with a champagne fountain and he spared no expense, it was totally amazing." Renee gushed. "I'm absolutely having the time of my life."

The details of Renee's favorite date continued to flow as Talitha just sat and listened to her speak as she quietly cast her mind back to her own first date with Bryson which certainly hadn't involved a champagne fountain and had been a lot more humble. In those days, Bryson hadn't been particularly wealthy, or even very financially stable but he'd taken her to the best Chinese restaurant that he could afford and she'd appreciated it immensely.

Some cute messages had been found inside the fortune cookies that they'd been given and they'd teased each other about them as they'd giggled and laughed. Straight after their first meal together, they'd walked down the quiet, empty city streets late at night hand in hand, until they'd found a street festival which they'd enjoyed for a couple of hours. First dates could be really exciting and magical and something that a couple would remember for years to come and perhaps even something that an individual would remember for the rest of their lives, regardless of how much money was or wasn't spent.

"What do you think Talitha?" Renee asked. "Do you think he has long term potential? He's slightly more mature than Simon was and our relationship so far has been a bit more sophisticated."

"Try to take your time with him Renee and get to know him a bit. Try to make sure that you're really sure." Talitha suggested as she rapidly crashed back down to earth as her thoughts were interrupted by Renee's pressing question. She smiled at Renee to encourage her. "Romance is a dish best served slowly casseroled and fully marinated."

"It's probably a bit late for that Talitha, we've

already been naughty and naked together, for a whole night." Renee explained.

"I just mean take your time in terms of your romantic commitment and your emotional attachment to him Renee." Talitha replied. "Let him earn you, don't let him take you for granted."

"You know Talitha, you've really changed my life." Renee said appreciatively. "And definitely for the better."

"I just want you to be happy Renee. If you leave here happy then I've done my job successfully." Talitha explained.

Approximately one hour later, once Talitha had applied the fix that Professor Heisner had prepared to Renee's body and mind and they'd discussed her follow up appointment, Talitha escorted Renee towards the reception area as she prepared to say goodbye. Due to the obvious satisfaction and appreciation that Renee had very clearly expressed, Renee's experiences provoked Talitha to consider the dead animal carcasses further as Renee stepped out of the building. Perhaps, Talitha deliberated as she began to walk back towards her consultation room, she was being overly sensitive and perhaps a few dead animals was a meaningful price to pay to bring heaps of happiness and joy into a human being's life. Although it had been very difficult to see those animal remains, perhaps somehow it could actually be understood and in some small way, actually be justified.

Lunchtime was a relatively quick affair as Talitha popped out, bought a sandwich and then returned to the Restructure building and her consultation room. Much to Talitha's surprise, when she returned she actually found Professor Heisner just outside her consultation room door waiting for her.

"Talitha, we need to have a quick meeting." Professor Heisner explained.

"Is anything wrong Professor Heisner?" Talitha immediately asked.

"No. Don't worry, everything's absolutely fine but I have some great news for you." Professor Heisner said as he smiled.

"Really that's good, good news on a Friday afternoon is definitely a good thing." Talitha replied as she quickly opened her consultation room door.

"I've found a solution for Saskia." Professor Heisner explained as he stepped inside the room.

"You have?" Talitha asked.

"Yes, I've managed to find a way to offer her a breast enlargement that is a double H cup." Professor Heisner explained as he sat down in one of the chairs next to Talitha's desk. "However, this is the biggest cup size that I can offer her and I'm really pushing the system as this definitely exceeds the usual safety standards."

"When should I implement the download procedure?" Talitha asked.

"You can do it today but this is a onetime Download and so it won't be accessible to anyone else. Once the procedure is complete, the Download will be destroyed so that it can never be utilized again." Professor Heisner quickly pointed out.

"Is it dangerous?" Talitha asked.

"It carries far greater risks than any of the other Download procedures we currently offer but I've let Marcus know and he'll have to explain those to Saskia and if she still wishes to proceed that's up to her really. I wash my hands of the situation." Professor Heisner replied.

"So I should do it today?" Talitha asked.

"Yes." Professor Heisner replied as he rose to his feet. "The things we do for those we care about. I've known Saskia since she was a child but she was very different back then. Such a shame really."

For an hour after Professor Heisner left, Talitha just sat and thought about her consultation with Saskia which would happen that same afternoon as she reviewed the potentially hazardous Download she was supposed to apply to Saskia's body inside the Restructure system. Inside Talitha's stomach, several knots began to form as she quietly contemplated what might actually happen, if the

Download procedure actually went wrong. Although Talitha wasn't really a fan of Saskia, the thought of something negative happening to her as a result of something that Talitha had implemented and put inside her body really wasn't a desirable outcome and that definitely worried Talitha profusely.

THE ROMANTIC AFTERMATH

Inevitably, the Friday afternoon progressed and at around three, at least thirty minutes after Saskia's consultation was due to start, Saskia finally turned up. The usual client pleasantries were faithfully performed as Talitha invited both Saskia and Marcus inside her consultation room and then offered them both a beverage as she prepared to begin Saskia's consultation. No apologies were offered for Saskia's lateness but Talitha expected none as Saskia wasn't really the kind of person that would offer an apology to anyone for her tardiness. A regard for punctuality was not Saskia's strong point, or something that she cared very much about and by now, Talitha had grown used to Saskia's attitude.

The cup of tea that Marcus had requested was placed down on Talitha's desk in front of him and the glass of apple juice for Saskia as Talitha silently celebrated the fact that Saskia was the last obstacle that she had to face before her weekend could be enjoyed. Upon Saskia's face there was a triumphant smile as she thanked Talitha for the apple juice which made a change as her face usually carried a scowl and Talitha immediately assumed that Marcus had already broken the good news to her about the second breast enlargement.

According to Professor Heisner's instructions, Saskia was permitted to have up to three Download procedures in any given session which meant, one of the procedures that Talitha had promised her would not be performed that day, due to the second breast enlargement. Due to those limitations, Talitha braced herself for a potentially angry outburst as she prepared to break the bad news to Saskia.

"Since you'll be having the second breast enlargement Saskia, I'm afraid I'll only be able to perform two other Download procedures today, so the other procedure will have to wait until your next consultation." Talitha explained.

"That's okay Talitha, I can wait a week. Everyone absolutely loves my new body and face." Saskia replied confidently. "Besides the breast enlargement really is much more important."

"Right, so since we'd planned to focus on your arms, chin and hips today but we can only do two of those which two would you like?" Talitha asked.

"I think I'd like my chin and hips today." Saskia said. "Those are the most important procedures. My arms can wait until next week."

Talitha nodded as she touched her screen. "Okay Saskia, I'll just start preparing the image selection for you now." She explained.

One thing comforted Talitha as she glanced at her screen and that was the fact that she no longer had to listen to, or tolerate Saskia's tantrums as she'd now passed that baton of responsibility onto Professor Heisner and he'd actually accepted sole responsibility for it. Whatever feelings of dissatisfaction that Saskia now felt, expressed and presented had become totally irrelevant to Talitha and Saskia's demands would no longer be a noose around Talitha's neck, or her problematic attitude a weight upon her very weary shoulders. Friday afternoons would no longer be a physical and mental drain for Talitha as Saskia's problems were no longer Talitha's problem, or responsibility and that in itself was extremely liberating.

A very heavy weight had now been lifted from Talitha's mind and the response 'Professor Heisner is dealing with this matter' had been like a spoonful of sugar to Talitha as Saskia's attitude had been a very bitter cup of coffee that Talitha had, had to drink every time the two women met. Very strangely, although Saskia had actually been a last minute addition to Talitha's initial client list and even though her father was one of Professor Heisner's personal friends, she'd definitely been the most trouble so far. Any tantrums that might now erupt, or negative ramifications from keeping Saskia waiting that loomed inside her dissatisfied mind, were now Professor Heisner's problem and Talitha relaxed in that one tremendous comfort.

Even if all of Saskia's current issues were resolved, Talitha quietly considered as she began to prepare the Download procedures and the fix she had to apply that day, Saskia would probably never be satisfied as she just couldn't seem to find peace inside herself. In terms of who Saskia was as a person, she was an impossibility and an irresolvable enigma of infinite demands that no one on earth could ever possibly satisfy, not even Professor Heisner and his miracle clinic Restructure.

Part of Talitha wondered for a moment what Saskia might do if one day she had to provide for herself, if that day ever actually arrived which Talitha was actually unsure it ever would. The Download clinic and Marcus had provided Saskia with the face and body that she'd wanted and it was far more likely that she'd probably just find a wealthy man to latch onto and marry that would provide her with the lifestyle that she was very much accustomed to living and enjoying. Despite all his good intentions, the reality was the guilt that

Marcus felt had contributed to this horror and the neglect that he'd inflicted upon his marriage had set of a chain of events that had resulted in less than desirable consequences.

Somehow, it was almost as if the whole family had become a victim to Marcus's dedication to his principles which stipulated that he should make as much effort as he possibly could to provide for his family financially. Perhaps once Marcus's wife had left, the principles that Marcus held dear had then been capitalized upon quite intentionally by Saskia as she'd exploited a heartbreaking situation and then utilized it as a justification to become who she'd always yearned to be. The excuses that Marcus made inside his own mind which seemed to relate to his guilt, somehow appeared to help him accept and accommodate the unacceptable, Saskia's very unreasonable, spoilt behavior and that was one thing a Download procedure, or three really couldn't change.

Ever since Professor Heisner had shared some of the intimate details with Talitha about their family history, she'd felt slightly better equipped and more able to understand the situation although she still remained unsure that she could actually help to change it. Some very negative, underlying currents ran deep below the surface of their interactions that flowed in a very destructive direction and being more informed and knowledgeable about why they existed, didn't actually solve any of the issues in isolation. Neither Saskia nor Marcus could now be lifted out of the rut of negativity they'd fallen so deeply inside, simply because Talitha was aware of their family history but to some extent that knowledge had helped her extend slightly more patience and understanding towards them both.

Knowledge of the past certainly couldn't change the present, or the future, not if the parties involved were unwilling to change anything and Talitha's awareness did not change the reality that their family relationship had fallen into a huge abyss of destructive negativity. Issues lay buried deep inside both their minds, underneath the rubble and debris of past pain and hurt that it seemed had formed an inescapable maze of interdependent guilt and exploitation for which it appeared, there was no simple way out or actual solution.

Perhaps Saskia's new body and face would provide both Marcus and Saskia with an actual way out, Talitha silently speculated as she touched the screen to confirm Saskia's preferences. Perhaps Saskia would find a partner that would be so attracted to her, he'd assume the burden of Marcus's guilt induced responsibilities, Talitha quietly considered as she rose to her feet and then began to lead Saskia towards the procedure room. Perhaps somehow, Professor Heisner had actually provided them both with a real solution that one day would actually be realized. Perhaps, just perhaps, by giving Saskia what she actually wanted in its entirety, Marcus had ultimately freed himself.

Inside Saskia's mind there definitely seemed to be some illusive standard of perfection that she was somehow attempting to live up to but Talitha doubted that attainment of that desired perfection would ever actually be realized. Tastes and fashions changed with the passage of time and different physical attributes were deemed as beautiful as tastes changed. Perhaps, Saskia would return to Restructure in the future when those changes occurred as she would seek to align herself with those changes and then she would become like a boomerang, thrown away by society through rejection and feelings of inadequacy once again.

A very sincere wish silently scurried through the passageways of Talitha's mind as she returned to her consultation room with Saskia, arranged her next appointment and then rose to her feet as she prepared to escort both Saskia and Marcus back towards the reception area. Saskia's attitude and happiness seemed to be completely reliant upon the attainment of physical perfection and so Talitha wished that one day, Saskia might actually mature and learn to be satisfied with her choices and that one day, Saskia would learn to actually accept herself. Deep down however, Talitha knew as she led them both out of her consultation room as she prepared to say farewell to the tired, worn down father and spoilt, demanding daughter for another week, Saskia's future was not Talitha's to cope with and that Saskia's future belonged only to Saskia herself.

Due to the fact that Saskia actually received a call as the three began to walk along the corridor that led towards the reception area, Saskia started to walk a few steps ahead, distracted by her conversation. The opportunity to speak to Marcus alone suddenly presented itself to Talitha and she quickly grabbed it by the horns as she attempted to provide him with a glass of advice and a portion of encouragement.

"You know Marcus, it's not easy bringing up a daughter on your own. I think you've done very well." Talitha encouraged as she smiled at him.

"I think I've failed Talitha." Marcus replied as he shook his head. "Do you really think I've succeeded as a parent?" He asked.

"Sometimes Marcus, I think people can get lost in the past and in what should have been and what shouldn't have been." Talitha advised. "And guilt can become like a debt that we carry around with us everywhere we go but that debt is never satisfied until forgiveness is given and sometimes that forgiveness is a gift we first have to give ourselves."

"Perhaps." Marcus said as he glanced at Talitha's face.

"I have to get back to work now Marcus I'm afraid." Talitha mentioned as the two stepped inside the reception area. "I have to write up Saskia's notes."

"Yes of course. I think Saskia must be waiting for me outside." Marcus quickly concluded as he glanced around the reception area and rapidly noticed that Saskia was not actually present. "Thanks for everything Talitha, you've really helped."

"I'll see you next week Marcus." Talitha replied as she smiled. "Enjoy your weekend."

"You too Talitha." Marcus said as he enthusiastically nodded his head.

Upon Talitha's face there was an amused smile as she quietly made her way back towards her consultation room as she began to think about the huge breasts that were now attached to Saskia's body. The breasts really were so huge that they might actually hit Saskia in the face when she turned or moved around, Talitha decided. Perhaps that wasn't a bad thing, Talitha quietly concluded as she stepped back inside her consultation room as perhaps that might knock some sense into her.

At the very least, Saskia had left the Restructure building that day satisfied, happy and content which meant, Talitha would never have to listen to her rants, tantrums, or complaints about larger breasts ever again. In some ways, Talitha considered thoughtfully as she sat back down at her desk and then began to write up Saskia's notes, Saskia was really a victim herself, a victim of a demanding society that demanded very high levels of physical perfection and especially from women.

For some inexplicable reason, women were placed under a physical microscope that men weren't and physical beauty was expected from them in every walk of life, simply because they were women. Men could get away with looking ruffled, untidy and messy and they could get away with being less attractive and less perfect and women often found their rough edges appealing. Women on the other hand had to be well manicured, immaculately presented and physically blessed with all the correct physical attributes that both men and the rest of society deemed to be both feminine and attractive. They had to possess all the things that were attributed to feminine beauty and this was usually reflected by the vast sums of money that many women spent upon cosmetic surgery, makeup, hair appointments, beauty treatments and various other cosmetic indulgences.

In society itself, a double standard definitely existed that Talitha had seen herself for many years in that men could get away with making less effort and women couldn't and for some reason, it was never questioned or disputed by anyone and least of all by women, who simply seemed to accept it. The idealistic physical imagery that surrounded women, discreetly dictated to them what was beautiful as it placed tremendous pressure upon them to be more beautiful and more attractive than they naturally were. Women in response, succumbed almost like obedient maids to those defined standards as they sought to physically sculpture their faces and bodies, according to the idealistic images of beauty in an attempt to actually live up to them.

Younger women were even more prone to the pressure, Talitha quietly concluded and she'd seen that inside the walls of the various cosmetic surgeries that she'd worked in as so many of their clients had been under twenty five years old. Life for younger women was definitely becoming more and more competitive and how they looked really seemed to have an impact upon their levels of confidence, the jobs they were given, the boyfriend they managed to attract and the standard of living that they enjoyed.

Rather unfortunately, Saskia's attitude was just a symptom of a greater disease that craved and demanded a perfection from women that in the long term was absolutely unrealistic, totally unattainable and completely unachievable. Someone else would always be deemed more beautiful and someone else would always possess superior physical assets and someone else would always be considered more physically attractive in one way or another and so women were ultimately fighting a losing battle against themselves.

Just a few more appointments actually remained with regards to Saskia's procedures, due to Professor Heisner's acceleration plan and then she would leave Talitha's client list for good but those were more of a formality than a necessity as Saskia had already received most of the procedures that she'd come to Restructure to receive. A smile crossed Talitha's face as she quietly reflected again upon Saskia's now absolutely huge breasts as they were so huge and Talitha began to speculate that she might even fall over as she walked along the street from being top heavy. Each breast was now a definite weapon that Saskia could utilize to disarm a whole room full of people, simply by presenting herself and her very huge boobs. Men would be powerless and women would no longer be a threat to her and Saskia would become the boob warrior of Shuttlesburg, Talitha thought as she submitted Saskia's notes and almost laughed out loud.

"She might never come back now." Talitha muttered as she began to shut down the Restructure system. "Now that is a very real possibility."

Funnily enough that day, Saskia had actually left Talitha's consultation room in a hurry, in all likelihood she'd been in a rush to show of her assets to the world and to seek human validation as quickly as possible but that was a good thing as Talitha wanted to leave work on time that evening. For once, Saskia consultation had been a lot less stressful and problematic and Talitha quietly concluded that Professor Heisner was definitely a genius and one hundred percent correct as it was much easier to just give Saskia exactly what she wanted and allow her be someone else's problem. Once Saskia walked outside Restructure's doors, she would indeed live her life with or without Talitha's input and Talitha really wasn't her social worker, mother or even her friend, she was just a consultant that had been paid to implement some beauty procedures to a human body and Talitha really had done her best.

When Talitha's working day finally ended and it was time to depart, she jumped up happily as she welcomed the thought of the weekend and the romantic possibilities it held.   Some dinner reservations had already been made for the evening ahead by Bryson as apparently, he wanted to tell Talitha something extremely important and Talitha was very excited about it as the venue was one of her favorite restaurants.   Despite the rather unpleasant nature of Professor Heisner's mistakes and the fix that Talitha had then had to apply to her client's bodies and minds, Talitha's week had actually been quite pleasant as she'd spent some of it with Dean and Renee, two of her favorite clients that now, she would greatly miss.

During their various meetings, Talitha contemplated as she crossed the room and headed for the door, Professor Heisner had never actually clarified how deeply involved Talitha should, or shouldn't become in the various complexities that surrounded her client's procedures and their very real lives and so that still remained quite a grey area. Just how far exactly Talitha should delve into those personal complexities, in order to ensure her client's needs were met, still remained totally undefined and really quite uncertain but it was something that Talitha often wondered about. One thing Talitha was sure of however as she opened up her consultation room door, time and experience would definitely shape her judgment and hopefully, provide her with further clarity and some of those answers.

Quite surprisingly as Talitha stepped out of her consultation room, she found Moses right outside the door and he gently placed his arm on Talitha's arm as he urged her to accompany him and then began to guide her in the opposite direction from the reception area. The long corridor which led towards Professor Heisner's laboratory around the rear of the building was quiet and empty as Talitha began to follow him and walk along it as Moses placed his finger on his lips and urged Talitha to be silent.

"Where are we going Moses?" Talitha whispered as she quickly glanced down at her phone to check the time as she was slightly worried that his detour might actually delay her journey home.

"To Professor Heisner's laboratory." Moses whispered back. "He's gone to a meeting."

"At some point Moses, I do need to actually go home tonight." Talitha explained as she gently shook her head, her priority that evening was Bryson and not a strange work colleague with mysterious patterns of behavior.

"I know, this won't take long." Moses replied.

Although his behavior was slightly strange, for some inexplicable reason, it slightly amused and intrigued Talitha as she followed him further along the corridor as in the past, he'd almost been like a wall of refusal, absolutely determined to hide things that he didn't want her to know but now, he suddenly appeared to be the exact opposite. Thoughts began to flood to the forefront of Talitha's mind as she began to wonder if Moses's strange behavior had anything to do with the animal she'd seen him release into the sea of junk.

Once the two arrived outside Professor Heisner's laboratory, Moses quickly unlocked the door as he stood in front of the eye retina scanner and it accepted his eye identification. A quick glance was cast over the interior of the room to check that it was empty and then Moses silently beckoned to Talitha to follow him inside. For the first time ever that Friday evening, Talitha ventured inside Professor Heisner's laboratory without the Professor actually being present and she virtually held her breath as she stepped inside the huge space that was littered with various pieces of scientific equipment. Just a few seconds later, Moses crossed the room and then opened up a wall like panel and he quickly urged Talitha to follow him as he prepared to step inside the secret hidden enclosure which she immediately did.

"Should I actually be inside here Moses?" Talitha asked as she stepped into the hidden enclosure. "Aren't you going home tonight?" She continued as she took the opportunity to bravely jump straight into another question that had occupied her thoughts for a while.

"I'm not like you Talitha." Moses replied. "I'm different."

"I didn't even know this room existed. What do you do in here?" Talitha asked as she began to inspect some of the animal cages inside the room. "I guess that's what you do in here, you test the animals here right?"

Moses nodded.

"What do you mean you're different Moses?" Talitha asked. "Why are we here?"

"There's something I want to show you Talitha." Moses replied as he touched his head and then started to peel off the layer of skin as he exposed a grey, shiny, metallic form just underneath it.

Every inch of Talitha's body immediately froze in shock and she almost winced in surprise as she watched Moses quietly as he peeled of the layer of skin right in front of her face. Total and utter shock seemed to paralyze Talitha for a few minutes as she simply stared at Moses's head, Moses wasn't even a nerd, in fact, he wasn't even human, he was a robot. A multitude of thoughts seemed to rapidly swirl around inside Talitha's mind which suddenly started to vibrate with confusion, she'd always thought Moses was quite strange but now it actually transpired, he was stranger than strange, he was actually a robot. Suddenly, everything about Moses made perfect sense, his lack of social interaction, his indifference to certain things and the lack of human emotions that he expressed which was purely due to the fact that he was not actually human at all.

"Moses, you're not human." Talitha observed in almost a whisper, she felt completely stunned by his sudden revelation.

"I know." Moses replied. "Professor Latimer built me with Professor Heisner. I'm a robotic being."

"No wonder you're so weird." Talitha teased as she began to nudge him playfully. "I thought you were just a nerd but I guess you really have got more personal issues than that. Dam you got even more personal issues than Saskia and I thought she had problems."

"No one else around here knows." Moses explained. "Only the Professor and now you."

"No wonder you haven't got a car, you probably don't even go home at night." Talitha concluded as she accepted the reality of who Moses really was. "Do you ever sneak out on the weekends and at night when everyone's gone home."

"Yes." Moses replied. "I've done that many times, I even built something special on the trash site."

"Built what?" Talitha asked.

"Something over the hill." Moses answered. "It's my secret. I'll take you there if you like."

"Have you ever thought about letting all of these animals go?" Talitha asked curiously as she walked towards a cage and then poked her finger through the wire front. "I mean would you dare?" She asked as she began to stroke the soft hair of a rabbit inside the cage.

Moses shook his head. "What would Professor

Heisner do if I let them all go?" He asked.

"He'd probably just buy more animals." Talitha replied as she grinned.

"Maybe he'd just do tests on the robotic frames instead." Moses said as he held onto Talitha's arm and then guided her towards the long grey cabinet on the other side of the room. He rolled back the sliding door and exposed the robotic frames inside it. "Professor Heisner uses these a lot too."

"What are these all for?" Talitha asked.

"The robotic frames Professor Heisner uses for tests and experiments, just like the animals but they can be attached to his own neural senses and can transmit the sensations that the various Downloads create." Moses explained.

"So fascinating but so very weird." Talitha replied. She began to stroll along the exterior of the cabinet as she touched some of the five robotic frames. "Are they your relatives?"

Nothing moved inside the cabinet as Talitha began to inspect each frame slightly more closely, some seemed to have human like skin and full body shapes whilst others didn't and she was absolutely intrigued and totally fascinated by it all. At one end of the cabinet there were some body cases that seemed to fit onto a physical human frame and Talitha glanced at them as she continued to inspect the interior of the built-in cupboard.

"I don't have any relatives Talitha." Moses replied solemnly. "I'm not like you."

"Well Moses, this is all very high tech and wonderfully scientific but I think since Professor Heisner is not here and we are, we should release all the animals today." Talitha suggested. "Do you look after them?"

"I do. I feed them every day and clean out their cages." Moses explained.

"Okay, so they're well fed and kept clean." Talitha replied. "But I still think we should release them."

"They're very well looked after Talitha. No one actually hurts them or anything." Moses insisted.

"What if we actually let all the animals go today?" Talitha asked mischievously. "Would Professor Heisner really miss them? He doesn't really need them, he has all those." She mentioned as she pointed towards the robotic frames and body cases inside the cabinet. "I need your help Moses." Talitha urged as she glanced at the cages and then drew closer to him. "I need you to help me set them free. Will you help me Moses?"

Moses nodded.

"First we have to make a plan, so that it looks like they escaped or something." Talitha explained. "I don't want you to get in any trouble."

"For robots like me there's no such thing as trouble Talitha. I don't fear humans." Moses replied. "The only thing a human being can do to me is reprogram me, if they feel I have malfunctioned."

"If we do this, Professor Heisner will probably reprogram you." Talitha insisted.

"That's fine." Moses quickly reassured her. "I'll simply be reconfigured and perhaps have a few programs deleted and I might even get some upgrades."

"Wouldn't you be worried about dying?" Talitha enquired softly. "I mean wouldn't that be a kind of robotic death?"

"I don't live and die Talitha." Moses explained. "I'm either operational and functioning, or I'm not. I don't miss living and existing. If I'm reprogrammed, I'm simply switched off until the upgrades and new programs that I need are installed."

"Okay, we'll still think of a plan though." Talitha insisted. "I'd rather you weren't reprogrammed."

"I could set of all the alarms throughout the building which will trigger all the doors to open and then it will look like the animals just escaped through the fire exit when I was cleaning out their cages." Moses suggested.

"Okay that's not a perfect plan but it could work." Talitha agreed. "You could also send me a backup file, just in case Professor Heisner decides to wipe your memory and reprogram you and then I could restore your rebellious side, so that you'd still be a robot with an attitude."

"Yes I'll do that and I have a cart Talitha, so we can put all of the cages inside that and use it to transport them, it'll be much quicker." Moses explained as he nodded. "We'll have to be really quick though, so no one sees us."

"What about the Night Watchman?" Talitha asked.

"I'll do something to the system, so that he can't see anything on the surveillance cameras." Moses quickly clarified.

"Okay, let's do this Moses." Talitha urged. "I really have to go home soon though as I have a dinner date with my fiancée tonight."

"There's an emergency exit inside Professor Heisner's laboratory, we could sneak them out of the building that way." Moses suggested.

"Sure Moses, if that'll be quicker." Talitha agreed.

Moses nodded. "I'll put some cages inside the cart and then there's a trolley, you can put some on the trolley." He explained. "We should be able to get them all out of here in about two or three trips."

The rather laborious task of emptying the hidden enclosure rapidly began as Moses brought his large cart and the trolley into the secret area and then the two quickly began to load up their means of transportation. Each cage was piled up inside the cart and on top of the trolley until about forty five cages were securely in position and then Moses set of the alarm just before the two rushed towards the fire exit. Quite strangely, the cart that Moses pushed actually looked as if it had been formed from bits of junk and it seemed as if Moses had made it himself from bits and pieces collected from the junk site and Talitha quietly began to inspect it as they exited the building and rushed towards the nearby hill.

Approximately fifteen minutes later, the two began their final trip to the other side of the hill as the alarms continued to sound out all around them inside the Restructure building. The animals inside the cages clambered around restlessly as they sensed a change in their environment and began to smell the fresh foliage around them and Talitha began to wonder for a moment if the tiny creatures would actually be okay. Differences in each creature's life span, care or treatment in comparison to other animals of their kind probably didn't actually mean that much to them as out in the wild, they might actually perish even sooner. Perhaps in the wild, Talitha began to speculate, they would be quickly torn apart by predators that would rip their flesh to pieces just to supplement their dietary needs and perhaps, just perhaps, they would suffer even more hardship.

Inside the walls of Restructure each animal was fed, watered and kept safe from harm each day and perhaps, Restructure and captivity wasn't really a worse fate than any other fate they could suffer naturally in the wild at the hands of nature itself. Yes, the animals were utilized to provide a deeper level of human comfort to mankind and to assist with scientific development but that wasn't really the worst life that an animal could live and Talitha couldn't actually deny that actual reality as she'd seen the dead animal remains in the ditch herself.

Once the animals had been freed, the two smiled at each other as Talitha absorbed the benevolence of their actions and tried to ignore the ditch of animal remains as in her heart of hearts, she definitely felt that they'd done the right thing that day, regardless of any potential predators. At least, they had tried and perhaps now, the animals would enjoy some part of their lives in the wild without any weird scientific experiments being performed upon their bodies, purely for the development and advancement of humanity.

"We should go back now Moses." Talitha suggested. "I mean we're done here right? It's starting to get late now and I really do have to go home."

"First Talitha, I'd like to you show you something. Do you mind?" Moses asked. "It will just take a few minutes."

"Sure Moses. Are you going to switch of the alarms now? The Night Watchman will probably be freaking out by now and searching the whole building for a fire that doesn't exist." Talitha joked.

"It's not a fire alarm Talitha." Moses explained. "I set off the poisonous substance leak alarm."

"Okay, whatever difference that makes, he's probably still searching the whole building." Talitha teased. "Since you did do me a huge favor today Moses, I'll give you a few more minutes."

"You can leave the trolley here Talitha." Moses insisted as he gently held onto her arm. "I'll sort that out later."

Some large piles of junk lay directly in front of the two and Moses quickly began to lead Talitha around one of them as he walked towards a much larger, huge pile of junk in the very center of the trash site. At one side of the junk pile that was almost as large as a small hill, there appeared to be a tunnel and Moses quickly led Talitha towards it as he urged her to follow him inside. Just a few meters away from the entrance of the tunnel, the tunnel suddenly disappeared and opened out into a huge space with a dome shaped ceiling and Talitha gasped in delight as she quietly observed that the interior had been molded from various types of glass and metal. Inside the huge circular space there appeared to be all kinds of metal and glass structures that adorned its interior and Talitha glanced at Moses's face as she silently marveled at her surroundings which were amazingly creative, extremely unique and very beautiful.

Suddenly Moses accessed the blue screen which lit up just in front of his face and some lights rapidly appeared and then began to bounce off each object inside the dome like space almost like fireworks. Curiosity and wonder rapidly began to fill every part of Talitha's being as she sauntered around the huge space and touched some of the carefully crafted objects inside of it.

"Who did all this Moses?" Talitha asked. "It's absolutely stunning."

"I did." Moses replied. "This is my home."

"Your home is very beautiful Moses." Talitha encouraged as she admired her surroundings.

A smile crossed Talitha's face as she glanced at Moses and accepted what lay all around her, this was indeed Moses's home, he'd built it, he'd made it and he lived in it and Moses wasn't just a robot, Moses was more human than Talitha could have possibly imagined.

"You have to go now Talitha." Moses suddenly reminded her. "You have a dinner date."

"Yes I do. I did send a text to say I'd be late but I really do have to go now. Thank you for inviting me to your home Moses." Talitha said as she smiled.

"Please don't tell anyone Talitha, no one knows about this place." Moses quickly clarified. "Not even Professor Heisner."

"I wouldn't dare tell a soul Moses." Talitha promised as she smiled. "This is something that you do outside of work, this is your private life and so, no one else at work needs to know about it."

"Thank you." Moses replied as he began to walk back towards the entrance to the tunnel. "We better go now."

"Thank you for helping me release the animals Moses." Talitha said as she began to follow Moses back towards the tunnel entrance.

"Yes, I don't fully understand your emotional attachment to small furry creatures Talitha but I was glad that I could help." Moses replied.

"Don't worry Moses, it's a girl thing. We like softy cuddly looking things although most of those animals would probably bite and scratch us, if we stuck our hands inside their cages." Talitha joked.

Approximately five minutes later, once the two reached the front of the Restructure building, they quickly parted as Talitha left Moses with the alarm, the trolley, the cart, the trash site and the Restructure building and made her way into the parking lot as she approached her car. Almost everything that happened around Talitha that day had been a total surprise, Saskia had been in quite a pleasant mood, Moses was a robot and they'd set free all the animals and the day hadn't even actually ended yet.

Life was definitely strange and Professor

Heisner was a very dark horse, Talitha quietly concluded as she entered inside her vehicle. Every strange thing about Moses now made perfect sense but he had seemed so geekily weird to Talitha in a very human way. In the very same building that Talitha spent every working day, it now transpired that Professor Heisner kept not only animals but also robots and Talitha hadn't even known and one robot, she even spoke to and interacted with on a regular basis. The work colleague that Talitha had interacted with many times and that she'd even considered extremely messy and in need of a beauty treatment, wasn't even human and she hadn't even known.

Restructure and Professor Heisner's work definitely involved some deep, very complex scientific elements that Talitha wasn't really supposed to know about and that had become more apparent as Moses had revealed some of Restructure's secrets to her in Professor Heisner's absence. Science really wasn't straight forward, Talitha decided as she began to drive out of the parking lot and she'd begun to realize and accept there really was a lot more to Restructure, the Professor and Moses than met the eye. One thing about Talitha's day however had absolutely delighted her and that was the fact that Moses had now become more than just an odd character that she had to speak to if she had technical problems and Moses had now actually become Talitha's friend.

Perhaps the lack of emotional connection to the world around Moses would be difficult to understand at times but where there was friendship, there could be understanding and Talitha could now extend the warm hands of friendship towards him. A mischievous smile suddenly crossed Talitha's face as she quietly considered for a moment that she had actually taught Moses that day to be a rebellious robot and that Professor Heisner would have her guts for garters, if he ever actually found out. Professor Heisner hadn't actually mentioned anything to Talitha about the animals which meant officially, she knew absolutely nothing about them and that of course would be her official position, if anyone asked her which she doubted very much they actually would.

Once Talitha arrived at home, she headed straight for the bathroom as she prepared to have a long soak in the bath and get ready for what she hoped would be a glorious romantic evening ahead spent at the side of the man she so deeply loved. In some people's sight, perhaps the stable, calm, loving relationship that Talitha had with Bryson would be considered boring but for Talitha, it really was the best relationship she'd ever had and it was boring in the best possible way. Tonight was about

Talitha and Bryson, not about Restructure, the animals it had contained, or even Professor Heisner himself as now, it was officially the weekend which was their time and right now, Bryson required all of Talitha's attention, devotion and dedication as he definitely deserved it.

A long soak in a creamy, frothy, foamy bubble bath rapidly began as Talitha started to pamper her skin and prepare for her delicious evening ahead with Bryson. Some curious speculations and excited questions began to flood through Talitha's mind as she quietly considered what Bryson might actually want to say to her later that evening as the reservations had been at a very lavish restaurant in the heart of the city, so it had to be something really quite important. On date nights and evenings out with Bryson, Talitha had several very special beauty routines that usually took at least an hour to perform but because she really wanted to look her best for Bryson that night, she was prepared to take the time that required to make that actually happen.

Meanwhile back outside Restructure the working day for Professor Heisner had not yet ended and his duties were far from over as he returned to parking lot, parked his vehicle and then began to make his way towards the entrance of the building. Quite shockingly as Professor Heisner made his way towards the main exterior doors, he found that they were actually open and that the alarm had been triggered in his absence. The Night Watchman, Giles was inside the reception area and Professor Heisner immediately rushed towards him in order to establish exactly what was going on.

"I tried to call you Professor Heisner." Giles quickly clarified. "But I couldn't reach you."

"Yes, I was driving Giles. My phone was in my briefcase and it was on silent as I've just come out of a meeting." Professor Heisner explained. "I forgot to switch the volume back on. What on earth happened?"

"I'm not sure Professor Heisner." Giles replied. "An alarm suddenly went off and then all the doors opened. It's not the fire alarm but I did a sweep of the building just in case."

"I know it's not Giles, it's the poisonous substance leak alarm." Professor Heisner quickly clarified as he touched a security panel on the wall behind the reception desk and the alarm immediately stopped. He grunted as he shook his head. "Where's Moses?"

"Inside your laboratory I think. I haven't actually seen him since the alarm went off." Giles quickly clarified.

"Right, I better go and speak to him." Professor Heisner replied as he began to walk briskly towards the corridor that led directly towards his laboratory. "He'll probably know what's going on."

Giles nodded.

When Professor Heisner entered into his laboratory, just a few minutes later, he found Moses right next to the door and he immediately began to question him as to what had triggered the alarm and as to what had caused the actual disturbance. The open security panel at the bottom of the laboratory suddenly caught his attention as the hidden enclosure was exposed and Professor Heisner quickly strode across the room towards it.

"What happened here Moses?" Professor Heisner demanded.

"Professor Heisner a rabbit escaped and when I started to chase it, I accidentally knocked over a bottle that contained Cyanide solution which smashed onto the floor and that immediately set of the alarm." Moses started to explain. "All the doors suddenly opened and then I bumped into some of the animal cages and the cages started to fall down and the cage doors opened up. All the animals escaped through the fire exit." He continued. "It all happened so fast, there was nothing I could do to stop them."

Inside the hidden enclosure, empty cages lay strewn and scattered across the floor but something about Moses's explanation still seemed slightly strange and a tad unbelievable as Professor Heisner began to quietly absorb his surroundings. The animals that usually occupied the cages had clearly departed and so Professor Heisner quickly sat down and then touched the screen on top of his workspace as although he had now deactivated the alarm, the doors of the building were still open and they needed to be closed through the electronic system. Just a few seconds later, all the doors in the building began to close as the security system immediately obeyed Professor Heisner's commands and the system was reset.

Strangely, there didn't appear to be any signs of the broken bottle upon the floor that Moses had referred to as Professor Heisner quickly scanned the ground with his eyes. The security system inside the building was designed to neutralize the air inside the hidden enclosure, if any poisonous gases or substances were accidentally released but there was no traces to suggest that any actually had been and that provoked his curious mind and generated a lot of unanswered questions. No actual shards of glass lay upon the floor and no animals seemed to have suffered from being exposed to the highly dangerous and extremely poisonous substance and so Professor Heisner was still slightly confused.

A silent realization suddenly began to creep through Professor Heisner's mind as he scrutinized the floor that surrounded him, there was no broken glass and no broken bottle and that meant, Moses had probably freed the animals himself in the

Professor's absence. Part of Professor Heisner suddenly began to feel quite annoyed about what Moses had actually done as it was an actual act of rebellion as Moses had done something that he did not have permission to do and that he'd not been instructed, or programmed to actually do. The animals had cost the Professor money and he'd lost a significant number that day which he usually required for his experiments and so it really was an inconvenience but the Professor began to internally deliberate further as he scrutinized Moses's face that perhaps it was one that could actually be forgiven as it was an intriguing inconvenience.

"Will you be buying more animals next week Professor Heisner?" Moses asked.

Professor Heisner considered the question thoughtfully and then shook his head. "No Moses, I won't be buying any more animals." He replied as he silently accepted that Moses had acted independently and made a moral judgment of his own. "The experiments that I had to perform are finished now as Restructure is up and running and well, animals aren't really the best method of testing anyway. Despite the many experiments that I've performed upon them, the side effects I later discovered hadn't even been noticeable or picked up, so there's really no need now."

Moses smiled.

For a few minutes, there was nothing but

silence between the two as Professor Heisner began to accept the strange events of the afternoon that had occurred in his absence. In some ways, he almost felt as if he'd slightly underestimated Moses as he'd simply viewed Moses as a mechanical, programmable assistant that just existed to follow his instructions. Through his very first act of rebellion however, Moses had very clearly clarified and confirmed to Professor Heisner that he was definitely something more than just an object that helped the Professor to achieve his scientific objectives and goals.

Today, Moses had proved that he was more than just a set of instructions and programs that Professor Heisner and his associate Latimer had created and given a physical form to and today, Moses had proven that he had the capacity to self determine his own future and ultimately that he possessed the intellect to make his own decisions. Everything about those realizations filled Professor Heisner with excitement as he silently began to consider the benefits that Moses could bring to his work, the possibilities of the future with regards to Restructure and even the advantages to Moses himself. Moses wasn't simply a predictable, mechanical being that obediently followed the rules that had been provided to him, Moses had evolved and that prospect held huge possibilities for not only Restructure and Professor Heisner but also for humanity itself.

Later that evening, once Talitha and Bryson had been seated inside the restaurant, ordered their starters, main courses and some drinks, Talitha quietly admired her very elegant, lavish surroundings with absolute delight as she rejoiced in her evening. The restaurant was extremely luxurious and as usual Bryson had impeccable taste as the food they served was truly scrumptious. A conversation began about Talitha's working week which had been slightly hectic and as she started to discuss it with Bryson, curiosity suddenly began to prick Talitha's mind as she steered the conversation into the topic of their own bodies. For Talitha, in some ways there was now an obvious temptation present every working day to actually enhance her own body and Talitha began to playfully seek out Bryson's views on the matter and whether he'd ever felt tempted to do so as their starters arrived and they began to eat.

"Do you think I need any upgrades to my body Bryson?" Talitha teased playfully.

Bryson glanced at Talitha thoughtfully and smiled. "Is this a trick question?" He asked. "If I say yes, will you be upset and refuse to make love to me later tonight and if I say no, will you really believe me? This is a tricky one."

Talitha laughed.

"Perhaps a tighter butt and bigger hips could

work. Huge hips like balloons are good for pushing babies out." Bryson teased. "Then we can have ten babies and I can grab your buttocks even harder when we make love. A tighter, harder butt is a tougher butt."

"Seriously Bryson. I'm being serious" Talitha replied as she giggled. She plucked a spicy grilled prawn from a plate on the table in front of her and then began to eat it. "What do you really think?" Talitha asked.

Several candles sat elegantly scattered across the table which flickered as Talitha glanced at Bryson's face as she began to inspect it slightly more closely, just to see if he was actually being serious as a waiter returned to deliver their main courses. Food and bowls were laid out across the table in abundance and Talitha's mouth rapidly began to water as the aroma from the dishes on offer wafted gently into her nostrils. A small pout began to cross Talitha's face as she waited for Bryson to respond, semi hurt by his response that had ever so gently scratched her feelings.

"Look Talitha, I love you and you are totally perfect for me, so don't you dare change a thing." Bryson suddenly replied as he broke the awkward silence that had somehow gathered between them. "I adore you, I love YOU and YOU represents you as you are: Yummy, Outstanding and Unbelievably gorgeous."

"Is my butt really flabby?" Talitha asked. "I could always go to the gym and you could come along too Bryson." She quickly suggested.

Bryson laughed. "Look Talitha, I'm far from perfect and I know it but together with all our imperfections, we've found something that is so totally perfect and that's us." He replied. "So let's not rush to change that because I believe in us, I'm happy with us and I love US."

Talitha giggled.

"There was actually a reason I brought you here tonight Talitha." Bryson began to explain as he slipped a hand inside one of his trouser pockets and then plucked out an envelope. "I would like us to make a date for our wedding, I've found the perfect location and I've saved up enough money now to invite all the people that we care about."

"Really?" Talitha asked.

Bryson nodded as he opened up the envelope and began to take out some photos. "I know you wanted to wait Talitha, until you'd found a new job but I really think we can afford to do it now." He insisted as he placed the photos down on top of the table. "And technically, you have got a new job now."

"This venue looks amazing Bryson. You really did your research, I'm impressed." Talitha replied as she gently touched the photos on top of the table and began to inspect each one.

"So is that a yes?" Bryson urged. "Or do I have to get down on my knees again, right here, right now?"

"You already did that bit Bryson when you gave me an engagement ring and asked me to marry you." Talitha teased.

"I can do it again." Bryson insisted. "I mean, if that turns you on and then I'll get lots of passionate pleasure later tonight."

Talitha giggled. "That's a definite yes." She replied.

Droplets of joy seemed to sprinkle themselves all over Talitha's body as her skin suddenly began to tingle with delight as she silently absorbed every word that Bryson had said. Inside Talitha, it was almost as if a fire of love and passion had been ignited as a warmth quickly surged through every inch of her body and her cheeks began to glow. Other people's opinions of them both as a couple, really didn't matter and Bryson was indeed absolutely correct as although they were both far from perfect in the physical sense, they loved, adored, enjoyed and appreciated every single inch of each other, even their imperfections.

Between the couple, they'd managed to find an impeccable kind of love that was truly irreplaceable and their enjoyment of that love was a dish that was delicious enough for them both to consume every single day and Talitha savored every single mouthful. To trade that beautiful enjoyment in just for a bouncier pair of breasts, or a more refined nose really wasn't worth it, or worth the love that they both shared. Everything that they currently were as a couple and as individuals was ultimately what made their union absolutely perfect and to change that would change the dynamics of their relationship and change their attraction to each other. The very natural purity of their love and relationship would ultimately then be destroyed and undermined by superficial irrelevancies that actually didn't matter and Talitha now fully began to understand and appreciate that beautiful fact as she glanced at Bryson's face adoringly.

Some women would perhaps consider Bryson's very large nose to be physically unappealing but to Talitha, it was absolutely adorable as when Bryson kissed her and it rubbed against her cheek, her whole body would tingle all over with excitement. A 'cosmetically perfect' nose just wouldn't have the same effect, or provide Talitha with the same kind of joy, comfort and pleasure that Bryson's natural nose gave her every single time he kissed her cheek. To add to Bryson's face what one might consider to be a perfect nose would ultimately in the end, take away from the enjoyment that his natural nose brought Talitha every single day.

The unnecessary pursuit of individual physical perfection would ultimately cost them both the imperfections that made their relationship the beautiful perfection that it currently was and by trying to add something else, they would only end up subtracting from their coupling and lose the most essential elements of the enjoyment that they shared. Each delicate imperfect piece fitted together immaculately inside the jigsaw puzzle of the life that the couple shared and the enjoyment derived from those imperfect pieces was a direct product of their love for each other and to change anything about that would destroy the perfectly completed jigsaw that had been pieced together with love every day for the past five years.

"You know Bryson, I never knew you were such a deep thinker." Talitha teased playfully as the couple finished their meal. "I'm starting to see all these hidden depths and layers to the wisdom inside of you and I think I like it."

"Does that mean we can have a marathon session tonight?" Bryson asked as he beckoned to the waiter to bring the bill. "Are you really turned on Talitha?" He whispered.

Talitha giggled.

Joy seemed to dance through every particle of air around the couple as Talitha's heart leapt with happiness and her mind enthusiastically embraced Bryson's words and his expression of love as he quickly paid the bill and the couple left the restaurant. Every part of Talitha knew that Bryson was irrevocably and wholeheartedly right and that the perfect love which existed between them both as a couple was something that millions of people all across the world would probably never have, or ever experience and they had both been truly fortunate to find each other when they did.

Each working day, since Talitha had joined Restructure, she'd observed the struggles of some of her single clients in their search to either find love, or to try and keep it once they'd felt they'd found it and she'd seen how painful that could be but Talitha had been lucky in love and Bryson was the physical manifestation of her luck. Somehow, luck had crossed Talitha's path and had brought the two together five years ago and since then Talitha had never looked back, not even for a second.

Several other potential suitors had attempted to court Talitha around that time but Bryson had always been her first choice and he'd been a choice that she definitely did not regret making. Over those five years life had thrown many things at them as a couple and as individuals that they'd often been uncertain about but the one thing they had both always been very sure about was each other. Their commitment to each other and their love had managed somehow to stand the test of time and there was absolutely nothing pretentious about their relationship which had provided Talitha with a blanket of comfort and a daily portion of reality as at work, she was usually completely surrounded by superficiality.

Two warm loving arms would be wrapped around Talitha's body every night as she snuggled up to Bryson that were appreciated immensely and Bryson had dedicated himself to Talitha in a way that no other man ever actually had. Every weekend the couple spent together and Bryson would ensure that they did something special and memorable and Talitha could always be certain that when she returned from work each day, weary and tired, Bryson's kisses would be waiting to re-energize her and to brighten up her day.

Only one thing had kept Talitha from walking down the aisle with Bryson and that had been financial worries but now, Talitha hoped that their finances would be slightly more stable and consistent. Although Bryson worked as a professional business architect for a partnership which had several other partners, a business that he'd started himself with some acquaintances in his late twenties and he created business models for clients that would invest large sums of capital, the couple were not actually rich themselves.

At times, Bryson's business dealings had been quite lucrative and so they had managed to purchase a home and take their first step out onto the property ladder but sometimes, Bryson's firm also suffered losses. During those more difficult times Talitha knew, Bryson would worry about their liquidity but she'd always tried her best to contribute to their position financially, if she could and now that Talitha had secure employment, she felt more than happy to make the lifelong commitment to Bryson that he truly deserved and in her mind had definitely more than earnt.

For Dean, his Friday evening held romantic possibilities firmly by the hand as he entered into the restaurant that he'd agreed to meet Janice inside and then began to scour the sea of stranger's faces for her pretty face. Quite intentionally, Dean had avoided making an arrangement to meet inside clubs, bars and alcohol laden environments that might encourage sexual liaisons and close physical proximity as he'd accepted Talitha's advice and attempted to apply it to his love life. Casual sex could happen very easily depending on whether or not the woman that Dean was meeting was up for it but he wanted to avoid that temptation for a while and get to know Janice slightly better first.

In terms of Dean's current position, he knew that his flesh was definitely weak and that if the opportunity presented itself to him, he might actually try to take it and right now that really wasn't in his best long term interests and so a fine dining experience had been very carefully selected. The relationship with Chantelle had now been completely abandoned as Dean had simply allowed it to peacefully lie inside the grave of rejection that she'd buried it in, never to be resuscitated, or revived ever again.   Inside that grave that deceased romance would remain lifeless and redundant, due to the hopeless and cruel realities which had so heartlessly sabotaged every inch of it.

Warm hands and a pleasant smile suddenly greeted Dean as he was approached by Janice and as she kissed his cheek, a waiter appeared and offered to show them both to the table that Dean had reserved. Fortunately for Dean, he'd somehow managed to find another attractive female that had a mutual interest in him and although Janice was not totally alone, in the sense that she had a daughter from a previous marriage, Dean had not been bothered by that potential responsibility. The two had agreed to meet at nine thirty that evening as Janice had arranged a babysitter that had only been available at nine and so Dean had made the most of his evening as he'd gone for a haircut just before their date had been due to begin.

Food and a bottle of wine were quickly ordered and the conversation between the two began to flow as they discussed their lives, interests and singleness and as Dean discovered more about Janice, he began to relax in her company. Every minute that Dean spent with Janice seemed almost magical as she brightened up the walls of his Friday evening with her lively conversation and decorated the start of his weekend with her gorgeous smile and colorful personality and Dean smiled as he silently accepted that when it came to dating women, Talitha was definitely right, it really was better to take your time. Inevitably, the conversation finally turned towards Dean's own love life and the lack of a marriage or children present within it and he swallowed slightly nervously as he prepared to discuss the accident that had rocked his world and thrown his life into complete turmoil.

"Why are you single Dean?" Janice asked. "You seem like a great guy and you've never been married before, or had any kids how come?"

"Well, first I had an accident, so that put my love life on hold for a while and then I suffered a couple of other setbacks." Dean explained as he glanced nervously around the interior of the restaurant as he wanted to ensure that no one else was in close enough proximity to their table to overhear their conversation. "I was in a very unique situation."

Quite frankly, Dean had absolutely no desire whatsoever to share any information with anyone about his recent troubles and he certainly didn't want to share that information with a room full of strangers but he searched deep within himself to find a way to communicate his problems to Janice. Such sensitive issues were hardly a suitable topic to digest along with a late evening meal but Dean attempted to address the issue somehow as he leant towards Janice and prepared to tiptoe across the rocky ravine of possible rejection and ridicule.

"There are a few issues at the moment really Janice. I have quite a large penis and some women don't enjoy that as it is quite large. I had a procedure last week to reduce it slightly." Dean explained in a whisper.

"Really?" Janice whispered playfully in response as she smiled. "Sounds interesting that could be rather fun. Perhaps they just don't know how to make good use of it."

Dean smiled. "Perhaps they don't." He agreed.

The couple's evening continued to saunter gently along the riverbed of companionship as the waters of flirtatious entanglements were more fully explored, eagerly engaged, bravely dived into and thoroughly enjoyed. Wine, good food and jokes were shared in abundance as the evening gurgled delicately along the river of romantic possibilities and the couple flirted with the notion of a passionate meeting inside the sea of romance. A sense of kindness and understanding had been shown to Dean that he wanted to nurture and explore and Janice seemed like a truly special kind of woman that might actually help Dean to overcome the obstacles that had recently caused him so much pain. What had been viewed as offensive to another woman would perhaps not be seen as so offensive in Janice's sight and that relieved Dean immensely.

When the two left the restaurant, Dean walked Janice to her car as he silently appreciated that since his recent mishap, this was the first time that he'd really spent a decent amount of time with a woman alone outside of work, except Talitha who didn't really count due to the professional nature of their relationship.

"Can I see you again Janice?" Dean asked as he paused beside Janice's car and then turned to face her. "I'd really like to."

"Definitely." Janice replied. "I'll be free next Saturday Dean. Maybe we could go and watch a movie or something." She suggested.

Dean his head nodded enthusiastically. "Yes that would be great." He agreed.

Inside Dean's heart, a spark of romance had definitely been ignited once more which was well on its way to becoming a soaring flame of passion, fuelled by Janice's mutual reciprocation and romantic interest in him. Quite fortunately for Dean, romance was definitely not dead but technically, the two hadn't yet faced the very thorny issue that had left a stain upon his last attempt at finding love and absolutely crucified the sapling of desire upon a cross of heartbreak and that worried him slightly. A gift of romantic hope however had now been provided by Janice and that was immediately tucked away inside Dean's heart as he began to cherish it and as the two parted, Dean appreciated the simple, enjoyable fact that he would now have the chance to love again.

Once again, Dean had been given the opportunity to indulge in the intricate complexities and enjoyment that romantic pleasures brought to a man's life and he'd been presented with another romantic chance. This time would be different, Dean silently vowed as he entered inside his car, he would take his time as Talitha suggested and hopefully this time, their romance would be able to weather any rough storms. Although that Friday night, Dean hadn't been swept along into the darkness on currents of heated passion, nor had he ridden upon any thrilling waves of sexual pleasure, he had managed to open up to Janice about the thorny issue that had torn his last attempt at romance to shreds and she hadn't actually run away.

Every fear that lay deep inside Dean's heart that evening had been quickly swept under the table that the two had been seated at, almost as if they were insignificant crumbs from a cake that had just been devoured. Inside Dean's heart the flames of hope had now begun to dance again as Janice had encouraged him that one day, someone would perhaps accept Dean in totality and that one day perhaps, Dean would be welcomed, accommodated and possibly even, actually appreciated.

On the Saturday evening, Renee's weekend took a rather splendid turn as she went out on another date with her slightly more mature lover as she avoided the arms of the much younger, sexually excitable males that had actively pursued her and that she'd recently engaged in some romantic fumbling with. In their attempts to satisfy their sexual hunger and Renee's, the younger men had made love to her vigorously, passionately and energetically but Renee had finally decided to attempt to find something slightly more serious and a more suitable partner, a bit closer to her own age group. Although Renee had enjoyed the eager, frantic fumbling of the younger men that she'd recently jumped into bed with and sought physical satisfaction from, in the longer term she knew that she would definitely appreciate this gentle meandering courtship, slightly more.

An evening of romantic refinement had been enjoyed by the two as they had flirted enthusiastically over dinner and satisfied themselves with verbal meanderings as visions of sexual gratification had danced through their thoughts, accentuated by gentle touches, seductive smiles and unspoken words that floated around just behind their lips. Subtle, tender, mature interactions had flowed in abundance throughout the entire evening and contact had been far less physical and a lot more focused upon romance and companionship.

Comfort had filled Renee's mind throughout the evening almost like a very close, warm friend as she'd appreciated the simplicity of her Saturday night and the lack of frantic sexual chaos and hectic sexual passions. Although those hectic nights of passion and desire had been exciting for a while, this Saturday night definitely felt a lot more natural as it was far less impulsive and a lot less animalistic. Deep down inside, Renee definitely felt as if she had a lot more control over the situation now which differed vastly from most of her recent romantic encounters which had been with red hot, sexually hungry, much younger males. This connection seemed much deeper in an emotional sense and that depth really suited her heart as she'd begun to yearn for something slightly more meaningful.

Due to the fact that it was a much more mature, well coordinated romantic evening the date had required an additional investment of effort on Renee's part in terms of the care, attention, time taken and preparation made but it had definitely been worth it, in Renee's sight. Once a splendid feast had been consumed at the very expensive restaurant that Aaron had taken Renee to, the couple had then begun to walk along the bank of a nearby river. All the one night stands that Renee had recently engaged in suddenly seemed to slip towards the back of her mind as each memory was gently placed upon the 'never to be repeated' shelf as Renee silently accepted that this date was definitely more up her romantic street.

Interestingly for Renee, although the casual one night stands had empowered her in the short term as she'd celebrated her sexual liberation and victory, they'd definitely lacked the emotional depth that she needed in the longer term. Another romantic, deeper connection had now arrived however and right on time as she'd really needed that change as she'd begun to feel quite emotionally empty and even slightly used.

Several small blue lights delicately hung down from some of the tree branches that lined the river bank and Renee smiled as Aaron slipped his hand into her hand as they walked. Somehow, the whole evening just felt extremely natural and for the very first time, since Renee had attended the Restructure clinic, she felt romantically at peace and as if her heart had found a desirable romantic equilibrium. Just on the romantic horizon of love, there was now it seemed, a possibility that Aaron and their dates would give rise to a deeper, much more meaningful, long term relationship and that pleased Renee immensely.

The thought of engaging in a more committed, loving, long distance test of endurance really appealed to Renee as opposed to simply participating in several very short one hundred meter sprints which usually left one out of breath and that were over in the blink of an eye. Short sprints definitely fell extremely short in terms of the longevity of one's life span which really demanded something more substantial and longer lasting and the marathon was in the longer term, the optimal outcome that Renee now wished to run alongside Aaron. A bottle of romance would now be collected at the starting line and Renee would put on her shoes of commitment, since the training session and initial dates had already actually taken place as she prepared to endure a marathon of love which would be as long in distance as both she and Aaron wanted it to be.

Internally, Renee's heart now felt quite hopeful and extremely enthusiastic as she prepared to embark upon the first real long term romance of her actual life. A ripe cherry of love now dangled down right in front of Renee's eyes and she quickly realized, now was her chance to pluck the fruit of love, cherish it and then gently consume it as although life hadn't provided Renee with many romantic opportunities finally, life had given Renee a real, long term romantic hope.

When the Sunday evening arrived, it was extremely pleasant for Charmaine as the couple relaxed at home and Lachlan lavished his attention upon her. The evening meal that they'd consumed that day, for a huge change had actually been cooked by Lachlan himself and that almost felt like a record breaking event as Lachlan absolutely never ever cooked. A bottle of chilled wine had been consumed alongside the food which apparently Lachlan had spent all week practicing to prepare during his lunch break inside the canteen in his father's offices and it was almost as if Lachlan had turned over a new leaf as Charmaine welcomed the positive change with very open arms.

Once dinner had been gloriously consumed, Lachlan eagerly pulled Charmaine towards him and then kissed her tenderly just before the couple left the kitchen with another bottle of wine and two glasses as they headed enthusiastically towards the bedroom. A flurry of passionate kisses were rapidly planted upon Charmaine's lips, neck and chest as Lachlan began to remove her clothes as he gently guided her towards the bed that the couple shared each night. Soft gasps of delight escaped from Charmaine's lips as she immediately embraced Lachlan's enthusiasm and his outburst of passion as his frantic hands began to explore every part of her body and she accepted his vigorous fondling and began to reciprocate his very passionate gestures.

Overall, Lachlan definitely seemed to be more physically attracted to Charmaine and she delighted in his appreciation as he appeared to be much happier and more satisfied in a sexual manner than he'd been for a very long time. Everything about Lachlan's satisfied state pleased Charmaine as she began to relax in the comforting thought that a satisfied Lachlan would be a more faithful Lachlan as he was far less like to stray, if he was happier at home and happier inside their bedroom. Just how long that satisfaction would last however, Charmaine didn't like to consider as she silently pushed any doubts to the back of her mind and enjoyed the moment for exactly what it was.

Before the couple could actually remove all their clothes, Lachlan thrust himself passionately inside Charmaine and she gasped in delight as she welcomed his hard, masculine hotness and her back began to arch with eagerness. Every thrust of desire made Charmaine moan with pleasure as she willingly accepted Lachlan's physical sexual adoration and every drop of sexual passion that he wanted to give. Electric currents of intense desire began to surge through Charmaine's body as she clung frantically onto Lachlan's naked sweaty flesh as he aroused and attempted to sexually satisfy her, until they both reached a climax.

Later that night as Charmaine lay inside Lachlan's arms as he slept, she began to think about how the couple had originally met and where they both were now as a couple. Despite Lachlan's flaws, their romance had begun and grown and now, they were almost inseparable and Charmaine didn't really want that to actually change. In terms of romance, Lachlan had been Charmaine's first love and also her first physical lover as she'd never even known another man sexually, or physically in that capacity.

The day Lachlan had initially stepped into Charmaine's love life, he'd swept her off her feet and eagerly reassured her that she had been totally perfect for him and ever since then they'd stayed together through thick and thin as they'd braved the world together, under Lachlan's lead. Despite Lachlan's flaws, the thought of actually facing the world alone without Lachlan and losing him really worried, scared and frightened Charmaine at times and she'd definitely made more compromises than Lachlan had during the course of their relationship. In Charmaine's attempts to secure and retain his romantic interest, commitment and devotion to her, she'd practically leant over backwards, sideways and even stood on her head but Charmaine felt that those compromises had in the end been totally worth it as Lachlan was still by her side.

A further reassurance to Charmaine had now

been provided by Lachlan's recent financial investment which he had made into Charmaine's body and that indirectly reassured Charmaine to some degree that perhaps one day, Lachlan would actually marry her and that was ultimately, what she really wanted to happen. Since the couple had been together for more than six years now, marriage was definitely a possibility but due to their age when they'd initially met, they'd both agreed to discuss marriage at a later point in time as Lachlan had said, they were both far too young to enter into such a huge romantic commitment. Well Lachlan had discussed it really, expressed his opinion and then Charmaine had accepted his position and the initial terms of their romantic relationship.

More than six years had gone by now, since the couple had first become a romantic item and Charmaine definitely felt that they were both much more mature, even though Lachlan didn't always seem to be but he'd definitely physically aged. Since Lachlan had completed college, he'd worked for his father within the family business and so money had never been a huge concern for either of them, or a problem as he'd climbed the corporate ladder extremely quickly. For Charmaine, the thought of starting all over again with someone else really didn't appeal to her very much as to invite another man into her heart, life and bedroom would in some way imply that she had built nothing meaningful with Lachlan and that somehow, she had perhaps romantically failed.

Several things were wrong with Charmaine's relationship with Lachlan and they predominantly revolved around his attitude towards her and although she yearned for Lachlan to change and for their relationship to improve, it had really been an uphill struggle. A more equal, committed romantic relationship was definitely desirable and one that was much more fulfilling to them both, not just to Lachlan as satisfaction from their romance leant very much in his favor.

Despite the fact that Charmaine hadn't totally wanted to make all of the physical changes that she had at Restructure to her body, her experiences there had been predominantly positive, she quietly concluded. The bodily enhancements that Charmaine had undergone at Restructure would now she hoped, either push Lachlan to make a lifelong commitment to her, or provide her with the strength and confidence she required to leave him forever and now at least, there was a finality in that reality that was very comforting.

Although Charmaine didn't really want to face the world alone, she decided as she closed her eyes and prepared to drift off to sleep, she could perhaps now win the overall war between them both that power, money and control had actually created. The access to masses of wealth that

Lachlan had and Charmaine's love for him had in the long term rendered her absolutely powerless but perhaps now that she had more choices and opportunities, she could be stronger. Perhaps now, Charmaine contemplated quietly as she began to drift off to sleep, she could stand up on her own two feet, stand up for herself and stand up to Lachlan and then she would no longer just be Lachlan's romantic doormat.

On the Monday morning, a pleasant surprise waited for Frank as he suddenly woke up and then made his way towards the kitchen as a familiar and much loved aroma wafted into his nostrils. The smell was strange in some ways as it was actually inside Frank's home and he could hardly believe that it was possible as his heart almost skipped a beat when he stepped inside the kitchen. Very interestingly, Frank rapidly discovered, the kitchen table had already been laid in preparation for breakfast which Maude was busy preparing but it was not the usual sawdust muesli and sour grapefruit offerings and a frying pan was actually being facilitated. A puzzled expression crossed Frank's face as he blinked, rubbed his eyes and then just stared at Maude in utter disbelief as he began to watch her.

"I made us breakfast Frank." Maude said as she began to place some fried food items onto two empty plates on the worktop right next to the cooker.

"You did Maude?" Frank asked. "But that's a fry up and you don't eat greasy, oily, fatty food."

"I've had a change of heart Frank." Maude replied. "I won't be running anymore races now and so I guess I just figured, what harm can a fry up do a few times a week?"

"Wow Maude. I'm absolutely astonished." Frank said as he scratched his head.

"Sit down and I'll bring you some breakfast. I've even bought some sauces there's ketchup, brown sauce and even some vinegar." Maude insisted as she picked up one of the now filled plates and began to walk towards the kitchen table.

"Thanks Sweetcheeks." Frank replied as he quickly sat down. "You don't need to ask me to eat a fry up more than once."

Maude laughed. "So now Frank, you don't need to sneak out to those greasy diners anymore because you can eat greasy, fatty, unhealthy food right here at home." She teased as she placed the plate of food gently down on the kitchen table in front of him.

"Now that is definitely something to celebrate." Frank said as he smiled and picked up a fork. "Will we still be doing the Mirror Test every morning?"

"Of course." Maude quickly confirmed. "I said I'd had a change of heart not a brain transplant."

Frank grinned. "Now that's the Maude I know

and love." He replied as he enthusiastically began to tuck in. "If I ever manage to save up enough money, I'll marry you one day Maude."

"Really Frank, you know I don't believe in marriage, it's just a piece of silly paper." Maude replied as she walked back towards the cooker, picked up her filled plate from the kitchen worktop and then carried it across the room towards the table.

"Maude, I really think we should get married." Frank insisted. "I cannot allow a woman who makes a gorgeous fry up like this to leave my side for more than a second and I want that in writing."

"Are you being serious Frank?" Maude asked as she sat down at the kitchen table beside him.

"Yes. To hell with divorces and to hell with what the world thinks. I want us to tie the knot and be painfully committed to each other for the rest of our entire lives." Frank replied. "Not that we've got a lot of years left but that's just a minor detail."

"Okay Frank, I'll think about it and I'll let you know in about ten minutes time." Maude teased as she grinned. "It's a very serious decision."

Frank laughed as he glanced at his wristwatch. "That's twenty seconds you've had already Maude. I'm timing you on this one." He joked.

Maude giggled.

For Talitha, her Monday morning was quite run of the mill as she arose at seven thirty, prepared for work and then made the journey towards the Restructure building. Once Talitha arrived at work, she quickly parked her inside the parking lot and then made her way towards the main entrance as she prepared for a slightly less hectic week than the previous week as this week, there were no more fixes to apply to clients bodies which meant, things were pretty much back to normal. When Talitha arrived inside her consultation room, she quickly switched on the Restructure system and then headed for the coffee machine as she prepared for her usual morning latte which was definitely required as it was like a liquid alarm clock that chased away the last remnants of sleepiness from the previous night.

Several unread emails awaited Talitha's attention and as soon as she sat down at her desk, armed with her cup of coffee, she noticed them and then began to inspect each one. One email was from Renee and there was another from Professor Heisner that requested her attendance at a meeting which he'd arranged for them both that morning. Due to Talitha's actions on the previous Friday evening with Moses, she began to feel slightly nervous about the fact that Professor Heisner had called a meeting that morning and her stomach rapidly began to tie itself up in knots as she quietly wondered if he'd actually discovered what they had actually done.

Since the email from Renee looked quite interesting and a lot less worrying, Talitha decided to spend a bit more time reading it as she quickly opened it up and then began to read the message it contained. Apparently and much to Talitha's utter delight, Renee's weekend date with the more mature man had gone exceedingly well and it seemed as if Renee had, had a romantic change of heart when it came to her approach to her love life which was very soothing news to Talitha.

Some worries had occupied Talitha's mind about Renee for a few weeks now, purely due to her dating choices as Talitha had felt that she was headed down a very destructive path that might undo some of the great things that Restructure had managed to achieve in her life. The good news and Renee's message was received like a ice cold drink on a hot summer's day as every word seemed to trickle through Talitha's thoughts and quench the parched dryness that had arisen inside her mind due to the empty physical, purely sexual liaisons that Renee had pursued and participated in up until that point in time.

Cheap sexual romps as Talitha knew, could be very damaging for women in the longer term and if Renee had continued down that path, all the positive things that the clinic had helped her to achieve would be rendered absolutely meaningless, null and void. An emotional emptiness often resulted from one night stands and that could be interpreted in the longer term as another form of rejection which Talitha feared, would only cause Renee more pain. Such self destructive actions would only inflict further wounds and would eventually scar Renee's outlook on life and instead of Restructure providing the healing that it should have resulted in, the bodily enhancements would then simply become another destructive weapon that would cause nothing but pain.

Thankfully it seemed however, Renee had now actually sought out a relationship that was much more substantial, in terms of the romantic commitment that was being offered to her and more emotionally fulfilling and that really appeased Talitha's mind. Finally and fortunately, the battle between Renee's sexual excitement and common sense had been won and her sexual hunger had been satisfied to some extent as she'd now selected a much more stable, steady, romantic partnership. Common sense in the end had indeed prevailed, Talitha quietly concluded as she quickly typed up an encouraging email response and Renee's long term romantic interests had ultimately been, absolutely victorious.

When ten that morning approached, Talitha nervously began to make her way towards Professor Heisner's office as she prepared for the meeting they were due to have that he'd requested that day. A lump of nervousness stuck inside Talitha's throat as fear began to run rampant through her body but really, there was absolutely nothing that Talitha could now do about anything as Friday had well and truly gone. If Professor Heisner did actually know about what she'd done with Moses on the Friday evening, just after work, he already knew and that could not now be changed and there really weren't any excuses that could be facilitated as Talitha had willingly freed the animals and it had actually been her idea to do so. The main worry for Talitha now was whether her actions would actually cost her the job that she'd just started to become comfortable in as if Professor Heisner had discovered what she'd done, it was a possibility as it could actually be considered a sackable offence.

Once Talitha arrived outside Professor Heisner's office, she tapped gently on the door and then waited for the Professor to invite her inside and within just a few seconds, the door swung open. A deep brave breath was taken as Talitha prepared to face the music and potentially Professor Heisner's anger as he held the door open and invited her inside. Silence filled the room as Talitha stepped through the door, crossed the room and then sat down beside Professor Heisner's desk as she waited for him to address her. The silent wait on Talitha's part that morning however, was a guilty silence not purely one due to respect.

"Good morning Talitha." Professor Heisner boomed as he sat down beside his desk and faced her. "We've managed to overcome the crisis and so things are pretty much back to normal now."

"Yes Professor Heisner." Talitha replied.

"So you know what that means?" Professor Heisner asked.

"More clients?" Talitha asked as a slightly confused expression spread out across her face as she internally began to wonder if his question was a trick question.

"Yes that as well but it means that all of our current clients are happy which is a very good thing." Professor Heisner boomed. "Happy clients means a very healthy, happy bank account Talitha." He teased. "We might not always agree with everyone, like Saskia and Lachlan but sometimes, we really don't have to."

"Yes Professor Heisner." Talitha agreed.

"And this week, I'll be adding some new clients to your client list so that the fun can start all over again." Professor Heisner confirmed. "I'll also be introducing some new bodily enhancements which will allow people to alter their physical height and their actual voice, so that's very exciting too."

"Professor Heisner the new clients, they won't be anything like Saskia right?" Talitha asked.

"Talitha, I very much doubt that you'll ever meet anyone quite like Saskia ever again." Professor quickly reassured her. "And we've almost finished with her request list now, so that thorn in our side should soon be gone but if you do, you now know exactly how to handle them. Give them exactly what they want and get rid of them as quickly as possible."

"Right." Talitha agreed as she smiled and nodded her head enthusiastically.

"Don't worry Talitha as I promised, I'm vetting all your clients for the first six months." Professor Heisner mentioned as he rose to his feet. "A few clients like Saskia at the same time and you'd probably be pulling your hair out in clumps."

"Very true." Talitha replied as she stood up.

"Right that's all for this morning Talitha." Professor Heisner clarified as he began to walk towards his consultation room door. "How are you finding the note system inside Restructure?" He asked.

"I think it's absolutely great Professor Heisner and very useful." Talitha replied.

"Yes, I wanted a system that would allow us to communicate in the most flexible way possible." Professor Heisner said as he neared the door. "A system that would allow you to send me direct, very detailed client progress reports which I could then analyze, review and provide precise feedback about each working day. My work inside the laboratory can be very intense and time consuming and so the note system just means, we don't have to juggle our schedules around to accommodate regular face to face meetings every day."

"I think it's extremely helpful." Talitha said as she nodded her head in agreement. "It certainly does all of those things."

"I better get back to my laboratory now Talitha, I have some experiments to conduct this morning and the clock is ticking." Professor Heisner explained as he opened his office door. "Get ready for next week Talitha, I'll be adding three or four new clients to your client list and some of them will have some very challenging issues."

"Yes Professor Heisner, I'll make sure I do that." Talitha agreed as she stepped out of his office. She sighed a huge sigh of relief as the door of his office closed and she was left alone once more inside the corridor. "Thank goodness." Talitha muttered as she began to walk back along the corridor towards the reception area.

Trouble had not stepped inside Talitha's life that day as Professor Heisner had absolutely no idea it seemed that Talitha had any part in the animals being set free the previous Friday. The nerves that had somersaulted through every inch of Talitha's body prior to and during their meeting, gradually began to subside as she walked back along the corridor towards the reception area and her consultation room and that wasn't the only blessing of that particular morning. Professor Heisner had also reassured Talitha that she probably wouldn't have another client like Saskia again, or at least not in abundant proportions and that meant, he would be vetting her clients with that in mind which was a total relief.

Due to Saskia's very demanding nature, Talitha had felt extremely grateful towards the other clients on her client list, who had been far less stressful and a lot less trouble as they had broken her in as a consultant gently and had provided her with a pleasant working experience. Deep down inside, Talitha hoped as she walked that her new client additions would all be quite similar in nature to Renee and Dean and absolutely nothing at all like Saskia. In terms of her client list, Renee and Dean had become two of her favorite clients as they had been the first two clients that had stepped through her consultation room door and they'd been the easiest to assist and work with. The ease of their consultations had been a total joy to Talitha as like well-oiled machines, both Renee and Dean had simply purred through each client session without any stress, or drama at all.

In her heart of hearts however, Talitha hoped as she walked that whatever she'd done for all of her clients, even Saskia, would bring them joy not more pain and that her work as a consultant would have somehow helped to alleviate the problems that had prompted them to seek out Restructure's services in the first place. The first set of adventures that Talitha had journeyed through at Restructure were now officially over as some of her initial clients would no longer even be on her client list and Talitha felt a definite sense of satisfaction about their departure as she had fulfilled their requirements and even changed some lives. A fresh set of faces, complexities and challenges would definitely begin that coming week but now, Talitha felt slightly better equipped to handle any issue that might arise as she'd applied Professor Heisner's training very precisely and she'd also managed to accumulate some real professional experience that would help to guide her along the way.

Life now for Talitha was as close to perfect as it could possibly be, she had a very supportive loving partner, a great boss that encouraged and believed in her, a job that really motivated her and she'd even made a new friend that wasn't quite human that didn't iron his shirts but that was just a minor technicality. One day perhaps, Talitha concluded as she stepped back inside her consultation room, Moses would learn how to iron a shirt as if Saskia could learn to say thank you which she definitely had and Lachlan could learn to appreciate

Charmaine's opinion which it seemed he had then truly, nothing was impossible.